SKY ON FIRE

DRAGON GATE, BOOK 5

LINDSAY BUROKER

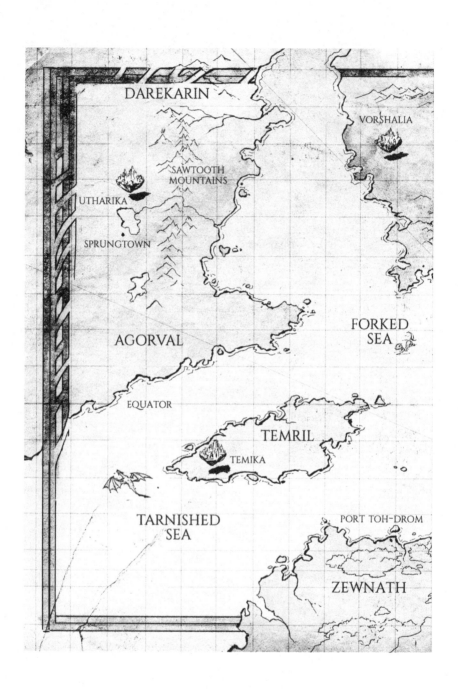

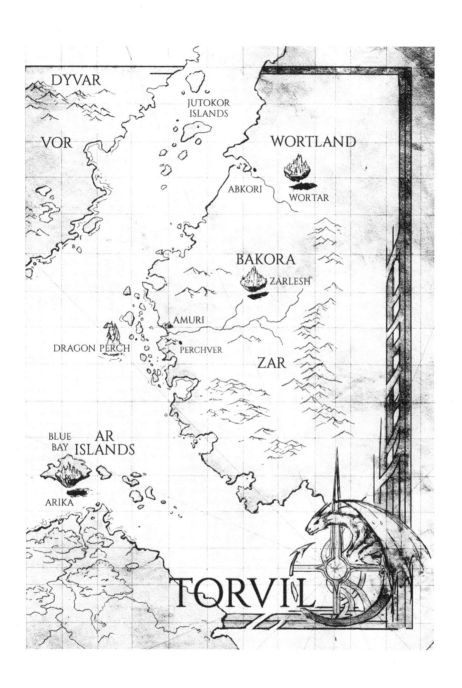

DYVAR

VOR

JUTOKOR
ISLANDS

WORTLAND

ABKORI

WORTAR

BAKORA

ZARLESH

AMURI

DRAGON PERCH

PERCHVER

ZAR

BLUE
BAY

AR
ISLANDS

ARIKA

TORVIL

1

THE FIREBALL HOVERED ABOVE THE RAILING AS THE *SERENE WATERS* flew north over the Forked Sea, clouds and blue sky visible through the meager flames. Jakstor Freedar, mage apprentice, cartography student, and surrogate dragon father, scowled. His fireball was so... wimpy.

When Rivlen, Malek, and other powerful mages conjured fireballs, they were huge, dense, and brilliant. Like spinning suns that could hurtle through the air to blast into enemies and incinerate them.

"And there's the problem," Jak muttered, having no desire to incinerate human beings or any other intelligent creature.

The first time he'd managed to conjure fire had been on Nargnoth, where hordes of deadly insects had descended on his dragonling charge—and the rest of the party. He hadn't minded incinerating *bugs*.

"Are you focusing?" Lord Malek, zidarr weapons master, mage, and loyal servant to King Uthari, stood beside Jak with his hands clasped behind his back as he alternately advised and watched the sky ahead for threats.

For *dragon* threats. Jak reminded himself that he needed to master this and whatever other attacks Malek taught him. Their world had been invaded by more than forty brown-and-gray mottled dragons that wanted to enslave or slay all of humankind. This wasn't the time to be squeamish.

"On my wandering thoughts, moral crises, and the impending doom our world is facing as we speak?" Jak pushed his hat down against a gust of wind. "Yes, I am. Assiduously so."

Malek slanted a sidelong look at him, the sea breeze riffling through his short black hair and tugging at his trousers and jacket. "Aren't you a little young to have moral crises?"

"No." At eighteen, when Jak had been immersed in his cartography studies at the university, laughing with friends, and awkwardly flirting with girls, he'd felt young. The adventures of the last few months seemed to have aged him ten years. "I'm morally mature for my age."

"Hm."

Clangs came from the mageship sailing to their port side, the *Star Flyer*. The deck was busy with mercenaries practicing with swords, as if such weapons would be sufficient against dragons. Fortunately, two members of Thorn Company, Tinder and Tezi, had dragon-steel axes that could cut through magic and otherwise impervious dragon scales. They could also cut through practice swords, as evinced by their scowling sparring opponents with broken blades littered at their feet.

The ship's captain, Xeva Rivlen, stood in the forecastle, her red uniform bright in the morning sun, her dark hair swept back in a bun. Her stance was similar to Malek's as she surveyed the sea a thousand feet below, as well as the other mageships in their fleet. All twelve vessels were flying in a cluster northward as fast as possible, returning to Agorval to defend their homeland from the world's newly arrived enemies.

Rivlen looked at Jak, her features elegant and beautiful despite their aloof coolness, and quirked an eyebrow as she glanced at the vestiges of his meager fireball.

Embarrassed now that he knew she'd been watching, Jak gripped the railing and turned his focus back to the task. As he so often did when calling upon his magic, he envisioned a map filled with familiar terrain features. He placed a forest in the center of it and imagined lightning from a storm striking a treetop. It started a wildfire that raged across the land, destroying all the foliage in its path as it charred the earth, but it also acted as part of the natural cycle, creating fertile soil and offering an opportunity for buried seeds to sprout and grow, with competing trees no longer blocking the sun's nourishing rays.

His fireball grew larger and larger, his cheeks now flaming from its heat rather than embarrassment, and he stepped back. He raised his arms as he willed it to rise in the air so the fire wouldn't char the railing or hull of the ship—and so Rivlen would be able to see its magnificence from her perch a hundred feet away.

Not that she would be impressed. She made entire *walls* of fire with a flick of her fingers. Still, when they'd met, he hadn't known how to do anything when it came to magic, and he liked to think she might find his progress a little impressive. Maybe even sexy. Though the sweat beading on his forehead—more from the effort required to use his magic than the heat of the flames—might not be as alluring as he would wish.

"That's better," Malek said.

"Thanks." Jak lowered his arms, letting the fireball extinguish, and glanced at Rivlen, hoping she would smile at him. She'd done so before, so he knew it was possible. On the surface, she might be the rigid and cool officer, adopting extreme military profession- alism to help her effectively command men who resented how quickly she'd risen through the ranks, but he knew she had a sense of humor, however dry, and that she was a decent woman.

Unfortunately, her first officer had joined her in the forecastle to report, and it had drawn her attention away from Jak. He slumped against the railing. Had she seen *any* of his success?

"I suppose that's one way to encourage you to focus." Malek trended toward dry humor as well.

"What?" Jak leaned back, though he feared the perceptive Malek was reading his thoughts. Even though Jak could now guard his mind from telepathic intrusion, he didn't always remember to do it.

"She's quite a bit older than you and career-focused."

"Only six years." Jak admitted it might be closer to seven, since he'd barely turned nineteen, but it wasn't as if he was the goofy kid he'd been back in school. He'd matured. He shaved semi-regularly. And he was even a father—of sorts—now.

"Uthari would probably tell me to encourage you, thus to further bind your family to him through those who loyally serve him." Malek's mouth twisted wryly as he waved a hand toward his own chest.

Jak grimaced, not needing the reminder that Malek loyally served his king—his megalomaniacal king whose obsession with synthesizing a life-extending drug was the entire reason the ancient portal had been erected and left open, even after mankind had learned of the terrible dangers that could enter Torvil through it. It was thanks to King Uthari that dragons were now razing cities all over the world and Jak and his mother and everyone they cared about might soon be dead.

"That said," Malek continued, "you might have more luck with the blonde mercenary girl."

"Tezi," Jak corrected, though Malek knew her name. They'd all gone on a mission to another world together.

Most of the time, Malek seemed much better than the other mages—*especially* better than the other zidarr—but he still carried that mage arrogance about him, that unwillingness to bother using the names of terrene humans, at least those who didn't have some value to his king. He'd had no trouble learning *Mother's* name. Though now that she'd been granted great magical power —a gift from the aged dragon Zelonsera—*every* mage seemed to know her name. Word had traveled fast.

"Yes. She's closer to your age and less ambitious." Malek gave Jak a significant look, a reminder that Rivlen had also been teaching Jak how to use his magic. It hadn't been out of friendship —or romantic interest—but because she longed to defeat the odious General Tonovan and believed Jak, someone who was outside of her fleet and the military chain of command, could help.

"I don't think she's that into me." Jak looked toward the mercenaries again and was in time to see Tezi, beautiful but fierce as she wielded her axe, slice through another practice blade and send her opponent skittering back with a curse. "I asked her numerous times for drinks, and she refused, despite my great handsomeness, charisma, and ability to draw an accurate map of any continent in less than a minute."

"Does that latter usually help in your campaigns to attract women?"

"It hasn't yet, but I remain hopeful that such a skill can't possibly go unappreciated indefinitely."

Tezi, Jak reminded himself, had been a sexual victim of Tonovan, as well as another mage, before she'd become a mercenary. When he'd been asking her for dates, Jak hadn't known the details of her past, but he had a feeling she wouldn't be that into *anyone* at this point. Of course, Rivlen seemed to have had run-ins like that with Tonovan too. If Jak were smart, he'd put thoughts of pursuing *any* woman aside until they defeated the dragons and his life returned to normal. Or as normal as it could be.

Shikari galloped across the deck, his blue scales gleaming in the sun, with something in his mouth. Was that... a feather duster? He stopped long enough to shake it like prey that he'd captured, feathers flying everywhere. A woman—one of Uthari's slaveband-wearing servants—shouted at him from a hatchway as she waved a scrub brush.

Jak dropped his face in his hand. It wouldn't be long before the quickly growing Shikari couldn't fit through the hatchways, but Jak doubted that would put an end to his mischievous streak—or his desire to chomp on everything that could possibly go in his mouth. Mother had a hypothesis that Shikari was teething, or the dragon equivalent. His horns were also growing, turning from the nubs they'd been a few weeks before into prongs that he liked to ram into objects—and people—before rubbing the velvety fuzz against them.

When is your dragon going to grow up enough to be an ally instead of a menace? an amused voice spoke telepathically into his mind.

Jak spun toward Rivlen, pleased to find her alone in the fore-castle again and looking at him. That was twice in five minutes. It *had* to connote interest.

He's a great ally. He's performed brain surgery on Malek, channeled power into me during battles, and shared his inborn knowledge of the ancient dragons with me.

He just annihilated that feather duster, and now he's turning a crate into a pile of splinters.

A shout came from one of the mage officers who patrolled the yacht, and he ran up to Shikari. He waved a sword and tried to use his magic to nudge Shikari away from the crate that he was pronging with his horns. As usual, the magic had little effect on the dragonling. The officer glowered at Jak, as if to put all the blame on him.

Shikari, Jak called silently, attempting to share an image of the dragonling backing away to sit sedately on the deck and help watch for threats. *Don't chew on things, please.*

Thus far, Shikari hadn't demonstrated that he understood the human language, but Jak often succeeded in conveying his intent with images. Whether Shikari obeyed the suggestions in those images was another matter.

After the briefest glance in Jak's direction, Shikari pounced on the officer's boots and latched his jaws onto the bottom of the man's sword scabbard. The officer shouted and swung his blade at Shikari.

Terrified, Jak rushed to form the mountain imagery in his mind that he used to create magical barriers, erecting one in the air above his charge. But Shikari was so fast that Jak needn't have bothered. The dragonling tore the scabbard free from the officer's belt and galloped away before the sword swung downward. It halted midair as it encountered Jak's barrier, which was heroically defending the empty deck.

Jak sighed. At least he'd gotten better at making barriers. Judging by the second glower the mage officer leveled in his direction, not everyone appreciated his progress. It didn't help that Shikari was running off with the man's now-perforated scabbard.

A menace, Rivlen repeated in Jak's mind, though she sounded amused.

He's just young and playful and full of vigor. Those aren't bad things, you know. Jak looked over at her, resisting the urge to point out that *he* was full of vigor. *Did you see my fireball?*

Assuming she hadn't, he conjured another one, once again focusing hard in an attempt to make it brilliant and fearsome. Jak's goal wasn't only to impress Rivlen but also to show the maligned mage that he had power—and that the man had better not attempt to hurt Shikari, or there would be repercussions.

Once more, the fireball grew large, the flames crackling as they radiated intense heat. As Jak held it in the air, he glanced over at Rivlen, but damn it, she'd been distracted again. Another officer had joined her and was pointing off toward the west where a couple of blue-hulled mageships were just visible, flying parallel to the fleet. If the leaders of the various kingdoms were wise, they would stop fighting with each other and focus on the dragon threat, but Jak doubted they were that wise.

Rivlen was wise. *She* ought to be in charge.

He held the fireball, still hoping she would see it, but his efforts were in vain. Oh, well. Using some of the skills the engineer Vinjo had started teaching him, he'd made her a magical trinket. As soon as he had the opportunity, he would give it to her and hope she liked it.

As he let the fireball fade and wiped sweat from his brow, Jak noticed someone else looking at him. His stomach sank.

General Tonovan, who'd lost his mageship during the dragon battle at the portal, was leaning against the railing near the bow of the *Serene Waters*, his arms crossed over his chest as he glared at Jak with his single eye, no patch covering the knot of scar tissue that was all that remained of his other eye.

Practice hard, boy, Tonovan spoke into his mind. *You'll need that power to defend yourself soon.* A cruel smile stretched against his face. *When King Jutok's fleet commander asked me what happened to Admiral Bakir, I let him know how Uthari's untrained wild one was integral in his officer's death.*

The memory of that battle haunted Jak—he'd endured more than one nightmare reliving the charring of Bakir's back under his flames—but that didn't keep him from wanting to blurt that *Malek* had landed the killing blow when Bakir had been trying to kill him. But Malek had been afflicted with those horrible bacteria at the time and out of his mind. Even if he hadn't been, Jak wouldn't have wanted to throw the onus on him. Besides, Tonovan knew full well what had happened and was intentionally being an ass. But, if it was true that he'd told Jutok's people that Jak had been responsible, Jak might have to watch his back for zidarr assassins from that kingdom.

I guess you can hide behind your mother's skirts if Jutok sends people after you. Tonovan's smile shifted to a sneer.

Malek might not have heard the telepathic words, but he noticed Jak and Tonovan trading glares. He rested a hand on Jak's shoulder and faced his nemesis, silently seeming to promise that he would protect Jak if trouble came. But Tonovan only shifted his glare to Malek, and it remained equally frosty. Jak well remembered the dragon battle in which Tonovan had tried to kill Malek, and he had little doubt that the vengeful general would try again.

Malek shifted to block Jak from Tonovan's view and waved toward the railing. "Create another fireball. You'll need to practice until it's as easy as breathing."

"I know. I will." Jak made himself look away from Tonovan, though he wished the man would go below so he could practice without anyone glowering at him. "Is it wrong of me to be envious of my mother? She seems to have gained all the knowledge she needs to use her power at the same time as she received it."

Malek's expression grew stern, and Jak expected Malek to remind him that he and every other powerful mage in the world had trained for years—decades—to learn their power. But all he said was, "You'd need a wise and powerful dragon to magically impart that ability to you, and I doubt it's something that happens often."

No, and Jak well knew the promise Mother had made to Zelonsera when she'd been chosen. What would happen if she couldn't find a way to get rid of the magical parasite that had infested the dragons' entire species and destroyed their culture, their way of life, and all that they'd been?

"Unless Shikari can do that for you," Malek continued, "you'll have to learn the hard way, with practice."

Shikari galloped toward them, talons clattering on the deck. He'd abandoned the stolen scabbard, but now he was draped with long strips of paper. Was that from the lavatory? Jak groaned, not certain whether one of the servants had flung rolls of the stuff at him or he'd found a stash and done it to himself.

"I think his days of wisdom and power are well into the future," Jak said.

"Indeed."

Shikari stopped in front of Jak, sat on his haunches, and gazed up at him. Worried he would have to protect his charge from more vengeful mages, Jak looked back the way he'd come, but nobody was running after the dragonling.

Shikari emitted a squeaky sound that wasn't as high-pitched as it had been a few weeks earlier but still wasn't like the deep roars of the adult dragons. He lifted his foreleg and rested his taloned foot on Jak's thigh.

"Do you want me to clean you off?" Jak asked. "Or feed you?"

On Nargnoth, with huge insects flying through the air left and right, Shikari had managed to feed himself well, but there were few options for hunting above the seas of Torvil.

But when Shikari shared a vision with him, it had nothing to do with food. In it, Jak and Shikari were underwater and swimming side by side through a dark lake or some other body of water. Perhaps the sea below? Rock pillars rose up all around them, the lumpy shapes covered with silt and organic material.

Strange sea life that Jak had seen only in books, if at all, swam past as he and Shikari maneuvered around the pillars. Here and there, larger shapes that might have once been walls rose up. Was this... some ancient ruin site? A lost settlement that had long ago been flooded?

The vision faded, and Shikari lowered his foot.

"Where was that?" Jak wondered aloud before remembering Malek stood nearby and might be wondering what he was talking about.

Shikari tilted his head in a questioning manner as a breeze swept through, rustling the paper dangling from his horns and one foot.

"You don't know? Why did you show it to me?" Jak removed

the paper for him and started to wad it up so he could throw it away later, but Shikari snapped his jaws and caught it. He chomped happily, as if it was as delicious as a steak or, in his case, a giant bug. "I'll make something for you to eat as soon as we're done training."

Shikari roared and spun around, whacking Jak with his tail, then galloped off to look for fresh trouble.

Jak frowned after him.

"What did he show you?" Malek asked.

"Some underwater ruins, but I'm not sure he knows why or where or what they mean. At the least, he didn't convey that to me."

"Does he often show such things to you?"

"No. Usually, he shares images of us hunting together, but this time, the Jak in the vision didn't have a tarantula dangling out of his mouth." Jak scratched his jaw. "Zelonsera, the dragon who gave Mother her power, said she imparted some of her memories and knowledge to Shikari, but she also said he was too young to learn much yet. I wonder if that was a hint about where we could go to help the dragons with their problem."

Of course, if the dragons had known where the answers to their problem were, they would have dealt with it themselves. They'd agreed to let Mother try because she might have different knowledge than they possessed.

"We have to deal with our *own* problem first," Malek said.

"Solving their problem might solve ours." If Jak and his mother could kill the parasite that made the dragons aggressive and terrible, they might leave Torvil alone and go back to their own world. Or they might even be turned into the allies that Jak had always dreamed dragons could be.

"That problem has remained unsolved for more than ten thousand years. Once we've rid the threat to our world, you can work on it, but for now, we need you to continue developing your power so that we'll have one more mage when we go into battle against the dragons." Malek nodded, then headed toward the double doors that led to Uthari's suite.

Those doors were open, and someone stood in the shadows. Uthari. Jak recognized his aura and wished he'd been paying attention earlier. How long had the old wizard been standing there watching? Somehow, his cool attention was even more unnerving than Tonovan's.

Uthari patted Malek on the shoulder when he entered, and the doors closed behind them.

It was unnerving, Jak decided, because Malek would do anything his king asked, including getting rid of Jak and his mother if Uthari decided they were no longer useful.

~

Dragon steel met dragon steel with a clang and a flash of blue light as Corporal Tezi sparred with Sergeant Tinder on the deck of the *Star Flyer*. The rest of Thorn Company was giving them room, more because they feared the magical blades than because of their weapons prowess, Tezi feared, but she was pleased at her progress.

"Be ready for the feint," Lieutenant Sasko called from where she leaned against the rim of the portal, the large circular artifact flat on the deck. Straps reinforced with magic crisscrossed it to keep enemy mages from sneaking in and using their levitation powers to steal it.

Tezi hoped all the mages in the world would join forces to deal with the dragon threat, and that they wouldn't have to worry about such incursions, but the portal had changed hands more times than currency on a sunny morning at the Perchver Market, so she couldn't blame Uthari's people for taking precautions.

"Tinder likes to feint high before slipping in low," Sasko

added. "A lot of enemies do. They know you'll instinctively guard your face."

The muscular Sergeant Tinder backed away, lowered her axe, and scowled at Sasko as she wiped sweat from her brow. Equally sweaty, Tezi did the same, glad for the break, even if she wouldn't admit it. Now that she'd been promoted to corporal, and had helped slay a dragon, the other mercenaries hadn't been teasing her as much, but she was the newest and least experienced member of the company. Maybe it was silly, but she still felt she had to prove herself.

"Why are you giving *her* all the tips and me nothing?" Tinder asked Sasko.

"Because when I give you tips, you always ignore me."

"I don't *ignore* you. I just like to think about your advice before deciding if it's right for me."

"She's been cogitating on your advice to stop letting dragons thump her for weeks now," Sergeant Words drawled from where she and Corporal Basher were taking a break from their own practice. She winked at Tezi.

"I think we *all* gave her that advice," Sasko said.

"Hilarious," Tinder grumbled. "Dragons are fast. It's not that easy to avoid thumping."

"Tezi managed it," Sasko said.

"*Tezi* had the invisible Colonel Sorath helping her and distracting their dragon," Tinder said.

"Sorath's face has been busted up more times than the furniture in the Rock Street Tavern back home," Sasko said. "It's not that distracting. Trust me."

"Really," said a mild voice from the side. Captain Ferroki was walking up with Captain Rivlen.

"Sorry, Captain," Sasko said. "I know some women like that broken-nosed, scarred look in a man."

"Whereas others prefer to get in bed with bony knees, grease-stained hands, and the absent-minded distraction of a man thinking about his tools instead of his woman?" Sergeant Words elbowed Corporal Basher, who managed to snicker while keeping her cigar firmly clamped between her lips.

Sasko scowled at them. "I haven't gotten into *bed* with Lieutenant Vinjo. And he thinks about his *projects*, not his tools."

"That must be *much* better for his lady friends," Words said.

"Does he *have* any lady friends?" Tinder wondered. "Besides Sasko, who's oddly into that kind of thing?"

Sasko bared her teeth at them, her lips peeling back like a wolf's.

"I don't think you're ever going to get advice from her again, Sergeant," Tezi whispered to Tinder.

"How ever will I survive without someone to tell me not to let dragons thump me with their tails?" Tinder asked.

That drew more snickers, not only from Words and Basher but from all the Thorn Company mercenaries within earshot.

Amazing that you were excited to rejoin this company of buffoons, Captain Rivlen spoke telepathically to Tezi, even as she and Ferroki pointed toward the eastern horizon and conferred.

There were other mageships out there, but they were too far away for Tezi to make out the hull coloring and identify which kingdom they were from.

They're good company and watch my back, ma'am, Tezi replied. *And in an all-female company, nobody, uhm,* bothers *me.*

That was vague, but Tezi trusted that Rivlen understood. Though the captain hadn't confided in her much during the times they'd worked together on missions, Tezi had a feeling they'd *both* been victims of General Tonovan. Rivlen wanted the man dead even more than Tezi did.

Not even that brutish sergeant? Rivlen glanced at Tinder.

No. Tinder's gruff, but she's a good person. And Dr. Fret keeps her in line.

Rivlen looked toward the railing of the ship, where the petite Dr. Fret was sitting and knitting with a mercenary from one of the other companies being retained by King Uthari.

By stabbing her with her knitting needles? Rivlen asked.

Tezi smiled. *If necessary.*

Ferroki pointed toward the long, narrow mageship sailing along behind the *Star Flyer*, the craft Lieutenant Vinjo had designed and built so that it could fly through the dragon portal. People had started calling it the *gateship*, though someone could have given it a more interesting name than that.

Rivlen turned her attention to it with a nod and spoke a few words. The wind caught them, so Tezi couldn't hear what the two captains were talking about. Officer stuff. She might be a corporal now, but that didn't mean the officers kept her apprised of everything. There weren't any rookies in the company currently, so Tezi didn't even have a squad of her own to command. Not that she craved leadership, but there were times when she thought wistfully of advancing up the ranks and being more than one fighter among many.

"Brace yourself." Tinder pointed her chin past Tezi's shoulder.

Tezi turned as two male mercenaries from Moon Guard Company walked toward her. She made herself lift her chin and meet their gazes, though she wanted to hide behind Tinder.

Before the dragons had come through the portal, three members of Moon Guard had tried to steal her axe. They'd died when the druid Grunk sneaked in and killed them to clear the way for his people to retrieve a prisoner. Tezi, who'd been caught in the middle of it, had told anyone who would listen the real story—especially that she hadn't been responsible for the deaths or been in collusion with the druids—but rumors persisted that she'd betrayed the camp. She'd been cringing, certain she would be targeted for revenge, ever since the Moon Guards had been ushered onto the *Star Flyer* along with Thorn Company. She almost wished they would run into one of the dragons, if only to keep everyone distracted and working against a common enemy.

"You're Rookie Tezi, right?" one man asked as they stopped in front of her.

"*Corporal* Tezi." Tinder stepped up to Tezi's shoulder to stand with her if the mercenaries started anything. "And if you can't tell her apart from the rest of the company, you're blinder than a Dyvarian bat." Tinder waved toward the bronze-skinned women of Thorn Company, then Tezi's sunburned pale skin and blonde hair.

Tezi blushed, hating to be reminded how easy she was to pick out among the desert-born Southerners. When she'd fled the north—and the repercussions for having killed a mage after he'd helped murder her parents—it hadn't occurred to her how much she would stick out, how easy it would be for someone who was looking for her to find her. She'd already gotten in trouble numerous times when mages had riffled through her mind and learned of that transgression. Would her past ever stop haunting her?

"She is a lot prettier than the rest of you," the man grumbled, curling a lip at Tinder.

Tezi tightened her grip on the shaft of her axe, reminded that she could take care of herself these days. And that Tinder and the others would back her up if she needed help.

"*Pretty* counts for a lot when fighting dragons," Tinder said. "What do you pigheads want?"

"Nothing from you. We wanted to say good fighting to your *corporal*." The mercenary nodded at Tezi. "We saw the dragon battle. You sank that axe into its back a bunch of times, and then right into its skull. That was brave. Some of our *own* people—" he tossed a scathing look over his shoulder toward his company, "—ran and hid in the jungle."

Tezi thought that was a fair way to react to a dragon, but she was so stunned that the man was complimenting her that she didn't know what to say. After all she'd endured, she couldn't help but wonder if this was a setup. As she recalled, the three Moon Guard mercs who'd died had implied someone had sent them to steal her axe from her. Was it possible that same person was trying a new trick by sending these two to try to disarm her?

"Thanks," Tezi made herself say as the men watched her expectantly.

The speaker nodded. "That was Colonel Sorath with you, wasn't it? With some magic that made him invisible?"

"Yes." Tezi almost added that they'd been working together to break Grunk out of Tonovan's brig when the dragons had arrived, but she didn't want to remind Moon Guard of her association with druids. Even Thorn Company had doubted her wisdom in helping the crazy Grunk, and it was probably only the fact that she'd been following Sorath's lead that had kept Ferroki from questioning her about the choice.

"Did Sorath tell you anything? Is there any chance he's coming back to help against the dragons?" The man's tone turned wistful. "We *need* someone like him to lead us. The mages don't care about us. They want to use us as cannon fodder in these battles and wouldn't mind if we all died. But if Sorath were here, he would come up with a plan. A plan to make sure we *won* and that dragons wouldn't destroy our kingdoms." He shook his head. "You can't count on these mages to come up with anything. They're as likely to squabble among themselves as work together."

Tezi hoped that wasn't true, but she caught Tinder sighing and nodding in agreement.

"Tinder, Tezi," Sasko called. "Over here."

She had joined Ferroki and Rivlen in their discussion and waved for them to come over to the group.

"I'm not sure where Sorath went," Tezi told the mercenaries, "but I also hope he'll be able to rejoin us."

How he would do that when Uthari wanted him dead and he'd been responsible for the murder of Queen Vorsha, Tezi didn't know, but the more people they had with dragon-fighting experience, the better.

She and Tinder left the Moon Guard mercenaries and headed toward Sasko and the others.

"What do you think that was about?" Tinder jerked a thumb over her shoulder toward the men. "Were they angling to get in bed with you, or something more?"

"I don't know," Tezi said. "Maybe they were genuine and just wanted to compliment me."

Tinder squinted at her. "Now that you're a corporal, you shouldn't be so naive."

Tezi smiled sadly. That word hadn't applied to her for a long time. "I was being hopeful, not naive."

"Well, quit it. It's not healthy for a mercenary."

Sasko raised her eyebrows, catching those last words as Tinder and Tezi approached. "What's not healthy for a mercenary?"

"Hope," Tinder said.

Sasko snorted but didn't disagree.

"Those are King Zaruk's ships on the horizon." Ferroki pointed toward the distant vessels matching their direction and pace. "His people *should* be heading toward their own city and kingdom to prepare for dragon attacks, but for some reason, they're sailing straight toward Agorval with us. Captain Rivlen believes they may make another attempt to get the portal, especially if we run into a dragon and are distracted."

Tezi eyed the artifact, the blue-black dragon steel seeming to absorb sunlight instead of reflecting it. She'd had enough of it and the creatures that came through it. It would have been better for the world if the artifact had never been unearthed.

"It's also possible they're trying to get their engineer back." Rivlen nodded toward the gateship.

Lieutenant Vinjo dangled against the hull, a panel open as he performed a midflight repair. He clunked his elbow on the side, dropped a tool, and frowned as it plummeted toward the sea below. Fortunately for the tool, he was a mage, and he stretched out a hand and used his power to levitate it back up and into his grip. Tezi wondered what would happen if *he* plummeted toward the sea.

"As hard as it is to believe," Rivlen finished dryly.

Sasko lifted her chin. "He's a very talented engineer and tinkerer, Captain. He's made all manner of unique and useful magical devices."

"Yes," Rivlen said, her tone turning to ice. "King Uthari is well aware of the stealth devices he likes to make and give to dangerous mercenaries so they can skulk off into the jungle after assassinating mages."

When Sasko opened her mouth, a rebuttal on her lips, Ferroki elbowed her and shook her head. Sasko closed her mouth. A good decision. Even though Tezi had formed a relationship of sorts with Rivlen—at the least, they had an understanding that if they got the opportunity to rid the world of General Tonovan, they would work together to do it—she couldn't forget that Rivlen was an officer in Uthari's fleet and loyal to him.

"Better he make them for your people than Zaruk's, is it not?" Ferroki asked calmly.

"That's been the consensus, though Uthari cares more about him keeping that ship flying and what tools he might make that could be of use to *mages*. He's forbidden Vinjo from making more of those stealth devices, and he said anyone we catch using one is to be put to death."

Tezi shifted uneasily, and Ferroki and Sasko exchanged looks. At the moment, Tezi didn't think anyone in Thorn Company had one of the devices, but they all knew that Sorath did. From what she'd heard, Sorath was back on Zewnath with the druids, but it was possible he was stowing away on the *Star Flyer*, using the stealth device to remain hidden until such time as he could step out and help the company. That would be almost suicidal for him, but... he cared about Ferroki and Thorn Company enough to risk his life. Frequently.

"If the king is irked with Vinjo," Sasko said, "and we're worrying about Zaruk's zidarr or whoever else attacking us to steal him back, why not let him return to his people?"

"King Uthari doesn't confide in me," Rivlen said, "but he must see some value in the engineer. Either that, or he's irritated with Zaruk and wants to vex him."

"You have to love the machinations of wizards," Sasko muttered.

Rivlen squinted but didn't berate her. "Whatever he wishes, it's not my place to question him, simply to obey orders. And he wants me to assign a couple of your people to keep an eye on Vinjo and his ship while I protect the dragon portal." Rivlen stood straight, her chin in the air, as if she were honored to have been assigned the duty.

Tezi thought both duties sounded like ways to get in trouble for failing and wondered why Uthari couldn't have his *own* crew watch the gateship. Maybe he was testing Rivlen and her ability to command. If so, Tezi felt affronted on her behalf. Were the *other* captains in Uthari's fleet being tested in such a way? There were eleven other black-hulled ships flying with them. Once, there had been more, but not all had survived the dragon battle.

"Ferroki," Rivlen said, "send a couple of your people, including one of your axe-wielders, to the gateship. They'll help defend it if there's a sneak attack from another fleet, and they'll also keep Vinjo alive in the event that we run into dragons."

"Is that expected?" Ferroki asked.

Unlike the mages, nobody in the company had the magical ability to sense dragons from afar.

"Sooner or later," Rivlen said. "If not out over the sea, then at home. I've heard that three have attacked cities in Agorval. The reports say they've spread out and are attacking settlements all over the world."

"Wonderful," Tinder muttered and rubbed her back—the spot where the dragon tail had smashed her to the deck a few days earlier.

Rivlen eyed her, then told Ferroki, "Your *other* axe-wielder will stay here and sleep snuggled up to the portal."

Tinder lowered her hand with a grimace.

"If mages attack," Rivlen continued, "my crew and I will deal with them, but if a dragon attacks, those are the only weapons that have proven capable of damaging them."

"The portal can damage them," Tezi pointed out, thinking of the red lightning Jak could command it to launch at enemies. That same red lightning had zapped Uthari in the back when he'd forced it to do his bidding, a memory that made her smile. The bastard had deserved that. It was only a pity that it hadn't killed him—and that Tonovan hadn't been standing beside him to get a share of the lightning too.

Rivlen looked over at her, and a surge of fear ran down Tezi's spine before she remembered that Rivlen shouldn't be able to read her mind while she carried the magical axe.

"It can," Rivlen agreed, "but after the *incident* during the last battle, Uthari won't rely on its power. Or so he's said. I suspect that if dragons show up, he'll send Jak over here and tell him to coax it into attacking."

Since Rivlen was watching her, Tezi stifled a smile. It had to gall the old wizard that the portal *liked* some kid who'd only recently learned he was capable of using magic, and it detested him. Tezi thought it was lovely.

"Maybe he should be the one sleeping snuggled up to it," Tinder remarked.

Rivlen looked toward the yacht, where Jak was riding with his mother and receiving instruction from Malek. Was her usually frosty expression slightly wistful, or was that Tezi's imagination? Back before Jak had left on the last mission, Rivlen had kissed him on the cheek. Or maybe she'd stumbled and fallen lips-first against him. Tezi had never been certain.

"That might happen eventually, but, for now, spread out the axes, and you two stay alert." Rivlen nodded curtly at Tezi and Tinder before striding off.

On the way to the navigation cabin, she snapped at an officer who'd been taking a break from repairs and leaning against the railing and gazing to the north. The mage winced and picked up his tools so quickly that he dumped half of them from his box. Rivlen scowled and continued inside.

Tezi decided that for Jak's sake, she would hope Rivlen *didn't* have any interest in him. He deserved someone sweet who appreciated his artistic side and his sense of humor. Rivlen was decent compared to other mages, but she was still a grouch.

"I'll go over there." Sasko pointed at the gateship. "Which one of you two wants to come with me?"

"I'd be aghast if I couldn't continue to enjoy your company and lack of advice," Tinder said.

"Aghast?" Sasko asked. "Are you sure you're using that word correctly?"

"Yes, but we can ask Words to verify it. She'll give us the etymology and everything."

"Won't that be a fun discussion?" Sasko muttered, heading off to collect her gear. Despite her grousing, she looked over at the gateship, caught Vinjo looking back, and lifted a hand toward him.

He was still hanging from the side of the ship, but he grinned and waved vigorously. So vigorously that another of his tools pitched out of his grasp. Distracted by Sasko's attention, he almost forgot to use his levitation powers to keep it from plunging into the sea.

Sasko shook her head, but she was smiling as she grabbed Tinder and convinced a mage to float them over.

A part of Tezi wished she'd been quicker and had volunteered to go herself, especially when she caught some of the Moon Guard mercenaries looking over at the company. Or... at *her*?

Why did she have a feeling she wasn't done with them?

2

—————

"THE DRAGONS MAY BE THE MAGES' PENANCE, IMPOSED BY THANOK to punish them for how little honest work they do and how little value they add to the world. And unfortunately, all of mankind will be punished right alongside them, through no fault of our own."

Jadora nodded to indicate she was listening and gave an *mmhmm* now and then when her father paused in his diatribe. They were in the makeshift laboratory that Uthari had given her belowdecks on his yacht, and she was filling pots with moist loam and peat moss and planting the spores she'd carefully scraped from underneath the fronds of the Jitaruvak she'd brought back from Nargnoth.

She hoped the plant was similar to ferns on Torvil and possessed the necessary male and female cells for germination. With the portal removed from Zewnath, it would be impossible to go back for more samples.

Once the spores did germinate, would they grow into prothalli? Or something she'd never seen before? And *would* they germinate here under Torvil's sun? Back on Vran, their magical greenhouse had contained special lights to nourish the plants they'd retrieved from other worlds with different suns. Creating such lights might be necessary here too.

As soon as her father left, and Jadora felt free to experiment with her magic, she would attempt to get them to germinate by less than natural means. Thanks to all the knowledge Zelonsera had poured into her mind, she had a few ideas about how to do that.

"Are you listening, Jadora?"

"Yes, Father. I agree that the entire world is now in danger because of the dragons."

She didn't mention Thanok, not being a believer herself, much to her father's consternation. Besides, as she well knew, Uthari was the reason the dragons were here. They could blame his insistence that she find the Jitaruvak and turn it into a compound that would supposedly grant eternal life—or at least extended longevity—to whoever drank it. Of course, he only intended to share it with his powerful mage allies and the handful of terrene humans who were deemed intelligent enough to contribute to society, as he'd put it.

Every time she remembered her conversations with him, she ground her teeth. At least she could now keep him from reading her mind. She wasn't consciously doing it, but Jak, Malek, and other mages had all informed her that they couldn't spy on her thoughts anymore.

"You must continue to work hard." Father pushed his fingers through his thinning white hair. "Don't let your change... change *you*."

"I don't intend to." Jadora rubbed her gritty eyes. She couldn't remember the last time she'd slept. Uthari had insisted she get to work right away.

She moved to the sealed glass dishes where she had samples growing. Some held the bacteria that the death darters on

Nargnoth had delivered via their long stingers. Now that she had the knowledge to destroy them if they infected someone, she wasn't that worried about them escaping containment, and she'd been experimenting on them with extracts from the various plants the team had brought back. If she found something that killed them without requiring magic, she would try it on the samples growing in the other dishes: the unicellular flagellate eukaryotes that she'd extracted from a dead dragon.

They were the insidious parasites that changed the dragons' personalities and their scale coloring, the parasites that the dragons themselves didn't know how to destroy. Once infected, the dragons stopped *wanting* to destroy them. They'd intentionally tried to infest Shikari with the parasites, to turn him into one of them.

Jak had warned her that the eukaryotes were dangerous to grow, that the parasitic organisms might escape of their own accord and jump into Shikari. Jadora didn't disagree, but the only way she could imagine learning what worked to destroy them was by experimenting on them. Not only did she need to figure out how to kill the parasite, but she ideally needed to find a way to do it without killing the hosts. That would be the hard part.

At least, thanks to her new power, she'd been able to enclose the parasites in magic as well as glass, so she wasn't entirely terrified by what she was doing, but she couldn't help but dwell upon her suspicion that the dragons themselves might have performed experiments such as these thousands of years earlier. Maybe they'd also believed they'd had the bacteria contained... and then something had happened, and they'd been infected themselves.

Jadora swallowed as she eyed the dishes under a microscope and took a few notes on the progress of the parasites in the growth medium. Thus far, she didn't think humans were susceptible—or of interest—to the parasites, but she wasn't positive. Just because they'd shown more interest in infecting Shikari than Jak or Malek didn't mean that humans were immune.

"You're lucky you missed the battle," her father said. "It was awful. So many people died, mages *and* terrene humans. The people who were there merely to serve their masters, forced to do so by magic and those soul-stealing headbands. I saw more than one mage push them out in front to use as human shields, hoping the dragons snapped the servants up instead of them. The cowards. Without their magic, they're nothing."

"Not all mages are like that," Jadora murmured, taking a few measurements.

Malek wasn't a coward, and he never would have pushed someone in front of him to use as a shield. If anything, he did the opposite. From what Jak had told her, the reason Malek had been infected by the death-darter bacteria had been because he'd been pulling Zethron out of danger.

He'd also risked Uthari's wrath when he'd opened the portal before it had been swooped up for transport on the *Star Flyer*, and they'd sent Zethron back to Vran. Zethron had hugged Jadora before he'd left, then hurried away, back to the world he called home, where he wouldn't have to worry about the horde of dragons that had arrived in Torvil.

Malek had watched the exchange with a bland expression, not the twinge of irritation he'd occasionally displayed when she'd gotten close to Zethron—or vice versa. Jadora didn't know if that meant he hadn't been concerned about Zethron's feelings for her because he'd been leaving or... if his own feelings for her had changed.

Since Zelonsera had given her the ability to use magic, Malek had been looking at her differently. All of the mages had. They knew how to guard their thoughts, so she couldn't read them, but she kept getting a sense for their feelings, a hint that they resented her and would prefer she go back to being a helpless mundane human. She almost missed that. Oh, she'd hated being a hapless prisoner, but her father hadn't looked at her with fear and pity, and she hadn't been certain people were scheming to knock her over the railing of the mageship.

"Please tell me you're not empathizing with them," Father said. "Not... *identifying* with them."

"No, but some of them are decent human beings."

Jadora flipped through her notes. She'd filled three entire journals on the way from the dragon cave on Nargnoth back to the portal, hurrying to decant the knowledge Zelonsera had shared with her before she forgot it, especially everything that might be helpful when it came to the parasite.

Father shook his head. "Not that Uthari. He had me kidnapped to use against you, and even after he promised to let me return to Sprungtown... here I am. Even though it's not my fault, I can't help but feel I've abandoned my congregation. And what of my gardens that feed those in the neighborhood who can't afford to buy fresh vegetables at the market? And Ms. Dwellker-ven's chair. I promised to fix it, but that was right before Uthari's henchmen swept me up. Do you think someone else helped her? Since she lost her husband and her eyesight, she's had so much trouble."

"I'm sure someone did, Father. You'll be back soon and can check on her. Even if Uthari doesn't want to let you go back to our city, I'll..." Jadora stopped before saying she would levitate him off the ship herself. He didn't want to witness or understand the power she'd been given, or believe she would change, and she'd gone along with his wishes and hadn't done anything magical in front of him. "I'll find a way to get you home," she said vaguely and turned back to her notes.

The words *Orbs of Wisdom* jumped out at her.

Jadora had almost forgotten about them. They weren't simply one among the thousands of things Zelonsera had shared in that great transfer of knowledge; she'd mentioned them specifically as a possible place to search for more information.

"*Yes.*" Father stepped forward and gripped Jadora's arm. "And you must come too. You and Jak. Back to Sprungtown and the university." His grip tightened as he gazed into her eyes, his brow furrowed with deep concern. "I see what they're doing to him, and you must too. The way he follows that *zidarr* around like a puppy, eager for his praise, learning his dreadful magic in the hope of a head pat. They'll turn Jak away from us, Jadora. You must see that. We *all* need to escape these foul people."

Jadora opened her mouth, torn between not wanting to argue with her father and desiring to defend Malek and promise that Jak wasn't a mindless pup who could easily be manipulated. Before she could speak, she sensed a powerful aura in the corridor outside. Uthari.

Grimacing, she held a finger to her lips. "He's coming."

"How do you—"

The door opened without warning—powerful mages seemed incapable of knocking—and Uthari strode into the laboratory.

There were bags under his eyes, and his skin seemed paler and thinner than it had before Jadora had gone to Nargnoth. She'd heard a rumor from the servants that the magical contraption that kept him alive long past the lifespan of a normal human being had been damaged in the dragon battle.

She had no idea if that was true—it was possible the old tyrant had a hint of a conscience and was being kept up nights, dwelling on how his ambitions had caused the problem the world now faced—but she wouldn't weep if he died. She couldn't bring herself to wish the death of another human being, but... her life would be simpler if Uthari were gone. Though she supposed Tonovan and other powerful mages would still be around, wanting to use her and her son. She sighed.

"Come with me, Professor," Uthari said, ignoring her father.

Father's hand tightened on her arm, as if he wanted to pull her to safety, to protect her. Jadora smiled sadly as she extricated herself from his grip. Unfortunately, it had been a long time since he'd had the power to protect her from that which threatened her.

Uthari strode back into the corridor, casting an impatient look over his shoulder. A childish part of her wanted to stay where she was, to test her new power and see if she could successfully resist him, but she tamped down that notion. She didn't want to fight with a wily old wizard who could kill her family members with a thought.

Jadora patted her father on the arm and joined Uthari in the corridor.

"You used to jump eagerly to obey me," he remarked.

"I assure you I was never eager, Your Majesty. Fearful, perhaps."

And she still was. Even if she could defend against his ire, what of Jak? Uthari and the other mages could hurt her through him. He was learning to use his power, but he still lacked the strength of those who'd been studying magic their whole lives. Even when he reached his maximum potential, there would always be those who were stronger. That was the way of the mages. The riches and rewards went to the strongest, and the weaker among them were vulnerable. She couldn't let herself get cocky just because she'd been granted power.

Uthari smiled briefly before heading down the corridor. "It would be foolish to be a brave mouse in a den full of lions."

She thought about pointing out that she wasn't a mouse anymore, but she didn't know if that was true. She couldn't envision herself launching any of the loathsome attacks the mages inflicted on each other. Her father wouldn't forgive her for using magic to hurt people—nor would she forgive herself.

"Yes," she said. "It would be."

Uthari led her out on deck, where she spotted Jak and Malek

standing side by side near the railing, Malek resting a hand on her son's shoulder as he instructed Jak. At first, the moment touched her, and her feelings for Malek filled her with warmth. She was glad he was teaching Jak and that they were developing a bond. But her father's words popped into her mind, the condemnation with which he'd suggested Jak was a mindless pup seeking praise.

Malek must have sensed her, for he looked back, their eyes meeting. Jadora made herself smile and nod, but she caught a smug smirk on Uthari's face—as if he was pleased Jak was growing closer and closer to Malek, his loyal servant. A cold brick of distress clunked down in her stomach.

Malek inclined his head toward her, though his eyes were curious as he glanced at Uthari. Wondering where he was taking her? If so, he didn't question her—or his liege. He merely turned back to Jak, lifting a hand and demonstrating something.

An odd twinge of jealousy arose in her, the thought that he was more comfortable with Jak now than with her popping into her mind. But she squashed the thought. Malek hadn't said anything about being bothered by her power. She was letting her own fears taunt her.

"This way, Professor." Uthari led her toward the wooden double doors that led to his suite.

Two of his officers stood guard to either side, men in their early twenties, each radiating a modest amount of power. Jadora now saw everyone as if with two sets of eyes. Her regular eyes and her magical eyes. Everyone she encountered with inherent power was like a candle or a lantern or a fire burning in a hearth. Or, in some cases, a huge crackling ball of flame that burned so brightly that she struggled to see their regular features through the power they exuded. The two guards were like candles. Many of the officers on board, mostly the lower-ranking ones, were similar, with a few lanterns among them. Rivlen and other higher-ranking officers were like hearths ablaze with power. And Uthari, Malek, and Tonovan were fireballs.

What, she wondered, did she look like to them?

Surprisingly, both of the guards eyed her up and down with interest. She'd seen them before when she'd been brought up to the yacht, and neither had so much as glanced at her, dismissing her as a nonthreat and nobody of interest. But now that she had power, that had changed. They had to see her as a threat and wonder if they should be concerned that she was trailing their king around.

No, she realized, as one focused on her chest and ran his tongue over his lips. It was more than that, at least for that man. It wasn't her status as a *threat* that had him considering her.

"Really, Orfar," Uthari said dryly as he passed the guard.

The man blushed, straightened, and looked away.

Jadora quickened her pace, wanting to get this field trip out of the way so she could return to the relative safety of her laboratory.

Once she and Uthari were in the wood-paneled corridor of his suite, the floorboards gleaming with freshly applied polish, the doors closed behind them. A female servant waited in the foyer with trays of iced water with orange slices floating in the glasses. A plate of frosted cookies rested beside the drinks, and Uthari waved toward them. "Will you have a drink? A snack?"

"I... I'm not thirsty or hungry." Jadora made herself smile and add, "Thank you."

"Perhaps afterward. I have a request to make of you, something you may find challenging. If you haven't already, you'll learn that drawing on a great deal of power can be as taxing as running twenty miles."

"Your Majesty?"

What did he want her to do?

When she'd previously visited his suite, the only room she'd been invited into had been his office, but he veered toward a different door this time.

The comment about using a great deal of power and being taxed made her think for a bizarre moment that he was taking her to his bedchamber and had sex in mind, but that was ridiculous. She blamed the lurid gaze from the officer outside for causing her thoughts to veer in that direction.

Thankfully, Uthari opened the door to a library, the walls lined with built-in bookcases, rather than a bedroom. Two cushy leather chairs sat near a porthole, but it was an apparatus in the center that he stopped in front of, resting his hand on a reclining chair that was tilted back amid liquids in glass flasks and columns with tubes running between them. Jadora had seen the contraption before in Uthari's castle and knew it was what infused a concoction of magic and chemicals into him to extend his life. Presumably, he had regular treatments.

"It's not working." Uthari watched her through slitted eyes.

So, the rumors had been true.

"It was damaged in the attack," he continued. "I found it knocked over on its side with many of the flasks broken and the frame warped. My doctor and I have replaced the chemicals and done our best to repair the damage, but it's still not working. A mage smith created it two centuries ago, but when I brought in my smith Homgor, he was at a loss. He's wonderful at crafting weapons. Medical equipment is beyond him."

"What do you want me to do?" Jadora asked.

"Repair it, of course. You can use your background in chemistry, combined with your new power, and I understand the dragon somehow transferred a great deal of knowledge to you as well?" Uthari arched his eyebrows.

Jadora did her best not to wince, knowing Malek must have shared everything with his king. She couldn't be surprised, and, since Malek had been loyal to Uthari for decades, she couldn't have expected anything else, but it felt like a betrayal. Emotionally, if not rationally and logically.

"Knowledge of things pertinent to dragons," Jadora said. "I don't think they overly concerned themselves with medical devices to lengthen human lives. If you would, however, like to know which worlds and climates are most desirable for dragons in the throes of their mating years, I can tell you all about that."

Uthari extended his hand toward the contraption. "Do what you can, Professor. If someone isn't able to repair my machine, I'll be forced to go back to the old rituals that require spilling the life force of human beings and magically transferring their energy to me. Alas, those who partook in the ritual with me tended to die. Surely, you don't wish me to resort to such vampiric measures?" He smiled at her. "I had this created so that I might continue my existence in a more humane way."

Jadora's stomach turned as she imagined him with innocent young people on their knees in front of him, sucking their lives from them via some vile dark magic. She wanted to scoff, but thanks to her new knowledge, she believed—no, she *knew*—that such rituals did exist and did work.

"I trust you'll do your best. There's a book in that drawer over there with schematics. Perhaps you'll find it useful if your new knowledge isn't sufficient." Something dark flashed in his eyes—resentment?—and reminded her of all the people who'd trained their whole lives and didn't have all that she'd been given in minutes.

It's not my fault, she wanted to cry to them.

"I'll check up on you in a couple of hours." Uthari strode out, shutting the door behind him.

She sensed him leaving the suite and walking out to join Malek.

Jadora glowered at the machine, wishing she could sabotage it so it would never work again, rather than fixing it. She gripped her chin and wondered if that was possible. Maybe she could figure out a way to alter it while making Uthari believe that she'd repaired it. If he *knew* it was broken, he would resort to those rituals.

But how could she sabotage it?

Jak was the one learning how to make mage devices from Vinjo, and she didn't have much knowledge related to engineering. Still, she knew a lot about herbs, tinctures, and chemicals. She could easily come up with a poison to slip into the liquids that would, when Uthari sat in the chair and his doctor slid a needle into his vein, ooze into his bloodstream.

Not an unappealing thought, but Uthari couldn't possibly trust her. After she tinkered, he would have his doctor check everything three times. She didn't know if she could sabotage the contraption in such a way that an expert wouldn't figure it out.

Even if she could, could she truly bring herself to *poison* Uthari? Or to arrange his murder through some other malfunction?

She had little doubt that the world would be a better place without him, and with him gone, there wouldn't be, as far as she knew, anyone else left to whom Malek had sworn his loyalty. Oh, he was zidarr and was likely supposed to serve whoever Uthari's heir was, but wasn't it possible he would let his feelings for her sway him? Maybe he would choose to stand with her instead of obediently swearing his allegiance to another conniving wizard.

It wasn't as if she wanted him to turn on his own people and start killing mages left and right. All she longed for was to find a way to fulfill her promise to Zelonsera and turn her kind back into the dragons they'd once been, friendly allies to humans, not vile creatures who preyed upon them. And if they did that, was it possible that what she, her late husband, and Jak had dreamed of would come to pass? That the dragons would help change Torvil and how it was governed by removing the wizards from power and letting terrene humans govern themselves? With dragons flying through now and then and monitoring the world, would mages *dare* continue to enslave humans and treat them like chattel?

It was a dream worth having, but if it relied upon her murdering Uthari...

Jadora shuddered, her father's voice sounding in her mind, delivering words from *The Teachings: If you must adopt the tactics and traits of your enemy to vanquish him, you will become that which you sought to defeat.*

As her mind whirred, Jadora found the book of schematics in the drawer and flipped through it. The engineering knowledge she hadn't thought she possessed came to her, and she absorbed and understood the text.

Who would have thought dragons would have been engineers with a deep understanding of building structures and machines? But it made sense. They'd built the portals, after all, and figured out how to travel to other worlds. Humans had no idea how those portals worked. Maybe it was delusional of her to believe that she could find a solution to a problem that dragons had been stymied by.

After studying the book, Jadora used her senses to examine the contraption. She did find damage, but it seemed superficial, as if an angry servant had taken a wrench to it. It was easy to fix. Barely stirring, she made a few adjustments.

She paused, however, when she determined a way she might sabotage the contraption. If she were to alter the syringe mechanism that delivered the substance, to send air into Uthari's bloodstream while *appearing* to deliver his medicine, that might kill him as surely as a poison. And it might even be deemed an accident. Oh, someone would suspect her of tampering, but if Uthari were dead, would it truly matter? Malek would stand beside her against the other mage officers.

Or would he? If he suspected her of killing Uthari, how would he react?

"Not well," she murmured.

A new thought struck her with the abruptness of a mallet hitting a gong. What if Uthari was testing her?

She lowered her arm as she stared at the contraption, at the repairs that had been simple, things that he or his doctor—or Vinjo, if they'd brought him over—could easily have fixed. What if Uthari was giving her this opportunity to tinker with his equipment to see what she did?

The resounding certainty that she was right came over her, and panic swelled in her chest as she realized she'd almost fallen into his trap. Not only would she not have succeeded in getting rid of him, but he would have learned that she couldn't be trusted. That she'd tried to *kill* him. How would he have reacted? By killing her? Or, if he couldn't get through her defenses now, by killing Jak?

Jadora gulped in deep breaths and tried to find calmness. She'd only thought about sabotage; she hadn't done it. He couldn't read her mind anymore, so he wouldn't know. He couldn't.

With shaking hands, she returned the book to the drawer and finished the simple repairs the machine required. Though she had no tools, she found her magic was sufficient to the task. More than sufficient. In minutes, she was done.

As if Uthari had been monitoring her, he returned right after she finished. He squinted at her thoughtfully as soon as he stepped in, then carefully eyed the machine. She could *sense* him examining it with his magic, little tendrils that swept out and probed it all over.

A smile crept across his face as he finished and looked at her. Though she couldn't read his mind any more than he could read hers, she knew she'd been right. It had been a test. It had very nearly been a trap.

"Good work, Professor," he crooned, stepping close to her.

With his wispy white grandpa hair and height no greater than hers, he wasn't physically intimidating, but she braced herself and prepared to raise her magical defenses.

He lifted a hand and rested it on her shoulder.

"You are wise to work with me instead of against me," he said softly. "You are one of us now. I would hate to have to command Malek to do what I discussed with him." He smiled at his vagueness, his eyes promising he wanted her to ask for clarification.

She wouldn't give him the satisfaction of showing that curiosity. To the Slavemasters in hell with him and his plans for her.

Uthari squeezed her shoulder, and magical power flowed from his fingers.

Again, she tensed and braced herself. Was it an attack?

She was on the verge of pushing it away—pushing *him* away—but his touch wasn't cruel. He delivered a wave of pleasure that flowed along her nerves. Not quite sexual but alluring, nonetheless, reminding her of the time she'd experimented with a mageband in school but far more intense.

"Loyalty comes with rewards," Uthari said softly, holding her gaze.

Jadora stepped back, using her magic to push his hand away. He only smiled wider, as if he knew he had her.

Jadora gritted her teeth and walked out. Let the bastard believe what he wanted.

The servant was still outside, holding her tray, her eyes vacant as she gazed blankly toward a wall. She made herself focus on Jadora.

"Water, my lady?"

"No, thank you." Still irritated with Uthari, Jadora used her magic to sabotage the woman's slaveband, to break the magic that controlled her through it, and give her back her free will.

It was petty and a pointless act of rebellion, as the servant wouldn't be able to flee anywhere when she was stuck on the yacht, and Uthari or one of his officers would notice sooner or later that the slaveband wasn't working, but it was all Jadora could manage as she strode back to her laboratory.

Power or not, she was still a prisoner here, a prisoner who dared not strike against her captor.

3

Colonel Sorath, a man without a company and currently without a mission in life, prowled the dirt-walled tunnels of the druids' underground complex. In the middle of the jungle on the southern continent of Zewnath, he was thousands of miles from his homeland of Zar, and hundreds of miles from Port Toh-drom, the nearest city where he might have found passage on a ship. Not that he longed to go back to the desert. Not with dragons ravaging the world.

He'd helped battle and slay one, and he wanted to continue to fight, to put an end to the threat to Torvil—and the threat to Thorn Company. After losing his own company, he hadn't intended to let himself get attached to another one, but he'd come to care about the all-female mercenary unit far more than he would have expected, especially in such a short time. Oh, he'd known Captain Ferroki off and on for years, but more often as an opponent than an ally. It had, however, been some time since he'd thought of her as an adversary.

Sorath sighed, wishing he were with Thorn Company now and heading into action instead of skulking in these tunnels.

Why he wanted to rush into battle again, he didn't know. He was far too old to take up a new career of fighting dragons. He'd long since passed fifty, his knees and back ached, and the stump where his hand had once been kept sending phantom pain up his arm. Still, what else was he going to do?

Before this had all started, he'd been retired and writing his memoir, but one could hardly sip octli and pen deep thoughts while dragons hurled magic at one's city. Besides, that life hadn't suited him well. His aching body might not appreciate it, but he was a man of action.

"Colonel Sorath?" came a woman's voice from behind him.

It was Kywatha, one of the few druids who understood Dhoran and spoke to him. The rest could communicate their intent telepathically, but they seemed disinclined to do so with a surly mercenary who was out of place in their nature-loving, magic-using, green-hair-dyeing community.

"Yes?" Sorath turned to face her.

Magical silver light emanated from the walls of the tunnel, making it easy to see her green hair, woven-grass clothing, and voluptuous figure. It was a testament to his distraction that he didn't pause to admire her—or maybe it was that he had another woman on his mind, one he'd shared a kiss with before taking Vinjo's magical stealth device and fleeing into the jungle, and one whom he hadn't seen except from afar since. Captain Ferroki's face floated into his mind. With her short hair, snub nose, and compact build, she wasn't the epitome of feminine beauty, but she was kind, wise, and understood him the way someone who wasn't in the business never could.

"You said you'd be willing to help fight more dragons, right?" Kywatha glanced at the dragon-steel dagger belted at his waist alongside his black-powder pistol.

The dagger didn't belong to Sorath, and he was surprised the druids hadn't asked for it back yet. Once young Grunk, the man who'd apparently brought it to their community, recovered from his wounds, he might ask for it.

"Yes. I was hoping to rejoin Thorn Company, though if they're still working for King Uthari, that might not be feasible." Sorath had tried to kill Uthari, and would have succeeded if Captain Rivlen hadn't leaped to his defense, so he was positive Uthari still wanted him dead.

"They've left the continent."

"Ah." Sorath had suspected as much. "Heading to Uth?"

The last he'd heard, the dragons had spread out after flying through the portal and were attacking cities all over the world. Would it be petty for him to hope that Utharika was destroyed? He wished no ill toward the terrene humans living below the sky city in Uthari's kingdom, but as far as he was concerned, every mage city could go up in flames before crashing to the earth.

"I believe so. There are dragons harassing their continent."

"Have you heard anything about dragons on Zar?" Sorath had spent most of his life there, only occasionally flying about on mageships and leading his men against forces on other continents. Even though his mother had been a roamer, she'd left the seagoing people to ensure Sorath had a stable childhood and good education. When he thought of home, it was the hot arid deserts of Zar, and his gut twisted when he imagined the people there being devastated.

"Some have been reported there, yes. But we have a more immediate threat." Kywatha touched her chest and tilted her head back toward the core of the druid complex. "Port Toh-drom is threatened. As we speak, a dragon is circling the city and might have destroyed it already, but a few druids in the area are helping the citizens. Surprisingly, some roamer pirates who were there when the dragon arrived are also helping."

"I'll assist if you can get me there." Sorath might have left the druid settlement days earlier if it hadn't meant walking on foot through a jungle without roads.

Kywatha nodded. "We're preparing our ship now."

Sorath blinked. "You have a *ship*? Like a mageship?"

He hadn't seen or heard of the tunnel-loving druids using such a craft.

"It's *like* a mageship." Kywatha smiled. "Perhaps more of a raft."

"A flying raft?"

"Essentially. And we've prepared it for travel. So, if you're ready..." She extended a hand toward him.

"I'm ready." It wasn't as if he'd been able to grab even a change of clothing before leaving the mercenary camp. One of the druids had offered him a grass vest, but it had looked scratchy and... *grassy*. He'd decided his clothing from home could last a little longer.

"Follow me, then. Grunk is eager to see you again."

"Oh?" Sorath had worked with the kid to infiltrate Uthari's yacht and kill Queen Vorsha—however inadvertently—but he wouldn't say they'd bonded. The bloody-knife-licking Grunk was unpredictable and more than a little crazy, not that Sorath minded that in a soldier. By the end of their adventure, Grunk had been speaking telepathically with him and hadn't seemed that bad.

"He told the story of how you heroically took down the *Dread Arrow* and slew a dragon. He's quite impressed with you."

"Huh. He was good in a fight. I take it your people got him all healed up?"

"Yes, he's ready to go into battle again. He hopes to slay his own dragon."

He would need his dragon-steel weapon back to do that. Sorath wistfully touched the hilt of the dagger, wondering if he might be able to find another one. Few other weapons could penetrate a dragon's defenses.

As Sorath trailed Kywatha into an upward-sloping tunnel, his hand on the dagger, a vision came to him. He saw the city of Port Toh-drom, buildings destroyed, people injured in the streets, and the docks along the river on fire. A brown-and-gray one-eyed dragon circled the area, looking at an eight-story tower on one of the hilltops in town, but four grass-tunic-wearing druids stood around a nearby monument with their arms raised and eyes closed. Every time the dragon encroached on the city, a beam of green light shot from the top of the monument and struck the intruder. The magical energy didn't seem to breach its defenses or hurt it that much, but it did deter the dragon, causing it to fly out over the jungle again.

Sorath braced himself, waiting for the vision to show him dying horribly in a battle against that dragon—the last vision he'd received from the dagger had shown him dying on the floor of Uthari's suite, and that had nearly happened. If not for Grunk, it *would* have happened.

But the vision merely swept out to let him see roamer ships anchored in the mouth of the river, the crew members firing arrows and magelock rifles at the dragon. Such weapons did nothing to harm the great creature, and it didn't even glance at its attackers, instead focusing on the druids and that tower, for some reason.

Sorath recognized it, for he'd battled Zidarr Yidar there while Jak and Jadora escaped. The stable that Yidar had brought down on Sorath's and Tezi's heads was still a flattened heap of rubble, much as he'd last seen it. With dragons invading the world, rebuilding probably wasn't a priority for the citizens.

"Sorath?" Kywatha touched his arm, and the imagery faded.

Though not sure what it had been trying to convey to him, if anything, Sorath happily released the vision. He liked that the dagger could pierce dragon scales while protecting him from magical attacks. Its other features were less appealing to him.

"Yes," he said.

"I said we have to climb up here." Kywatha pointed to a ladder leading up ten feet to an opening with muted daylight beyond, the dense jungle canopy visible far above. "Can you make it?" She glanced toward the pickaxe attachment at the end of his left arm.

"Of course." Sorath frowned at the suggestion that he might not be a fully capable man. Even if he hadn't had the tool, he could have managed a simple ladder. "Your dagger was enlightening me."

Not explaining further, he passed her to climb up first, making sure his pace was suitably swift. The sound of his pickaxe clinking on the rungs reminded him that he might not climb ladders as *stealthily* these days, but the mageships had all left to deal with the dragons, so he doubted he had to worry about enemies waiting outside.

They emerged on a tree-filled hillside, the ground carpeted with fallen leaves and ferns, but at the bottom of a slope, the foliage had been cut back. Sunlight beamed into a clearing filled with people. With people and a huge... raft. Kywatha was right. That was the word that came to mind.

Almost as large as one of the mageships, it was made from logs bound together with vines, with nothing save for what might have been a navigation cabin or engineering room—or both—rising up from the back of the flat platform.

"I guess nobody gets a private cabin," Sorath said, though he'd never been offered a private cabin on one of the mageships either. Mages all seemed to believe hired mercenaries should sleep out in the open on the deck, even in rain-loving and bug-filled Zewnath.

"No cabins. We're a simple people." Kywatha led the way down the slope.

As Sorath followed her, he spotted Grunk among a number of druids boarding and setting packs on the center of the raft. Though he favored the same green hair as most of the other druids, his pale skin stood out among the darker-skinned Zewnath natives, a reminder that he'd come from the north, perhaps even from Vorsha's kingdom. Sorath hadn't gotten the full story, but Grunk had intimated that he'd been a slave for her people—maybe even for her personally—forced to fight for the amusement of his masters.

Someone walked close to him, brushing his shoulder, and Grunk spun, his knife in hand before he caught himself. The druid skittered back, mumbled an apology, and gave him a wide berth after that.

"He's a damaged young man," Kywatha murmured.

Sorath, who well understood what war and fighting did to people, only shrugged. "A lot of us are. Those who aren't probably will be by the time this is all done." He waved toward the sky to indicate the dragon invasion.

"You're a cheerful man, Colonel."

"Yes, mercenary leaders are known for their ebullience."

When he climbed onto the raft, Grunk spotted him and jogged over. He put his knife away, though he squinted around at anyone who stepped close to him. Surprisingly, he smiled at Sorath. That did little to soften his face, since he—or one of his former masters—had filed his canine teeth to points. If the kid ever wanted to attract a woman, he had better learn to smile with his lips sealed.

We will go into battle again, Colonel, Grunk shared telepathically instead of speaking aloud.

Sorath hadn't yet heard him speak, though he'd seen him lick knives, so he knew Grunk had a tongue. "Dragons this time."

I prefer to kill mages and wish dragons could be friends, like Shylezar was in the olden days, but to fight is good. Grunk whipped out his knife again and shadow sparred with his imagination.

"You'll need a better weapon than that to take down a dragon." Reluctantly, Sorath drew his borrowed dragon-steel dagger.

Beside him, Kywatha exhaled. In relief? Had she believed Sorath wouldn't give it back?

Sorath clenched his jaw. He was an honorable man. He did not *steal* that which didn't belong to him.

Yes. Grunk faced him, clasped his hands together in front of his chest, then bowed before reverently accepting the weapon.

Despite his thoughts, it was a challenge not to snatch it back. Without it, Sorath would not only be vulnerable to magical attacks, but he wouldn't have the means with which to pierce a dragon's defenses.

Given that the dagger had shown him that a dragon was waiting for them... relinquishing it made him especially uneasy. He had no inherent magic and couldn't summon power from within an ancient druid monument. How was he supposed to help in the coming battle?

A knock at the door to the laboratory made Jadora straighten, her neck and back stiff from hunching over the workbench for hours. Hoping for Malek or Jak, she reached out with her senses, but she didn't know the name of the officer standing outside. She recognized his aura, as she'd been on the *Serene Waters* long enough to encounter most of the crew, and wondered what message Uthari had sent the man to deliver.

"Come in," she called, sweeping out more broadly with her senses as she did so, wanting to make sure Jak was all right.

It had been hours since her little act of rebellion—breaking the magic of the servant's slaveband—and Uthari hadn't barked any warnings into her mind, but that didn't mean it had gone unnoticed.

Jak was up on the deck, no longer training with Malek, but

Shikari was with him. Hopefully, that meant he was safe. The dragon, his head—horns—barely above Jak's waist, hadn't yet grown into the fearsome creature he would one day be, but he had the ability to help defend her son.

The door opened, and a red-uniformed officer walked in with a tray, a cloche covering a plate. It looked like the meal trays the servants had been bringing by, and Jadora was surprised one of the officers would deign to partake in such a lowly task.

"Good afternoon, Professor Freedar." He bowed to her over the tray, the act almost startling after the mages had spent weeks ignoring her or treating her like gum stuck to the bottom of their boots. But she'd changed since then, to them if not herself.

"Hello, uhm, Lieutenant."

"Brathanik." He bowed again. "I told the slave girl that I would bring you your lunch. Someone like you should have company when you dine." He set the tray on her workbench, bumping a couple of her pots but too oblivious to notice. He didn't stare at her chest, like Uthari's young guard had, but she sensed him probing her with his magic. Was that how mages checked each other out? "*Stimulating* company," he added with a lazy smile, his magic apparently liking what it saw in her magic.

By Shylezar, she hadn't had this much male attention when she'd been unmarried, available, and far younger than she was now. Did her *power* somehow make these men indifferent to the fact that she was over forty and had a grown son?

"I'm stimulated sufficiently by my work." Jadora lifted her palm toward him, hoping that would be a sufficient deterrent. "And I've got a lot of it to do. Thank you for the meal, but I must ask you to leave now."

"Oh?" Brathanik propped an elbow on the workbench. "Are you sure? I come from a good family. Our children would be very powerful mages."

"Our *what*?" Jadora gripped the workbench for support. "I'm not— We can't. How could you even— I haven't even been able to propagate plants yet." She flung a hand toward her pots.

"Propa-what?" Brathanik blinked slowly.

"*Propagate*," a familiar voice said from the doorway. "To breed specimens of a plant or animal by natural processes from the parent stock."

Brathanik spun toward the doorway. "Lord Malek! I was just— Uhm, I mean, I brought our guest her lunch. I thought she'd be hungry."

"For you, no doubt." There was a hint of dryness in Malek's tone, but his face was hard and his gaze cold as it speared the lieutenant.

"*No.* Er, I wasn't sure. I wanted to ask in case she was... I'm from a good family, my lord!"

"Leave her alone, Brathanik." Malek stepped aside, leaving a clear path to the door.

"Yes, my lord." The officer sprinted out, almost bouncing off the far wall as he propelled himself down the corridor.

"I'm a guest now instead of a prisoner?" Jadora slumped against the workbench, though she eyed Malek with more wariness than usual. What if *he* strode forward with thoughts of propagation on his mind? No, he wouldn't make any clumsy passes, she was certain. If anything, he'd been avoiding her. Unfortunately. She missed his company, even if he had told Uthari everything about their ordeal on Nargnoth. "I guess I should be relieved."

"I don't think Uthari has officially changed your status. It's likely Brathanik elevated it due to his newfound interest." Malek walked into the room, but he stopped several feet from her and clasped his hands behind his back.

There was that distance again. It saddened her, but she supposed it was for the best.

"A number of people—*mages*—have developed an interest, it seems," Jadora said.

"Are you all right?" Malek asked softly.

"Just rattled. I preferred it when they were all indifferent."

"Power isn't the sole deciding factor in whether a mage is attracted to another mage, but for many, it can be a large part of the equation."

"But not for you?" Jadora raised her eyebrows, reminded that Malek had felt something for her long before she'd received her power.

He hesitated, then smiled sadly. "Whatever zidarr feel in regard to attraction matters little, since they're not supposed to act on it."

"Right." Jadora supposed that meant she shouldn't walk over and slump against him, hoping for a hug. "What did you and Uthari discuss in regard to me? Can you tell me?"

Earlier, she'd noticed that the stealth device Vinjo had given her back on Nargnoth was gone. She'd had it tucked in the bottom of the magical pack Malek had created for her weeks earlier. She didn't know who had taken it, but she suspected Uthari. She wondered if Jak still had the one Vinjo had made for him.

"I reported the details of our mission," Malek said, "as I always do."

"When he dragged me up to his suite to test me, he said there was something you discussed that he might command you to do to me. He was deliberately vague."

His eyes narrowed. "What do you mean *test*? What did he do?"

Jadora explained the supposedly broken medical contraption and how she'd been positive it had been a test—a trap. It had almost been easier when Malek had been able to read her thoughts and see everything that she remembered and was thinking about for himself. Would he still trust her now that he couldn't read her mind? Or would he, like Uthari, feel the need to test her?

Malek frowned, stepped forward, and lifted a hand, as if to touch her shoulder—or maybe her cheek? But he lowered it again. "I suppose I'm not surprised that he would arrange a test. He's wary of you and your new power."

"He has Jak and my father here on his yacht. I can't believe he thinks I would do something that would put them in danger." Though she very nearly had, hadn't she? She'd almost been seduced by the possibility of putting an end to Uthari. And of having Malek to herself, the way she had for moments here and there on their missions. At the least, she'd had the *illusion* of him. Maybe that was all it had been. His heart and soul had belonged to Uthari long before he'd met her.

"I can't either," Malek said. "I told him as much, that you weren't the type to murder people, no matter how much they might deserve it." The sad smile returned.

He was thinking of Tonovan, of course, not Uthari. She didn't need to read his mind to know that. Despite his honorable nature, he couldn't see what everyone else saw, that Uthari was as much of a villain as Tonovan. Maybe he was more of one. After all, Uthari knew what Tonovan was and employed him anyway. And his machinations affected the entire world.

"As to what he asked me..." Malek turned his palm toward the ceiling. "He said he wouldn't ask me to kill you—" he grimaced, "—or try to do it himself, as it might no longer be possible unless you were caught off guard..."

Jadora's jaw sagged in horror as she imagined Malek and Uthari discussing how her death might be accomplished.

"But he did ask me to force you into exile on another world," Malek continued, "if you turned out to be a threat to him or mages or our way of life. I guess he thought... you'd let me do it."

"Lovely," she whispered, her voice raspy.

It was the idea of the men calculatingly discussing her fate that disturbed her more than the thought of exile. She was fairly certain she now had the power and the knowledge to activate the portal even without a key—those had been made for the humans who worked with dragons, after all—and almost told him as much. But if Malek and Uthari hadn't guessed that, it was better not to point it out to them.

Besides, if they forced her through the portal and took it down again afterward, she truly would be exiled. She might be able to travel among the other worlds in the portal network, but she would never be able to return home again, never see her son or her father again, never walk the hallways at the university or putter around in her lab there.

Even though they might only have been musing, and Malek wasn't threatening anything at the moment, Jadora couldn't keep from tearing up with emotion. She turned her back to him, not wanting him—not wanting *any* of them—to see her weakness. No amount of dragon power could change that she was human and could break down emotionally as easily as the next woman.

"Jadora," Malek said softly, stepping closer. "I'm sorry. Nothing will come of it. I know you're doing as he asks and won't work against us, at least not while we have this common threat."

His words suggested he remembered that she'd once shared her husband's dream of using the portal to find dragons who would help mundane humans oust the wizards from power. She *still* dreamed of that, and she knew Jak did too. But Malek was right. As long as there was a greater threat to humanity, Jadora had to help the world deal with it. Even if it meant working with mages and for Uthari.

"I know you won't see it this way," Malek said, "but he meant it as a favor."

"A *favor*?" She spun back, but he'd stepped closer, so she ended up speaking to his collarbones. "Not to *me*."

"No. To me, I guess. He knows I wouldn't kill you." His voice lowered to a growl. "Or allow anyone else to do so either."

This time, when he lifted his hand, he did touch her cheek.

"Even him?" Jadora lifted her gaze to Malek's eyes.

"Nobody." He stroked her cheek with his thumb as he returned her gaze. "I told you I would protect you, and I will."

"Except from exile."

"I trust it won't come to that."

She wished she could be sure. What happened the next time Uthari set a trap for her? What if she wasn't clever enough to see through it twice?

"Although, you've thus far been protecting *me* as much as I've protected you." His sad smile returned, a ghost of a genuine smile, and she tried to remember if she'd ever seen him throw his head back and laugh as he looked at the world in pure delight. Maybe zidarr weren't allowed to do that. "I don't think I thanked you for curing me of those dreadful bacteria."

"You were too busy asking me to jump up and down to see if my pockets jangled with vials."

His smile widened slightly. "To see if you'd *changed*."

"I'm not sure what you think a dragon could do to me that would keep me from carrying sample-collection spatulas and vials in my pockets."

"Do you have them in there now?" He lowered his hand and quirked his eyebrows as he looked toward her pockets.

"No. We're not off on a mission exploring another world now. All I've got is a pen and a few vials." She didn't specify vials of *acid* as she delved into her pocket to pull out what she found to demonstrate her collection to him. She'd gotten in the habit of carrying those around to defend herself from mages and didn't quite trust that her new power would last, that she would never need them again. "A folding ruler," she added as she found more than she expected in her pockets and laid it on the workbench.

"Rubbing alcohol, activated charcoal, a protractor, starter yeast for my dishes, peat pellets..."

Malek propped his chin on his fist and watched, his eyes twinkling, as she inventoried her pockets. "A pen and a few vials, hm?" he asked when she finished, a stack of items piled on the counter.

"I was generalizing."

"I see. I'd ask what's in your backpack, but removing everything inside might take the rest of the journey."

"Ha ha."

"Where was I? Oh, yes. Allow me to formally thank you for saving my life on Nargnoth. And on the frozen world we first visited. I admit to being chagrined that I, a powerful zidarr trained from his earliest days to defeat all foes, needed saving not once but twice." He shook his head slowly.

"How much of that zidarr training involved instruction in arrogance?" Jadora asked, amused that anyone could be chagrined that a *dragon* had nearly defeated him. She could see being a little more sheepish about being laid low by bacteria. Even Zelonsera had seemed chagrined when speaking of dragon hubris and how they'd caused their parasite to mutate and adapt their magic due to their own actions.

"That was a daily part of my lessons."

"You mastered it well."

"I came to express my gratitude to you and shoo away suitors from good families and you respond by teasing me."

"Sorry. I like teasing you. Your eyes get delightfully indignant when I do it, and it makes me want to..." She stopped herself from finishing, from saying *kiss you*. Instead, she stepped in and hugged him, burying her face in his shoulder. She appreciated that he'd come and that he wasn't completely avoiding her, and she didn't want him to think she had changed. She hadn't, damn it.

"I know," Malek said softly, returning her embrace and resting his head against hers.

She closed her eyes, enjoying the moment, the closeness, though the dangerous urge to kiss him on the neck came over her. The neck, and then the mouth, as she slid her hands under his tunic and over his muscular torso. Would he allow it if she did? Or would he step away and speak of the Zidarr Code? At the least, he would point out that kissing on Uthari's yacht wasn't a good idea. This time, they weren't far off on another world where Uthari might not find out.

Still, the rebellious part of her that had snapped the magic of the slaveband arose within her again. She kissed the side of his neck, her lips lingering on his warm skin as she inhaled his masculine warmth.

Malek grew still. "We can't do anything, Jadora," he murmured, though he stroked the back of her head, delicious warmth spreading through her as his hand slid down her hair.

"I know."

"Not today," he added, as if there would be some day when they *could* be together.

Since Uthari might live forever, Jadora couldn't foresee that day, but when he slipped his fingers through her hair to rub the back of her neck, she leaned her chest against his and let herself fantasize.

"Someday?" she whispered, tilting her head back to enjoy his massage. "Do zidarr ever get to retire?"

Malek snorted softly. "I'm not sure. Most don't make it to the age where one might normally do that."

His forehead creased, as if he were trying to remember if a zidarr had *ever* made it to such an age. More likely, they slowed down as they grew older, and some enemy's blade inevitably found their back.

Distressed by the thought, Jadora touched his jaw, afraid that would happen, that he would die before they got a chance to be... something.

Malek met her gaze again, and maybe he saw a hint of her thoughts in her mind—or in her eyes—for his face softened. He opened his mouth to speak but instead leaned closer for a kiss. It was a bad idea, and they both knew it, but she didn't hesitate to tilt her mouth toward his.

But he froze and frowned at something past her shoulder.

"What?" she whispered, longing for the kiss.

"What is that?" Malek nodded toward the workbench.

Unless something under the cloche had sprouted legs and was walking off her plate, she couldn't imagine what had distracted him, but she turned to look. His gaze was focused on the sealed dishes that contained the unicellular flagellate eukaryotes.

"I started growing samples of the dragon parasites." Hadn't she told him about that? She'd told Jak, but maybe she'd started this project when Malek had been afflicted by the death-darter bacteria. "I know it might not be that wise, but I've magically sealed the dishes. I'm experimenting on them and trying to find something to kill them that won't also kill the hosts."

Jadora was trying to find something to kill them *period*. Back on Vran, Malek had used fire to incinerate the parasites riding on floating, glowing motes toward Shikari, but thus far, the bacteria she was growing were resistant to heat. She hypothesized that the organisms Malek had succeeded in destroying had been weakened from the death of their host, but it was also possible he'd only destroyed the magical motes that had been carrying them and that the parasites had fallen to the ground and remained alive. If the latter, they'd been lucky to have gotten out of there before the organisms could find another way to infect Shikari.

"I know about that, but look." Malek pointed at a dish in the back.

Jadora leaned toward it as she reached for a magnifying glass, but she froze. She didn't need magnification to see what he'd spotted, and a boulder of dread dropped into her gut.

Glowing softly within the dish was one of the motes that could float through the air and carry the parasites to a new host.

Until that moment, she hadn't known if the motes were something the parasites created or something that naturally existed inside a dragon's body that they'd coerced into helping them spread. Now, she had her answer. And now, she knew that the parasites she was growing had plans to find a new host.

4

As the sun set, Captain Rivlen finished helping with the last of the repairs the *Star Flyer* had needed after the dragon battle and headed to her cabin. The vessel hadn't taken as much damage as some of the ships in the fleet—the memory of Tonovan's *Dread Arrow* utterly destroyed and crashed behind the portal could still make her smile—but she wanted the *Star Flyer* in tiptop shape for the inevitable battles that were coming.

Battles? Or an all-out war?

Rivlen didn't know.

The fleet was flying as fast as possible back to the Kingdom of Uth, and she felt both trepidatious and determined as she anticipated fighting more dragons. They were terribly powerful enemies, and facing even one without help could result in her death and the destruction of the *Star Flyer*, but she couldn't shy away from her duty.

That morning, when she'd met with King Uthari, General Tonovan, and the other mageship captains, she'd learned there were three dragons razing their kingdom, destroying cities and killing hundreds, if not thousands, of people. Thus far, they'd been targeting hapless towns and villages on the ground, terrene-human habitats not protected by mages, instead of the well-defended sky city of Utharika.

Rivlen's parents lived there, and she was glad they hadn't yet been attacked, but it seemed inevitable that the dragons would soon challenge the city. They might enjoy preying on easy targets, but they hadn't shown any fear of humans wielding magic.

Had so many mageships not been down in Zewnath these past weeks, forces would have already been marshaled to fight the dragons terrorizing the kingdom, but... no. Rivlen shook her head. She wouldn't allow herself to think of the mistakes the king had made. It wasn't her place to judge, and the past didn't matter. What mattered now was killing those dragons before they could do more damage and destroy Utharika. At the least, the fleet had to show them that their kingdom was too powerful and dangerous for them to harass.

As Rivlen was hanging her uniform jacket and preparing to have dinner, a knock sounded at her door. To her surprise, she sensed Jak in the corridor outside. Earlier, Uthari had been contemplating sending him over to the *Star Flyer* to be close to the portal, in case someone attacked them, but the last she'd seen, Jak had been training with Malek on the *Serene Waters*.

Had something happened? Were Zaruk's ships creeping closer?

As she called, "Come in," she swept out with her senses in the direction of the other fleet.

The blue-hulled ships out there were still maintaining their distance and pace. If Rivlen hadn't known their city was to the northeast and not northwest, like Utharika, she might have thought they were simply heading in the same direction, but unless Zaruk's commander planned to help Uth fight off its drag-ons, they were going the wrong way. And she *knew* that wasn't what Zaruk's people were up to. From what she'd heard, their kingdom had its own dragon problem.

The door cracked open, and Jak poked his head in. "Hello, Captain. May I join you?"

"Is there a destructive dragonling with a penchant for chewing on everything with you?" Her senses told her Shikari wasn't in the corridor; she detected him up on deck near the portal. Since that was made from dragon steel, it ought to be impervious to fangs.

"Not currently. He went to say hello to the Thorn Company mercenaries. Specifically, the Thorn Company mercenaries who were breaking out their rations for dinner."

"What's he eating out here over the sea? There aren't many bugs for him to catch." Rivlen waved for Jak to enter.

He'd cut his hair since returning from Nargnoth, so it wasn't dangling boyishly into his eyes anymore. Its shortness made his face seem more angular. Stronger. Or maybe that perception came from his increasing power. As he'd further learned to access it, his aura had grown more noticeable.

When Rivlen had first met Jak, she'd barely been aware that he had power, though she'd gotten a few glimpses of his potential, such as when he'd been communicating with the portal. His aura had shone brighter then, like a shuttered lantern cracked open in the night. Now, his shutters were fully pulled back, and he beamed as brightly as many of the higher-ranking mage officers in the fleet.

As someone who'd grown up in Utharika and lived her whole life around mages, Rivlen should have been used to and unimpressed by such auras, but Jak was one of the few who didn't think highly of himself while he was creating fireballs with the power to incinerate small towns. It was possible it was because he didn't yet *know* he could do that, but she doubted he would change much even when he did. He would still crack jokes and make silly comments in the face of danger, and, unlike so many of the officers she worked with, he would see her as an ally rather than someone to compete against or resent because she'd been promoted over them.

"I do think he misses the jungle," Jak said, "but his tastes have broadened, and he's willing to eat more than bugs now."

"Like mercenary rations?"

"Well, they're eating fish. He likes fish."

"And table legs and feather dusters, from what I've seen."

"That's more about teething, I think. Those things can't be that nutritious." Jak stepped inside, but he didn't move far beyond the door, as if he wasn't sure he was welcome.

He'd acted similarly when she'd invited him to her cabin so she could ask him for all the details of his mission—and of how his mother had abruptly become as powerful as Uthari. He'd burbled and cheerfully shared far more than she would have learned by asking Malek or Tonovan. To let him know she'd appreciated the information, she'd thought about asking him to join her for dinner, but she couldn't *date* him. Jak was far too young to be of interest to her, and besides, Uthari wouldn't like it. Since the portal had lashed out at him, Uthari had been especially uptight when referring to Jak, and Rivlen was a little surprised he was allowing Malek to continue training him.

She supposed Uthari was too smart to let a resource get away. Once Jak fully developed his power, he could be a strong ally for the kingdom. Rivlen remembered that she'd originally thought of using him against Tonovan. That had been before she'd struck up a deal with Tezi—Tezi and her deadly dragon-steel axe—but if Tonovan ever attacked Rivlen while Jak was nearby, she trusted he would help her. He was reliable like that. Reliable and loyal.

"Did Uthari send you over?" Rivlen waved him toward the only chair in the room as she sat on the bed.

As the captain of the *Star Flyer*, she could have had a larger cabin, but she'd followed Malek's lead. Even though he frequently flew aboard the ship, his cabin was small and sparsely furnished. The double cabin that was *supposed* to belong to the captain had been most recently used by Tonovan, and it had his stink about it —not to mention suspicious stains that the servants hadn't been able to fully scrub out. As soon as Rivlen was sure he wouldn't return—she *hoped* he never had reason to set foot on the ship again—she intended to use magic to thoroughly sanitize those spots.

"No." Jak looked at the chair but remained standing. "I don't think he knows I'm here, actually."

"So you snuck over for a sunset tryst with me?"

"*No*," he blurted, his eyebrows flying up. "I mean, I'm not opposed to trysting, but I came because I wanted to check on you and, er, bring you something." His hand strayed to a pocket.

"*Check* on me? I'm a mageship captain in one of the most powerful fleets in the world, survived a recent battle with a dragon unscathed, and have the ability to incinerate almost anyone who vexes me. What kind of *checking on* could I possibly need?" Rivlen hadn't meant the words to sound quite so arrogant, but she hated when people thought she couldn't handle herself as well as a male officer of the same rank—or a male officer in general—and she was quick to grit her teeth at any perceived affront.

Jak shrugged. "I thought you might be lonely."

That wasn't the answer she'd expected, and she lowered her hackles. Out of habit, she did try to read his thoughts to see if he meant that or if he was angling for something. But he'd finally gotten better at walling off his mind from others, and she couldn't get anything, though his eyes seemed sincere. A part of her was tempted to press against his barrier, to test him and see if she could get through, but he wasn't an enemy, and he hadn't asked for a magic lesson.

"Because you're the captain," he continued, though she hadn't asked for an explanation. "You seem apart from your other officers, like you *have* to be, because you're in charge, and also because..."

"They don't like me?" she offered.

Rivlen didn't care if the crew liked her, though she hoped they were learning to respect her. She'd successfully led them into battle multiple times, and the *Star Flyer* had come out victorious. Even when captains from her own *fleet* had conspired against her.

"They haven't come to fully appreciate your wit and other fine attributes," Jak said.

"My attributes, huh?" Rivlen looked down at her chest.

"I meant your *leadership* attributes. Though those are nice too." He waved to her chest, then seemed to realize it might be offensive and jerked his hands behind his back.

"You're really bad at flirting, aren't you?"

He winced. "Yes. I'm not sure how to tell before I open my mouth if I'm about to give unappealing flattery or a well-received compliment."

"How about you just stand beside me in battle and funnel some of your power into me when we're outmatched and I'm flagging?"

That was something he'd gotten good at doing and that nobody else had ever done for her before. She hadn't forgotten what a relief it had been to receive his extra charges of energy when she'd needed them. She'd hated that she *had* needed them, but these past weeks had forced her to accept that even though she was a powerful mage by the standards of humans on Torvil, there were more powerful entities out there in the universe.

"That's something that makes you... appreciate me?" Jak asked.

"A lot more than your awkward praise."

"Oh. Good. I'll remember that."

"Excellent. I'd hate to have to dismiss you as quickly as the drunken louts who proposition me at the tavern."

Jak arched his eyebrows. "Do you spend a lot of time at

taverns? You don't seem to be someone who relaxes that often. Or who would enjoy such dubious locales."

"When we're not at war, there are required social gatherings for officers in the fleet." She wrinkled her lip. She *didn't* enjoy such dubious locales.

"So the drunken louts are your colleagues?"

"Often." The professional straight-to-business part of her thought about asking why he'd truly come, since *trysts* didn't seem to be the reason, but the part of her that *was* a little lonely wanted to wave him to the chair again and listen to more of his awkward attempts to flirt.

"I did come for another reason besides checking on you." Jak stuck a hand in his pocket.

Had it been a pocket closer to his crotch, she might have found the bulge in it alarming. Or possibly flattering. But it was a jacket pocket, and he withdrew a round bronze sphere with a slight magical signature. It had segments, almost like an orange, that looked like they might spread open to reveal something inside.

"It's a gift. If you want it. Or would find it useful. I made it." He winced again. The words not coming out as smoothly as he wished? Or had rehearsed?

She smiled at his continuing awkwardness. Normally, she was far more drawn to men like Malek, who strode around supremely confident and completely indifferent to the interested gazes from women, but Jak was a vast improvement over those like Tonovan and the backstabbing Captain Ular, who simply assumed they were amazing and that any woman they desired would fawn all over them and beg to serve their needs.

"I didn't know making bronze balls was a hobby of yours," Rivlen said.

"Maps, actually. You do know about that."

"I do, but that doesn't look much like a map."

"You have to activate it and say what you want to see." Jak

placed a finger on an indentation at the top. "The Kingdom of Uth."

The segments of the sphere unfurled, and an illusion formed in the air above the device. It was indeed a map that showed the middle of the continent of Agorval, with Utharika floating in the sky above Sprungtown Lake and the Sawtooth Mountains. Though tiny, the representation of the city had remarkable detail.

"If you tap something on the map, it'll highlight it and display a larger version." Jak poked Utharika's castle, and the illusion shifted, the continent fading into the background as the city enlarged to show all the details of the castle buildings, courtyard, and even gardens and fountains within its walls.

It was so detailed, Rivlen could easily imagine seeing people walking on the castle wall and manning the guard towers. She rose from the bed to look more closely. There *were* people in those towers.

"They're just representative of what I saw the last time I was there," Jak said. "It's not an accurate display of where people are right now. I *wish* I knew how to make a map that did that. That would be *amazing*. And imagine the military uses if you could see exactly where encroaching enemies were." He shook his head. "I don't know if even with magic it's possible to make something like that, but I'll have to look into it. I'm just learning how to make devices."

"This map is quite good." Rivlen waved at the details, including cobblestone streets, market stalls, and the architectural flourishes on buildings. "It isn't one I've seen before."

"Well, I made that particular map. It's based on the ones that are already out there, since it's not like I had the opportunity to wander the city and take measurements when I was there as a prisoner, but I did add touches from my personal experience. Most of the maps in the device are copies of ones I found in atlases, but if I have time someday, maybe I can draw some more myself." Jak smiled wistfully, as if he wished he were back in cartography school at that very moment. "I constructed the device so that it can be updated."

"Well done." Rivlen ran a finger along the outline of castle walls, and the illusion shimmered slightly, reacting to her touch. It was more than a map; it was art. She wasn't a connoisseur of such things, but it was impossible not to appreciate the talent. "You said it's a gift? For me?"

When had he had time to make it? She knew he'd been as busy as she.

"Yes. Here." Jak set the sphere in her hand. "Try saying another place. I drew the Zewnath map too. Though I left the portal off, both because it's moved and, uhm, where it goes might be secret information or something. I mean, almost all the mage fleets know about it now, but I didn't want to include any intelligence that Uthari might object to. I didn't detail the interior layout of his castle or anything, though I *did* see a lot of that when I was there."

"I'm sure he'll appreciate your thoughtfulness," Rivlen said dryly.

"I'm sure he won't, but as long as he doesn't flog me, I guess I'll survive."

"*Flogging* isn't typically how mages deliver punishment."

"Well, Malek won't talk about what happened when he was punished, so my imagination has to fill in the details." Jak grimaced.

"*Malek* was punished? When was that? And why?" Rivlen couldn't imagine it. Hadn't Malek led the teams to the other worlds and brought back everything Uthari had asked for and more?

"My mother didn't give me all the details, but I think because we're... she's... Uh, more she than me, I think, but Uthari doesn't like either of us."

It took Rivlen a moment to parse the vagueness, but then she remembered that startling realization she'd had back on Vran, that Malek seemed to care for Professor Freedar. At the time, she'd found the notion flummoxing—why would a powerful zidarr like Malek care about a middle-aged terrene woman who always had her nose in a book?—but now that Jadora beamed power like a sun, Rivlen would be shocked if male mages weren't falling all over themselves, wanting a taste of her magic. Not that she could imagine Malek acting so foolishly, but an attraction would make more sense now.

"Uthari punished his prize zidarr because he likes a woman?" Rivlen was well aware of the Zidarr Code and its rules about zidarr not marrying or having romantic relationships that went beyond pure physical release, but if anyone should be given some slack after all his years of loyal service, wouldn't it be Malek? He was so loyal to Uthari. Rivlen couldn't believe the king would risk losing some of Malek's devotion by punishing him.

"Something like that." Jak shrugged. "Until recently, I was kind of oblivious to that and still prefer not to think of my mother liking anyone or *being* liked by anyone."

Rivlen almost made a comment that there was nothing wrong with older people having relationships, but she remembered that Jak had lost his father. To Jak, it probably felt like a betrayal for his mother to like someone else, even if her husband had been dead for years.

"If they're smart, they won't act on any feelings they have," Rivlen said, and realized she shouldn't let herself act on any feelings for Jak either, not if Uthari was displeased with him and his mother.

The last thing Rivlen wanted was to have her king mistrust her because she'd been cavorting with someone he still considered a prisoner, a prisoner who'd been a wild one until recently, and who'd dreamed often about overthrowing mages instead of becoming one of them. Just because Jak could hide his thoughts now didn't mean those thoughts had changed. All it meant was that he was more dangerous.

"Yeah," Jak said glumly.

It took her a moment to realize that was in response to her last words and not what she'd been thinking.

"Anyway, I hope you like the map." Jak stuck his hands in his pockets. "Since you have to fly all over the world on missions, I thought it would be useful. You squeeze the sides when you're done, and the segments close up."

She nodded and did so. The segments snapped closed, and the map disappeared, but another illusion appeared in the air. This time, it was a drawing instead of a map. Right away, she recognized the dark form of the ancient ziggurat on Vran. In front of it, a dead dragon was sprawled among the ferns, with a woman standing with one foot up on its tail and her arms across her chest.

"Is that me?" Rivlen asked dryly, though the drawing was good enough for her to tell without asking.

"If you like it, it is. If not, that's of a random woman who was wandering through the forest after the battle and paused for a sketch."

"Of course. I didn't do much to help slay those dragons, you may recall." Unfortunately. Rivlen wished she *had* been able to single-handedly take one down.

"You led them off through the trees on a skyboard so we could finish Malek's surgery. And you and the mercenaries worked together to keep one busy until we could wake up the power of the ziggurat." Jak smiled. "You were integral."

"I'm not sure I agree, but thanks. For the drawing too." Rivlen waved at the illusion as it faded. Would it appear every time she closed down the map device? She hoped so. "It's nice. And good." Rivlen grimaced, the words sounding inadequate and awkward to her own ears. And here she'd been teasing Jak for that.

"Yes, I can see from your beaming glow that you're delighted." He smiled, though he didn't seem sure if she liked it.

"I am." Rivlen wiped away her grimace and kissed him on the cheek. Though for all the time he must have put into the gift, he deserved more than that. She eyed his mouth, thinking of the kiss she'd given him on Vran and of the warmth of his magic when he shared it with her. He deserved...

A knock at the door startled her, and she stepped back, jamming the sphere into her pocket. She hadn't sensed anyone approaching and still didn't detect anyone out there, nobody with a magical aura anyway. It had to be one of the mercenaries. Or a mundane assassin.

Frowning, she readied her magic and called, "What?"

The door didn't open.

Exasperated, Rivlen strode toward it and yanked it open. She'd been about to chastise whoever it was, but the serene Captain Ferroki stood there with her hands at her sides. Perennially calm, Ferroki always looked more like someone's mother than a deadly mercenary, and yelling at her had a tendency to make one feel like a heel.

"What is it, Captain?" Rivlen asked, marshaling her own calm.

She wasn't agitated, after all, just annoyed that she'd been interrupted when she'd been about to...

About to *what*? Rivlen glanced back at Jak. She'd already decided that she should have nothing to do with him. He wasn't her type. And he was far too young. A boy, not a man. A *nice* boy, but still.

"There are several wrecked sailing ships in the waters ahead," Ferroki said. "Some are burning, and one looks like it was bitten in half and smashed by a tail."

"By a dragon tail?"

"That's my guess. I thought you might want to collect the

survivors and question them. They may have some intelligence worth knowing."

"Beyond that there are dragons in the world, and they're destroying everything?" Rivlen already *knew* that.

Ferroki lifted a shoulder. "Perhaps."

"I'll come take a look." Rivlen grabbed her uniform jacket.

The fact that neither Uthari nor any of her officers had said anything to her about the wrecks suggested no one but terrene humans were onboard, and nobody in the fleet had any intention of stopping to *collect the survivors*. But it wouldn't hurt to look.

Rivlen waved for Jak to follow her, less because she wanted his opinion than because she didn't want to leave him alone in her cabin. Not that he was the type to root around in her underwear drawer or pry into her personal effects in her absence, but he would probably draw another picture of her while he was waiting. Though she appreciated the one he'd built into the map device, and liked the gift, she didn't want to encourage his interest. They couldn't do anything—*be* anything.

Ferroki led the way to the deck, joining several of her mercenaries at the railing.

"Hi, Jak," Tezi said when he and Rivlen stepped up beside them.

She smiled at him. It wasn't a flirtatious smile, and Rivlen didn't think Tezi had any interest in Jak or any other man, but when Jak returned it, heat flushed Rivlen's cheeks, and she had to bite back the urge to stand between them. She wasn't some besotted teenager, damn it. She'd *just* decided there couldn't be anything between them. If Jak wanted to smile at and draw every woman in Thorn Company, that ought to be fine with her.

Huffing at herself, Rivlen peered over the railing.

Far below, four smashed ships lay helpless, cast about by the ocean waves, wreckage strewn across the waters. All of their masts were broken, so they wouldn't be able to sail anywhere, and the last Rivlen had checked a map, the fleet was more than a hundred miles from land. They had opted to sail straight north before cutting toward home, staying over the Forked Sea, rather than traveling over the well-guarded island Kingdom of Temril. Other kingdoms tended to get nervous—and aggressive—when enemy fleets flew over their land.

One of the mercenaries handed her a spyglass, though Rivlen could already tell there weren't any magical beings among the wreckage. It hardly seemed worth a closer look.

"There are a lot of dead people down there. And some still alive and injured who might die if they're not helped." Jak's quiet voice was full of empathy. Of course, *he* wouldn't consider terrene humans useless and worth ignoring.

Rivlen sighed as she looked through the spyglass, wondering how long it would take Jak to grow out of associating with them. Even though he'd just started learning to use his powers, he had the potential to be great. He was far superior to those hapless humans below.

"Roamers." Rivlen curled a lip at the tattooed faces and wild hair of the people clinging to the wreckage and the remains of their ships.

A few of those faces looked up at the fleet, but none of the roamers waved for help. They couldn't expect it, not from the mages their entire people thumbed their noses at. Considered worse than other terrene humans, they refused to swear fealty to any of the kingdoms and settle down on land and pay taxes and contribute to society. A few ships full of roamers wouldn't be missed by anyone.

"There aren't that many of them," Jak said, "and the *Star Flyer* easily has room."

"Room for what?"

"Survivors." Jak waved at them. "Can you take the ship down to pick them up?"

"Why?"

His forehead furrowed. "To save their lives. They'll never be able to make it to shore."

"They're *roamers*, Jak."

"So?"

"You might have noticed that roamer pirates are currently being employed by our enemies."

"The only enemies we need to focus on right now are the dragons, and I'm sure *they're* not employing pirates."

"Trust me. Those aren't our only enemies." Rivlen couldn't see the blue-hulled ships that continued to pace their fleet, but she could still sense them out there.

"Those are fishing vessels." Ferroki pointed at the wrecks below. "Not all roamers are pirates."

"But *all* roamers are unaffiliated with any of the kingdoms and contribute nothing to the world," Rivlen said.

"I'm sure they contribute to their own culture and ways," Jak said. "Just because they like to live free of mage rule doesn't mean they're evil. Or deserve to die."

"Do you even *know* any roamers?" Rivlen highly doubted he was familiar with the belligerent people, beyond whatever he'd read in books.

"I know Colonel Sorath."

"Oh sure. He's a paragon and a lovely person."

"He's been decent to me."

"He tried to kill Uthari," Rivlen snapped. "*Twice.*"

She didn't have to read minds to tell Jak was thinking that wouldn't have changed his opinion of the colonel. Her fingers balled into fists. How could someone with his burgeoning power *side* with the mundanes? With a disloyal mercenary?

Jak didn't appear fazed by her irritation. All he did was look toward a hatch. Shikari ambled out, as if he'd called the dragonling. Maybe he had. What did he think Shikari could do? Fly

down and pick up the survivors? Rivlen didn't think the dragonling even knew how to fly himself yet. Even if he did, he wasn't
large enough to give a *monkey* a ride, much less a crew of human
beings.

"They may have valuable intelligence on the dragons," Ferroki
said. "Isn't it worth picking them up, if only to question them?"

"No, or my superiors would be doing it." Rivlen waved toward
the ships ahead of them, Uthari's yacht and half the fleet already
well past the wrecked vessels.

Not only were they *not* flying down to pick up the survivors,
but Tonovan or Uthari would likely have some choice words for
Rivlen if she wasted her time doing so when their kingdom was in
danger. Or at all.

"It's worth picking them up, because they're human beings,
and it wouldn't be that big of a deal for us to go out of our way to
do so," Jak said, looking toward Rivlen again. He met her eyes, his
own eyes earnest and imploring. "If we can't divert to take them to
Temril or another nearby land mass, then they can ride along
until we get to Uth. I'm sure they would prefer to find a way back
to their people from there to being dead."

Shikari sat at Jak's side and joined him in gazing imploringly
up at Rivlen. She didn't think he was trying to use magic to manipulate her—she doubted the dragon even knew what was going on
—but their combined gazes made her feel like she would be an ass
for leaving the people. The mercenaries were all looking at her
expectantly too. What the hell? How had she ended up
surrounded by all these do-gooders?

I'll draw you another picture if you go down to get them, Jak said,
switching to telepathy, as if he thought he would have better luck
changing her mind through a private conversation.

Rivlen snorted. *I'm going to get chewed out for doing this. You'd
better promise to give me a full-body massage and rub my feet every
night for a week.*

Jak blinked. *Uhm, I'll rub anything you like. Whenever you want.*

You're an amenable boy.

An amenable man. *With the deft hands of an artist.* Jak raised his eyebrows and wiggled his fingers in the air.

"Is he casting a spell on her?" Tezi whispered.

"To melt the frost off her?" another mercenary whispered back. "I hope so."

Rivlen, aware that her jaw was clenched and she doubtless *did* look frosty, forced her face to relax. But she shot the whisperers the hard look their comments deserved.

Tezi merely gazed back at her. Since she'd acquired that axe and learned how to use it, she'd gotten more confident in herself.

"Fine, Jak," Rivlen grumbled and sent a telepathic command to the officer in navigation. "Stand next to me and be prepared to share your power with me if Tonovan comes over on a skyboard to kick my ass."

"Gladly," Jak said without hesitation.

Ma'am? the helm officer replied uncertainly.

You heard me. Go down there. We're picking up the survivors to question about the dragon attack. Rivlen knew Ferroki had only said that because she'd thought it would be more likely to sway Rivlen —she couldn't believe roamer fishermen had any information worth learning—but maybe if she used the same excuse, Tonovan and Uthari wouldn't give her a hard time.

"Wishful thinking," she muttered as her officer replied, *Yes, ma'am.*

The *Star Flyer* descended, turning since they had already flown past the wrecks.

Rivlen braced herself for the inevitable contact from her superiors. She should have asked for permission before leaving the formation, but she had little doubt they would have denied it. Further, she knew she would get in trouble for this. Her jaw clenched again of its own accord.

"Thank you," Jak said softly, touching her hand.

She glowered at him. "Your idealistic do-goodness is going to get me kicked out of the fleet."

He pulled his hand back but didn't say he was sorry. A disappointed, "Ah," was all he voiced.

Disappointed in her? Or in her fleet? Or in the fact that it meant a lot to her to excel and climb the ranks in that fleet?

Where are you going, Rivlen dear? Tonovan's snide voice spoke into her mind.

Rivlen swore. She hadn't wanted to talk to Uthari, either, but he would have been better than Tonovan.

To pick up the survivors and ask them about the dragons that were clearly responsible for destroying their ships.

To pick up roamers? What could they possibly know? Tonovan sent an image of himself along with his words. In it, he was shirtless with a leg sprawled over the armrest of a chair. It was one of the chairs from his cabin on the *Star Flyer*. That wasn't a promise that he was heading over to her ship, was it?

They have eyes, she replied, not commenting on the imagery. *They'll know how many dragons attacked and which way they went.*

Who cares? Three dragons have been reported in our kingdom. That's all that matters to our fleet.

Just because there are three there now that we know of doesn't mean more won't head that way.

I suppose that's true. Perhaps I'll come over tonight to join you in questioning these roamers. The Tonovan in the image rubbed his bare chest suggestively, then shifted his hand lower. *And afterward, you can enjoy my company. It's been a long time, Rivlen dear.*

Not long enough. Nobody on this ship wants your company, and I'll take my own life before getting into your bed.

'Ware your tongue, Captain. Uthari is watching you and also wondering what you're doing. It would be a shame if I told him what I suspect is the truth, that you let your feelings for that boy influence you.

Rivlen realized Tonovan was on the deck of the *Serene Waters* and looking down at them. At *her*. Had he been there the whole time? And seen that hand touch Jak had given her?

Her stomach roiled with unease.

Would Uthari be annoyed with her for that? She'd saved his life back in Zewnath, protecting him from Sorath after the portal attacked him, but she didn't know if Uthari had been conscious and seen that. Nor did she know if it was enough to keep him from being irked that she hadn't tried harder to kill Sorath. She'd even worked with him to bring down Yidar—something Uthari might have learned about by now.

Have my cabin prepared for my visit, Captain, Tonovan drawled into her mind. *Maybe you and the blonde merc can both join me tonight.*

What, so she can poke out your other eye?

Watch yourself, Captain. You don't have that many allies in the fleet, and that boy doesn't have the power to help you.

She should have kept her mouth shut, but her temper demanded a retort. *You might be surprised.*

We'll see tonight.

5
_____

JAK WATCHED RIVLEN WARILY AS HE ENVISIONED GEYSERS IN HIS MIND and summoned his power to levitate the first of the shipwrecked roamers to the deck of the *Star Flyer*.

Captain Ferroki, who understood some of their language, especially a part that relied on hand gestures, had communicated their intent to the roamers. The beleaguered people appeared more worried than grateful at being picked up by a ship full of magic users, but they were injured, waterlogged, and weary, and none of them resisted. Few of them had weapons beyond nets and fishing spears.

Ferroki had been right. These weren't pirates. The dragon attack must have been horrible for them.

Rivlen ignored Jak, her gaze locked on Uthari's yacht as it kept traveling, leaving the *Star Flyer* behind. A man in a black cloak stood at the railing of the *Serene Waters*, looking down at her. Jak grimaced, able to sense Tonovan's aura.

Was he berating Rivlen for her choice? For *Jak's* choice that Rivlen had given in to?

Jak refused to feel bad about that, since he was certain they were doing the right thing. Ferroki and the other Thorn Company women thought so too. Even mercenaries had kinder hearts than mages, it seemed.

No, that wasn't fair. Rivlen wasn't as cold as she pretended to be. But she *was* stuck operating within the confines of her chain of command. She'd known she would get in trouble for taking an unauthorized detour, and that was why she'd objected.

Jak chose to believe that. He knew she and the other mages didn't feel terrene humans were worth their time, but he didn't want Rivlen to be completely heartless. He *liked* her. Maybe it wasn't wise, but he liked her. It didn't hurt that she was beautiful and he was drawn to that hint of vulnerability deep within her, the part of her that she never wanted to show to anyone but that he knew existed.

"Are you the only one willing to lift them?" Tezi asked.

With the first roamer deposited on the ship, Jak turned back to levitate another. "I guess."

Most of the mage officers were watching with disinterest or looking at Rivlen and waiting for orders. Jak wished he knew how to lift multiple people at a time, but he wasn't sure if he could adjust the geyser imagery he used to raise an entire crew.

"Shikari," Jak said as the dragonling nosed around the uncertain roamer woman hunkering on the deck, water dripping from her sodden clothing. "Will you help me?"

Shikari licked a piece of kelp off the woman's sandaled foot. She gaped at him and looked like she wanted to sprint away, but when she eyed the cold-faced mage officers, she must have found the young dragon less scary.

"He's more like a puppy than an ally, isn't he?" Ferroki murmured.

"You have to entice him with treats." Jak spotted fish in nets on the deck of one of the roamer ships—they must have been in the middle of hauling up a catch when the dragons had shown up—and shared images of fat flounders with Shikari.

"So that's a yes, right?"

Jak shrugged. "Yes. But he's a very *smart* puppy."

The fish imagery prompted Shikari to gallop to the railing. Jak levitated another survivor to the *Star Flyer* while trying to convey to the dragonling that he should do the same.

Shikari picked up the net full of fish and levitated *that* to the *Star Flyer*.

"I'm not sure you're the dragon from Zelonsera's vision that she believed would save all of her kind," Jak murmured to him.

After the fish-filled net had been deposited on the deck, Shikari swatted Jak with his tail and used his own magic to levitate up one of the survivors.

"Good dragon. Thank you." Jak patted him on the head between the horns.

That earned him a squint, a confirmation that Shikari was far more intelligent than a puppy. Jak suspected it wouldn't be long before Shikari learned to speak telepathically to him, as the other dragons they'd met could.

More survivors rose from the water and the wreckage. At first, Jak thought Shikari was responsible, but the gateship with Vinjo, Sasko, Tinder, and a few mages had descended to float behind the *Star Flyer*, both vessels about ten feet above the waves.

Jak waved to Vinjo, who waved back. He and a spindly mage with spectacles were responsible for the increase in the number of survivors being levitated aboard. The other mage had grease smears on his face and red uniform. Maybe Vinjo had found an engineer in Uthari's fleet to lure over to help him.

"Find out who the leader is," Rivlen said, coming to stand beside Ferroki and Jak, "so we can question him or her."

Her cheeks were flushed, and she looked even more annoyed

than she had ten minutes earlier when Jak had been pleading with her to bring the ship down.

Are you all right? he asked telepathically as Ferroki said she would and walked up to the growing collection of soggy roamers.

Rivlen looked darkly at him.

I'm sorry if you're getting in trouble.

But not so sorry you wouldn't guilt me into picking these people up? Uthari and Tonovan both *chimed in to ask me what in the Slavemasters' hell I was doing. These roamers better have some scintillating intelligence to share. That may be the only thing that saves me from a demotion when this is all over.*

Jak rocked back. *Uthari's going to take your command away? Because you helped people?*

Because I'm letting a kid he doesn't much like influence me. Tonovan made sure to point that out to him.

Jak touched his chest.

Yeah, you. Why don't you stop scheming against your own kind?

"My own kind?" he mouthed, wondering if it was possible she'd learned about the kerzor. He hadn't attempted to make one yet, but he kept his mother's schematics in his pocket and looked them over often. The desire to create such devices was what had prompted him to ask Vinjo for engineering lessons.

Mages. Rivlen glared at him as more dripping roamers floated over the railing to join the others on the deck. *Uthari is allowing Malek—one of the most powerful zidarr in the world—to teach you. And you'd happily screw both of them to help terrene people you don't even know.*

That's not true.

Isn't it?

I wouldn't do anything to hurt Malek or get him in trouble.

Was that the truth? If Jak did succeed in making a kerzor, Malek would be angry with him and might end up in trouble—a *lot* of trouble—with Uthari.

Just Malek? Rivlen asked.

Uthari is a megalomaniacal ass. I understand that you like being a fleet officer, and you're good at it, but serving someone like him is—

"You, Jak Freedar, don't understand half as much as you think you do." Not waiting for a response, Rivlen turned her back on him and stalked toward the navigation cabin.

"I don't think she's going to invite me to give her a massage tonight," Jak murmured sadly.

"No?" Tezi asked. "She needs one. She seems tense."

"She's always like that."

"I've noticed."

Jak looked toward the *Serene Waters* and the rest of the fleet as they continued flying north, clearly making a point. The *Star Flyer* had the portal, so Jak doubted the others would go far before stopping to wait. Too bad. He wished he could get Rivlen away from her chain of command. She'd been more relaxed—more pleasant to be around—back on Vran.

You and Tezi had better stay belowdecks and out of sight tonight, Rivlen spoke into his mind, though she'd disappeared from sight. *Tonovan promised to come over, and he has some delusions about what he thinks is going to happen in his cabin tonight.*

Uh. I'll let her know. Thanks, Rivlen.

She didn't respond.

Jak's cabin was back on the *Serene Waters*, and he could have returned to it—and probably should have, since he'd left without telling anyone except his mother that he was going—but he couldn't imagine leaving if Tonovan was coming and intended to harass Tezi and Rivlen. He'd promised to stand at Rivlen's side if Tonovan challenged her, and he would.

He fought down the urge to run after her and let her know, instead turning his attention back to plucking up survivors. There were shark fins in the distance, and he was sure the roamers would appreciate getting out of the water before anything tried to bite them. Anything *else*. Jak eyed the dragon-maw-sized hole in one of the ships.

Jak? His mother's voice sounded strongly in his mind.

Yes. I'm still on the Star Flyer. Originally, Jak had only intended to be gone long enough to give Rivlen his gift.

I know, and Shikari is with you, right? I think... you should stay over there.

Why? And would that be allowed? Jak deliberately hadn't asked for permission from Malek or anyone else before leaving. He'd been afraid the answer would be *no*.

I doubt Uthari cares which ship you're on when we're all flying together, but... Mother shared an image with him of one of her enclosed bacteria-growing dishes.

Normally, Jak couldn't tell one fuzzy splotch of bacteria growing on a medium from another, but a single glowing mote in the middle filled him with uneasiness. And certainty.

The dragon parasite? he asked.

Yes. The mote appeared a little while ago. I'm contemplating tossing the dish over the side of the ship and into the ocean, but then I wouldn't be able to continue to study the parasite—and try various magics and extracts on it in an attempt to eradicate it.

Jak rubbed the back of his neck. When Mother had first started growing her specimens, he'd said it was a bad idea, that there was a chance they could escape, but if she couldn't experiment on the dragon parasite, they would never find a way to destroy it.

Shikari is the only one we have to worry about catching the parasite, right? Jak asked. *If so, as long as I keep him away from your lab, there shouldn't be anything to worry about.*

Thus far, when infected dragons have died in the proximity of humans, the parasites haven't tried to jump to them and take them as new hosts, but that's not conclusive proof that they can't.

So, we should all *stay away from your lab?* Jak tried to keep his telepathic tone light and convey a smile, but it was hard. He glanced toward Shikari to reassure himself that his scales remained blue and there weren't any magical motes floating around him.

Possibly. I'll keep you apprised.

Thanks. I'll see if Captain Rivlen has someplace I can sleep over here.

Aren't the mercenaries all sleeping out on the deck?

Yes, but I gave her a gift. She might think I deserve a bunk.

We're still prisoners, you know.

I didn't say the bunk wouldn't be in a brig cell.

A female roamer cried out, and Jak spun to check the group. He'd allowed himself to be distracted from pulling people aboard, but everyone had been removed from the wreckage and was huddled on the *Star Flyer* or the gateship. The woman who'd cried out sat on the deck with her legs stretched out and her hand pressed against her thigh. Blood dripped between her fingers.

"Dr. Fret?" Ferroki waved her medic over. "This woman was bitten by one of the dragons that attacked."

None of the mage officers were doing anything to help— instead, they were touching their weapons and eyeing the roamers suspiciously. As if they were in a position to take over the ship. Jak snorted.

Since Malek had started teaching Jak about healing with magic, he walked toward the group, hoping he could help. Shikari was sniffing around the roamers, and he cocked his head as the woman gasped and groaned. Jak thought about asking if he could heal people, but he froze as a thought slammed into him.

Mother?

Even though the *Serene Waters* had continued on and wasn't waiting for them, her power was so great that it was easy for him to sense her. He could pick out her aura and also Malek's—maybe they were in the lab together contemplating that mote.

Yes?

Do the parasites have to be transferred to a new host on those motes? Or is it possible… if someone was bitten by a dragon, could they be infected with the parasites and pass them along to someone else? Or another dragon?

I'm not certain, but I've wondered that myself. It's possible the bacteria could be transferred through saliva—like rabies. You better keep Shikari away from those people, just in case.

Jak conveyed the information to Shikari, then knelt beside Dr. Fret and the woman. There were numerous injured roamers who needed assistance. So far, he'd only learned to heal small cuts, but he did his best to apply his knowledge to the larger wounds. He was aware of Rivlen walking out on deck, but he decided to wait until later to mention that he might be a permanent visitor.

"The roamers fled from Temril," Ferroki, who'd been speaking with one of the men, told Rivlen. "They'd been at one of the roamer-friendly villages on the east end of the island when dragons flew overhead. Most headed for the more populated west side and the sky city, but some attacked the village. The roamers fled in their ships and thought they were far enough away but sailed out to deep waters just to be safe. However, they *weren't* safe. The next day, two dragons found their fishing ships and attacked."

"How many dragons attacked Temril?" Rivlen asked.

"The roamers saw three different ones but heard there might have been as many as eight."

"I wonder why so many went to such a small kingdom. And if there are a lot more than the three we've heard about in Uth." Rivlen grimaced.

The man who'd been speaking to Ferroki gestured and said more. Ferroki frowned and repeated a word as a question. The man nodded and outlined something long and thin in the air.

"One of the dragons tore open the hull of their leader's ship to get at their musician," Ferroki translated.

"Their *musician*?" Rivlen asked.

"A roamer with a little magic who plays work songs for the crew. Years earlier, he'd acquired a dragon-steel *hylnonom*. A musical instrument their people use. Something like an oboe, I believe."

"A *dragon-steel* musical instrument?" Rivlen looked at Jak. "I've never heard of such a thing."

"Uthari had a decorative dragon-steel plate in his lavatory," Jak said. "And there's a big pillar on Agathar Island in the Tarnished Sea. We know dragon steel was used for things other than weapons."

"Uthari used the dragon steel from Vran to have bars made on a cell." Tezi was kneeling next to Fret and holding things for the doctor as she worked, but she frowned darkly, as if she had personal experience with that cell.

"I'm aware that it can be made into things besides weapons," Rivlen said, "but it's extremely rare, Uthari's chest that we brought back notwithstanding."

Jak wondered what had happened to that chest. He hadn't sensed the bars of dragon steel since before he'd gone to Nargnoth. Had the chest and the mage learning to work the dragon steel been sent ahead to Utharika?

"It's strange that someone would have wasted such a precious resource on music," Rivlen added.

"Some might argue that music is an important part of culture and not wasteful," Jak murmured.

Rivlen gave him another dark look. "So, what happened, Ferroki? The dragon didn't like that man's music and singled him out to kill him?"

Ferroki shook her head. "The dragon *did* kill him, but it also took the instrument and flew away after it had it."

The roamer said a few more words and pointed toward the west—toward Temril?

"He thinks it's the reason the dragons came after their ships," Ferroki said. "They had nothing else of value."

"Except munchies." Jak looked at Shikari, who sat in the middle of the net he'd recovered, and was happily noshing on the fish.

"Can't the dragons *make* dragon steel?" Rivlen asked, ignoring him. "Why would they care about our baubles?"

"They make it out of that ore we saw on Vran, ore that, as far as I know, isn't found on Torvil. Even though they *can* make it, they probably can't make it here. And without the portal, they're trapped here for now and only have access to what's on our world."

Jak decided he had better contact his mother and let her know about this new information. He doubted Uthari was sharing the reports he received from his commanders with her.

"Why wouldn't the dragons try to get the portal itself instead of lesser knickknacks?" Rivlen waved toward the ancient artifact strapped to the deck.

Until that moment, it hadn't occurred to Jak that the dragons might want it, but just because they'd come to Torvil to invade the world and kill and enslave humans didn't mean they wouldn't want the ability to leave at some point. Uthari had ordered the portal removed so that no more dragons could come through, but what would happen when the ones who were already here decided they wanted to go home?

"For all we know," Jak said, "they're on their way to get it now."

And he'd voluntarily come over to the ship carrying it. He shook his head bleakly. Well, he'd promised that he would stand beside Rivlen. It seemed like he might get that chance soon—and against more than a cranky one-eyed general.

~

Malek stood in Uthari's office, his hands clasped behind his back as Uthari listened to King Temrok speak via his dome-jir. The king's bald head and torso floated in the air above the orange crystal, his hands visible as he alternated wringing them and tugging at his sleeves. Tonovan was also in the office, one leg slung over the armrest of the chair he lounged in.

Outside, the sun was setting and the fleet had come to a stop, waiting for the *Star Flyer* to finish collecting and questioning the roamers. Uthari had been peeved that Rivlen had detoured without asking for permission and had intended to continue on until Malek pointed out that the portal was on the *Star Flyer* and dragons and Zaruk's ships were in the area.

Originally, he'd come to Uthari's suite to tell him about the mote that had grown in Jadora's dish and to alert him of the possible danger. But this was the third dome-jir discussion with the third king that Uthari had engaged in, so Malek hadn't gotten a chance to speak. Given all that was going on—the other monarchs had also reported dragon problems in their kingdoms—the parasites seemed irrelevant.

"My mages have had to flee the other cities to make a stand in Temika," King Temrok was saying. "I've lost five mageships, and the dragons ravaged the Sarlon Croplands. I don't know what they want. They say nothing when we contact them telepathically, only making occasional threats as they kill us and kidnap my subjects. They're wantonly destroying my entire kingdom, and they won't *leave*."

"A difficult situation," Uthari said.

"That's the understatement of the century," Temrok snapped, then took a breath to pull himself together. "I know they are in your kingdom as well, Uthari, but you have greater forces than I, and your fleet is less than a hundred miles from here. I implore you to send some ships to help. I understand you also have warriors with dragon-steel weapons and that those are effective against these terrible beasts. Our magic was not. I've never faced such powerful foes."

"They are difficult to kill." Uthari rubbed his back, though it had been the portal, not a dragon that had zapped him. "I am empathetic to your problem, but I can't divert my ships to your island. My kingdom needs them. It sounds like it's too late anyway."

"It's *not* too late. Temika still floats in the sky and contains thousands of refugees. We will continue to fight the dragons, and once we drive them away, we can rebuild our other cities, but we need them to *leave*. I've heard you and your portal are the reason they're here. That makes you responsible for getting rid of them."

"*All* of the rulers wanted the portal erected to explore the other worlds," Uthari said coolly.

"But only your team went through and gained dragon steel. I may not have sent ships to pant around that portal, but I knew what was going on in Zewnath. And I know that the archaeologists you kidnapped were responsible for finding the artifact and placing it. Don't deny it."

Malek shifted uneasily, not pleased to hear that kings whose fleets hadn't even been in the area knew about Jak and Jadora.

"I don't deny that we placed the portal," Uthari said. "But as to being responsible—"

"You have people who can fight the dragons. Send them. Send them and I'll..." Temrok looked around in desperation, likely seeking something of value that he could offer from his kingdom that had been ravaged and likely had little of value left.

"Give your allegiance to me?" Uthari suggested. "And send troops to fight alongside mine in the future when Uth is targeted again by ambitious enemies?"

Temrok blanched. "I will agree to an *alliance* with you, and I will share whatever information I'm able to gather with you free of charge. *If* you can get these dragons out of my kingdom."

"I'll send a few ships and see what can be done," Uthari said.

That surprised Malek. Since Temril had so little to offer, and Uth had a dragon problem of its own to deal with, why would Uthari split his forces? Or was he simply telling Temrok he would help while having no intention of doing so?

"Thank you, Uthari." Temrok bowed, and the dome-jir went dark.

Uthari stroked his chin as he regarded Tonovan and Malek.

"You wish me to take the *Star Flyer* and a few other ships, Your Majesty?" Malek asked.

Tonovan sneered at him, no doubt prepared to accuse him of kissing up. Though Malek would prefer to fight the dragons assailing Uth, all of the dragons in the world would have to be dealt with sooner or later, and he was one of few with experience battling them. Battling them and *killing* them.

"You will stay with me and the forces returning to Utharika," Uthari said. "We'll take the portal home and ensure it and our kingdom are safe. Besides, I need you to keep an eye on your magically enhanced professor." Uthari's smile wasn't friendly. "She must also return to Utharika so she can finish her work. I trust she's making progress on the plant?"

"She had some pots with soil in them in her lab. Preparing to grow it, I presume."

"You presume? You didn't ask for details when you were down there?" Uthari squinted at Malek.

"I was distracted by something else."

"Her lips and ass," Tonovan said.

Malek lifted his chin. "The parasite she's also growing, per the request of the dragon who gave her that power."

When he'd reported to Uthari after their last mission, Malek had explained the encounter with Zelonsera to the best of his ability, but since he'd been largely insensate during it, he hadn't been able to share an eyewitness account.

"I don't care about that," Uthari snapped. "The *plant* is her priority."

"She's working on both."

Uthari clenched his jaw.

"Who do you intend to send to Temril?" Malek asked to change the subject. He didn't want Uthari to start mulling over exiling Jadora again.

Uthari leaned back in his chair. "The *Star Flyer* with the mercenaries with those axes. Perhaps another ship or two. I have no intention of committing a large number of forces to assist Temril. In fact, I have little interest in *assisting* that kingdom at all."

Malek bit his tongue to keep from pointing out that their actions, under Uthari's command, *had* been responsible for the arrival of all those dragons. Even though he didn't know how they could defeat them all, Malek felt obligated to try, on behalf of Uthari and their kingdom.

"Why send people then?" Tonovan asked.

"It sounds like Temril is weak and at its knees after being ravaged by the dragons. This could be an opportunity for us." Uthari gazed at Tonovan. "*You* will lead the mission, General. If you see the dragons, destroy them. But what I would like... is Temril for myself. For *us*, and Uth's continued dominance on the world stage."

"Temril Kingdom has little of value, Your Majesty." Malek kept his face carefully neutral, but the idea of taking advantage of a people who'd been decimated by the dragons Uthari had unleashed disturbed him. It wasn't honorable. He understood that the monarchs of the world constantly schemed and plotted against one another—that was, after all, why the zidarr existed— and that one king trying to take over the lands of another was nothing new, but in this case, he found it distasteful.

"Except its location. It's the nearest significant land mass to Zewnath, the place where, if I understand what our archaeologists learned well enough, the portal must be placed in order to operate. As was demonstrated on numerous occasions, the druids make setting up camp on their continent tedious, but if we possessed Temril, perhaps, after the dragons have been dealt with, we could store the portal there, then take it in and set it up for brief periods of time for missions. Once our teams had returned, we could remove it again before the druids could marshal their forces against it."

"To what end?" Malek asked. "We obtained that which you sought. I didn't think you had further need for the portal."

"Creating the life-extension drug *is* the legacy I want to leave the world, but why stop there?" Uthari asked. "There are more worlds out there to explore, more dragon steel and other resources we might obtain. Items that could ensure our kingdom grows into the greatest kingdom in the world—and beyond." Uthari smiled contentedly.

Tonovan matched his smile. No doubt, he fancied himself as the highest-ranking military commander in the greatest kingdom in the world. Malek had noticed, however, that Tonovan's face had been troubled at the revelation that *he* would be sent to deal with dragons.

Uthari quirked an eyebrow at Malek. "Do you disapprove of my ambition, my zidarr?"

Malek had thought he was keeping his expression neutral and unreadable, but after all these years, Uthari knew him well. "It is not my place to approve or disapprove, Your Majesty. I am prepared to serve you in whatever capacity you deem proper."

"So politic, Malek," Tonovan drawled.

"Go to the *Star Flyer*, General. You know what I desire. See to it that it happens." Uthari held Tonovan's gaze for a long moment—adding some additional telepathic instruction? "And do see if you can keep your trousers buckled on your mission. I would hate to see you return with more missing body parts."

Tonovan scowled but didn't offer a rebuttal. Malek wondered if Uthari had learned about the vial of acid that Jadora had broken in his smallclothes and how much damage it had done. If Tonovan had needed the services of a healer after that, he hadn't come to Malek for it. Fortunately.

"I have no problem focusing on the mission, Your Majesty." Tonovan rose from his chair and bowed to Uthari. "And I *perfectly* understand what you wish accomplished."

"Come back successful, and I'll see to it that a new flagship is built to replace the lost *Dread Arrow*. A newer and better ship, as befitting the commander of the fleet of the most powerful kingdom in the world."

"Excellent, Your Majesty."

"You are dismissed."

As Tonovan walked out, Malek waited to see if he would also be dismissed, but Uthari hadn't yet given him a task, so he expected more. He was curious, as well, what Uthari had added silently to Tonovan but had to accept that Uthari would have said it out loud if he'd wanted Malek to know.

"Why is Jak on the *Star Flyer*?" Uthari asked.

Malek lifted a shoulder. "I don't know why he originally went, but Jadora believes he—or at least Shikari—should stay over there so that there's no chance the dragonling will be infected with the parasite she's experimenting on."

"*Jadora* believes. Goodness, Malek. I didn't realize *she* was in charge now." Uthari watched him through slitted eyes.

"When it comes to that parasite, we would be wise to heed her warnings." Once again finding the desire to change the subject, Malek asked, "Is there anything you wish me to do? Other than arranging the transfer of the portal from the *Star Flyer* to one of the ships continuing north? I assume you prefer it not be on the *Serene Waters* with you." Malek realized he might have implied that Uthari now feared it—especially when

Uthari's squint deepened—and added, "It is, after all, rather large to be transported on your yacht without impeding the crew."

"Indeed," Uthari murmured. "All I want from you, Malek, is to be prepared to defend the portal if someone attempts to steal it. And to tell me... what I can do to rectify the mistake I've made."

"Your Majesty?"

"I must speak confidently and without doubt in front of Tonovan, for he will only follow someone with strength and power, and I also cannot admit weakness—or... fallibility when I deal with the other kings, but I hope you know it was never my intent to let dragons into our world. As soon as that giant worm flew through, I recognized the danger of having the portal in place, but I believed the Jitaruvak was worth taking a risk for. And, though it wasn't my original desire, when I saw you come back with that chest of dragon steel, I admit to being seduced by the idea of retrieving more resources to cement my reign and my place in the history books."

"Yes, Your Majesty," Malek said.

"But I acknowledge, if only to you, that the destruction now being wrought on the world is... my fault." Uthari gazed toward the porthole, night falling beyond the glass. "I want to rectify it. We will seek out the dragons and kill them one by one if necessary, but I have been wondering... if perhaps your professor, with her knowledge of plants and chemistry—and now what the dragons themselves collectively knew—might come up with another solution. A solution in which we don't have to sacrifice ships and mages in battles to the death."

Malek leaned forward, hope rising in his chest. "You want her to focus on the parasite? On finding out how to kill it, in the hope that doing so would turn the dragons from enemies into possible future allies?"

Uthari turned his gaze back to Malek, several seconds passing as his face grew thoughtful. "I don't think we can know that's what would happen if she *did* manage to destroy that parasite."

"True." Malek knew Jak believed that any dragons that weren't infected would be allies to *terrene* humans, rather than mages, but Malek doubted there was proof either way. He thought dragons would be more drawn to those with magic, those who'd been altered by exposure to the very dragon steel that their kind had once made.

Uthari's hand strayed toward his back again, reminding Malek that the portal did not love him. And hadn't Jak mentioned the possibility that the souls within the portals belonged to the elder dragons, or had at least been imbued by them long ago?

Maybe Uthari would prefer a world where dragons didn't exist at all and terrene humans had no hope of finding allies powerful enough to overthrow wizard rulers. Malek could never forget that Jak and Jadora had longed to overthrow the existing regimes since long before they'd met him. And, as surprising as it was, their views didn't seem to have changed once they'd acquired power of their own.

"As long as she's studying parasites that affect dragons," Uthari said, "perhaps she could see if there's one that could *kill* dragons."

"Your Majesty?"

"Maybe the parasite she's growing right now could be altered to do so. Then, instead of you and other warriors risking your lives going after each dragon, we might need only infect one, and then they could spread the deadly parasite to each other. Eventually, our problem would solve itself, and my conscience would no longer need to be plagued."

"I don't know if that would be possible, but I can ask her what she thinks about it." Malek held back a grimace as he thought of Jak and how devastated he would be by such a thing, especially if Shikari were killed. Though perhaps they would be able to keep him from being exposed.

Uthari was watching him intently. Malek knew his mental barriers were in place, and nobody could read his mind, but it was possible he was allowing evidence of his thoughts to creep onto his face.

"Ask her if it's possible, and suggest it's a good idea," Uthari said. "You have a lot of influence over her."

Malek snorted. "Less than you'd think. She's a stubborn woman." He managed not to smile as he said that, knowing Uthari didn't approve of Malek's appreciation of Jadora's attributes.

"But you could sway her if you tried, I'm sure. Perhaps while delivering the caresses of a lover."

Malek rocked back. What was Uthari suggesting? That he would *allow* that? That he would even *encourage* it?

Before a hint of elation could blossom, Malek stifled it. If Uthari was encouraging him to have a physical relationship with Jadora, it was only so he could get what he wanted. Still, Malek couldn't help but want to give in to the temptation to take Jadora to his bedroom for a tryst, a tryst fully sanctioned by his liege. He wouldn't *have* to try to influence Jadora. It wasn't as if Uthari would know if he had or hadn't. After all, he could have tried and failed.

His honor protested the thought of lying, but temptation... tempted.

"Think about it, Malek," Uthari said. "I know what you want, and I'm trying to think of a way I can give it to you, when the Zidarr Code forbids it, and I'm not sure it's wise."

"I understand," Malek said, though it occurred to him that Uthari was manipulating him as much as he had Tonovan.

For Tonovan, who craved power and glory, Uthari had been the strong and scheming ruler out for world domination. For Malek, who wanted to follow someone fair and honorable, Uthari showed his vulnerabilities and suggested he wanted to atone for his sins.

But did Uthari truly care? What had he told Tonovan in private? Something that Malek wouldn't approve of?

Disturbed by his thoughts, Malek bowed and walked out, a part of him wondering if Jadora was right for calling Uthari a monster.

Malek owed the king his life and, after all the years Uthari had devoted to his training, Malek owed him even more than that. But for the first time, he wondered if all that Uthari had given him was enough to ensure his unquestioning and eternal loyalty. He couldn't imagine acting against his king, but once the world was safe from the dragons, Malek might have to spend some time dwelling on the future, and what his place in it should be.

6

UTHARI WAS HAVING THE PORTAL MOVED TO ANOTHER SHIP. Watching from the deck of the *Star Flyer*, Rivlen couldn't help but frown as the straps were released, and mages on the *Soaring Eagle* levitated it into the air. She hadn't been told the reason for the change, but since the rest of the fleet was in view again, she trusted the captain wasn't acting of his own accord, with plans to steal the portal and flee from Uthari.

Night had fallen, and the *Star Flyer* and gateship were back at a thousand feet and ready to continue the journey home. They now had roamers to drop off somewhere, but Rivlen would figure that out later. After they'd dealt with the dragons. Though her ship would now have to battle them without the possible help from the portal. Oh, well. She still had two mercenaries with dragon-steel axes.

A pair of mageships left the fleet formation and sailed toward the *Star Flyer*. Rivlen frowned again as she sensed Tonovan's aura on one of them. Earlier, when he'd been threatening her about coming for a visit, he'd been aboard Uthari's yacht. What was he up to now?

Captain Rivlen, Uthari spoke into her mind.

Yes, Your Majesty? She braced herself.

When she'd opted to fly down to the roamer wrecks, he'd spoken with her, but it had been brief. A perturbed *what are you doing.* He hadn't even acknowledged her explanation.

If you've completed your unauthorized altruistic side trip, I have a new mission for you.

His tone was drier than the desert, and Rivlen couldn't help but wince at the implied disapproval.

I have, Your Majesty. We learned that the dragons are seeking out dragon steel, so the Soaring Eagle *captain may want to be careful with that portal. It's likely it'll be targeted soon.*

They're seeking dragon steel?

Musical instruments, at the least, but it seems more likely that it's dragon steel itself that they want.

Interesting. Uthari's tone grew less dry and more contemplative. *You learned that from questioning those roamers?*

Yes, Your Majesty.

It's possible it was a good idea to pick them up. I admit I thought you were being oddly swayed by sentiment. Or perhaps someone else with sentiment.

No, Your Majesty, Rivlen said, telling herself that Jak didn't have that kind of influence over her. It had merely been the logical argument that he and the mercenaries had made that had convinced her.

Good. I prefer that my commanders act rationally and not be moved by emotion. Or young men with goofy smiles.

I also prefer rationality.

Though Uthari shouldn't have been able to read her mind, especially from a distance, Rivlen carefully did not think about Jak. She wasn't moved by his smile, regardless. The gift... had been practical and lovely, but it wouldn't affect her command choices. *He* certainly wouldn't.

Excellent, Captain. I am aware that you stood between me and that oaf, Sorath, while I recovered from the shock of being attacked by the portal.

Rivlen exhaled in relief. She had wondered if Uthari knew. She had acted on instinct, not out of a desire to curry favor with him, but if it kept him from punishing her for other times when she had failed, or at least not succeeded to the extent they both desired, that would be a good thing.

I've also had reports from my intelligence officers trickle in and am aware that you worked with Sorath to kill Yidar.

She winced again. She hadn't tried to hide that, but she'd also hoped that in the chaos of the dragon attack, Uthari wouldn't ever learn exactly what had happened to Yidar.

That's not precisely what happened, Your Majesty. When Yidar showed up, he was with Zaruk's ships, and the zidarr Night Wrath was looking on. Because of his past betrayal, I believed Yidar had turned against you again and was working with Zaruk's people. At the least, she'd *hoped* that was correct, that she'd interpreted Yidar's arrival with those ships accurately. *I admit I was trying to protect Tezi, since her mercenaries have been working for us, but I didn't see Sorath or know for certain that it was he.* A lie. She grimaced, fearing Uthari would see through it. *I did suspect he was the one fighting Yidar,* she amended. *But Yidar's opponent was invisible.*

I see.

Damn it, how had they gotten onto this subject? Uthari had said something about a mission. A new chance to prove herself?

Rivlen had worried that Uthari ordering the portal removed didn't bode well, but maybe it was because he wanted her to fly off and fight dragons that were razing parts of the kingdom far from the capital, the direction the fleet was heading.

If you wish, Your Majesty, I will lower my barriers so you can see what truly happened. The thought scared her, since he might find fault in her actions that night, but at the least, he would see that she hadn't openly been working with Sorath.

I will accept your offer, Rivlen. Lower your guard to me.

A shiver went through her, but she'd made the offer and had to obey. She looked around, making sure no enemy was nearby to take advantage.

Jak, who was helping Dr. Fret with the injured roamers, must have sensed her gaze, for he looked over and raised his eyebrows, as if to ask if she needed help. None that he could give. Not this time.

Rivlen gripped the railing for support. *I'm ready, Your Majesty.*

Uthari's mental touch whispered through her mind. For most mages, they would have to be in the same room for this, but it didn't surprise her that the powerful Uthari could read her mind from thousands of feet away.

With the king nudging her thoughts along, Rivlen let herself dwell on her actions that night, the trek through the druid tunnels, her reluctance to attack the terrene refugees they'd found, and her disgust when Yidar had jumped down into their cavern and started hurting them. Her grip tightened on the railing as she worried Uthari would think she'd been weak—*sentimental*—and that she shouldn't have let her feelings influence her. She *certainly* shouldn't have sided with Sorath against Yidar, not when she hadn't known what he'd been doing there.

Uthari's touch wasn't painful, but Rivlen couldn't help but find the experience excruciating. Why had she volunteered for this?

I believe you made some poor decisions that night, Captain, Uthari said.

Yes, Your Majesty. She dared not object or make excuses.

You would be wise to distance yourself from the mercenary girl—from all of them. They are only tools, fodder to be placed to distract our enemies while we use our power more freely. And I absolutely forbid you from teaming up with the girl to attack Tonovan.

Fear clenched Rivlen's heart like a vise. She was positive she hadn't been thinking about that. How could Uthari have chanced across that thought?

I am sending Tonovan to lead your mission, and you will obey him without question. That doesn't mean you have to get into his bed if he wishes it, but when it comes to the mission, you will do as he says and help him to the best of your abilities. I've already lost one of my zidarr; I will not lose my general. Whatever you think, you are far from ready to command the fleet. If Tonovan dies on this mission, I will personally lead the investigation and find out if anyone conspired against him. If you *conspired against him. Do you understand?*

Yes, Your Majesty.

As I said, you will help him to the utmost of your abilities. I'm sending you to Temril. They've requested assistance with the dragons. It's likely too late for them, but we must destroy these dragons before they destroy our world, and you, under Tonovan's lead, will be responsible for bringing down the ones in the area while the rest of the fleet handles the threat to Uth. Do you understand?

I do, Your Majesty.

As I said, I appreciate that you defended me after the dragon's death. Because of that, I will not punish you for your questionable choices, or the fact that you've let feelings *influence your decisions. But if Sorath shows up again, and you don't do your best to kill him, I will not be so lenient with your failings in the future. I need you to be an officer I can count on. And I know* you *need to be the kind of officer your father will be proud of.*

Yes, Your Majesty. Rivlen leaned forward, sagging against the railing, afraid she'd dug herself into a hole that she wouldn't be able to climb out of.

It's not irrevocable, Captain, Uthari said, his telepathic voice softening. *Do everything you can to help Tonovan defeat the dragons and complete his mission, and we'll take another look at your actions. For now, you remain in command of the* Star Flyer. *If you perform well going forward, I'll see to it that you're rewarded. And I'll ensure that your family sees me reward you. Your father will know what a powerful mage you've become and that you serve me loyally.*

Thank you, Your Majesty. I understand, and I won't make the same mistakes going forward.

Good, Captain. Carry on.

As his presence faded from her mind, Rivlen grew aware of someone standing next to her. Jak.

By habit, she pulled herself together and wrapped her mental defenses about herself again. She doubted Jak would pry into her mind, but it was hard for her to let her guard down around anyone. Even someone who wouldn't take advantage.

"Are you all right?" Jak asked quietly.

She stood still, torn between wanting to jump away from him in case Uthari was monitoring her and wanting to lean against something—someone—more supportive than the railing. Though her conversation with Uthari hadn't been long, she was exhausted, as if she'd run miles instead of enduring a brief mind reading.

"Tonovan is coming." Numb, Rivlen waved toward the two approaching mageships, then pointed to the west, the direction they would be heading. The gateship was tagging along with the *Star Flyer* as well, though she didn't know if Uthari had assigned it to the new mission or if it was staying close because some of the Thorn Company mercenaries were on it. "Before, I think he just wanted to hop onboard to torment me, but there's actually a mission now. He's leading us and a couple of other ships to Temril to deal with the dragons that attacked that kingdom."

"Oh good. Maybe we can get the roamers their instrument back."

Rivlen scowled at him. "Yes, that's my primary concern too."

Jak managed a sheepish smile. "Well, if we did, it would mean we'd defeated the dragons."

"That *is* the goal. That and... enduring Tonovan." Rivlen couldn't keep from baring her teeth.

Jak's forehead furrowed. "Enduring him *how*?"

"Not in bed. Uthari made it clear I didn't have to give in to *that* kind of order."

"Magnanimous of him," Jak murmured.

"But I must follow him in every other way and serve obediently on this mission. No plotting his death." Rivlen sighed. "Somehow, Uthari knows I've been fantasizing about using one of those axes to cut off the rest of his body parts."

"I think everyone fantasizes about that."

She snorted. "Yeah, but Uthari doesn't care about *their* thoughts."

Uthari must have believed that Rivlen had the power to make her fantasy a reality. With the help of Jak and Tezi, she might have. Maybe at some future date, she could, but she dared not act against Tonovan now.

Worse, she had to make sure he didn't die on this mission, or Uthari would blame her. She propped her elbows on the railing and dropped her face in her hands, dreading the idea of an *investigation* in which Uthari scoured her mind—and maybe the minds of everyone around her—to make sure she hadn't colluded, or even stepped aside to let fate happen, in Tonovan's death.

"I'm sorry." Jak rested a hand on her back, some of his supportive magic seeping through her uniform and into her body.

Rivlen wasn't in a battle and didn't need her reserves recharged, but... it felt good, and she had to fight the urge to lean into him, to *let* him support her. Especially here, on the deck of her ship, with her officers around. What would they think if they saw her cuddling up to a prisoner?

"For what?" Rivlen made herself straighten so that Jak's hand would drop from her back.

"For finagling you into picking up the survivors. I can't regret doing that, because it would have been cruel to let people die when we could save them, but at the time, I wasn't thinking about the ramifications to you—that Uthari might be angry. I didn't mean to get you into a tough situation with him."

Rivlen sighed again. Maybe she should have been angry with Jak, since that was exactly what had happened—though Uthari's true ire was a result of the choices she'd made when Jak hadn't been on Torvil—but she couldn't muster the emotion.

"And if Tonovan turns out to be... a *problem*, I meant what I said. Just because Uthari told you not to kill him—I suppose that's not an unreasonable request—" Jak smiled wryly, though his eyes remained grave throughout their conversation, "—doesn't mean you have to take his crap and let him torment you. Maybe it's delusional to believe that I have enough knowledge or power to make a difference, but I'll come stand beside you and support you whenever he's irritating you. Or... any time at all. And Shikari has funneled his power into me before, the same way I've learned to do it for you and others, so maybe with *both* of us standing at your side, it would make a difference."

Gratitude welled up in her throat, and she tried to swallow down the emotion, Uthari's words about her being affected by her feelings fresh in her mind. "You think your belt-height dragon will stand up to Tonovan, huh? I heard he hides behind your legs when real dragons show up."

"Tonovan is no dragon, and Shikari isn't afraid of him. Shikari whacks him with his tail every chance he gets."

"Doesn't he whack *you* with his tail too?"

"Yes, but affectionately." Jak's second smile was warmer, and he raised his hand and lifted his eyebrows.

Offering his touch again? That warm supportive magical touch?

Since she'd pushed it away before, he didn't presume to touch her a second time without permission—how different he was from so many of the mages she'd worked with over the years—but his eyes seemed to say that the offer was there.

Maybe it made her weak, but she stepped closer and dropped her elbows to the railing again. It was dark. If the crew was paying attention to them, they wouldn't see much. And so what if they did? Jak wasn't *really* a prisoner anymore. He was Malek's apprentice. And he was a civilian, so there weren't any rules about fraternization that would apply to him. If she wanted to take him off to her cabin, it wasn't anyone's business.

Jak rested his hand on her back again, and she closed her eyes and leaned into his warmth. This close, she could feel the growing strength of his aura, and she realized that he might be able to give her the extra boost she needed to match Tonovan's power. If only she hadn't let Uthari into her mind where he'd chanced across her desire to get rid of the general. Well, she could survive one mission with him. And maybe he would be useful against the dragons. With all the power he had, it seemed he would *have* to be.

But after the mission, after the dragons were gone and Torvil was safe from further threats, maybe then Uthari wouldn't care as much about what happened to his general.

Come to my cabin later, Jak, she caught herself saying into his mind.

The magic stopped flowing from his fingers, and she sensed his surprise.

You promised me a massage, she added, though that wasn't what she'd had in mind. Maybe it should have been. Anything else would be foolish, given that Uthari didn't like Jak. Rivlen still didn't know why he'd agreed to let Malek train him. Possibly because Malek wished it, and Uthari did seem to value his senior zidarr.

I'll be happy to come, Jak said. *I should warn you, however, that I don't have a lot of experience giving massages to women.*

You favor men?

No. They don't usually invite me to touch them either. When Shikari is muddy, he lets me rub down his scales with a towel.

So, your primary experience in this area is with juvenile dragons.

It is. He's very discerning. If I don't wash him off just right, he whacks me with his tail and eats the towel.

Doesn't he do that no matter what?

Well, possibly. But I'll do some research on massaging women. Maybe I can find a book or something...

Rivlen straightened, amused by the image of Jak one-handedly massaging her while flipping the pages of an anatomy book. "What you were doing just now will be fine," she said before her gaze was drawn by the approach of the two ships.

General Tonovan stood in the forecastle of one, staring down at the *Star Flyer* with a curl to his lip. His scathing gaze was for the roamers huddled together on the deck rather than Rivlen, but she had no doubt she would have an unpleasant experience with him before the mission was over. Likely before the *night* was over.

She hoped Jak found his book, because she needed a good massage more than ever.

Sorath did pushups and crunches as the druid raft flew north over the Zewnath jungle. With no railings on the strange craft, he was careful to stay away from the edges. The druids appeared unconcerned by the lack of railings—or the five-hundred-foot drop to the ground far below, but they could use magic and levitate each other to safety.

He hoped they could also create magical barriers around the raft to defend against mages and dragons. The thought of going into battle on it daunted Sorath. There were no cannons, magical or otherwise, nor had he spotted ammunition that he could use to resupply his black-powder pistol. He would have to be careful with the shots he fired, making them count. Not that a pistol would help against a dragon. Without a dragon-steel weapon, he might be relegated to offering tactical advice.

Would the druids listen to him? He'd spent his career commanding terrene mercenaries, not magic users, but he had a good idea of the tactics that worked with their kind.

There. Grunk, who was crouching nearby, pointed to the north.

Port Toh-drom and the Forked Sea had come into view, as well as something flying above the city. The dragon.

The dozens of druids aboard the raft were already facing in that direction, having doubtless sensed it with their magic.

Sorath pushed himself up, the round logs making for awkward footing, and wiped sweat from his brow. He tapped a pocket, making sure his handful of remaining pop-bangs were tucked safely inside, then also checked his pistol. If nothing else, his weapons might distract the dragon while those with the ability made killing blows.

The dragon flew up high, banked, then dove for the city, disappearing from Sorath's view.

"Many in Toh-drom are injured or dead," Kywatha said gravely, her eyes closed. "Two of our kind have also been lost. The dragon has been attacking for hours."

"What's it after?" Sorath asked.

"It is a dragon. It simply wishes to destroy humanity. Its kind came through the portal to hunt and feed on human beings."

The dragon flew back into view and circled the city.

"It doesn't look like it's feeding on anyone now," Sorath said.

"This is not a joking matter, Colonel."

"I'm not joking. Are we *sure* harassing humanity is all it wants? All they *all* want? I don't know about your people, but the dragons haven't shared their plans with me." Sorath had heard them making threats to all those guarding the portal, and he admitted that Kywatha's conclusions were plausible, but he thought of the vision the dagger had given him and wondered if the dragon wanted something. It had been trying to avoid the monument and the druids while getting close to that tower. "Can you speak with the druids defending the city?"

"Yes," Kywatha said. "I'm communicating with them now."

"Ask them if the dragon is still trying to get to the tower."

"The tower?" Kywatha looked blankly at him.

Maybe she didn't know Port Toh-drom that well. Her people lived deep in the jungle hundreds of miles away.

"It's eight stories high, vine-covered, and used to have a big metal gong hanging at the top." That had fallen when Jak and Jadora had been escaping, and since Sorath hadn't seen it in the vision, he assumed it was either still lying at the bottom inside or the priests who maintained the tower had taken it away to repair.

"Ah. The Tower of Thanok. Our people do not go there, and few citizens of Port Toh-drom do either. It is a relic from the time the zealous priests of Thanok tried to convert our people to their religion."

"Ask them if the dragon is interested in it."

Kywatha frowned at him but closed her eyes and reached out.

How will we kill the dragon, Colonel? Grunk swiped in the air with the blue-black dagger. He'd been too injured in the last battle to partake, but he appeared eager to fight now.

"I doubt you want to throw your dagger, so you'll have to jump on its back, run up its neck to its head, and plunge your blade into its eye."

As eager for battle as Grunk was, he paused and peered at Sorath, as if he thought he was joking. Why did everyone think that today?

Sorath spread his palm toward the sky. "You can try to wedge it in between its scales, but the dagger won't be long enough to dig into more than muscle. The axes are ideal for deep and more damaging cuts, but Thorn Company has both of those."

He didn't point out that striking the dragon in the eye wouldn't be easy and might not be enough to kill it, since its head was so large that its brain could be deeper than the dagger could reach. Still, if his vision had been correct, that dragon had only one eye. Knocking out the other ought to blind it.

"It does seem to be fixated on the tower," Kywatha reported, her eyes still closed.

"Is there anything special about it?"

"The gong is magical—our people can sense it from many blocks away—but many things are magical. And dragons have such powerful magic of their own that it would be odd if they cared anything about things humans had made."

"It's not made from dragon steel or something special, is it?" Sorath didn't know what other *special* alloy might attract a dragon, and he was merely grasping at possibilities. He'd seen the gong before it fell, and it had been golden, not blue-black, so he didn't think dragon steel was involved.

"The religion of Thanok does not acknowledge dragons as anything other than mythological beasts, and dragon steel isn't mentioned in their *Teachings*," Kywatha said.

"That's not what I asked," Sorath said.

Kywatha frowned at him. "I'll ask. I— Uh-oh. It's attacking the druids head-on now." She called out in her own tongue to someone in the navigation cabin, and the raft surged forward.

Sorath crouched, bracing his boots against two logs. As they sailed closer, more of the city came into view, as did the river, burning docks, and roamer ships, which floated in the water between the docks and the mouth of the river.

With harpoon launchers and cannons that were firing up at the dragon, the roamers appeared to be pirates, not fishermen. Pirates who were in trouble. Two of their ships were listing to one side, and one had sunk, with only part of the deck remaining above the surface. That wasn't keeping the crews from fighting, yelling, and waving their tattooed arms as they fired flintlock weapons and harpoon launchers.

Sorath shared one predilection with his mother's kin—he also preferred not to rely on mage-made weapons. Unfortunately for the roamers, black-powder firearms did even less against dragons than magelock rifles.

At least their winged enemy was focused on the druids. It arrowed downward, darting to the side to avoid a beam of energy from the monument, then snapped at one of the green-haired women in the square.

She shrieked and threw herself to the ground, rolling away from her attacker as the other druids tried to protect her with a barrier. The dragon landed in the square and whipped its tail at the monument. When it struck, the rectangular slabs of stone that leaned together at the top shuddered. The dragon roared and smacked it again and again.

Shouts came from all around Sorath on the raft, the druid crew indignant at this threat to their monument. They hurled magic, green lightning, and balls of energy surging toward the dragon.

Their combined might must have hurt it—or at least irritated it—for the dragon sprang into the sky, but not before the damage was done. As it flapped away from the druids, a shattered slab gave way, and the others toppled. The green beam that had been firing from the top of the monument disappeared as it crumbled, rock dust flying up and leaving the square hidden in a hazy cloud.

The dragon flew over to the tower and perched atop it, its single yellow eye glaring at the approaching raft.

"Well," Sorath said, "we've got its attention."

The dragon's long neck bent as it lowered its head to sniff at the walls of the tower and the open door at the bottom.

"Or not," Sorath mused.

Nobody seemed to be listening, but Kywatha abruptly spun to look at Sorath. "There *is* dragon steel in it."

"In the tower? Or that gong?"

"The gong. We're close enough that I can examine it more thoroughly with my senses. It's covered in gold, but there's a disc of dragon steel in the center. The priests must have built it in for luck or—knowing them—they wanted to take the symbol of a supposedly lesser religion and swallow it with their own."

"Why do you think a dragon would want dragon steel?" Sorath mused, stroking his chin.

Clunks and clangs came from the distant tower. The dragon leaped from its rooftop perch and roared. In frustration?

"I don't know, but what is it doing?" Kywatha asked.

Sorath almost laughed. "I think it's trying to figure out how to get the gong out. Last time I was here, it fell down inside. It should fit through the opening at the top if it's tilted just right but not the door. I—"

A great *crack* sounded, and the walls of the tower blew outward. It was as if someone had detonated explosives inside, but it had to be the dragon using its power. Under the assault, the tower crumbled, all eight stories of it collapsing.

Before the rubble settled completely, the chunks of stone started shifting around. The dragon levitated pieces away as it sought to uncover the gong.

"I don't know why it wants that thing," Sorath said, "but it might not be a good idea to let it have it."

Kywatha called an order in her own tongue, and her fellow druids unleashed their power again, sending their attacks at the dragon. Green balls of energy bounced off its defensive barrier, not bothering it in the least. Rubble continued to shift aside, and Sorath glimpsed the gold of the gong gleaming in the moonlight.

The raft was getting closer, and he flexed his muscles, suspecting the dragon would turn to deal with them eventually. It could ignore the roamers with their harpoons and cannonballs—the weapons still arcing over the city toward it—but the combined might of the druids ought to be more of a threat to its defenses.

The rubble stopped shifting, and the dragon spun in the sky to face them. Its wings barely stirred, but through its magic, it remained aloft.

Its single yellow eye scanned the raft. The other was nothing but the scaled version of scar tissue, and Sorath couldn't help but wonder what enemy it had tangled with that could have done that. Another dragon? A druid kid with a dagger?

An easier target, the dragon spoke into their minds.

Kywatha and several other druids, as if offended by the comment, raised their arms and sent more green lightning bolts streaking toward it. As before, they bounced away, deflected before they touched its scales.

Nice of you humans to bring it to me.

Was it Sorath's imagination, or was that eye focused on him and Grunk? They crouched shoulder to shoulder on the raft, weapons out as they faced their scaled foe, but the druids were a far greater threat.

Unless... Sorath glanced at the dagger in the kid's grip. The *dragon-steel* dagger.

"I think it may want your blade, killer," Sorath said.

Grunk nodded, as if he wasn't surprised in the least. *I am ready to give it to the dragon.* He made a jabbing motion.

Leaving the tower, the dragon flew toward them. Sorath pulled out a pop-bang.

The druids continued to cast magical attacks as the dragon flew closer, and its single eye narrowed, as if it were doing the dragon equivalent of a human gritting his teeth in determination.

Kywatha shouted something, then the translation for Sorath. "We're wearing it down. We're getting through."

The dragon roared and flew straight toward Grunk.

"We've got a barrier up, but—" Kywatha broke off with a gasp.

Most of the crew gasped, their knees giving out as they crumpled to the deck.

Even without the ability to sense magic, Sorath knew the barrier protecting the raft was down.

As the dragon arrowed toward Grunk, Sorath shouted a warning to the kid, then threw his pop-bang and dove to the side. As his shoulder hit a log, the wind from the dragon's wings battering him, he saw it snap its great fanged maw toward Grunk.

Grunk waited until the last second, and he barely dodged in time. A wave of power blasted into the logs, snapping vines and hurling other druids away, but Grunk's blade protected him from the attack. As soon as he sprang out of the way, he leaped back in, slashing at the dragon with the dagger.

He didn't come close to its eye. Instead of flying past, like an eagle snapping its beak for a fish, the dragon landed. It spun toward Grunk, jaws opening again as it tried to bite his head off— or steal the dagger from his grip.

The pop-bang Sorath had thrown struck the dragon's side and exploded, surprising him by getting through its magical defenses to blow up against its scales. But the dragon didn't turn its focus from its prey. It snapped its jaws repeatedly for Grunk. With impressive agility, he danced away each time, but his eyes were wide with fear.

As quick as the kid was, he couldn't evade those rapid strikes forever. All the druids attacked the dragon, unleashing so much power that it made Sorath's arm hair stand on end. Their strikes made it through to the scales, the air crackling with the magical energy, but the dragon endured it all. It continued to snap at Grunk, backing him toward the edge of the raft as its tail thumped down. The tip hammered into the roof of the navigation cabin, smashing it inward.

Grunk's heel caught on an uneven log, and he pitched backward.

Fear for the kid surged into Sorath, and though he didn't have a weapon capable of hurting it, he ran and leaped onto the dragon's tail. It shifted and moved under him, but he used his pick and fingers to find handholds between the scales and ran up to the dragon's back.

Someone got a barrier up over Grunk, protecting him from what would have been a killing blow. He rolled to the side but was only safe for an instant. The dragon summoned its power and ripped the barrier away, the nearby druids responsible for it gasping and grabbing their heads.

Sorath threw a pop-bang at the back of the dragon's head.

"Get down!" Kywatha yelled. "We can't target it with you on it."

Despite her warning, numerous druid attacks assaulted the dragon, and the air sizzled around Sorath. If one missed and struck him...

His pop-bang exploded, wreathing the dragon's head in smoke. It was too busy trying to get at Grunk—at his dagger—to take its focus from him.

An idea sprang to mind, and Sorath continued along the dragon's back toward its head. The slick scales shifted under his feet, threatening to knock him off, but he kept going.

"Grunk," he called. "Throw me the dagger."

Yes, here, Colonel. Not hesitating, Grunk tossed it above the dragon's back.

The blade spun slowly in the moonlight, and Sorath focused on it as he reached up, afraid he would cut his hand off with the sharp weapon. Underfoot, the dragon shifted, and it nearly derailed him, but Sorath managed to snap his fingers around the hilt.

With the deadly weapon in hand, he did as he'd instructed Grunk, running up the dragon's long neck. Navigating a balance beam would have been simple compared to staying on the slick scales, but momentum carried Sorath to the head. The neck jerked upward, and he lost his balance and flailed. He managed to catch hold of a horn before he would have tumbled off the head.

Wood shattered as the tail struck down again. Wind whistled past Sorath—a magical attack. The dragon had realized he was there, that he represented a threat. But the dragon steel protected him, and Sorath flattened himself atop the head, the horns framing him to either side.

Look out for the tail, Grunk shouted into his mind.

Sorath ducked low, afraid a pinpoint strike would smash him like a gnat, but it swept overhead, more like a whip than a mallet. Air whistled again, another magical attack aimed at him. Impervious, Sorath belly-crawled forward, hooking his boot on one of the horns and hanging down the front of the dragon's face. He lifted the dagger as that huge, cold eye focused on him. The angle was horrible for a powerful strike, but he did his best.

As the dragon crouched and sprang upward, Sorath drove the dagger toward its eye. But his enemy spun in the air, flipping upside-down. Sorath barely scratched the scale beside its eye before gravity caught up to him. Though he tried to keep his boot hooked around the horn, the dragon continued to spin, and he fell.

A dozen lightning bolts struck the creature as soon as Sorath dropped. He twisted in the air and managed to land in a crouch, ready to dodge an attack. But instead of going after him, the dragon roared and flew into the air. Sorath had barely scratched it, but the combined attacks from the druids might have injured it more substantially. It flapped its wings without trouble, so it wasn't mortally wounded, but Sorath sagged in relief as it dove away from the raft.

I'll be back for you, human mercenary, the dragon said.

The words chilled Sorath as he realized they'd been directed solely at him, not at everyone present.

Next time, I won't miss your eye, he replied, figuring bravado would be better than collapsing in a quivering heap on the raft.

Next time, I'll tear your head from your body and hurl it into a volcano.

As long as I get your eye first. I'll pluck it out, pin it to the ground in the desert, and let the ants come out to devour it.

After your head is gone, I'll feed your body to the young of crawler mites.

Sorath had no idea why he was engaging in this bizarre exchange of threats, but he had some notion of getting the last word, as if that would make things better. *I'll come back from the dead and haunt your eyeless remains until you go mad.*

Foolish human mercenary, dragons are already *mad!*

No shit.

Rubble shifted, rocks clattering in the city below, and several of the druids shambled to the edge of the raft to peer down.

"It got the gong," Kywatha said wearily, "and is flying to the south."

"At least it didn't get Grunk's dagger." Sorath flexed his foot. In the landing, he'd twisted his ankle, but considering how much worse it could have been, he was happy to have survived with only a small injury.

"What city is it going to harass now?" Kywatha wondered, then switched to her native tongue.

Alarmed calls came from the half-smashed navigation cabin.

We're going to crash. Grunk shook his head, shaggy green hair falling in his eyes.

Sorath wanted to say that things would be fine, but he realized the raft already *was* crashing. Albeit slowly. It had lost altitude, and the tops of the trees outside of the city were above them now. They were sinking to the ground—no, to the river. The roamers on the decks of their grounded ships watched their descent, several whispering and pointing at the raft. Or... at Sorath?

That had to be his imagination. It wasn't as if he'd slain the dragon or done anything notable.

"We'll have to do repairs before we can go after the dragon," Kywatha said. "I can't believe that with all our power, we did so little to hurt it."

Since Sorath had done the equivalent of giving it a splinter, if that, he couldn't speak. He only shook his head, wishing for one of the dragon-steel axes that Thorn Company had, and wishing he were fighting with them. The druids had more effective firepower than terrene warriors, but he missed the mercenaries—and being with his own kind.

"Here." Sorath held the dagger out hilt-first to Grunk.

The kid looked but didn't reach for it. *You are a better fighter. You should keep it for the dragon battles.*

"You're a good fighter. That was some fast footwork. I thought you were going to end up an appetizer for a dragon gullet."

You are more experienced. And climb dragons like a spider. Grunk grinned, flashing his pointed canines.

Sorath shook his head and tried to return the dagger again.

Grunk lifted his hands and stepped back. *Return it when all the dragons are gone from the world.*

"We didn't even succeed in killing one."

Next time, we will get it.

Sorath would prefer there not be a next time, especially with a mad dragon who *knew* it was mad, but he doubted he would be that lucky.

7

Once the roamers were settled down and Thorn Company had eaten dinner, Tezi knelt beside Sergeant Words and Corporal Basher to arrange her blanket for the night. She thought longingly of a soft bed with pillows, but she'd gotten used to the mercenary life and knew such luxuries were few and far between.

"How're you liking your new rank, Corporal?" Basher puffed at a cigar as she leaned against her pack—the closest thing any of them had to pillows.

"It seems about the same as before," Tezi admitted, "but I'm glad to officially be back in the company."

"Once we're done with this mission, the captain will do some recruiting, and we'll get some fresh blood. Then you'll get some people to push around and razz." Basher curled her tongue and blew out a smoke ring. "You'll love it."

"The proper thing to do with new recruits is to instruct them on the ways of the military, how to use their weapons, and what to expect as a mercenary," Words said.

"While pushing them around and giving them a hard time, the same as we did with Tezi. It's the circle of life."

"That's not what that expression means," Words said. "I suppose one could argue that hazing is an integral part of the military hierarchy and designed to inure new recruits to a harsh life, so they're prepared for the difficulties of battle and loss and death when they come."

"Yup. That's what I said. Circle of life." Basher elbowed Tezi but paused to frown at something behind her.

Dropping her hand to her axe, Tezi turned. Three armed women from Moon Guard Company were walking up to them.

As her fingers rested on the haft of the axe, a vision flashed before Tezi's eyes. It had nothing to do with the mercenaries but was of a starry night sky over the sea, a half-moon spilling a silvery beam onto the dark waves below. A winged shape flew in front of that moon—a dragon. No, *two* dragons.

The brown-and-gray mottled creatures would have been magnificent if they hadn't been so menacing, so cruel. Their maws hung open, long fangs visible, as they flew side by side, their powerful wingbeats in sync.

With no landmarks beyond the stars, Tezi couldn't tell which way they'd come from and where they were going, but as the vision faded, she knew with certainty that the axe had given her a warning for a reason. The dragons had to be coming this way.

Tezi lurched to her feet, intending to warn Captain Ferroki, and almost ran into the three women.

"Sorry," Tezi said, looking around the deck. She ought to warn Rivlen too.

"What do you want?" Basher asked the women.

They exchanged nervous glances with each other.

"We were hoping to talk to your captain," one said.

"We were wondering if you were recruiting," another said.

"From Moon Guard?" Basher withdrew her cigar and looked them up and down dubiously.

"Yes. We're all looking for a change."

"Moon Guard was spreading some ugly rumors about one of our soldiers." Basher nodded toward Tezi. "Not to mention some of them tried to kill her for her axe."

"That wasn't us."

"That's *why* we want to leave. Some in our company are... Well, a lot of the men think that just because you're a woman..."

"We'd prefer to work for your company since you're *all* women. We reckon there aren't a lot of internal... problems."

Basher looked at Words, who only shrugged back.

"I need to talk to Captain Rivlen." Tezi pointed, only half-listening to the conversation. Rivlen had come out on deck and had her head up and shoulders back as she faced four uniformed mages on skyboards leaving one of the other mage-ships and heading toward theirs. One of them was General Tonovan.

"Hurry back," Basher said. "We might be getting some new recruits for you to razz."

The three women didn't seem to know whether to be worried or encouraged by that comment. When Tezi jogged away, Basher was directing them toward Ferroki.

Tezi hurried to Rivlen, wanting to warn her before Tonovan arrived and distracted her. Tezi hoped the general wasn't going to command the mission from the *Star Flyer*. Ever since she'd stabbed him in the eye, she'd done her best to avoid him, but that would be hard to do if they were on the same ship.

"Captain," Tezi whispered, coming up beside Rivlen.

"Not now." Rivlen's gaze was locked on Tonovan.

He wore a smug and pompous expression as he descended toward the deck with his officers beside him.

"Dragons are coming," Tezi said.

That broke Rivlen's gaze. She spun a circle, scowling out at the night, before frowning at Tezi. "I don't sense any."

"My axe warned me. It's possible it won't be tonight, but they were flying over the sea, and we've turned west to head toward Temril, haven't we? So, we'll make land by morning?"

Nobody had filled Tezi in on why they'd changed course, but earlier, the *Star Flyer,* gateship, and two other black-hulled vessels had broken away from the main fleet and were flying west. At first, she'd thought it was to drop off the stranded roamers, but it had to be more than that.

"That's right." Rivlen eyed the axe in Tezi's grip.

Tezi grimaced, hoping Rivlen would believe that it was a legitimate warning. The dragon-steel weapon hadn't shared a lot of visions with her, but it had given her enough useful insights that she believed its magic could see the future. Or at least possible futures.

"How many dragons?" Rivlen asked.

"I only saw two, but..." Tezi spread an arm. Two was a lot. And they didn't have Malek with them this time.

"I'll alert my officers to keep an eye out. Tell your mercenaries to expect trouble too. When they show up, bring your axe and fight with me."

"Yes, ma'am."

Well, isn't that delightful, Tonovan drawled into Tezi's mind. *Two eager women awaiting my approach.*

Judging by Rivlen's grimace, she heard the comment too.

The only one eager for your approach is Jak's dragon, Rivlen replied. *He hasn't had any enemies to smack with his tail for a while.*

Tonovan and his three officers arrived, hopping off their skyboards and landing on the deck.

Tonovan sneered at Tezi. "How is it that you're still alive?"

"I have a big axe that likes to protect me while it kills mages." Tezi had used it more frequently to kill *dragons,* but she had a feeling it wouldn't mind cleaving off Tonovan's head.

"You better sleep and piss with it, or someone will steal it from you." Without warning, Tonovan lunged for her. No, for her *axe.*

Though startled, Tezi sprang back before he could grab it. The weapon would protect her from magic, as she'd promised, but she had to rely on her own skill to keep another warrior from physically taking it from her.

She landed in a crouch, the weapon raised as she faced Tonovan. If he wanted it, he would have to fight her for it.

He snorted and faced Rivlen. "I'll be riding on the *Star Flyer*. I trust you've had my suite prepared for me."

"It's as you left it, suspicious stains and all."

"I do enjoy having a good time when I'm on board."

"I suggest you use your bed for rest tonight, General," Rivlen said. "We may be flying toward a pair of dragons."

"Sounds like a reason to do something more enjoyable than *rest*. If there's a chance that we might all die before sunrise..." He smiled and stepped closer to her but hesitated and glanced toward a hatchway.

Jak was striding toward them, his eyes cool, his chin set with determination.

Tezi had always thought of him as academic and a little goofy, not as a deadly mage, but as he approached, cloaked in the same kind of power that the great mages and wizards had, she realized he'd changed since this had all begun. As a terrene human, she couldn't usually sense magic, but with some of the stronger mages, even she could feel the power that radiated from them like heat from a fireplace.

Shikari, who'd been sleeping on Dr. Fret's blanket the last Tezi had seen, spotted Jak and trotted over to join him. Together they strode closer until Jak stood at Rivlen's side, with Shikari on his other side. The dragonling's tail swished as he eyed Tonovan and the newcomers.

"Is this your new *bodyguard*, Rivlen?" Tonovan waved at Jak. "A boy who can barely wipe his butt with his power?"

Tezi knew Jak could do a lot more than that with his magic, but she didn't comment, only shifting to stand closer to Rivlen's other side. The chat they'd had back on Vran came to mind, when they'd discussed possibly working together to one day take down Tonovan. Had that day come?

Rivlen held up a hand to Tezi, as if she knew what she was thinking.

"A boy and his scaled hound." Tonovan laughed and looked at the mages he'd brought with him, officers Tezi had seen in passing. They weren't high-ranking, but they also had that palpable power about them. Tonovan had probably brought them to back him up if there was trouble.

Shikari hissed at him.

"Who thinks he's part snake," Tonovan added.

The hiss turned into a roar. Thanks to his size, it wasn't the most ferocious roar, but Tezi wouldn't want to irk a dragon of any age.

Jak tapped Shikari on the back and must have conveyed some message, for the dragonling tilted his head as he looked at Tonovan. A couple of seconds later, his belt unbuckled. Tonovan swore and grabbed it before the weight of his sword and dagger could drag it to his ankles. Too bad.

"You're the *last* one here who should be cocky, boy," Tonovan growled at Jak. "Under the power of a real attack, your defenses will wilt faster than paper in a fire."

Jak lifted his hands. "*I* didn't do it."

"Enough of this nonsense," Rivlen said. "General, the—"

Tonovan swore and jerked a hand up to cut her off as he peered toward the horizon.

With dread settling into her gut, Tezi looked, expecting to see those two dragons. She didn't yet, but that didn't mean they weren't out there. The mages could sense things farther away than a person could see.

Rivlen and Tonovan's officers seemed to detect them too. Frowning, they all turned toward the same railing.

Tezi let her gaze be drawn in the same direction, but she wasn't so distracted that she didn't notice Tonovan stepping closer to her. As Rivlen called to her officers to ready the ship for battle, Tonovan stared into Tezi's eyes, his empty eye socket a garish reminder of what she'd done to him—and that he had to hate her for it.

You've committed countless crimes, not just against me but against other mages, Tonovan spoke into her mind. *You've killed our kind. It's appalling that Malek gave that blade back to you. You don't deserve it. You don't deserve anything. The second you let go of that axe, I'll use my magic to crush your heart and tear it from your chest.*

You can try, Tezi replied, though she dreaded going on this new mission with him.

If they had to fight dragons, it was possible the weapon would be knocked from her hand, or pulled away when it was lodged between scales. If he was watching for an opportunity to pounce, he might very well find it.

Jadora stifled a yawn as she sprinkled water into the pots holding her spores and adjusted the light source she'd created. She'd combined magic with dragon engineering to make a lamp that could float above the soil. Whether it emitted the right type of light that mimicked Nargnoth's sun, she might not find out until her spores germinated—or didn't. Until she knew she could grow more Jitaruvak, she was reluctant to do too much experimentation with the samples she'd brought back.

It was a long-term project, one that hardly seemed important in the face of the dragon threat, but it was the one Uthari wanted prioritized. Besides, she was able to work on it on the *Serene Waters*, whereas her experimentation on the parasite was at a standstill. Until she had access to a full lab and a vast library of scientific literature, there were only so many things she could think to attempt.

She'd tried all manner of heat, cold, plant extracts, and magic on the parasite, and nothing had disturbed its growth. And it was *rapid* growth, especially given how little sustenance she'd provided. Thus far, the dishes, which she'd reinforced with her power, were keeping them confined, but she worried that *magical* parasites might find a way to escape, so she checked them often.

As she worked, she grew aware of a presence in the distance, miles—if not dozens of miles—behind the yacht. A dragon.

She stretched her senses toward it, wondering if the mages onboard had detected it yet. It seemed to be following them. Or closing on them?

She also swept out to the west to check for Jak's aura. When she'd encouraged him to stay on the *Star Flyer* to keep Shikari away from her experiments, she hadn't realized that ship would be sent off on another mission. Nobody had come by to update her on that, but when she'd asked Malek telepathically, he'd said the *Star Flyer* and a couple of other ships were being sent to assist with dragons in Temril.

The thought of Jak flying into battle without her around to help made her uneasy. As did the knowledge that Uthari was no humanitarian—if he'd sent ships to another kingdom, it was because he hoped to gain something.

She'd been tempted to leave the yacht and catch up with the *Star Flyer* but doubted Uthari would have allowed that. He'd made it clear that he wanted her here, working on his drug. And that Jak would be in danger if she tried to use her power to disobey Uthari.

Jadora sensed Malek walking down her corridor.

Come in, she spoke into his mind before he reached her door and knocked.

Malek stepped inside, fully dressed and with his weapons belt on. Not that she would have expected him to show up in pajamas, but it was late, and he looked like he was ready to go into battle instead of to bed.

"You sense the dragon?" she asked.

He had his magical armor wrapped around himself too, as if he expected a dagger in the back at any moment. Tonovan wasn't on the *Serene Waters*, so she hoped that wasn't likely, but since she'd gained power, she'd noticed that he always had a protective barrier wrapped around himself, even when it was just the two of them. She was positive he didn't believe she was a threat, so she assumed he simply protected himself like that every waking hour of the day.

"Yes," Malek said. "And I've had word from Uthari that the *Star Flyer* is about to engage in a battle with two other dragons."

Jadora winced, worried anew for Jak.

"I thought you should know," Malek said softly.

"Thank you."

"If we're attacked, stay down here." Malek waved at the little lab.

"You don't think I could be of assistance in a battle?" Jadora asked, though she had a hard time imagining herself throwing fireballs. The knowledge and power might be within her now, but she didn't have the experience of a warrior. And possibly not the heart. She was a mother and an academic, not a battle mage.

"I am certain you could be, but Uthari would prefer you to stay somewhere safe until you've completed his project." Malek extended a hand toward the pots. "And *I* would prefer you remain safe indefinitely."

If the dragon destroyed the *Serene Waters*, and the yacht plummeted to the sea a thousand feet below, it wouldn't matter where onboard she was, but she didn't point that out.

"Thank you," Jadora said. "But if I see an opportunity to be of assistance, you know I'll have to come up and do something."

Malek smiled faintly. "Will you attack the dragon with magic or throw vials of acid at it?"

"Can't I do both?"

"Certainly." He glanced toward the door but hesitated.

She wished he would stay, but she supposed he had to prepare for battle. Another presence approached. Uthari. Jadora grimaced, hoping he was heading off on some errand and not coming here, but Malek stepped aside, and Uthari soon opened the door. Two guards had accompanied him, but they waited in the corridor.

Uthari looked at Malek, likely saying something telepathically, for Malek nodded into the silence. The same type of barrier that Malek kept wrapped around himself enveloped Uthari. He had personal bodyguards and was on his own ship, but—even though the dragon was still far away—he apparently felt the need to protect himself. Maybe it was habitual, and she simply hadn't noticed it before. Why she was noticing it now, she didn't know, other than that she was tired and the two men seemed tense.

"We may see battle, Professor," Uthari told her. "Make sure your specimens can't be damaged if the ship is thrown around."

"I will," she said.

"Are you making progress?" He eyed the pots rather than the dishes with the parasites.

"I'm trying to figure out how to grow the plant on our world. I can attempt to synthesize your drug from the samples I already have, but you'll want to be able to grow more in the future."

"Yes. We'll be back in Utharika soon. You'll have everything you need for such pursuits there."

"Even if the city has been ravaged by dragons?" Malek murmured, concern in his eyes.

Had they heard reports of that happening? What about Jadora's home of Sprungtown? She imagined finally getting her father safely back to the city only to find out that it had been destroyed.

"The dragons have sent scouts to investigate Utharika, but they haven't yet attacked," Uthari said. "Their ravaging has been confined to the terrene-human towns below."

Jadora stared bleakly at him. That meant Sprungtown was in danger.

"Their attacks are interrupting our supply chains, food sources, and making it difficult for the kingdom to operate efficiently," Uthari said, "but you'll have whatever you need when we arrive, Professor. I'll see to it."

"How many have died?" Jadora wondered softly. So far, as they'd flown north, she'd only heard secondhand reports. She hadn't witnessed the devastation herself.

"How many of our people?" Uthari said. "Only a handful of mages, but since Tonovan is about to lead his troops into battle against two dragons, that number will likely go up. I hope the dragon trailing behind us doesn't attack until we reach the better-defended sky city."

"I meant *all* people."

Uthari looked blankly at her.

"Terrene humans," Malek told him.

"Oh." Uthari lifted his eyes toward the ceiling, then shrugged. "I don't have those numbers. Malek, discuss what we were talking about with her, will you? I need to prepare for battle and see if I can coax that obstinate portal into responding to my commands again." He stepped back into the corridor, his guards moving out of the way so their barriers wouldn't bump against his. "Keep your lab safe, Professor. Those specimens you brought back are our only ones right now. We can't lose them." He met Malek's gaze, maybe also tasking *him* with the chore, before closing the door and walking away.

A flash of insight came to Jadora. "I think I've realized why all mages are such asses."

She barely realized she'd voiced the words out loud until Malek dryly said, "Do tell."

"When Rivlen started teaching Jak to use his power, before you took over, the first thing she taught him was how to make a barrier around himself."

"It's an early lesson for mages."

"How to put on armor."

"Essentially." Malek tilted his head. Fortunately, he seemed more curious than hostile in regard to her epiphany.

That made her regret that she'd unintentionally included him in the category of *all mages are such asses.* But even he lacked empathy when it came to terrene humans.

"The first thing you learn is how to make yourselves invulnerable," she said.

"To survive in a world full of other mages, who are at the worst your enemies and at the best your competition, you have to be able to protect yourself."

"I think..." Jadora spoke slowly, working through her thoughts. After all, she was a chemist, not a psychology professor. "I think that when you don your armor, you're not just walling yourself off from physical attacks but from other people on every level. You'd almost have to. It's an act of distancing yourself. When you make yourself invulnerable to the sticks and stones that your rivals might throw, you also make yourself invulnerable to the pain, suffering, and fear of others. You might be able to observe it from a distance, the way a scientist observes insects in an experiment, but you can't feel their pain on a visceral level, not the way you could if you allowed yourself to be close to them."

"You should now know that when you have the ability to communicate telepathically with others and read their minds, it also comes with the ability to sense everything they're thinking and feeling. You *have* to wall off your mind, or you'd go crazy from being inundated with all that."

"Yes." She smiled sadly. "I've seen how you armor your minds as well as your bodies."

"It's necessary for our sanity."

"But it keeps you from feeling what others feel, from having true connections and developing bonds with others. Have you ever let down your guard, Malek? Removed your magical armor?"

"Not voluntarily, but in that dungeon cell on Vran." He waved at the spot where the kerzor had been embedded in his temple. "And when that dragon almost killed me on that frozen world, my barriers were down. Also when that bug flew through my armor and infected me with bacteria that nearly stole my sanity. Nothing good comes from letting down your guard."

"No? Those are the times when you were the most human to me. The most vulnerable. The easiest for me to identify with. Those were the times when I realized... I love you."

Malek opened his mouth, but he didn't seem to know what to say. Funny how speaking aloud that she loved him made *her* feel vulnerable, open to rejection, scoffing, pity.

"I haven't known you that long," Jadora said into the silence, "but you've changed in the time I have. And I think it's those events that changed you. In those moments, you glimpsed what it is to be human, not simply an invulnerable zidarr impervious to all attacks, mental and physical. I'm sure Uthari doesn't think it's a good thing, since he hasn't the faintest idea anymore what it is to be human, if he ever did."

"I'm sure he would say that *you're* responsible for any changing I've done," Malek said.

It wasn't exactly an accusation, but he didn't seem as delighted by her epiphany as she was, and she resolved to wrap it up. Though it was interesting that he didn't deny that he'd changed. Maybe he knew.

"It's impossible for one person to change another. That's something that has to come from within you." Jadora took a deep breath, her senses informing her that the dragon had flown closer. Maybe it intended to attack during the night. "I doubt Uthari has any interest in changing. I understand if you don't either, though because of how I feel about you... I keep hoping that you will, that you'll realize it would be the right thing to walk away from him."

Malek shook his head.

"It's not the magic itself that makes mages indifferent to the rest of humanity," Jadora said. "It's what it allows. The power it gives them to live in their sky cities, apart from the rest of the world, separate from the suffering and pain of others, of anyone and anything that might remind them that deep down they're human, they're vulnerable, and they're mortal." She snorted. "At least until Uthari gets his potion."

"I only came to warn you about the dragon," Malek said.

"Not for a lecture? Distressing. I miss having students to deliver my diatribes to." Jadora looked toward the wall and, with her senses, through it toward the dragon. "It's coming for the portal."

"It's spoken to you?"

"No, but Jak told me that another dragon swooped in and attacked the roamers to take a dragon-steel artifact. The portal is pure dragon steel, so if they're collecting it, they'll want it too."

"Why would they be collecting it?"

"I don't know. What did Uthari want you to tell me?" Maybe she shouldn't have asked. She doubted it would be anything good.

Malek straightened and nodded, seeming relieved to change the subject. "He wants to know if you can use your new knowledge to alter the parasite or create some *other* parasite that would feed off the dragons' power or their blood—whatever it would take to kill them. It would have to affect only their kind and be transmissible between them so that it would wipe out their species without our people having to battle them. Maybe it could build on the parasite that already infests them." Malek waved to a dish where two motes were now glowing atop the growing parasite population. "If you could create something that would kill the dragons, at least the ones who've invaded our world, we could eliminate the threat without losing so many people to them. Mages *and* terrene humans."

Jadora leaned back against the counter, the hard edge cold through her dress. "Even if that were possible, I don't think I could do it."

She imagined innocent Shikari being caught and killed simply because he was a dragon.

"Why not?" Malek asked.

"Even in war, there has to be a line that one cannot cross because it's too vile, too evil. I draw that line well before genocide."

"They want to enslave all of humanity and kill who knows how many of us along the way, Jadora. They already *have* killed a lot of us."

"That doesn't mean it's acceptable for me to do the same to them. There's a quote from *The Teachings* that's been in my mind lately. If you must adopt the tactics and traits of your enemy to vanquish him, you will become that which you sought to defeat."

"Philosophizing can come after the fighting, after the threat to our world is gone."

"If it doesn't come *before* the fighting, we're already doomed."

Malek sighed at her and walked out.

She gazed sadly at the door for a long time after he was gone, distressed that the times she'd felt the closest to him, the times she'd loved him the most, were times he considered the most detestable. Would she ever see him vulnerable again?

He hadn't responded to her statement that she loved him. Maybe because he wouldn't—couldn't—ever feel such emotions himself, not for her and not for anyone. Uthari wouldn't allow it. *Malek* wouldn't allow it.

8

"You know, when the captain sent me over here, it wasn't to hold your tools," Sasko said.

She didn't know if Vinjo heard her. He had his head stuck through an open panel under the console in navigation, grunting as he made adjustments to who knew what. Clinks and clanks interrupted a buzzing noise that had been going on for the last five minutes.

"Was it to fondle my leg?" Vinjo asked. "Because I'd be amenable to that. Other parts too, though I'm not sure how much of me you can reach."

Sasko eyed his bare feet and the grass trousers he'd made back on Zewnath, the hems rucked up to his knees. His waist and half of his torso were also in view—he wasn't as embedded in the ship's workings as he might think.

"Your bare knees are visible," she said.

"Oh, knee fondling is nice. I—" Vinjo broke off as something clanked, and his body jerked, a groan leaking out afterward.

"Do you want me to get the first-aid kit?" Sasko asked dryly.

"No, I'm fine. I just hit my head. But my head is hard. Callused on account of how often I bang it against things."

"Head calluses, how sexy."

Vinjo wriggled his lower half as he pushed himself out from under the console. Grease smudged his cheeks, and cobwebs and dust blanketed his tousled hair.

A few weeks earlier, the gateship hadn't existed. Sasko had no idea how it could have acquired cobwebs so quickly, though she'd heard Nargnoth had been swampy and filled with killer bugs. Maybe some of those bugs had been web-spinners.

"I love it when you talk dirty to me." Vinjo beamed up at her.

"If you think that qualifies, I'm not sure you know what *talking dirty* is."

"Talking to me while I get myself dirty?"

She snorted, smiling despite herself. He was a complete goof.

His expression grew more somber as he met her gaze. "I appreciate you coming over here to watch out for me."

"The captain sent us, and I think Sergeant Tinder's axe is what's going to protect you if trouble shows up." Sasko tilted her thumb over her shoulder toward the corridor, though Tinder was up on deck with some mages Rivlen had also sent over.

When they'd first come aboard, Vinjo had given everyone a tour of the cabins, navigation, and engineering room, all accessible off the corridor that bisected the long, narrow ship, but it had been tight, especially for people walking around with weapons hanging from their belts. Almost everyone had gone back up to the deck to keep an eye out for trouble.

A few roamers that Vinjo had magically plucked up from the shipwrecks were up there too. Most of their people were on the *Star Flyer*, but a dozen had landed on the gateship and laid out their meager belongings to make a camp of sorts. Sasko assumed the roamers would be set down in Temril. Nobody had filled her in on why the gateship and a portion of the fleet was *going* to

Temril, but she wagered the roamers would appreciate getting away from mages.

"I assume," Vinjo said, "if you hadn't wanted to come over to this ship, you wouldn't have."

"Sure. That's how mercenary companies work. The captain *asks* if you want to do things. There are no orders given, and objections and discussing things committee-style is encouraged."

Vinjo smiled, refusing to be daunted by her sarcasm. "You won't regret coming over. The gateship has some decent armor to it, and I infused the hull with a senses-scrambling field."

"What does that do?"

"It's a magical camouflage that makes it so dragons don't notice us. Sort of. They're pretty bright and observant, but it did make it a little harder for the ones on Nargnoth to find us than it otherwise would have been."

"So, you're saying I was wise to volunteer to come over here?"

"Hah." Vinjo snapped his fingers and pointed at her. "I *knew* you came of your volition."

That wasn't quite how it had happened, but Sasko gave up on arguing and brushed her fingers through his hair to scrape out the cobwebs. He leaned forward to give her easier access and perhaps because it felt good. She didn't mind rubbing his head. Despite the dust, his hair was soft.

"Do you think my people will come for me and try to kill me?" Vinjo whispered in a rare serious moment.

"I don't know anything about them, but Captain Rivlen thought it was a possibility." Sasko hadn't noticed the blue-hulled ships on the horizon since the *Star Flyer,* gateship, and two other vessels had split off from the fleet. She hoped Zaruk's people had continued after the majority of the ships, since the fleet had taken the portal with it, but if Vinjo's people wanted him back more than they wanted the portal, or if they wanted to attack an easier and less well-protected target...

"It wouldn't be so bad if they kidnapped me—maybe—but I've done so much work for Uthari now that... I'm afraid of what will happen if they take me back to my king alive."

"You're Uthari's *prisoner*. It's not like you've been given a choice." Sasko waved to his grass pants—he'd made them and a skirt so he could avoid wearing the red uniform that Uthari's mages had tried to foist on him. After being tortured, he'd reluctantly agreed to work for them, but the trousers had apparently been the line he wouldn't cross.

"I could have let Uthari kill me. Or killed myself." Vinjo stared glumly at the deck. "That's what's expected of military officers. Working for the enemy is treason."

"Even when you're a prisoner?"

The mercenaries had their own code of conduct and rules they were supposed to obey, but nobody who worked for coin was expected to be as fanatically loyal as the soldiers who swore oaths to their monarchs when they signed up.

"Even then, yes." Vinjo sighed and leaned back against the console. "The problem is that I like being alive. And I like building things. Being told to make a ship—" he waved to indicate the vessel he'd designed and almost single-handedly built in the middle of the jungle, "—isn't the most onerous thing. I may have even liked doing it." He bit his lip. "They're going to kill me for sure."

"Not if they don't find you."

"If I never go back, they'll consider me a deserter. I'd never be able to return to my kingdom, to see my parents or friends or anyone from back home."

"Sorry." Sasko could have pointed out that he'd already likely passed that point and wouldn't be allowed to go home, but that wouldn't have been helpful. His expression was so bleak that she wished there was something heartening she could say. "Maybe when this is over, you can join Thorn Company."

"Isn't your unit exclusively for women?"

"Yeah, but you've got a grass skirt. You're halfway there."

"I think it's the half *under* the skirt that might be against the rules."

Sasko patted him on the shoulder. "If you need a place to hide out, we can make it work. The captain likes you."

"She does?"

"Well, she asked *me* to like you."

"And that's working... right?"

"Yeah, it's working."

Vinjo smiled, clasped her hand, and pulled her down to the deck with him. Sasko knelt and kissed him, glad they had some privacy in the navigation cabin. Tinder would have teased her mercilessly for this, but Vinjo was a surprisingly good kisser for someone so absent-minded. It was probably those little tingles of magic that came with his touch. She hadn't figured out if he consciously used his magic to give her pleasure, or if mages simply exuded it when they were intimate with someone else, but she found him far more enticing to kiss than she ever would have expected.

It crossed her mind that there weren't any rules saying they couldn't do *more* than kiss. Perhaps Vinjo had that in mind as well, for he pulled her into his lap, but he abruptly jerked his head back, clunking it against the console—again.

"What's wrong?" Sasko asked.

"I sense something."

"Besides how alluring it is to kiss a mercenary?"

"Yes. I mean, that *is* alluring, since you're an amazing warrior woman, but, uhm." He shifted her aside, stood up, and peered through the large navigation porthole.

Sasko didn't see anything, but he groaned and flung open the hatch, sprinting for the ladder.

Weapons in hand, Sasko followed him. On the deck, everyone

was sitting or lying quietly, settled in for the night, with only Tinder standing guard as she leaned against the railing. Whatever Vinjo had sensed must not have been in view yet, for Tinder raised her eyebrows in surprise at their arrival.

Shouts came from the *Star Flyer*. It and the two other mageships were sailing along ahead of them. The wind muddled the words, but Sasko thought she heard calls to prepare for battle.

"Dragon?" she asked glumly, the vision she'd received from the druid woman's future stone coming to mind. It had shown her a battle in the sky, dragons versus mageships, and Captain Ferroki had been killed in it. Had that vision been accurate? Was it about to come true?

Maybe not. It was night, and the vision had shown a daytime sky. Sasko hoped that meant none of Thorn Company would die tonight.

"*Two* dragons," Vinjo said with a groan.

"Any chance that camouflage you mentioned will keep them from seeing us?"

"They might focus on the other ships before us, but... that's not good for them either."

Sasko gazed toward the *Star Flyer* where Thorn Company was readying itself for battle and wished she could bring her comrades over for their protection. But even as she had the thought, she knew Ferroki wouldn't agree to that. They were mercenaries, and it was their job to fight.

"But not dragons," Sasko whispered. "We didn't sign on to fight dragons."

Vinjo glanced at her, but Tinder shouted, "Look!" and that drew their gazes forward.

The two dragons had flown into view, the half-moon gleaming on their scales as they flapped their powerful wings.

"Mages," the senior-ranking officer on the deck of the gateship called, "get ready to put up a barrier!"

Sasko readied her magelock rifle, though she had no delusions about the weapon harming dragons. "Did you bring any grenades, Tinder?"

"I've *always* got grenades." As Tinder slung her axe off her shoulder, she patted a bulging pouch on her weapons belt. Dr. Fret had knitted a dragon onto the front of it. Hopefully, that meant the grenades inside would have great luck at hitting dragon targets.

"Mind sharing?" Sasko asked.

"Of course not."

"Uhm." Vinjo raised a finger. "If you let me see those, I might be able to enhance them."

"My grenades don't *need* any enhancements," Tinder said.

"I could add magic so the explosions are even bigger and stronger."

Tinder hesitated, still appearing affronted by the idea of enhancements, but she admitted, "I do like bigger and stronger."

She unhooked the pouch and handed it to Vinjo. Sasko stood beside him as he knelt to wriggle his fingers over them.

The two dragons flew closer, but they either hadn't noticed the gateship yet or didn't care about it. They also weren't aiming toward either of the two mageships that had come along. Instead, they flew straight toward the vessel that carried Thorn Company. The *Star Flyer*.

Sasko shook her head bleakly as the mercenaries fanned out along the railing closest to the approaching dragons. Grim-faced but determined, they readied magelocks, grenades, and swords.

Tezi's blonde hair stood out, gleaming in the moonlight, and she hefted her big axe. It also gleamed under the influence of the moonlight. Or maybe its magic caused that glow.

Was it Sasko's imagination, or were the dragons looking at Tezi? Maybe at her *axe*? If they'd gone out of their way to steal a dragon-steel musical instrument, that axe might be an even greater prize.

Rivlen, Tonovan, Jak, and Shikari hurried up the stairs to the forecastle, the young dragon half flying, half running. He didn't charge to the railing with the others but hunkered down behind Jak and peered around his legs. Rivlen and Tonovan lifted their arms and hurled flaming walls of fire at the dragons as they came within range.

"They're attacking instead of focusing on keeping their defensive barrier up?" Sasko asked as someone shouted for Thorn Company to fire.

She tightened her grip on her rifle, though she waited for the mage officer in charge of the gateship to give an order.

"I don't think Captain Rivlen is one to hide behind a barrier when attacking is an option," Vinjo said, his head down as he focused on the grenades. "Though I'm sure they'll be forced to raise their defenses. They're probably trying to get a first strike in."

Even from hundreds of feet away, Sasko could feel the heat of those walls of fire as they roared toward the dragons. The flames washed over the great creatures but didn't harm them through their scales and magical defenses. That didn't keep Rivlen and Tonovan from launching a second round.

Jak lifted a hand, but if he attacked the dragons, Sasko couldn't tell. Rivlen seemed to straighten, her flames growing even brighter, so maybe he was assisting her in some way.

The dragons roared, the pure power sending shivers down Sasko's spine.

"We haven't raised defenses yet," the mage officer in charge said, "if you want to fire."

Sasko licked her dry lips and raised her rifle. From the deck of the *Star Flyer*, Thorn Company was already firing, the magelock blasts bouncing off the dragons' defenses.

Though she doubted it would do any good, Sasko joined in. If nothing else, maybe she could distract the dragons so the mages had a better chance of getting through their defenses.

"Are you sure drawing their attention is a good idea?" Tinder waited in a crouch, her axe ready.

"No, but I can't stand here and do nothing."

"I'd be all right with that." Despite the words, Vinjo stood and handed Sasko two grenades. He returned the pouch containing the rest of them to Tinder.

The grenades didn't glow or tingle in Sasko's hand, or do anything that promised great power, but she trusted he'd done something to make them better. Somewhere along the way, she'd started to believe that he could fix or improve anything he touched.

"Barrier up!" Rivlen cried, lowering her arms.

"Here too," the lead mage on the gateship yelled.

A second later, the *Star Flyer* shuddered as an invisible wave of power hit it. The barrier kept the ship from being blown to pieces, but several of the mages on deck dropped to one knee, staggered by the effort required to maintain it.

Some of that wave of power passed over the *Star Flyer* and clipped the gateship. A mage near Sasko swore, and the deck rocked under their feet. She wished she could fire again, but with the barrier up, her attack would be deflected back toward them.

Where is it? a voice boomed into Sasko's mind.

The dragons had reached the *Star Flyer* and snapped at the barrier, trying to bite the people on the deck, but it held against their fanged attack. They roared again as they circled the ship, seeking an opening. With the dragons' focus on the *Star Flyer,* the officers on the other two mageships risked lowering their barriers to launch attacks at their foes. Fireballs slammed into the dragons' sides, but they appeared impervious.

"Is it just me, or are those dragons even stronger than the one we battled at the portal?" Tinder asked.

It was here, another cry sounded in Sasko's mind. *I smell it under the human stench.*

"You and Tezi need to get close enough to be able to use your axes." Sasko recalled from her prior battle that only the magical weapons and the lightning from the portal had hurt the dragons.

"Always a smart idea," Tinder muttered.

"Lower the barrier to attack," their officer said as the dragons continued to focus on the *Star Flyer,* snapping at its barrier.

Rivlen, Jak, and Tonovan all stood in the forecastle with their arms up, channeling their power into it. Their efforts were effective, and the dragons couldn't get through, but how long could their stamina last?

"Our barrier is down," the gateship mage said. "Everyone, fire!"

Sasko squeezed her trigger twice, but the dragons were close enough now that she might be able to reach them with the grenades.

"Let's see what kind of enhancements we've got here." Sasko switched her rifle to her other hand, armed the grenade, and took a running throw.

As the projectile hurled toward the closest dragon, a fireball from one of the neighboring ships almost took it out, but it sailed over the flames. It struck the back of the dragon and exploded, pink, green, and pale blue brightening the usual whitish-yellow flare of light.

"It looks like he enhanced it with a little girl's crayons," Tinder said.

Whatever Vinjo had done, the explosion didn't bother the dragon any more than the fire attacks had. It kept snapping at the barrier, trying to get through to the deck below—to where Tezi waited with her axe.

"Give it a moment." Vinjo held up a finger. "Also, boys like crayons too."

"I'm sure *you* did," Sasko muttered, squinting at the dragon. Some of the pale colors had appeared on its scales, as if its backside had been spattered with paint.

"It's more of an acid," Vinjo said, glancing at Sasko.

"Are you reading my mind again?" Sasko raised the second grenade, wondering if she could hit the other dragon with it.

"Just monitoring you to make sure you aren't in distress."

The dragon reared back, its wings flapping erratically as it twisted in the sky and nipped at its hindquarters. Like a dog biting for a flea, it tried to remove Vinjo's acid.

Rivlen pointed at Tezi, and a deck board under her feet ripped free to launch her into the sky as if from a trampoline. Sasko stared in surprise, hoping that had been planned and that Tezi was ready.

She must have been, for she rose straight up toward the twisting dragon and swept at it with her axe. She only managed to clip one of its talons and, judging by the grimaces on the mages' faces, cut through their own barrier in the process. Nonetheless, the deadly weapon drew blood.

The dragon shrieked and whipped its head toward Tezi. It cast a magical attack that blew past her without stirring her hair, but it knocked half the ship's railing away behind her. As she landed in a crouch on the deck, Sasko stared in confusion. How had Rivlen used magic on Tezi when the dragon's power hadn't touched her?

Another deck board ripped up to launch Tezi aloft. Ah, indirect magic.

After failing to hurt her, the dragon flapped its wings and turned away. Tezi lunged for the only part of it still within reach, and her axe cleaved off the tip of its tail.

The ensuing shriek of rage, pain, and indignation was so loud that Sasko staggered back and half the crew of the *Star Flyer* covered their ears. With its huge wings flapping hard, the dragon wheeled away from the ship.

Unfortunately, the other one came in, taking advantage of the *Star Flyer*'s barrier being down. Tonovan and Rivlen poured streams of flame into its face. Jak rested one hand on Shikari's head and the other on Rivlen's shoulder, and her gout of fire grew stronger and brighter than Tonovan's. He glanced over with a disgusted sneer and must have managed to find even more energy, for his also grew brighter.

"Mage pissing contest," Tinder muttered and hurled a grenade.

Sasko did the same, targeting the same dragon as Rivlen and Tonovan.

Her explosive hit its flank as the creature shook its head, a roar turning into a screech. It flapped its wings so hard that Sasko felt the breeze from afar, and it rose into the air, tail rigid as it flew away from the ship.

Unfortunately, the first dragon had recovered. Tezi waved at Rivlen, yelling for her to throw her into the air again, but their enemy didn't attack the *Star Flyer* this time. It flew up a few dozen feet, sniffed as its head swung slowly from side to side on its long neck, then focused on the gateship.

Whatever Vinjo had done to camouflage it, the dragon had finally sensed them.

"Shit," Tinder swore as that dragon's gaze landed on her. Her and her axe.

Sasko reached for Tinder's pouch and another grenade as their lead mage shouted, "Barrier up!"

Earlier, his voice had been calm. Now, there was a panicked note to it as the dragon flapped its wings and flew toward them. Unlike on the bigger ships, they only had a few mages to maintain that barrier.

Sasko gripped her grenade, waiting to see if their defenses would hold. On the *Star Flyer,* Tonovan dropped his arms and shouted in the direction of the dragon that was fleeing. Some smug, triumphant slander? Since the other dragon was still here, that was premature.

Rivlen and Jak looked toward the gateship. She pointed,

sending a fireball at the dragon while commanding others on her ship to join in.

Ignoring the flames, the dragon roared, and its power blasted into the gateship. Their lead mage cried out and crumpled to his knees.

"The barrier's down," Vinjo blurted. "Look out!"

Sasko threw her grenade, then dove to the side as the dragon flew straight toward the deck.

The grenade blew, striking it in the neck, but the colorful acid that splattered against its scales didn't bother it right away. The dragon landed, talons sinking into wood as it came down with wings spread. Ridiculously huge on the narrow deck of the gateship, it roared in what sounded like triumph.

The unarmed roamers sprinted for the back of the ship, huddling in fear. Sasko couldn't blame them. Even armed, she would have done the same thing if the dragon had glanced at her.

But its focus was on Tinder, and it snapped its jaws toward her.

Springing to the side, Tinder swung her axe toward those jaws. Vinjo lifted his hands and launched a fireball at the dragon, but Sasko knew his power was meager next to mages like Rivlen and Tonovan, and she feared it wouldn't deter the dragon. Indeed, it ignored him completely.

Out of grenades, Sasko lifted her rifle and fired twice. The magelock charges blasted the dragon in the shoulder but bounced uselessly off into the sky.

The rest of the mages onboard cast fireballs, though several of the officers glanced toward the hatch—and over the railing—as if they wanted to flee. The dragon stomped after Tinder, who swung as she backed up, trying to keep it at bay. Her blade sliced through the creature's defensive barrier, popping it like a bubble, but even that didn't make the dragon pause.

"Its defenses are down," someone yelled. "Keep firing."

Sasko, down to her last three charges, did so, but she wished she had more enhanced grenades. Especially since the dragon appeared injured. Though it continued to snap at Tinder, its scales rippled with involuntary spasms, like a horse's flanks with flies pestering it.

Powerful streams of flame came from the *Star Flyer*, from Rivlen and others. The dragon screeched in irritation, still trying to get to Tinder, as mages pelted it with attacks. Sasko took careful aim at one of its eyes, hoping that might be a vulnerable spot.

Tinder kept backing until she bumped into the railing. That startled her, and she glanced back. In that second, the dragon's neck snapped forward like a striking cobra. Sasko fired, her shot just missing its eye and pinging off its scaled cheek. Ignoring it, the dragon snatched Tinder up and sprang into the air.

"No!" Sasko cried and fired her last two shots.

They struck but once again did no good.

A battle cry came from the *Star Flyer*, from the mouths of Rivlen, Jak, Tonovan, and others. They all unleashed their power, wind, fire, and raw energy striking the dragon.

It screeched in pain and spat Tinder out. Sasko ran to the railing, realizing Tinder wouldn't land on the deck, and stretched out a hand.

But Tinder fell past too far away for her to reach.

"No, damn it," Sasko shouted, tears of frustration springing to her eyes as the dragon flapped its wings and flew off to the south, heading in the same direction as the other.

They'd driven it off, but Tinder...

Sasko leaned over the railing, though the last thing she wanted was to see her friend die by hitting the sea far below with bone-crunching force.

To her surprise, a flailing Tinder was rising up instead of plummeting down. As if pushed into the air by a geyser, she shot up and landed in the middle of the deck.

Sasko looked to the *Star Flyer* in time to see Jak lower his arms and slump against the railing. Had he saved Tinder? If so, Sasko would buy him a beer later. If they ever returned to a world where such mundane things could happen.

Tinder groaned, grabbed her arm, and rolled onto her side.

"We need Dr. Fret over here!" Sasko called to the *Star Flyer* as she knelt by her friend. "Tinder, did you break anything?"

"*Everything*," Tinder rasped.

"I hope that's an exaggeration."

"So do I, but it hardly matters." Tinder rolled onto her back and flopped limply on the deck as she stared bleakly upward.

Only then did Sasko realize that she didn't have her weapon anymore.

"The bastard got my axe."

"At least it didn't get you." Sasko patted Tinder gently on the shoulder, but she couldn't help but look toward Thorn Company.

Tezi still had her axe, but for how long? And how would they defeat more dragons if they lost all of the weapons capable of breaking through their defenses? Hell, they hadn't even defeated *these* dragons. Not really. As soon as they licked their wounds—or the acid off their scales—they would be back for the other axe. And whatever else they were looking for.

Sasko dropped her face in her hand, wondering if this would ever end and if she would live to see her homeland again.

9

"THE MERCENARY WOMAN LOST ONE OF OUR AXES?" TONOVAN ASKED in disgust. "I knew those two bumbling oafs wouldn't be able to keep those weapons."

Bumbling oafs? Jak would never call Tezi or Tinder that. They were solid warriors, and Tezi's skills improved every day.

"I thought *mages* would take them from them, not dragons. This is even worse." Tonovan spat over the railing, then glared not at Tinder on the gateship but at Tezi on the deck of the *Star Flyer*.

"At least they're alive," Jak said, not wanting to pick a fight with him—no matter how tempting it would be to shove him over that railing.

"Better we have those weapons than a couple of powerless mercenaries." Tonovan made a chopping motion with his hand. It reminded Jak of an executioner's axe coming down. "They can't be trusted to keep them. They never should have had them in the first place."

Captain Rivlen, who'd been directing men to get to work fixing the broken railing and the deck boards she'd torn up, turned back to Tonovan and opened her mouth to speak. Before she could, he sprang down from the forecastle and landed in a crouch behind Thorn Company.

"Look out!" Jak barked, having no idea what Tonovan intended but fearing he would do more than berate the mercenaries.

Tonovan threw a scathing look over his shoulder as he strode toward them. *Stay out of this, boy.*

Jak glanced around to make sure Shikari was nearby. During the battle, the dragonling had helped him funnel power into Rivlen, giving her enough strength to finally blast through their enemies' defenses. Jak might need Shikari's help again now.

"What is he doing?" Rivlen groaned.

"You." Tonovan stopped near Ferroki, Basher, and Tezi and thrust a finger at Tezi. "You people can't hold such valuable axes. A *mage* wouldn't have lost one of the only weapons we have that can cut through a dragon's defenses." He thumped himself on the chest.

"Tezi did not lose her weapon." Ferroki gazed at his angry red face with impressive calm. "She struck two blows on the dragon and even severed its tail."

Tonovan snorted as he glanced at the deck where four inches of the tip of the tail lay limp, blood spattered under it. "Yes, that mighty blow will incapacitate it for life."

"It's as much as you did, General." Tezi lifted her chin and met his eyes.

Jak was glad she had the courage to stand up to him, but he also worried. As Rivlen had proven with the boards, the axe couldn't protect Tezi from physical objects hurled by magic. Tonovan might figure that out—if he didn't already realize it—if they were to do battle.

"I did great harm to them with my fire attacks," Tonovan snarled. "To their *bodies*, not the tips of their tails. The dragon will grow that back by the end of the day."

"Not sure I noticed him doing *great harm*," Rivlen muttered.

Jak agreed. None of the mages had gotten through until Shikari had thrown his power into Jak and Rivlen. Even then, none of them had done substantial harm. Unfortunately. If, with all these mages, they couldn't slay a single dragon, how would they deal with the forty that had invaded their world? Jak hoped his mother was having some luck figuring out how to get rid of that parasite. Uthari might not want to accept it, but Jak believed that destroying it and altering the dragons' personalities might be their only hope.

"Give the axe to me." Tonovan held out his hand to Tezi.

"What?" Tezi stepped back. "No."

"You will not defy me," Tonovan said. "You people work for my king, and I'm in charge of this mission, so you work for me. *Give me the axe.*" He roared the words, and Jak felt the power—the magical compulsion—in them.

But the dragon-steel blade protected Tezi from his magic, and all she did was take two more steps back and lift it, prepared to defend herself.

"Tell your soldier to give me the axe," Tonovan told Ferroki, the same compulsion in his words.

She didn't have a magical blade to protect her, and she lurched toward Tezi like a marionette.

No, Jak thought into her mind, trying to add compulsion of his own, though he hadn't had any instruction on that yet. *Don't listen to him. He doesn't have the right to make such demands from your people.*

Jak didn't want to make things worse for the mercenaries, but he didn't want to see that brute gain such a powerful weapon. Tonovan had already tried to kill Malek with his magic. If he added a dragon-steel blade to his arsenal, Tonovan would be even more of a threat.

Besides, Tezi deserved that axe. She might have originally

found it by happenstance, but she'd been practicing with it and had survived numerous battles. It belonged to her.

When Ferroki didn't obey Tonovan, he snarled again. Without warning, he sprang for Tezi and snatched for the axe, as if he was such a superior fighter that he could simply rip it out of her hands.

But she was ready for him and blocked the grab. She twisted the axe to rap the haft against his hand. She *could* have used the blade.

Jak almost wished she had, that she would put an end to the loathsome general. But there would be repercussions for that.

Tonovan drew his sword. "You want to fight for it, girl?"

"No, but I will."

Jak looked at Rivlen. "We have to do something. If Tezi ends up killing him..."

"Uthari will demand her death and possibly mine for allowing him to be killed on my ship." Rivlen clenched a fist in frustration. "But I can't *order* him to stand down. He's my superior officer."

"He's a superior asshole."

"General Tonovan," Rivlen called as the mercenaries backed away, giving Tezi and Tonovan room for what seemed an inevitable fight. "The dragons could return at any time. We need to repair the ship and get ready."

"I'll be ready with that axe in my hand."

"General." Ferroki had recovered from his attempt at manipulation and lifted a hand. "Please. Tezi is worthy of the axe. She helped kill the dragon at the portal battle last week. She—"

"Silence!" Tonovan waved his sword, and Jak sensed him drawing upon his power.

A wave of energy crushed down on the mercenaries like the ceiling of a cave collapsing. They gasped, stumbling and falling to their knees. All save Tezi were affected.

Her eyes widened in fear, but she raised her axe and stepped toward Tonovan.

A snap sounded, and a piece of the broken railing flew across the deck toward Tezi. Out of the corner of her eye, she saw it coming and got the axe up. The blade cleaved it in two, and the pieces flew harmlessly past her head, but Tonovan was already launching a second projectile at her. One of the huge lifeboats broke free from its mount and soared toward her.

Tezi gasped and flattened herself to the deck.

Cursing, Rivlen used her power to halt the lifeboat before it could fly over the side and be lost into the sea below. "I said we needed to *fix* the ship, not destroy it further."

Tonovan lunged at Tezi before she could jump back to her feet. Snarling again, he stabbed his sword toward her eye.

"No!" Jak blurted, jumping down from the forecastle.

Tezi managed to dodge the blow but barely. A tuft of her blonde hair floated to the deck.

Jak leaped for Tonovan, having no idea what he would do beyond grabbing the man and distracting him. He didn't even have a weapon.

But Tonovan sensed him coming and launched power at him without so much as glancing back. Jak wrapped his own power around himself to form a protective barrier, but Tonovan was still the stronger mage. *Much* stronger. Jak's defenses partially cushioned him from the blow, but it struck like a battering ram and hurled him against the wall under the forecastle.

Tonovan glared back at him. "*You* don't have a special axe to protect you, boy, so you'd best kiss my ass and tread carefully. I haven't forgotten that you were integral in Admiral Bakir's death. Had he been one of *my* officers, you'd already be dead."

A shadow passed overhead as Jak straightened, doing his best to strengthen his defenses. Rivlen landed lightly on the deck between Jak and Tonovan.

"General." She lifted her hands in a placating manner though her tone was firm and exasperated. "We can't fight among ourselves when there are greater enemies. A *lot* of greater enemies."

"Agreed. Once the girl gives me that axe, I'll help with repairs and we'll continue on our way." Tonovan put his back to Rivlen and Jak, as if to say they weren't threats that he had to worry about.

Rivlen clenched her jaw, her fingers balling into fists again.

Tezi readied herself for another attack, but Tonovan, realizing it wasn't easy to get at her, smiled and looked at the mercenaries again. They'd pushed themselves to their feet as soon as his focus had shifted from them, but they eyed him with great wariness. Several had pulled out swords or magelock rifles.

Ferroki hadn't drawn a weapon, but that didn't keep Tonovan from singling her out. He lifted a hand toward her, and Ferroki gasped and dropped to a knee, her back rigid with pain.

"Give me the axe," Tonovan told Tezi, "or I'll kill your captain in front of your eyes."

He applied more pressure and Ferroki crumpled to the deck, clutching her chest.

Rage blasted into Jak, and he created a fireball, a great orange blaze that could have incinerated a man. He started to hurl it at Tonovan's back, but before it reached him, something like a hurricane gale swept across the deck and batted it over the railing where it dissipated, useless.

"Mind your puny boy, Rivlen," Tonovan growled as he continued to torment Ferroki and watch Tinder. "He's not half the mage he thinks he is. Dribbling power into a superior magic user doesn't make one a wizard. He's a *mock* mage." Tonovan laughed shortly at his own wit.

"Rivlen." Jak turned imploring eyes on her. He knew she shouldn't strike at her superior officer, but *someone* had to. Tonovan would kill Ferroki—maybe *all* of the mercenaries—simply to get Tezi's axe.

Rivlen was so furious she was trembling, but she couldn't act—or wouldn't.

Jak glimpsed Shikari coming down the steps from the forecastle. *Shikari, will you help me against him?*

And if he did, would it be enough? If Jak and Shikari combined powers, they might best Tonovan, but without Rivlen...

More power blasted from Tonovan. It almost caught Jak off guard. His barrier was up, but, once again, Tonovan's strength overwhelmed him. The power thrust him against the wall so hard that boards broke behind him and he felt the pain. His barrier gave way. Tonovan's angry, raw power tightened around his throat like squeezing hands. The magic shoved him against the wall again and again.

Jak struggled to reestablish his barrier. It was impossible with pain pummeling him, but then a great wave of energy flowed into him, sharing not only power but the concentration to allow him to get his defenses back up. Better defenses than before.

He was about to take that boost of energy—a gift from Rivlen—and launch a counterattack, but Tonovan cursed. It was almost a scream.

Jak focused on him in time to see Shikari yank the officer's boot off, then bare his teeth, as if to promise the foot would come with the next bite.

"You scaled menace," Tonovan snarled and threw his power at Shikari.

But it affected the dragonling no more than it had Tezi. Shikari roared. He'd gotten bigger, and that roar was getting deeper and more effective than it had been even a few days ago. Power accompanied it, power that sent Tonovan stumbling.

For a moment, his back was to Tezi. She glanced at Ferroki, who still lay crumpled on the deck and gasping, then gritted her teeth and hefted the axe.

"No." Rivlen lifted a hand toward Tezi. She'd been levitating the lifeboat back to its spot but hadn't stopped watching the confrontation. "I can't let you kill him."

Tezi frowned at her, appearing almost confused by the statement. Tonovan spun back toward Tezi with rage flaring in his eyes.

"And I can't let you kill *her* either," Rivlen told Tonovan. "Any of them. If you try, I'll have Jak sic his dragon on the rest of you."

Shikari sat on his haunches as he chewed on his prize. Jak couldn't imagine thinking a sweaty, stinky boot a prize, but his charge found it pleasurable to chomp on.

"You overstep your bounds, *Captain*," Tonovan said, not pointing out that neither Jak nor Shikari was in her chain of command. Maybe he knew that Jak would do what Rivlen asked, especially if it was an order to attack Tonovan, and that Jak had influence over Shikari.

"My orders are to get to Temril and fight the dragons. With all of my troops there to help." Rivlen tilted her head toward the mercenaries. "I'll do whatever it takes to obey our king. And I assume you will as well."

Tonovan squinted at her. Shikari spat out the lump of soggy leather and lace that was all that remained of the boot.

"We'll discuss this further later, Captain." Tonovan snatched up the disgusting boot. "In private." He shot Tezi a dark look, as if to promise he would be visiting her *in private* too.

Jak's insides clenched at the thought of Tonovan showing up to harass them in the middle of the night, but the ship wasn't that large. If Jak heard someone cry out, he would grab Shikari and show up in time. He hoped.

When Tonovan walked below decks, not staying to help with the repairs, Jak slumped against the wall. Maybe it was premature to feel relief, but they'd survived Tonovan and they'd survived the dragon attack without losing anything worse than a weapon. His body and head ached from being battered against the wall, but he didn't think he'd broken anything. As soon as he caught his breath, he would grab a skyboard and take Dr. Fret to the gateship to help Sergeant Tinder.

Rivlen walked over and dusted pieces of wood off his rumpled tunic. "Are you all right?"

"Just a few bruises." Jak held back a grimace as an experimental rotation of his shoulder drew pain. Maybe he would ask Dr. Fret to look him over after she helped Tinder.

"You may be the one who needs the massage tonight."

"If that's an offer, I accept."

"We'll see." A smile ghosted across her lips, but it faded as she looked toward the hatchway Tonovan had disappeared through. Rivlen set her jaw and walked off to direct repairs, but Jak knew she had to be worried about her commanding officer.

He was worried too and caught himself looking toward the gateship. Maybe after he dropped off Dr. Fret, he would have a chat with Vinjo. Since returning to Torvil, they had been separated and hadn't been able to continue their lessons on engineering and magical-device construction, but Jak couldn't help but feel that, more than ever, it would be handy to have a working kerzor.

A curious peep came from Shikari. With his boot chew-toy gone, he'd wandered over to investigate the limp piece of tail the dragon had left behind.

At first, Jak didn't think anything of it—what kind of threat could a severed tail be?—but then Shikari drew back, issuing higher-pitched peeps and an alarmed shriek that caused heads to turn. A couple of glowing motes rose up from the tail, and fear slammed into Jak like an uprooted tree in a cyclone.

At the beginning of the fight, he'd told Shikari to stay behind him so the other dragons couldn't get close, but when they had proven more interested in the dragon steel than the dragonling, he'd forgotten about the threat of the parasite. But the awareness of that threat returned in full force now.

Jak sprinted over to put himself between Shikari and the motes, even as he brought up his wildfire imagery in his mind. The two motes sparkled in the air and floated toward him—him and Shikari.

"What is it?" Rivlen called.

Jak willed a fireball into existence right on top of the motes, putting everything he could into making it huge, hot, and capable of incinerating everything within its bounds. He was aware of Rivlen walking closer and the mercenaries exchanging looks, as if he were a weirdo, but he kept the fire burning, possibly far longer than was necessary. Though he'd barely sensed the tiny magical motes, he knew how dangerous they were to Shikari.

Finally, with sweat beading on his forehead from the heat—and the effort—Jak stepped back and let the flames fade. The deck under the spot where his flames had hovered was charred. Later, he would apologize to Rivlen and fix it, but first, he had to make sure he'd succeeded in eradicating the threat.

To his horror, the motes still hung in the air. Hadn't his fireball been strong enough?

After a pause, they continued toward Shikari.

"No!" Jak rallied his strength to try again—this had worked when Malek had done it back on Vran—but Rivlen summoned a different kind of magic.

A stiff wind swept across the deck and caught the motes, pushing them out over the railing. She must have given a telepathic order to the navigation officer, for the *Star Flyer* surged away from them, continuing toward Temril. The other ships in their little fleet did the same, and the glowing motes soon faded from view.

That they were still out there disturbed Jak, but he supposed as long as the mageships could outrun them, it would be all right. Eventually, without a host, they would die. He hoped.

"Good idea," he told Rivlen. "Thanks."

She pointed at the deck that he'd charred. "You're as much of a threat to my ship as Tonovan and the dragons."

"Sorry, but you didn't see the motes—and the parasite that rides on them—back on Vran." As Jak recalled, he, Malek, and Mother had been the ones to witness the threat to Shikari. "They're what make the dragons aggressive. Crazy. *Evil.*"

Jak realized the tip of the tail still lay on the blackened deck. It hadn't been charred by his magic, and he thoroughly investigated it, afraid that more of the parasites might remain within it.

"I don't sense anything from it," Rivlen said.

"Hopefully, we got the only parasites." To be safe, Jak crouched, picked up the limp tail between thumb and forefinger, and strode toward the railing with his arm stretched as far from his body as possible. He flung the tail toward the sea and didn't turn his back until it disappeared from view. Even then, he shuddered as he thought about how close those motes had been to infecting Shikari.

"Well, damn," Corporal Basher drawled as she relit the cigar she'd been enjoying before the battle. "I was going to bronze that thing and hang it around my neck as a lucky charm."

"Trust me," Jak said. "That's not the kind of luck you want."

In the stern of the *Serene Waters*, Malek stood with his hands on the railing, gazing into the dark night and watching for the dragon he knew was out there. Thus far, it remained miles back and out of sight, but it had gradually been closing the distance. He felt certain it would pick up speed and attack before dawn. He wished it would do it now. That would keep him from having to stand alone in the dark with his thoughts. With the thoughts Jadora had stirred up in his mind.

She'd told him that she loved him. It wasn't the first time, but before, it had been in a desperate moment when she'd believed she might lose him—or he might lose his mind—forever. This had been in a calmer time, and he knew she'd meant it.

He'd had the impulse to say the same thing to her, but he'd hesitated because she'd implied that she loved *vulnerable* Malek. A man he did not like being. Did she feel the same about nearly impervious Malek?

That was the man he preferred to be. He hadn't trained for decades, seeking perfection and to be better than all of his opponents, only to easily accept that he had hidden weaknesses. Or that there were worlds that were full of stronger opponents. That still galled him. He *hated* having weaknesses, being vulnerable. It bothered him that Jadora had *liked* it when he'd been those things.

Why couldn't she love Malek the zidarr who followed the Code to perfection? Who defeated his enemies without trouble?

He found it hard to believe that one had to be vulnerable to love or be loved. But... it wasn't a feeling he'd experienced. Not since his mother had died and he'd started his zidarr training. Love hadn't been allowed, not then, and not now. No wife, no children. He didn't even have colleagues that he was close to. His colleagues were as much his rivals as his allies.

Only Uthari had shown appreciation for him over the years and had occasionally expressed affection. But was that love? Had it even been genuine? Or, as Jadora had implied, was Uthari incapable of tender feelings for another person? Was everything he did, as Malek had observed earlier in the day, about manipulation? Maybe Uthari had made a conscious choice to be the father figure that Malek had needed as a boy. And maybe that he even needed on some level today. For his entire life, Malek had only had Uthari to lean on and confide in, but as Uthari had admitted from their earliest days together, he'd raised Malek to be a weapon. A tool.

For the first time, Malek found himself wondering what he'd given up to become a zidarr.

His senses prickled, and he squinted into the gloom. Shouts sounded on the deck of the yacht and from the other ships in the fleet. The dragon was approaching.

When Malek drew his weapons, it was with relief. Better to fight than to spend the night mired in his mind.

More mages stormed onto the deck behind him, and as the dragon came into view, a dark winged shape in the night sky to the south, they raised a barrier around the yacht. Diamond-strong and enhanced by their combined efforts, would it be enough?

With the rest of the fleet there to help, it ought to be. The other ships flew closer together as the threat approached, and Malek sensed their crews also raising barriers. For now, there was only one dragon. Would it try to steal the portal?

Malek checked with his senses to ensure Jadora was in her laboratory. She was. Good. He'd joked about vials of acid, and he suspected she *could*, with her new power, help against the dragon, but he would prefer that she remained safe.

As the creature flew closer, the mages collectively braced themselves. With their barriers up, they couldn't attack, and Malek could only crouch patiently with his weapons, waiting to see if his services would be needed.

There is the portal, a raspy voice spoke into his mind—into everyone's minds? *I will report to the others that I've found it.* The dragon sounded smug.

How many others were there, and how far away were they?

As the yellows of its reptilian eyes came into view, the dragon launched its first attack. Claws of magic raked at the barrier around the *Serene Waters*.

The barrier held, but Malek frowned. It was singling the yacht out from the rest of the fleet. That was odd, since the portal was on another ship, and the dragon had just expressed interest in it.

Malek funneled some of his strength into the barrier, adding to its power. He rubbed his thumbs against the hilts of his sword and main-gauche, ready to do more.

The dragon attacked again, silver sparks showering the air as its magical claws struck the barrier. Once more, the yacht was its target. It seemed to be testing them. Or was this a feint so the mages protecting the portal would let their guard down?

Give me your passenger, humans, the dragon said. *Or I will tear your ship to pieces.*

Their *passenger*? It couldn't be referring to the portal, could it?

She has been given something that your kind have no right to. A human shall not possess the knowledge of the dragons.

A chill went through Malek. It was talking about Jadora.

The dragon launched a different kind of attack. Instead of a great raking swipe, a pinpoint battering ram of magic burst toward the side of the yacht. Malek hurried to help the others shift their defenses to protect against the attack, but it was difficult to alter the shape of a barrier generated by many. Malek managed to get his power up in that spot, but when the battering ram struck, it was like a dagger plunging into flesh. It ripped through even his ability to maintain their barrier and punctured the starboard hull of the yacht.

That was the side with the laboratory.

Malek ran toward the railing above the puncture, as he and others struggled to reinforce the barrier in that spot, to drive the dragon's power back. A cry of alarm came from below, and Malek sensed Jadora's fear as he recognized her voice. She'd gotten a barrier up around herself, but that didn't keep the dragon from using its magic to extract her from the yacht.

Malek reached the railing, longing to plunge his dagger into the dragon's eye, but it was too far away. He might be able to reach it with a jump, but he spotted a skyboard and levitated it toward him.

"Stop it!" someone cried as the dragon's magic pulled Jadora out through the hole in the hull.

Dozens of mages combined power to try to break the grip or sever the invisible rope of power pulling Jadora away from the ship. Malek envisioned great shearing scissors cutting through it. But he might as well have been trying to cut dragon steel. The dragon kept reeling Jadora in, the barrier she'd formed around herself protecting her from being crushed but not from being kidnapped.

As Malek jumped onto the skyboard, he remembered the Vran mage who'd protected herself within a bubble from the dragons who'd kidnapped her. She'd managed to keep herself alive for hours that way. Hopefully, Jadora could do the same. But the power of this dragon worried Malek. It had so easily broken through *all* of their combined might.

I'm coming, Jadora, he called into her mind as he sailed after her on the skyboard.

Thanks. It's trying to crush me to death. Even via telepathy, she sounded breathless, and her face was scrunched with concentration. Concentration and fear. *I'm not sure how long I can keep up a barrier.*

Unfortunately, the dragon's power created a buffer around Jadora, and Malek couldn't get close enough to grab her. He marshaled his own power, attempting to wrench her away, but once again, he faced an opponent who was stronger than he.

Jaw clenched, he flew past her. As the dragon kept reeling her in, Malek hacked at the invisible rope of power with his sword. If he'd had a full dragon-steel weapon, maybe he could have cut through its magic, but his lesser-dragon-steel blade wasn't as effective. Why had he given that axe back to Tezi instead of keeping it for himself?

Attack the dragon, Malek barked toward the mages in the fleet, sensing they were largely focused on reinforcing their barriers to protect their ships.

They needed to get Jadora back. Didn't they know how much they needed her? How much *Malek* needed her?

Besides, the dragon was distracted by pulling her in and fighting back against the power she was applying to try to free herself. This was their opportunity to deal with the creature.

A fireball roared past over his head, brightening the night as it blasted into the dragon. The creature's scales protected it, but it roared in indignation.

Though he was reluctant to move far from Jadora, Malek turned and sailed toward the dragon. More fireballs struck it as mages on some of the ships lowered their defenses to attack it. But after the first blow, the dragon wrapped a barrier around itself, and the fireballs bounced off. Malek checked Jadora, hoping it had released her or lessened its grip, but the dragon was still reeling her in. Unlike humans, their kind had the mental capacity to perform many kinds of magic at once. Unfortunately.

Since the fireballs were aiming at its side and head, Malek directed the skyboard toward its belly. He had to avoid its long wings, though he took an angry swat at one as he passed near it. His blade bounced off, but it got closer than he'd expected. The dragon's barrier seemed to be shrinking inward under the assault of so many mages.

Malek flew up under the belly, though it bothered him to let Jadora out of his sight. Attempting to emulate the battering-ram attack it had used on the ship, he sent a pinpoint blast of energy toward its expanse of brown-and-gray mottled scales.

The belly moved abruptly, almost as if his strike had caused the dragon to hiccup. He plunged his blade upward, hoping to take advantage and slip through its defenses. As fireballs blasted into the dragon's flanks, Malek's sword dipped between two scales.

It only sank in a couple of inches before the dragon rolled sideways like a barrel.

Malek lowered the skyboard as fast as he could, but a wing smacked him as the dragon kept spinning. Its long neck twisted, and its maw came into view, fangs leering toward him. Malek wrapped power around himself and the skyboard as he crouched, weapons ready to attack. But a full barrier encompassed the dragon again, and he feared his blades would bounce off.

Get ready, Jadora spoke into his mind.

She hung in the air thirty feet away, still trapped by the dragon's power, but she'd stopped moving closer to it. Between Malek and the fireballs coming from the fleet, the dragon was thoroughly distracted now.

"By its desire to kill me," Malek muttered. *Ready,* he replied silently to Jadora.

He didn't know what she intended to do, but as those fangs lunged closer, he braced himself.

As fireballs continued to sizzle through the air, some bouncing off their scaled foe and some missing it altogether, a great power swept toward the dragon's head. Like a hurricane gale, it ripped away the barrier protecting the area around its eyes and snout. Jadora's power.

Malek darted aside as the jaws snapped for him. He flew up, leaping off the skyboard and onto the dragon's snout. Not giving it time to react, he drove his sword into its eye. It screeched and jerked back. Its tail spasmed and swung, smashing into Jadora.

"No!" Malek cried.

He yanked his blade out, wanting to drive it into another vital target. But the dragon's magic blasted him away from his perch, and he tumbled through the air. That time, he'd done more damage, but as he flew backward, he worried it wouldn't make a difference. The dragon still had another eye.

As gravity caught up to him, and he started to fall, Malek used his power to call his skyboard back to him. He'd dropped below the dragon, and more fireballs flew past above him, slamming into the dragon. It jerked its head around, blood and ichor dripping from its burst eyeball.

Malek looked around for Jadora, then swore. She was falling. Had the tail knocked her unconscious so that she couldn't levitate herself?

He angled downward and sped after her. Falling into the ocean from this height would kill her as surely as if she struck land.

With his heart in his throat, he sped faster as he summoned his own power to levitate her. It *should* have worked, but something about her—about her lingering defenses?—kept him from getting a good grip. It was almost like when he tried to use magic on someone holding a dragon-steel weapon.

As the wind whistled past him and he urged the skyboard to top speed, he shifted his focus, attempting to stiffen the air underneath Jadora to hold her up that way. Her descent slowed, but would it be enough? They were rapidly approaching the great dark expanse of water.

Above, the injured dragon flapped away from the attacking mages.

I'll be back with my comrades, it snarled, *and we'll take that portal and destroy you. We'll destroy* her.

Jadora stirred and looked around in confusion as she tumbled. Malek reached out a hand as he drew closer to her. A little bit closer. *There.*

He caught her wrist and pulled her onto his skyboard as he shifted it from a vertical descent to horizontal movement. Waves crested just below, sea spray spattering their faces.

Jadora slumped against him, and he wrapped his arms tightly around her, pressing his face against her tangled hair as the dragon's last words rang in his mind.

"Why do they want to kill you?" he whispered. "Because another dragon gave you some power?"

Lots of people had power. Why single her out?

"Maybe, but it specifically spoke of my new knowledge." Jadora slid her shaking arms around Malek, hugging him back. "They could be worried that I learned something that could destroy that parasite and either revert them back to the dragons they once were... or kill them."

"I would accept either." Malek stroked her hair and made himself direct the skyboard back up toward the fleet, though a part of him wanted to remain there and simply hold her a while longer. "Thank you for the help in getting through to its head."

"Thank *you* for coming to get me. I thought I would be relatively safe in the lab and was caught off guard." She wiped water— or tears?—out of her eyes. "I didn't even have time to grab my vials."

"Something that surely would have turned the tides of battle earlier."

"*Surely*." She smiled and kissed him on the cheek.

Malek thought about kissing her *not* on the cheek, but they were nearing the yacht, and dozens of faces, including Uthari's, peered down at them.

Reluctantly, Malek arranged his arms into a more professional I'm-just-holding-her-so-she-won't-fall grip. As she shifted her own arms away from him, she winced.

"Are you injured?" He swept over her with his senses to check and grimaced.

Several of her ribs were cracked. He immediately felt guilty for having hugged her so tightly.

That dragon had been trying to crush her to death, not simply capture her, and if not for the power she had now, she would have died. But as strong as she might be compared to the mages of

Torvil, she was no match for a dragon, not in sheer raw power. None of them were.

"It's fine. I mean... it's not, but I'll be all right. At least until that dragon comes back with friends."

"We'll reach Utharika by then," Malek said, "and be able to better defend against dragons."

Jadora nodded, but her eyes were dark with uncertainty.

Malek couldn't blame her. If the forty dragons that had come through the portal banded together and came after her, would all of the mages in Utharika be enough to deter them? He feared they would not.

10

As night deepened, clinks, thuds, and mutters came from the partially reconstructed navigation cabin on the druids' raft. It floated in the river near the charred remains of the docks.

Sounds of sawing emanated from the jungle beyond Port Tohdrom, though its rubble-filled streets lay quiet. Sorath hadn't seen many citizens while he'd been sitting on the raft earlier in the day, offering to help with the repairs but mostly being told to stay out of the way because *magic* was required. He suspected most of the residents had fled into the jungle when the dragon had first shown up, but a few healer druids had gone out to help the injured, so some remained.

Murmurs and the sounds of oars dipping in the water reached his ears. Two longboats full of roamers were heading upstream toward where the raft floated, its substantial size taking up half the river. Dark-skinned and dark-haired, the men were hard to see in the depths of night, and Sorath had no idea what expressions marked their faces. He also had no idea if they were armed, with pistols pointed toward the raft.

He stood up, hoping the roamers wouldn't be trouble, but after he'd identified them as pirates, he was wary. They might be some of the very pirates who'd been hired by King Zaruk and the various mage fleet leaders to attack Uthari's people and attempt to steal the portal.

Sorath had no loyalty to Uthari and had been forced to work for him against his wishes, but the pirates might not know that. He hoped that after they'd all fought against the dragon together, the past would be forgotten.

"Greetings, Colonel Sorath," one called, using accented Dhoran instead of their native tongue.

Sorath had barely spoken the roamer language since his mother passed, and before that, only with her. He supposed he should have been relieved not to have to test his memories of pronunciations, but he wouldn't have minded hearing it again. It had been more than fifteen years since his mother's death, but in the quiet dark of night, with the trees moaning in the breeze, he missed her. Right now, he missed almost everything about the past, when life had been simpler and unoccupied by dragons.

"Greetings," he replied, watching them warily.

"I am Captain Tengo. May we come aboard?"

"I'm not in charge here."

"No?" The captain sounded surprised.

"This is a druid raft. In case that wasn't obvious from the magical vines tying themselves around freshly cut logs."

"Yes, but we assumed you led them."

Sorath scoffed softly—he led nothing these days—and looked around for Kywatha. A few magical lamps glowed green and provided illumination for the raft, but he didn't see her.

"Anyone care if these men come up?" he called, hoping some of the other druids understood.

Be careful, Grunk spoke into his mind. *They may want to steal the dagger.*

A week earlier, Grunk had distrusted him and thought *he* wanted to steal the dagger. Sorath didn't point that out, saying only, *I'll be careful.*

Whatever the roamers wanted, they didn't sound angry and belligerent. At least the captain didn't. Even if they had some nefarious plan in mind, the druids had the power to stop it. Some of them were probably already reading the men's thoughts.

"I guess you can come up, Captain," Sorath said. "What do want?"

"To speak with you." The first boat bumped against the raft, and Tengo climbed onto the logs.

"More than we're already doing?"

Tengo faced him, pushing back thick ropes of black hair, then crossed his arms over his chest and bowed in a traditional greeting of respect to one's superior. Tattoos of waves and chains and jagged patterns stretched across his cheeks, curving down the sides of his neck and disappearing under a coarse cotton tunic.

Sorath arched his brows, positive he'd never met the man before.

"We were at the battle for the dragon gate," Tengo said. "And we lost men to the dragon. The mages used us as fodder to throw at the creature. We knew they would. We said no when they wanted to hire us, but they used their foul magic upon us. On *me*." Tengo clenched a fist, then pointed a finger at the side of his head. "We had no choice."

"I know how that is."

Tengo looked toward the handful of druids watching them—most were busy with repairs—and lowered his voice. "They do not control you, do they?"

"No."

"But you do not command them? We know you slew the dragon and crashed one of the mageships. You were invisible, but we know. Our seer saw it all and told the story." Tengo waved toward the deck of his half-sunken ship. Without magic, they wouldn't be able to repair their battered vessels nearly as quickly as the druids.

"I was *on* the mageship when it crashed," Sorath said, "and I had help with the dragon. A lot of help."

"Of course." The way Tengo smiled made it seem like he didn't believe Sorath, that he was certain Sorath had single-handedly—quite literally single-handedly—been responsible for all that himself. What had this seer been telling his or her people? And why? "Because our ships were destroyed by the one-eyed dragon, we are stuck here, but we wish to go to the kingdom of Temril. Many of our people sail in waters around that great island, and the natives in a couple of villages let us camp on their northern shores during the winters. Many of our women are there now. But they're in danger."

"Everyone is in danger."

"You don't understand. Dragons are attacking Temril right now. Our seer told us. Our women and all who've been kind to us, even when their mages forbade it, are in danger."

"What do you want from me?"

"A ride to Temril on this funny mageship. And then for you to join us in battle. To *lead* us in battle."

Sorath leaned back, startled by the man's earnestness and belief that he could help.

As a young man, whenever Sorath had encountered roamers in the coastal ports, they'd sneered and spat at him for having turned his back on his people and the sea. Since then, he'd done his best to avoid them. Now, he searched for deception in the captain's eyes—was it possible his people were still working for Zaruk or another wizard king and had been sent to lure Sorath into a trap? He didn't, however, see any sign of deception. Besides, how could Tengo have known Sorath would show up in Port Tohdrom?

"I think the druids will want to keep their raft here and defend Zewnath," Sorath said, though a few days earlier, Kywatha had admitted that her people had made a mistake in not helping fight against the dragons as they came through the portal. She'd said mages and druids would have to work together to protect Torvil from this new threat.

"You must convince them to go to Temril. There are many dragons there, and their kind are plotting to take over our world."

"How do you know where they are and what they're doing?"

"Our seer has the gift. She knows much."

She hadn't known that Sorath hadn't crashed General Tonovan's mageship, so she didn't know *that* much. Unless she'd exaggerated the truth to make her people want to work with him. But if so, why?

"I'd like to meet your seer," Sorath said.

"That will happen if you take our people aboard your raft and we all fly to Temril."

"Let me talk to the druids."

"Yes." Tengo bowed again, then clasped his hands behind his back. Intending to wait right there?

Sighing, Sorath walked off to look for Kywatha.

Grunk found him first, a bone dagger in hand as he squinted suspiciously at the pirates. *What do they want?*

A ride.

They could be after the dagger. Grunk waved to the blade sheathed once more at Sorath's waist.

Can you read their thoughts?

I'm not that good at that. More fighter than druid. Grunk thumped his chest.

Kywatha stepped out of the navigation cabin, magical engine components glowing inside, and Sorath continued toward her.

"Do you know if there are a lot of dragons on Temril?" he asked her.

"I'm not able to sense them from that far away, but I have heard there are. We're receiving messages from druids all over the world, describing the dragons' forces and what they're doing. All continents are being threatened—or have already been attacked."

"Well, those roamers are hoping we can take them to Temril and help fight the dragons there." Sorath pointed out Tengo and his men. "That's what they told me anyway. Maybe you can read their thoughts and see if it's the truth."

He expected Kywatha to scoff and reject the suggestion outright, but she gazed over at them, her eyes growing glassy.

"They have allies and families over there who are threatened," she said quietly.

"That's what they told me."

"And they believe you can lead them to victory against the dragons, and that once they're defeated, with the roamers prominent in taking them down, their people will finally have the respect of the world. Then, they will have an easier time finding ports in which to winter without mages trying to force them to obey their rules and swear fealty and pay taxes to their kingdoms."

"I believe they want that," Sorath said.

"They also think you were chosen by Shylezar to lead them into these battles against the dragons, and that as long as they have you with them, they'll be victorious."

"Uh."

"A seer has been speaking of these things ever since their people were rounded up to fight for the mage fleets and they saw you with Thorn Company. She'd heard of you as a mercenary commander who'd won battles against mages, and then you defeated a dragon, and she knew you were the one." Kywatha arched her eyebrows.

"Did they also hear about how mages tricked me last year and killed my entire company?"

"That's not in his thoughts, no."

Sorath rolled his shoulders and gazed up at a dark, cloudy sky that threatened rain. He didn't want to be anyone's messiah. He wasn't the right man for that. After his failures, he shouldn't be leading a squad, much less a company or a horde of pirates.

"Since I know nothing of this seer," Kywatha said, "I don't know if she truly has the gift of sight, but we have people among our kind who do. And there are also those who own dragon-steel or lesser-dragon-steel weapons and receive insights from them."

"Yes, I've experienced that."

Kywatha switched to her language and called softly back into the navigation cabin. A couple of older men stepped out, and she conferred with them. They pointed north several times. Or perhaps northwest? Toward Temril?

One man nodded thoughtfully, but the other shook his head and issued objections.

Sorath rested his hand on the dagger hilt, wondering if he could coerce it into giving him another vision—or some guidance —about the future. So far, he'd had no control over whether it shared with him, and he didn't expect anything to happen now, but as the druids continued to argue, their voices faded from his awareness, and he saw rocky terrain full of destroyed buildings, with dragons flying overhead. Fires burned across the land, and people lay dead in the streets of charred and crumbling villages. Mageships flew toward the dragons, three large and one small.

Sorath's breath caught. One of those ships was the *Star Flyer*, and Thorn Company was on the deck, preparing to engage in battle. The mercenaries' faces were set with determination, but fear lurked in their eyes, and he glimpsed Captain Ferroki at the head of the company.

The vision faded as the tiny fleet sailed toward the dragons. Were those events happening now? Or would they happen in the future? Sorath had no way to know.

"We agree that we need to go out and help the world with the rest of the dragons," Kywatha said, "and find the one we battled today but failed to kill, but we are concerned that we won't have the power to defeat them in lands where there are no monuments to call upon."

"That monument didn't seem to be doing much today."

Kywatha frowned at him. "It harried the dragon and kept it from reaching its goal until the end."

"But in the end, it *did* reach it and destroyed that tower in the process. And killed a lot of people."

"At least it was something. There are no druid monuments in Temril."

"But Thorn Company is there, and they have two dragon-steel axes. If we combine that with this dagger..." Sorath patted the sheath. "And add in all of your power, maybe it'll be enough."

"Thorn Company flew off with Uthari's ships."

"Yes, but now they're in Temril." Sorath frowned. Wait, *why* were they in Temril? In his vision, he'd seen four ships, not their whole fleet, but they'd definitely been crewed by Uthari's people. For the most part. That smaller vessel had been the gateship that Vinjo had built.

"How do you know?" Kywatha asked.

"A vision, thanks to Grunk's dagger." Sorath tilted his head toward the kid—he'd come over to listen. "Either that, or I'm becoming a seer."

She squinted into his eyes, and he didn't attempt to protect his thoughts. Let her see what he'd seen.

Then he realized the dagger would protect him from mind-reading, so he set it on a log and stepped back. Kywatha nodded in understanding of what he was doing—or what she saw in his mind.

"Even though I see what you saw, and I don't read deception in the roamer captain's mind, it is possible someone is trying to lure us into a trap," Kywatha said. "It could even be Uthari's people. The king hates us, and I believe he hates you as well."

"Oh, yes. Vehemently. And don't forget Grunk. He slew Uthari's date."

Grunk nodded and showed off his pointed teeth.

"That makes a trap seem even more likely," Kywatha said.

"I considered that myself," Sorath said, "but I don't know how Uthari could have foreseen us showing up here so that the roamers could make contact with us. With me."

Kywatha looked pointedly at the dagger. "I'm sure Uthari has dragon-steel weapons that give *him* insights into the future as well."

"Oh." Feeling foolish, Sorath picked up the dagger and sheathed it. That was a good point.

Uthari hadn't received warning about his and Grunk's attack, but perhaps he'd seen this meeting of people.

"So, you won't take your people—or their people—to Temril?" Sorath wondered if there was a way for him to find a ship heading that way. He could understand the druids not wanting to risk themselves, but he wanted to be reunited with Captain Ferroki and Thorn Company. For good or for ill.

Kywatha blew out a slow breath as she looked at her colleagues. They'd stopped speaking but hadn't left the area. "We will go, and we will take the roamers. Temril is the closest kingdom to Zewnath. If the dragons take it over, they'll have a convenient launching pad to our continent."

Sorath suspected the dragons could easily *launch* themselves from anywhere in the world, but he nodded in agreement. He could see why the druids wouldn't want enemies so close to their homeland.

"Tell the roamers," Kywatha said, then smiled briefly. "Maybe you'll get to meet this seer who thinks so highly of you."

"A dream come true," Sorath murmured.

Jadora closed her eyes, basking in the healing power of Malek's touch as his hand rested on her abdomen, his magic flowing warmly into her to knit her broken ribs together. She lay on his bunk in his cabin, alone with him. He'd taken her there instead of the yacht's infirmary, and she hadn't objected, stopping only long enough to ask one of the servants to let her father know she was all right. Meanwhile, the fleet was underway again, heading north as quickly as possible.

Before she and Malek had descended belowdecks, she'd glimpsed land on the horizon, the southeastern edge of Agorval. Maybe she should have been relieved to return to her homeland, but it was hard to feel anything but dread, knowing enemies awaited and had already attacked the cities there. Worse, the dragons knew of her existence and wanted to snuff out her life, to kill her because of some threat she might possibly represent.

Premature, she thought. So far, she'd made no progress toward finding a way to destroy the parasite. The words *Orbs of Wisdom* kept floating in her mind, and she was beginning to think she'd made a mistake in not requesting to go back through the portal before it had been taken down. Maybe they should have immediately traveled to the world with those orbs. Even though she doubted the answer was there, there might be clues. Zelonsera had suggested as much.

"Malek." Jadora lifted her head, her abdomen tightening and a stab of pain causing her to gasp. She dropped her head back onto the pillow and closed her eyes. Maybe a discussion could wait.

"Yes?" Malek left his hand on her abdomen but lifted his other to her face and touched her cheek. "I'll be done soon, but don't stir yet."

His tenderness warmed her as much as his magical healing, and she turned her head to rest her cheek against his palm.

"Did I tell you about the Orbs of Wisdom?"

"You said the dragon mentioned them as a place to visit for research."

"It might be a good idea to go visit them now."

"We have to deal with the dragons here first. Uthari won't let us take the portal to set it up again until after we've accomplished that."

"If I can find an answer to the parasites, it might also provide the solution to our dragon problem," Jadora said. "If their kind were no longer aggressive and cruel, we might not *need* to fight them."

"And you think the answer is there? In a place the dragons knew about all along?"

"I think something might be, something that could help me, with my background in herbs and chemicals, in a way that it didn't help them." Was she vain to believe that? Maybe, but it was worth trying.

"Such a journey would also remove you from this world and keep the dragons here from attacking you again," Malek mused. "That's something I'd like to see, though I doubt Uthari would allow that either."

Jadora was tired of worrying about and being influenced by what *Uthari* would allow, but she didn't say the words to Malek. Nothing, she knew, had changed for him.

"Sometimes, I can still guess your thoughts by your expression," Malek said. "Either your digestive system is ailing you, or you want Uthari to stuff himself in a dragon's maw."

"Both of those might be true," she muttered, relaxing as the pain in her ribs faded.

"I'll call him down, and we can ask. If he permitted it, I would have to get the gateship back from the other fleet, but with it, I could take you through the portal. I don't disagree with you that eradicating the parasite would be far easier than battling all those dragons—if it works. I believe you're right, and it's worth taking a shot to see if it will."

"Thank you." Jadora rested her hand on his. That was the first time he'd admitted that he agreed with her. If having a dragon single her out and try to kill her had helped flip him over to her way of thinking, maybe it had been worth it.

"You are welcome." He leaned down and kissed her on the cheek.

He started to pull back, probably realizing it was a mistake— Uthari might already be grumpy simply because Malek had taken her to his cabin instead of somewhere less intimate—but he lingered and gazed into her eyes.

"When I realized the dragon was targeting you," he whispered, "I was terrified for you. And terrified that I would lose you."

"It disturbed me too," she whispered back, watching his lips, longing for him to kiss her on the mouth—and more.

She lifted her hand to his head, pushing her fingers through his hair and tempted to pull him back down. Would he allow it?

She didn't have to. He lowered his mouth again of his own accord, his warmth and power infusing her as he kissed her on the mouth.

We can't do anything here on Uthari's yacht, he spoke into her mind as his lips made her want nothing more than to pull him tight and wrap her arms and legs around him.

I know. We could if we went off to find those orbs together.

I thought you wanted to save the dragons, not sneak me off to a private world to have your way with me.

A lady can't want both?

A knock at the door startled them.

In the past, Malek had jerked away whenever someone had

approached while they were sharing an unsanctioned kiss or even a touch, but this time, he hesitated. Maybe because he sensed, as she did, that it wasn't Uthari or anyone with a magical aura. Or was it possible he'd stopped caring?

Reluctantly, Jadora put a hand on his chest and pushed him back. She wished *she* could stop caring, but she remembered Uthari punishing Malek because of her, his cries of pain as great power wracked through him, tormenting him in a way that even a dragon's fangs could not. Pain from an ally, from a mentor, was far greater than pain inflicted by an enemy.

Even though she pushed him away, her fingers curled in his shirt, and she wanted badly to pull him back down, to ignore whoever wanted to disturb them. If Uthari tried to punish Malek again, she could stop it, couldn't she? She hadn't tested herself against him and had no idea if she would be his equal, but if she and Malek *both* fought against him, they could force him back. She was sure of it.

As Malek kept gazing into her eyes, she wondered if he was thinking something similar. Or maybe he was thinking about how much he would like to have sex. She would enjoy that too. Very much.

The knock sounded again, along with a throat clearing.

Jadora recognized that voice. It belonged to her father.

Malek sighed and leaned back. With his help, Jadora scooted into a sitting position and smoothed her rucked-up dress.

"Come," Malek called, his voice calm, no hint in it that they'd been engaged in anything inappropriate, though he gave her a long look up and down before the door opened.

Someone in the corridor spoke to Father, so a moment passed before he stepped warily inside. By the time he did, Malek stood beside the bed, his hands clasped behind his back. He was only her healer, his stance said. Not the man she'd been forbidden to love and who seemed more and more inclined to break his king's command on that subject. But she couldn't let him.

"Jadora." Father took a step toward her, raising his arms to smother her with a hug. But he paused and looked at Malek, as if he were some fearsome guard dog that would snap at him if he got close.

Malek *did* look fearsome. But he always did. He stepped to the side so that her father could get close.

"I'm all right, Father," she said. "Did you get my message?"

"Yes, and I saw the battle, but I had to make sure. I couldn't believe it when the dragon plucked you out of the ship through the hull, and when it struck you with its tail..." He came forward and hugged her.

How did *the dragon strike you with its tail?* Malek asked silently, his head turning curiously. *The last I saw, you were successfully protecting yourself with a barrier.*

Jadora looked sheepishly at him over her father's shoulder. *It flicked up so fast that it startled me. My instincts took over, and I jerked my arms up to protect myself—and my concentration lapsed. The dragon may have given me knowledge and power, but...*

Experience counts for a lot.

Yes. I'm glad you were there for me.

I always will be. Malek seemed to mean it, but Jadora couldn't help but add to his words in her mind. *Until Uthari decrees otherwise.*

She sensed Uthari coming and grimaced, releasing her father.

"Were you injured?" he asked.

"Yes, but Malek healed me with his magic."

Father frowned but made himself turn and bow to Malek. "I am relieved you were there to protect my daughter. Thank you."

When Malek gazed at him without comment, Jadora mouthed, "*You're welcome,*" reminded that he rarely used social niceties and had only started doing so with her because she'd given him a hard time about it.

Malek opened his mouth, but his door swung open first, revealing Uthari standing outside. He thrust a finger toward the bed, as if he'd been certain he would find them entwined inside and planned to say, *Ah ha!*

Since Jadora and Malek *had* been on the verge of getting entwined scant moments before, it *had* been a possibility, though she liked to think that both she and Malek would have sensed Uthari coming and broken apart in time. Admittedly, his kiss *had* been distracting. Had it gone much further, she might not have been paying attention to her senses at all.

"Why did the dragon target you?" Uthari lowered his finger and waved for Father to leave. Though his jaw clenched, he patted her on the shoulder and did so. "Was it about the plant?" Uthari added when he was gone.

Jadora almost snorted. As if the dragons cared about the Jitaruvak.

"We didn't have a prolonged conversation," Jadora said, "but it seemed to be because of what Zelonsera shared with me. The dragons must see me as a threat now."

"Because of your power," Uthari reasoned.

"Because I may have the ability to kill that parasite. Once I research further." Jadora licked her lips, remembering what she and Malek had been discussing. "Is there any chance you'll let Malek and me take the portal back south and use it one more time for a mission? I know it would be dangerous, since more enemies could come through, but... the female dragon spoke of these Orbs of Wisdom and recommended them as a place to do research."

"The portal will *not* be going south, and neither will you. Either of you." Uthari eyed Malek, as if the idea might have partially been his. "The library in Utharika is well stocked with titles from all over the world. I'm certain it will be sufficient for your purposes, and don't forget what *I* want, Professor." Even though he spoke to her, he kept eyeing Malek.

"Yes, Your Majesty," Jadora said. "I'll synthesize your drug."

She had a feeling he wouldn't consider letting her go to the privy alone, much less to another world, until she'd done that. She just hoped that when she did, it wouldn't be too late to deal with the dragons—and all that they threatened.

"A word, Malek." Uthari tilted his head toward the corridor.

Malek nodded and headed for the door. "Take as long as you need to recover, Jadora."

Don't you need to sleep in this bed? Jadora asked telepathically as the door shut.

I suspect Uthari will be berating me soundly for the next two hours.

It sounded like a joke, but she wasn't sure, and the memory of the last time Uthari had punished Malek came to mind again. *For kissing me or for not performing adequately in the battle?*

She'd found him to be *extremely* adequate and far more effective than the rest of the mages. If Uthari didn't agree, she would march out there and lecture him until he changed his mind.

For not quashing your notions of taking the portal and going off on a journey when he has a duty for you. He shouldn't know about the kiss unless you told him.

Oh, yes. I chatted him up as soon as he came in. I let him know that you have the lips of one of the gods-descended-from-the-heavens in an Egarath the Eternal play, and that my female parts get tingly whenever you're close.

Careful, you're getting me excited.

I guess I'd better make sure I'm not still in your bed in two hours then. She rested a hand on the single thin pillow. It wasn't a luxurious bed—nothing in Malek's sparsely furnished cabin spoke of luxury—but she would happily have waited for him if it meant they could spend the night together.

If you are...

She held her breath, waiting for him to finish that sentence.

But he sighed into her mind and said, *Nothing can happen. I should have volunteered to go with the other ships to Temril. I don't know why I said* some mages are drawn to those with great power, *as if I were excluding myself. I was drawn to you before, and now you're even harder to resist. It's almost as bad as when I was under the influence of that drugged juice.*

I'm sorry. Jadora hadn't asked for the power and didn't want it. Maybe after she did as Zelonsera had asked, the old dragon could take it back and leave her as she'd been. *But I wouldn't care to be here without you. I like your company. Besides, there wouldn't have been anyone here to save me from the dragon.* She would have liked to think she could have saved herself, but all her power was still insignificant compared to what those great creatures wielded.

I like your company too, Jadora.

Rivlen was finally sitting down in her cabin to eat a late dinner when someone knocked at her door. She lifted her head and reached out with her senses, hoping it would be Jak—and that it *wouldn't* be Tonovan.

Massages were no longer on her mind, but she wouldn't have minded company—someone to rant to. But whoever was in the corridor didn't have the aura of a mage. She sensed Jak over on the gateship—he'd flown the mercenary doctor over there and was probably helping to heal people.

"Such a do-gooder," she muttered but smiled as she rose. She would take a do-gooder over the *anti*-do-gooder Tonovan any day. "Come."

The door inched open. "Ma'am?"

"Come in, Tezi," Rivlen said, though the mercenary wasn't the company she'd had in mind.

She had a feeling she knew what Tezi would bring up, and she didn't want to discuss it. She was disgusted that she'd finally gathered the allies she needed to overpower and maybe get rid of Tonovan... and Uthari had forbidden it.

Logically, Rivlen knew they needed all their powerful magic users to deal with the dragons, but that didn't make it any easier to stomach having Tonovan on the *Star Flyer*. Why couldn't the bastard ride on one of the *other* ships?

Tezi stepped into the cabin, her axe in hand, though it hung loosely at her side. She probably slept with the thing these days. Rivlen couldn't blame her.

Tezi shut the door behind her. Wanting a private conversation?

"Thanks for sticking up for me against him tonight, ma'am." Tezi tilted her head in the direction of the cabin—the spacious *suite*—that Tonovan had claimed for himself.

"You're welcome, though it was Jak's dragon that made the difference. I hope he chewed off a few toes while he was removing that boot." Alas, Rivlen hadn't spotted any blood seeping from the general's sock.

"I'm starting to love that dragon." Tezi smiled, though it didn't reach her eyes. Something was troubling her.

Rivlen snorted. Something was troubling *all* of them. "Even though he ate half your doctor's knitting bag?"

Tezi shrugged. "She can knit herself a new one. Dragons are handy to have around."

"Ally dragons, sure. I could do without the rest."

Tezi nodded, then met her gaze. "Ma'am? I thought..."

Rivlen sighed. She'd been right and knew what Tezi would ask even without the ability to read her thoughts. "I know, but we can't."

"Tonovan?"

"Yes. We need him to fight the dragons."

Tezi wrinkled her nose. "He didn't do that much, did he?"

"He helped." Rivlen hated to admit it, but it had taken her, Tonovan, *and* Jak and Shikari to make a dent in the dragons' armor with their fire attacks. "And Uthari knows I want him dead, and he forbade me from acting on that desire."

"Oh."

"It's more than that. He said he would hold me responsible and that he would personally lead an *investigation* if Tonovan died on this mission. I can't conspire against him. Not right now."

"Oh." Tezi's shoulders slumped. "It's not that I want to scheme and plan a murder, but today, when he was attacking my captain..." She swallowed, and her voice dropped to a whisper. "I wanted to kill him so badly."

"I know." Rivlen walked to her porthole to gaze out into the night. The running lights of the gateship were visible as it flew behind the *Star Flyer* off to the starboard side. She wondered what was keeping Jak over there. "Maybe we'll get another chance after we've dealt with the dragons."

"Do you really think we'll be able to *deal with the dragons*?"

"Yes. We have to."

"There are so many of them, and they're so much more powerful than we are."

"We've killed their kind before." Rivlen didn't clarify that the semi-sentient dragon-steel ziggurat on Vran had been responsible for the first two she'd helped kill. Besides, several ships of mages working together—along with Sorath and Tezi—*had* slain one. "If they keep attacking in ones and twos, we've got a chance."

Rivlen didn't mention the possibility that the dragons were merely scouting and exploring the world right now—while absconding with all the dragon steel they could find—and would band together and attack cities en masse once they were ready. She didn't know if all the mages in the world could stand up to forty dragons working as a unit.

"Yes, ma'am." Tezi sounded skeptical but didn't question her further. "Will you get in trouble from that *investigation* if Tonovan happens to die and you weren't involved?"

Rivlen snorted again. "Probably."

"Oh."

Catching the disappointment in Tezi's tone, Rivlen faced her again. "You're not contemplating murder, are you?"

"I'm contemplating that I would... defend myself if he tried to do the things he said he would." Judging by Tezi's expression, Tonovan had managed to slip vile comments into her mind while they'd been fighting.

"I'd like to hope that such an investigation would involve mind reading and would be effective at protecting the innocent, but I'm not sure. I don't think you should challenge him without allies anyway. Allies that he can't compel to turn on you during a fight." Rivlen wondered if Tezi knew how close her captain had been to obeying Tonovan's compulsion and grabbing her.

"I know, but I might not have a choice," Tezi said glumly.

"Don't let yourself be caught alone with him. And yell if there's trouble."

"Yes, ma'am."

The slump to Tezi's shoulders remained as she walked out, and Rivlen wished she could have offered better advice—and a promise that she would cleave off Tonovan's head if he tried to touch either of them.

She looked out the porthole again, trying to tell what Jak and the mercenaries and officers on the gateship were doing. From her angle, she couldn't see everything, but it didn't look like anyone was up on the deck. Had it been necessary to take Tinder down below to heal her? And what had happened to her that would have taken more than two hours to address?

Jak? Rivlen called out, sensing him inside and toward the back of the gateship.

Hi, Rivlen! he blurted. For a fleeting second, a hint of panic seemed to accompany the words.

Maybe that was her imagination, and she'd merely startled him. *What's taking so long?*

Nothing. Uhm, are you eager for me to give you a massage? Or to give me *a massage?*

Yes, I lie awake nights, dreaming of rubbing your shoulders.

He hesitated. *You started to get me excited, but I think you're being sarcastic.*

I was being sarcastic, but I'm sure you're excited anyway.

Well, maybe. I was helping Vinjo with some repairs.

Was he? He'd said *nothing* at first. Though Rivlen didn't want to mistrust Jak or believe he was scheming against her or the fleet in any way, she checked again with her senses, looking for Vinjo this time.

Ah, he was right there with Jak. And she also sensed magical devices around them. The engine and power supply for the ship? Most likely.

Rivlen shook her head, telling herself that she didn't need to doubt Jak. He wasn't Tonovan. He'd stood beside her every time Tonovan had threatened her or even glowered at her. And during the battle, Jak had lent her the support and power to make a wall of fire stronger than Tonovan's, strong enough to make the dragon flinch. Even though her enemies were all she should have paid attention to during that battle, she'd caught Tonovan's scowl as he realized they were collectively stronger than he.

One day, as she matured as a mage and her power grew, Rivlen would be stronger than he was all by herself, but for now, she was glad that she had Jak. That she could lean on him and rely upon him. And maybe she *was* fantasizing about rubbing his shoulders.

He wasn't the muscular and finely honed weapon of a man that Malek was, but he *was* handsome, with a charismatic smile and eyes that were always quick to twinkle with good humor. More, she'd never in her life had anyone stand beside her the way he did. He wasn't even in her chain of command. He was *supposed* to be a prisoner, though with Malek teaching him, Jak's status was nebulous. He didn't love mages and shouldn't have any love for her. And yet...

She closed her eyes, envisioning what it would be like to have sex with someone who cared, who didn't just want to sate his urges. Someone who respected her and understood how she'd struggled to rise up through the ranks even as men accused her of sleeping her way into her promotions. The first time they'd met, he'd seemed to grasp what others couldn't—or didn't care to. She wasn't entirely sure why he did, but she wanted to thank him for the support he'd offered.

She snorted at herself, at the supposedly selfless thought. No, she wanted to have sex because she craved it and wanted to see what creative ways he could find to put his magic to use. Hands—and magic—that could craft that beautiful map device would surely know how to touch a woman.

Finish up the repairs, Jak, and come see me.

Oh? Yes, ma'am. I'll be right there.

Even though he sounded eager, Rivlen was surprised by how quickly Jak arrived. She'd taken off her uniform jacket and boots, and unbuttoned her shirt enough to entice his imagination, and she was lounging on the bed and contemplating taking off more when the knock came. She sensed his aura, more powerful and more appealing every day, and unbuttoned another button on her tunic, leaving her fingers to rest just so.

Tonovan might have called him a mock mage, but that had been bluster. Jak's power had matured quickly, and one day, he might even surprise Tonovan—should the general survive long enough to see that day. It would almost be worth getting into trouble with Uthari to see that.

No, she couldn't give up her captaincy and all she'd worked for because she had a vendetta. She had to be patient. One day, Tono-van's end would come. For now, she would find ways to ignore him, to do her duty, and, when there was time, to enjoy herself.

"Come in, Jak," she called.

"Sorry I took so long." Jak walked in, looking at some papers and nudging the door shut with his foot. "I asked Dr. Fret for advice on massages and where the good parts are to rub. She drew me an anatomy chart." He looked up as he waved the papers but froze when he saw her lounging on the bed, with more skin on display than she'd shown him before.

Usually, she preferred utter professionalism and not so much as a button undone or a pocket flap askew, but she was off-duty, and he... ogled her with open and flattering appreciation. None of that bland indifference that some men offered, as if they'd seen it all a thousand times before and usually better.

"I would hope you can find the *good* parts without a chart, but I'm open to letting you explore." Rivlen pushed aside her shirt, showing him the curve of her breast.

She watched the wonder in his eyes shift to desire—arousal—and expected him to burble nervously. That would have been all right—and he could be cute when he did that—but she didn't know how much time they had, as it was possible the dragons would return before the night was out. She used her magic to tease his nerves, as if she were already physically running her hands over his body, a promise of what would come.

"Rivlen," he whispered hoarsely and set the papers aside, aiming for and missing a bookcase. They fell to the floor, but he strode toward her without noticing. His eyes burned with desire and unveiled intent, all hints of the burbling boy gone as his power crackled in the air about him.

She sat up with intrigue and interest, spreading her arms, pleased to see the strong and capable mage coming to her bed. Even before he touched her, he used the same strokes of magic

that she had to send fire racing along her nerves. A gasp of pleasure escaped her lips.

"You're a fast learner," she whispered with approval.

"I want you to enjoy this." Jak slid his arms around her as he
sat, his lips taking hers with more confidence and certainty than
she'd expected from him.

The charts, she decided, had been for massage instruction, not
because he didn't know where the parts were—or what she
enjoyed having touched. She pushed her hands through his short
hair, digging her nails into his scalp as she kissed him back. Hard.
And with more longing than she'd realized she had. She always
kept her desires buttoned down as tightly as her uniform, afraid to
let them out, to admit they existed.

When she occasionally took a man to bed to satisfy her needs,
she never let her guard down. She was always afraid that her lover
would turn into an adversary and use her vulnerability against
her. But she trusted Jak not to take advantage of her, not to hurt
her. He'd helped her too many times for her to believe he would
turn on her, and she found herself letting him get glimpses into
her thoughts so he would know what she liked, know where to
touch her.

And he did everything she wished, leaving her panting and
groaning as their auras mingled, the experience enhancing their
pleasure as they pushed aside clothing and brought mouths to
sensitive flesh. She hadn't been joking when she'd called him a
fast learner, and he was intuitive too, stroking her and using his
magic to touch her places she hadn't known she craved to be
touched.

He let down his guard as well, the way he'd let her glimpse
his thoughts before he'd learned to wall them off from everyone,
and she basked in his appreciation for her and how much he
enjoyed being with her. As they writhed together on the bed,
sweat slick on their warm bodies, she couldn't remember ever

letting her mental barrier down to such an extent, and she hadn't known how much satisfaction she would feel when she did.

When he shifted atop her, she sank her nails into his shoulders, begging with her grip and her mind for him to fill her, and trusting that he longed to do so, that he preferred her over all others. Who would have thought, when he'd been joking about his chest hair, that someone so young could be everything and more for her than others with far greater experience?

When they came together to their shuddering releases, she slid her arms around him, pulling him down on top of her and kissing him with gentleness she hadn't known she possessed. He nuzzled her neck and sent supportive waves of magic through her, silently promising to continue standing with her against dragons, generals, and anyone else who threatened her.

She tightened her grip, doubting fate—or Uthari—would allow them to stay together for long but vowing to enjoy this time with him—and bring him to her bed every night. As he settled drowsily against her, brushing his lips against her ear, she doubted he would mind that.

Aren't you glad you didn't stay over there all night, fixing things with that goofy engineer? she asked silently.

Yeah.

He hadn't raised his mental barriers yet, and she glimpsed the thought her words evoked, him and Vinjo hunkered in the engineering cabin, a toolbox open at their feet. She started to smile, but the Jak in his thoughts opened his hand as he looked intently at the engineer and asked something.

Rivlen froze, the pounding of her heart the only movement in her body. She recognized the device in Jak's hand. It was one of those awful kerzor from Vran. Had he somehow brought one back? Or—certainty slammed into her between one heartbeat and the next—had he and Vinjo *made* that?

You're an amazing woman, Jak added, the words half-slurred as he dozed off.

After glimpsing his thoughts, sleep was the furthest thing from Rivlen's mind. She stared at the ceiling with wide eyes, tempted to wrench Jak awake and demand to know if he had a kerzor. If he'd made one—if he knew how to make *more*—he was a threat, a threat to Uthari and mages all over the world.

And a threat to her?

No. She couldn't believe that. Not after they'd made love and she'd seen in his thoughts how much he cared for her and respected her and wanted to be with her.

Rivlen grew aware of someone with a familiar powerful aura walking down the corridor outside and abruptly knew exactly why Jak and Vinjo had made a kerzor. Tonovan.

Her mind kept whirring as she stared at the ceiling, Jak oblivious and breathing evenly in sleep. He had to be thinking about trying to embed it in Tonovan's temple to steal his magic from him. Those kerzor wouldn't work on a dragon, even if someone could somehow get close enough to try to embed one; she was sure of it. And nobody else on the *Star Flyer* or the other ships was threatening Jak. There weren't any other mages he should want to rob of their magic.

Tonovan paused outside of her cabin. She ratcheted down her mental barriers and spread the protection around Jak. It was unlikely his dreams would betray him, but it *was* possible.

You took that boy to your bed? Tonovan laughed into her mind. *Instead of a real man? How pathetic.*

Actually, he wasn't. Continue to your cabin, General. Nobody wants you in their bed tonight.

Or ever, she thought but didn't add.

He remained outside her door, contemplating who knew what dreadful thoughts, and she worried she would have to spring out of bed and fight him. But, despite his condescension toward Jak, he wasn't a complete idiot. He had to realize Jak was growing stronger and that the two of them together might be able to best him. If Shikari showed up, and she believed he would if Jak was in trouble, they would absolutely be a match for Tonovan.

Pathetic, Tonovan repeated, then continued on.

A distant thud sounded as he entered his cabin and shut his door. Unfortunately, Rivlen couldn't relax, not after what she'd seen in Jak's mind.

11

DARK GRAY CLOUDS FILLED THE SKY AS RAIN PATTERED ON THE DECK of the *Star Flyer*, as well as the ruined remains of a town on the island nation of Temril below. A hundred miles north to south and two hundred miles wide, it was a large island but one of the smaller kingdoms. Or at least it had been. As Jak peered over the railing, he wondered how many of the cities and towns—and people—had survived the devastating attacks.

Most of the buildings were made from stone and adobe, but fires burned anywhere the construction had involved flammable materials. The rocky island didn't have many trees, but here and there, sturdy pines and junipers rose up from boulder piles. Many of them had been burned, their charred black skeletons still wafting smoke.

The attack had been recent, perhaps the night before. What would the *Star Flyer* find when it reached the sky city of Temika?

They hadn't seen any dragons since their battle at sea the night before, but Jak could sense two farther inland, in the direction they were flying. Another encounter was inevitable.

He looked around the *Star Flyer*, eyeing their forces. Thanks to the rain, they didn't appear formidable at the moment. The roamers were sitting with Thorn Company and another mercenary unit, blankets and tarps erected in an attempt to keep water off their heads.

Jak thought about asking Rivlen if she would let the soggy men and women go belowdecks, but when one of the mercenary officers had made a similar request, Tonovan had barked something snide about passengers not being permitted access to restricted areas. Jak had been tempted to point out that *he* had been allowed belowdecks many times, but he didn't want to interact with Tonovan more than necessary—or at all. Besides, if Jak brought the subject up, Tonovan would doubtless decide Jak shouldn't be allowed down there either, and he would end up huddled with the mercenaries and a wet dragon.

He much preferred where he'd spent the previous night and couldn't keep a goofy smile from sprawling across his face at the memory. His gaze traveled to the forecastle where Rivlen stood at the railing, ignoring the rain falling on her shoulders as she surveyed the terrain below for trouble. Her uniform was buttoned, her boots polished, and her dark hair back in its usual tight bun, but he couldn't help but imagine her as she'd been the night before, her hair tousled about her shoulders as she lay in bed, barefoot and eventually bare-*everything*.

The memory got his libido humming, and he forced himself to look away and take a few calming breaths before someone noticed him panting in her direction. Though Rivlen—Xeva, he reminded himself, though she hadn't yet invited him to use her first name—had been a far warmer lover than he'd dreamed and had seemed to enjoy their experience as much as he, Jak was positive she would give him a scathing look if he suggested she shirk her duty so they could go to her cabin for a midday lovemaking session.

Besides, Jak was worried that he might have let something slip the night before. When Rivlen had first reached out to him, he'd been locked in the gateship's engine room with Vinjo, putting the finishing touches on the kerzor they'd made. No, the kerzor that *he'd* made. Vinjo had made it clear that he would advise on general magic-crafting principles but that he wouldn't assist in creating a device that could steal a mage's power—permanently. Jak had precisely followed his mother's schematic, which she'd made while studying the Vran versions of the devices under magnification, which meant he'd included all the minuscule hooks that embedded themselves in the brain so that the kerzor couldn't be yanked out, not without causing hemorrhaging and possible death. It had chilled him to create such a thing, and he'd almost backed away from the project numerous times, but if the device could be easily removed, it would be of no use. He had, however, after consulting Vinjo for suggestions on how to accomplish it, embedded a warning system that would let the person wearing it know what would happen if it was yanked out.

Assuming the kerzor worked. Vinjo had been dubious, suggesting they might need a talented mage blacksmith. Jak had stubbornly worked with the metals and wires they'd had, determined to emulate the device on the schematic. But had he succeeded?

There was no way he could test it without implanting it in someone's brain, and nobody would volunteer for that, so he wouldn't know until he tried. His senses could tell that he'd imbued the device with magic, and that it felt similar to the ones he'd seen on Vran, but was it the same?

He didn't know, but the very fact that he'd attempted to make such a device would condemn him in the eyes of Uthari, Tonovan, and likely all mages in the world. Even Rivlen. Perhaps *especially* Rivlen, who might see it as a betrayal of her trust and the freedom she'd allowed him to go back and forth between the ships.

When she'd invited him to her cabin the night before, he'd almost panicked and said he couldn't come. He'd been afraid he would inadvertently drop his mental barrier and let her see into his thoughts. And now he worried that he had. She hadn't reacted, but that didn't mean she hadn't seen what he'd been up to. Once he'd arrived in her cabin, he'd been focused on *her* and not Vinjo or magical devices, but he didn't know if he'd completely kept her from finding out about the project. After they'd started kissing, he hadn't wanted to worry about keeping his defenses up. She'd started sharing her thoughts and feelings and what she enjoyed, and he'd wanted to do the same, to trust her.

He hoped that hadn't been a mistake. The fact that she hadn't said anything that morning, merely kissing him and getting out of bed early to wash and dress for work, had been promising, but he could still slip up. It would be best if he avoided getting close to her for the rest of their mission. Even if he hadn't let condemning thoughts escape the night before, that didn't mean he wouldn't if they slept together again. Avoiding her would be safest.

Unless that would be suspicious. Would it?

He'd been undeniably eager the night before. Would she find it odd if he didn't come visit her again? Did she *want* him to come again, or had she simply invited him because she'd had an itch she needed scratched, and now she would be sated for the duration of the mission?

"Too much thinking, Jak," he muttered to himself and considered joining the mercenaries for some training. A few had left their tarps and were jogging and performing calisthenics between the puddles on the deck.

If Jak found a moment alone with Tezi, he might pull her aside and confide in her about the kerzor. As much as he would like to spring on Tonovan from behind and jab him with the thing before the general could react... that was wishful thinking. He would need help. The day before, Tonovan had almost crushed him offhandedly while he'd been in the middle of fighting with Tezi.

Rivlen looked down at Jak as he walked toward the mercenaries, and his steps faltered. Would she grow irritated if he drew Tezi aside? She seemed far too beautiful, powerful, and sure of herself to succumb to feelings of jealousy, but she did know he'd had a little crush on Tezi at one time, and she might misinterpret things if he suddenly took her off to plot in private. Maybe Jak needed to put aside all thoughts of the device for the time being.

He looked down at the deck boards, as if they might be to blame for his little stumble—though the crew had already repaired the ones Rivlen had wrenched up in the battle—then altered his path and climbed into the forecastle.

"Good morning, Captain Rivlen." Jak clasped his hands behind his back as he came to stand beside her. Given how professional she always was, he assumed she wouldn't want him to do anything in public to suggest they'd been together the night before.

"Such formality today." Rivlen cocked an elegant eyebrow, and he wondered if he'd assumed incorrectly.

Still, he couldn't imagine she wanted him to swat her on the butt or wrap his arms around her and nuzzle her neck. They might be alone in the forecastle, but a dozen of her crew—not to mention all the mercenaries—were out on deck and could easily see them.

"I was contemplating hugging you and nuzzling your neck," he said quietly, "but I assumed you would throw me overboard if I did that in front of your crew."

"That would be the appropriate response. I'm not even sure what your status is with King Uthari currently. Prisoner? Student? Young mage that he's manipulating for his own ambitions?"

Jak snorted. "That's everyone's status in his eyes, isn't it?"

Rivlen squinted, her gaze cooling, and Jak wanted to smack himself in the forehead. She was loyal to Uthari, the same as Malek, and he couldn't forget that. She might not care if he called

Tonovan an ass, but the monarch she'd dedicated her career to serving was a different story.

"It's a wonder your mouth hasn't gotten you killed yet," Rivlen said.

"I know. It's why I have to take a dragon everywhere with me for protection."

"Convenient that you were able to find one."

"Yes."

"What were you doing last night in the engine room with Vinjo?" Rivlen asked, her eyes challenging as she stared into his.

Jak struggled to keep his face neutral and his mental barriers up as panic blossomed in his chest. She *had* seen something in his thoughts the night before.

"Helping Vinjo with repairs of his ship. He's been teaching me a few things about engineering and making magical things. He's the reason I was able to craft that map device." Jak smiled, hoping she appreciated the gift and would allow herself to be distracted by fond thoughts of it.

"I didn't know you had an interest in creating magical devices." She was still looking into his eyes.

A tickle at his mental barrier told him she was also trying to read his mind.

Jak swallowed, torn between wanting to back away and avoid this conversation, doing nothing, and confessing everything. He didn't want to lie to her. But she was loyal to Uthari. She might even side with Tonovan against someone who'd created a device that could steal a mage's power.

"I tend to get interested in a topic quickly if someone starts showing me intriguing things about it," Jak said, amazed that his voice came out steady. "I never wanted to be a mage, but then you and Malek showed me that I could use my power to defend myself and my mother, and that helped me gain interest very quickly."

Rivlen gazed toward the gateship, her face cool as the wind

batted at her bun, successful in tugging a couple of strands of hair free. He longed to touch her cheek and stroke her hair, to return to what they'd been the night before. He didn't want her to be suspicious of him or to consider him anything but an ally. When he'd decided to make the kerzor, it had been to protect her. Her, Tezi, and anyone else Tonovan had ever used his power to dominate and hurt.

"What repairs did that ship need?"

"Pardon?" Jak lowered his hand. He hadn't realized he'd started reaching for her.

"I saw the dragon snatch Tinder up and take her axe, but it didn't seem to do any damage to the ship."

"Oh." Right, what repairs *had* he been helping Vinjo with? "I don't think the problems were caused by the dragon attack. That ship was put together in a hurry in the middle of the jungle with few quality parts, and it was battered and stuck in a tree for a while on Nargnoth." That much was true. "It's had pieces falling off ever since." A lie. Vinjo was a master at keeping the thing in working order. "I'm amazed Vinjo is willing to fly anywhere in it."

Jak tried to smile, but his lips wouldn't cooperate. He hated lying to her. *Especially* after the wonderful night they'd spent together. And especially when she squinted suspiciously at him again.

"I'm sorry, Rivlen. I... need to tell you something." Jak took a deep breath, afraid of how she would react, but he wanted her trust. He wanted to *deserve* her trust. And maybe when he explained that he'd made it for Tonovan and only Tonovan, she would understand.

Rivlen folded her arms over her chest and raised both eyebrows this time.

"I..."

"Fire in the sky city," a mage with a spyglass called from the aftcastle.

Rivlen dropped her arms and spun to look ahead of the *Star Flyer*. The sky city of Temika was still miles away, but it was visible on the horizon, a miles-wide and miles-long platform that magically floated a thousand feet above land. In some ways, it was similar to Utharika, but it was dominated by spires, obelisks, and elegant towers, with no castle-like city walls surrounding it.

Fires burned in those spires and towers, and some had been toppled, rubble filling the streets. Plumes of smoke even darker gray than the clouds wafted above the city, and Jak first sensed and then saw a dragon perched atop a broken building.

From such a distance, it was hard to tell, but he thought its head was turned in their direction, watching their approach. Did it sense Tezi's axe and want another stab at it? Jak couldn't tell if it was one of the dragons that had attacked them the night before. There was another one out there, flying through the smoke behind the city, casting attacks that knocked down walls.

The mages inside the city should have been raising a barrier and protecting it, but maybe they had been battling all night and were too exhausted to keep up their defenses. Or maybe they were all dead. The *Star Flyer* wasn't close enough for Jak to sense the auras of mages, if they were there, but the way the dragon perched fearlessly on the building suggested it wasn't worried about anything.

"Are we too late?" Rivlen asked, her interrogation of Jak forgotten.

With all the destruction below and ahead, and who knew how many thousands dead, Jak shouldn't have been relieved that Temika had distracted Rivlen, but he couldn't help but be glad he didn't have to finish his confession. Maybe with time, he would think of a better way to explain his actions. Or maybe he would save her life in battle and she would forgive him for all of his transgressions.

"Yeah, right," he muttered.

Rivlen looked at him. "What?"

"I can't tell if people are alive in there or not," Jak said, waving away his other comment. "What's the mission, exactly? Drive away the dragons and save the city? And all of Temril?"

He feared it was too late for the rest of the island kingdom, but if they could defeat the dragons, more of the citizens might survive and have the opportunity to rebuild.

"As far as I know, our mission is to assist King Temrok and his people," Rivlen said. "Tonovan is in charge and has more detailed orders."

As if they'd summoned him by speaking his name, Tonovan strode out from belowdecks. As he walked, he buckled his belt. Jak hoped he hadn't found an innocent servant to force into his bed.

Tonovan looked up at them, and Jak made sure his mental barrier was locked down hard. Sensing the dragons must have been what brought Tonovan up, but he smirked at Jak and Rivlen as he climbed into the forecastle. They weren't holding hands or standing that close, but certainty socked Jak in the stomach like a punch that Tonovan knew they'd been together the night before. It was the cruel amusement glinting in his eyes.

"Did your mock mage keep you entertained in bed, Captain? I imagine it was a *short* night." Tonovan's smirk lingered as he looked dismissively at Jak.

"What are your orders, General?" Rivlen asked, ignoring his question. "Continue to the city and engage the dragons in battle?"

Tonovan huffed out a breath as he looked at the smoking Temika. "Yes, but we need to be careful. There's a *lot* of damage here." He waved at the ruins below and back toward the demolished towns they'd already passed before pointing at the sky city. "More than two dragons could have been here—and might still be here."

"I don't disagree, but I wonder why," Rivlen said. "On the worldwide stage, this island kingdom isn't that important, nor is it known for its natural resources. Though I suppose dragons don't crave the same natural resources as humans do. Who knows what they value, beyond…"

"Dragon steel," Jak finished as she trailed off. "Is there much of it on Temril?"

"Not that I've heard of."

"The king has a little dragon-steel dagger that he fondles whenever you threaten his fleet or suggest his kingdom is small." Tonovan shrugged. "There could be a few other relics in his kingdom. He only has two zidarr, and they both carry lesser-dragon-steel blades, like Malek. I have no idea if the dragons care about those or why they'd be collecting dragon steel in the first place."

"That's the question of the week," Jak murmured.

Tonovan frowned at him. "Why are you in this meeting, boy?"

"Because I was standing here when you walked up."

"Well, go stand over there. This is a military discussion for loyal fleet officers."

Jak bristled and glanced at Rivlen, hoping she would value him and want him to stay—after all, he'd been studying dragons and the artifacts they'd left behind on Torvil for more than five years. His knowledge was valuable.

But maybe she agreed with Tonovan that this was a military discussion, and he wasn't supposed to be privy to such. Or maybe —his gut tightened with unease—she was wary of Jak now because of the kerzor. Either way, she didn't say or do anything to counter Tonovan.

Reluctantly, Jak left the forecastle, climbing down the stairs to join Shikari, who was licking from puddles on the deck. Jak glanced at the water bucket he'd set up for the dragonling, making sure it wasn't empty. It wasn't. Glistening clean water filled it, but apparently puddle water was more appealing.

"Sometimes," Jak told him, "it's easy for me to see the great, noble, and intelligent dragon that you'll one day become. Sometimes, you act like a puppy who's going to grow into a big, floppy-eared hound dog."

Shikari rolled onto his back and lifted a hind leg to scratch his side.

"Exactly," Jak said.

Tezi walked over to join him, her axe in hand as she alternately looked at Tonovan and the sky city. As they flew closer, the smell of the smoke grew noticeable, as did the auras of the two dragons.

"Thorn Company is ready to fight," Tezi said. "And I'm ready to lop off another tail."

"I think it's the *heads* that we should try to remove."

"I'm game." Tezi squinted not at the dragons but at Tonovan, probably fantasizing about removing *his* head.

Jak couldn't wish for that, not when it would get Rivlen in trouble. Though every mage in the world might disagree, he believed his kerzor solution was best. If it worked. If it *did*, it would be worth Rivlen's ire to make Tonovan impotent and keep him from ever again hurting people with his magic. Jak would hate to make an enemy of Rivlen, but if it was for the greater good...

"Look." Tezi's attention had shifted toward the city, and she pointed to the dragon perched on the building.

It sprang into the air, smoke wreathing its wings as they flapped.

"Get ready to fight," Rivlen called to her mages and the mercenaries, then waved to the captains of the other ships in their little fleet.

Now that the *Star Flyer* was within a mile of the sky city, Jak could sense mages alive among the rubble. He could also sense the magic of the great engineering system that kept the massive platform and all that was built atop it in the air. Some of those devices were pulsing intermittently. By design? No, he realized. They were *flagging*.

It was likely some of them had been damaged in the battle.

With his new engineering knowledge, Jak was certain there were backups with redundancy built into the system, but if enough of the engines and power sources failed, the city would fall out of the sky. The dragons might have damaged Temika to some extent, but it would be completely obliterated if it plummeted a thousand feet to the ground.

Surprisingly, the dragon didn't fly toward them. It met the other dragon behind the city, the smoke making their movements hard to see, then they both flew off toward the south.

"I don't understand." Tezi lifted her axe. "I assumed they would be drawn by the dragon steel again and attack us."

"They could be going to get reinforcements," Jak said grimly.

Tezi's shoulders slumped. "Oh."

Jak didn't know what exactly the fleet's mission was, but if they were going to assist King Temrok and his people, Tonovan and his officers had better act quickly.

Lieutenant Sasko watched from the deck of the gateship as Captain Ferroki led Tezi, Basher, and a squad of Thorn Company mercenaries off the *Star Flyer* and into the sky city of Temika. Jak, Tonovan, and Rivlen strode ahead of them, and the dragonling was also on the excursion, running from side to side of the rubble-filled road, sniffing everything. Fires still burned, and smoke hazed the city, so Sasko didn't know what Shikari could smell beyond that.

When they had arrived, none of the locals had come out to greet Utharika's little fleet, and all four ships had glided unopposed into docks at the edge of the city. A few mageships from Temril were moored there, but they were all damaged. Others that had presumably launched to battle the dragons were wrecked on the rocks far below.

Sasko shook her head, worried for her comrades. With all the damage they'd witnessed as they flew over Temril, she had a feeling more than two dragons were in the area.

"Not good." Vinjo joined her at the railing and tapped it nervously with a wrench. "This is not good."

"You think those dragons will be back? With others?"

Vinjo's eyebrows flew up. "I hadn't thought of that. I figured they left because they were afraid of us. Well, more General Tonovan, Captain Rivlen, and your Corporal Tezi than me, but that's what I was hoping. That the fleet made an impression on the dragons, and they don't want to tangle with more mageships and axe-wielders."

"Let's hope." Sasko cocked her head as she regarded him. "What were you saying *not good* about if it wasn't the dragons?"

"The perpetual engines and the *subliminuthers* that hold the city aloft."

"The what?"

"The magical devices that keep it from falling out of the sky. Many are broken. Others appear to be failing." Vinjo lifted his wrench, as if he might run into the bowels of the city to repair them.

Could he? Sasko imagined that such a task would take a whole platoon of engineers. And a few more platoons to clear rubble and pull people out of collapsed buildings. She shook her head, glad she hadn't been invited along on the trek to wherever their comrades were going. As a mercenary, she'd seen plenty of death, and she'd delivered her fair share, but seeing people in pain never got easy.

"What happens if the devices fail while our party is in the city?" Sasko asked.

"About what you'd guess." Vinjo pointed downward. "Hopefully, the mages can levitate everyone safely back to the ship."

"Hopefully, they care enough to do so." Sasko grimaced,

doubting Tonovan would bother with Thorn Company. If anything, he would happily let Tezi fall, then fly down to collect the axe once she was dead. Sasko swore as she realized the mages might not even be able to help Tezi as long as she held the dragon-steel weapon. "I'll hope even more that the city stays right where it is for at least a few more hours."

Vinjo nodded. "Me too. Do you think I should volunteer my services?"

Sasko spotted a few glowering faces in towers near the docks, beleaguered men and women with weapons. A few gripped mage-lock rifles and looked like they were contemplating firing upon Uthari's fleet.

"Let's wait until we hear back from Ferroki." Sasko gripped Vinjo's shoulder, reminded that she'd been sent to protect him. Just because they hadn't spotted Zaruk's blue-hulled ships since leaving the main fleet didn't mean he was safe. "The locals may not yet know we're here to help."

Vinjo followed her gaze to the armed locals. "Ah, yes. I see."

"But maybe you could tell Captain Rivlen that you'll volunteer. If you were able to keep King Temrok's city from falling out of the sky, I imagine he would be appreciative. Maybe he'd even invite you to stay here and work for him. In case you're seeking refuge but foolishly turn down my invitation to hike up your skirt and join Thorn Company."

"I'm wearing trousers today."

"That's an optimistic name for those." She plucked at a frayed piece of grass sticking out of the loose weave.

"Because you're fondling my leg, I'm not going to find your words insulting."

"That wasn't a fondle."

"In my mind, it was." He winked at her.

"I can't believe I find you amusing rather than offensive."

"I can't either, but it delights me to no end." Vinjo patted her shoulder, letting his hand linger, though his eyebrows went up, as if he was asking for permission. "I'd rather join Thorn Company than take up residence in a remote city without any warrior women."

"It's possible they have warrior women." Sasko leaned against him and waved toward the glowering locals. "That girl there has a homemade bow."

"She can't be older than ten. I prefer my warrior women to be more mature and..." Vinjo trailed off with a frown, his gaze toward the docked ships rather than the locals or their own party, though Tezi, Ferroki, and the others had disappeared from view.

"What is it?" Sasko squinted through the smoky haze and spotted a few red-uniformed men and women leaving one of the other mageships. She hadn't been aboard it before and didn't know any of the crew.

"I sense... those officers are carrying weapons."

"Wouldn't you when going into a city full of people who don't yet know that you're not an enemy?"

"Those are more than weapons for protection. It's not their swords and magelocks that I sense. I can tell..." Vinjo closed his eyes.

The smoke made it hard to see anything, but a couple of the people were wearing backpacks, and a pair of men carried a trunk between them.

"I don't understand. I think some of those packs contain explosives. Maybe *all* of them do." Vinjo looked at Sasko with haunted eyes. "Are you sure Uthari's fleet is here to *help* these people?"

Sasko sighed as she watched the officers disappearing into the smoky city. "No. Mages don't tell mercenaries their plans."

Maybe the officers planned to set traps for the dragons, should they return, but Sasko wouldn't be surprised if Uthari wanted his people to take *advantage* of Temril's plight instead of assisting the kingdom. That was the way of the wizard rulers. They spent their whole lives conniving, manipulating, and trying to one-up each other.

"If explosives go off while your people are in the city," Vinjo said, "the *subliminuthers* are going to be even more likely to fail."

"Let's hope Uthari's men are smart enough not to blow up the city they're standing in."

The concerned frown that Vinjo slanted her suggested he doubted it.

12

SORATH SAT CROSS-LEGGED ON THE EDGE OF THE RAFT AS IT FLEW northwest across the sea, a briny breeze blowing across the logs. Since a couple hundred roamers had joined the dozens of druids onboard, bringing their weapons and their packs with them, there wasn't much room. Sorath had been forced to overcome his unease about being close to the edge, though it was hard to glance at the water hundreds of feet below and not think about falling.

Even though he had no magic himself, his instincts warned him of someone approaching from behind, and he shifted to look.

A barefoot woman in a colorful toga approached, her eyes milky white with blindness. She used a staff to pick her away across the logs and around backpacks toward him, managing the task surprisingly well.

Sorath rose to help her if she needed it. With hair as white as her eyes, she appeared to be in her sixties or seventies, an unlikely person to find among the rough-and-tough pirates.

"You must be the seer." Sorath held out his hand and pickaxe, careful to turn the point away from her in case she grasped it.

She stopped outside of his reach and leaned on her staff instead of him. "What gave it away?"

"Well, you're blind, and that seems to be a prerequisite of the profession, at least if one goes by the fables and myths of old."

"Prerequisite." She threw back her head and laughed. "You definitely weren't raised on the sea and tutored by fishermen and pirates."

"Were you?" he asked curiously.

She didn't have Tengo's accent, and her Dhoran was flawless.

"I came and went." She smiled cryptically. "Married, had children, lost them. Returned to our people. They needed me. I'm Jary." She offered her hand. "Don't prong that with your pick, eh?"

"I don't do that unless people greet me with weapons."

"I do have a staff." Jary thumped it on a log, and it dented the wood. Caps on both ends were the blue of lesser dragon steel.

"A most ferocious weapon." Sorath leaned forward and gripped her hand gently. "May the seas and Shylezar bless you, Jary," he said, one of the traditional roamer greetings. Not all of the nomadic tribes followed Shylezar, some preferring their ancient sea gods, but unlike the followers of Thanok, most roamers at least believed the dragon god had once existed.

"We're nearing Temril."

"Yes. This druid raft isn't slow, given its lack of aerodynamics."

"It oozes magic. I rubbed my butt on a vine earlier—" Jary nudged one of the tendrils binding the logs together, "—and it made my cheeks tingle. The *lower* ones." She laughed again. It had the hint of a maniacal cackle.

If the fables and myths he'd mentioned were to be believed, sane seers were even rarer than sane dragons. The thought made Sorath remember his odd conversation with the one-eyed dragon, and he shook his head, hoping he never encountered the creature again.

"Are you a mage?" Sorath remembered Kywatha saying that

some of her people had clairvoyance, but those lesser-dragon-steel caps on Jary's staff would also be able to convey visions, perhaps often enough for her people to label her as a seer. He supposed one could make a lot of predictions and need only have a few prove right to be held in high regard.

"Nah. I'd toss them all to the sharks if I could. I just get a few glimpses of the future now and then." Jary thumped her staff again. "A few with you in them you lately."

"Interesting." When Sorath had received visions from Grunk's dagger, they had usually involved him rather than focusing on someone else. Why, when Jary had never met him, would she receive visions revolving around him?

"You seem to be, yes." Jary cackled again. "In one of them, you're leading these druids and my people into battle against dragons. In another, you're *riding* a dragon."

"Riding? Are you sure I wasn't crawling up its back in an attempt to get to its head and drive a dagger into its skull?"

"It looked a touch more peaceful than that. It was soaring through the clouds with you on its back. A big dragon with one eye."

Sorath shook his head, certain the one-eyed beast he'd fought had no intention of inviting a human onto its back for a ride. Especially one who'd done his best to destroy its other eye.

"A beautiful blue one-eyed dragon," Jary continued. "Flying against the blue sky, its scales gleaming like the insides of abalone shells."

"Oh, that's a different dragon then." One Sorath had never seen. The only *blue* dragon he was aware of was Shikari. The brown-and-gray mottled scales of the others weren't what he would call beautiful against a blue sky—or anywhere else.

"Better find him or her and make friends, eh?" Jary puckered her lips and made kissing noises.

"I don't think that vision is going to come to pass, but the other, perhaps. I don't suppose you have any insight into whether this trip to Temril is a good idea? Your people believe so, and maybe you do too, but I know Uthari's ships are there, and I'm concerned it's a trap." Maybe he shouldn't have been so honest with Jary, but she'd openly said she hated mages—he presumed wanting to feed them to sharks sufficiently conveyed that. It was hard to imagine her snuggling up to and colluding with Uthari or General Tonovan to ensnare him.

"Might be a trap, but you'll spring it if it is and get away." Jary nodded firmly.

"What makes you so sure?"

"Visions." She thumped the staff again.

"Well, that's reassuring."

A call came from the front of the raft—Sorath had a hard time thinking of the front end of the rectangle as the *bow*—and a druid pointed toward land visible ahead of them. If they'd flown straight and direct, it ought to be the southeastern edge of Temril.

Already, Sorath could tell that dragons had been there. Dozens of fires smoldered, sending smoke up into the sky, and a village of stone buildings on the coast had been reduced to rubble. The raft was too far away for him to see people—or bodies—but he suspected they were there.

Kywatha walked up to Sorath, only glancing at Jary before saying, "Our most sensitive druids are able to detect the dragons ahead of us. They're inland another fifty miles or so."

"How many?"

"Three that they can sense, though they aren't right next to each other. If they're indifferent to us, we may be able to fly close to one, battle it, and finish it off before the others arrive."

Numerous problems with that plan jumped to mind, not the least of which was that they hadn't managed to *finish off* the other dragon, even when it had been alone.

"Maybe we can lure one closer to us and farther from the others," Sorath suggested.

"With what?"

He raised Grunk's dagger. "Can you speak telepathically with the closest one and put thoughts of the dragon steel in its mind? I don't know why their kind want or need it, but they seem to desire it."

"Just because we choose one to speak with doesn't mean it won't relay our words to the others."

"True. Are you able to tell if Uthari's mageships are here?" Sorath still didn't know if the vision he'd been given had been of the present or the future. If it had been of the present when he'd received it, the *Star Flyer* and Thorn Company might have left the area by now. Or... they might have been slain, leaving the mageship shipwrecked somewhere.

"We're not sensitive enough to sense mage auras from that far away." Kywatha hesitated. "This vessel does have a communications device. If I knew a potential *ally* that I could reach out to among Uthari's people, perhaps I could, but..." She spread her hand.

"Captain Rivlen?"

Kywatha curled her lip. "She was among the mages who sneaked into our compound to kill the refugees there."

"She protected Tezi and me when we fought against Zidarr Yidar, and I don't think she was after the refugees." Sorath admitted that he didn't know Rivlen well, and she was undeniably loyal to Uthari, but she seemed professional, not cruel or vindictive like Tonovan, and he would choose her to communicate with over any other of Uthari's officers. "You did point out that we'll have to work together with the mages to defeat the dragons. This could be an opportunity."

An opportunity or their only chance to survive against three dragons. Sorath grimaced.

So did Kywatha, perhaps for different reasons. "I'll attempt to reach out to her. In the meantime... be ready to fight."

"Always," Sorath murmured as she walked away. "I suppose there's no safe belowdecks to send you to," he told Jary.

"With dragons, nowhere is safe."

"Sadly, that's true. What will you do during the upcoming battles?"

"Cower behind large men with my butt on the vines."

"To enjoy the tingling?"

"I'm getting to the age where *tingling* is pretty damn exciting."

Sorath smiled faintly as she walked away, guided by the staff. But his smile faded as they flew over Temril and the extent of the damage—the *carnage*—came into view.

In a couple of days, the dragons had destroyed villages, farmlands, and vineyards in this part of the kingdom, if not across all of Temril. He wondered what their sky city looked like and if their mages had been successful in defending it, or if it too had fallen. If so, that didn't bode well for the rest of the world.

Tezi carried her axe in both hands as she walked beside Ferroki, Basher, and ten other women from the company. They were trailing Tonovan and Rivlen and an equal number of their officers through the smoldering city. Here and there, buildings still burned, filling the rubble-strewn streets with heat and smoke. Tonovan strode along confidently, apparently knowing their destination and the way to it.

Jak and Shikari were also with the party, though the young dragon bounded off frequently to investigate everything from piles of rubble to collapsed buildings to smashed fruit from an upturned vending cart. Bugs buzzed in the air around the latter, and Shikari used his magic to sweep them into his maw, then chomped happily.

Jak swatted him on the backside and pointed to their party, urging him to quit dawdling. Shikari ran past, bumping him in the hip and knocking him into a rubble pile. He paused to look back, tail swishing like a cat's, and used his magic to float Jak out of the pile. Then he ran off, as if he expected to be chased.

"At least somebody's having a good time," Ferroki murmured.

She also gripped her weapon—her magelock rifle—in both hands and looked around with unease. The smoky sky city would have been unsettling to walk through even if there hadn't been a chance that the dragons would return.

Now and then, their group startled injured citizens, but they ran away instead of asking for help. The red uniforms of Uthari's people stood out here, where so much was charred and covered in soot, and the locals had to wonder if this was an invading fleet.

Tezi *hoped* that wasn't the case—she'd heard that King Temrok had asked Uthari for assistance—but so far, none of the mages in their party had stopped to help anyone. Only Jak had, occasionally finding someone trapped by rubble or too injured to run from him. He'd knelt, waving for Shikari to join him, and the dragonling had assisted him as he'd used his magic to free the people. Tezi didn't think he'd had time to heal them, since Tonovan hadn't slowed the procession or even glanced back, but at least the injured men and women had been able to move when Jak and Shikari had finished.

When the party had left the *Star Flyer*, Ferroki had tried to bring Dr. Fret along, but Tonovan had said noncombatants would wait on the ships until they were needed. He'd glowered at Shikari as he'd said that but hadn't attempted to make the dragonling stay behind.

They passed through a wide intersection littered with upturned vending carts. A fountain in the middle had been smashed, a large piece of rubble breaking the side so that water flowed out, creating puddles the group had to walk through. Nearby, a baby cried as a mother tried desperately to shush it.

"Why do I feel like part of an invading army?" Tezi whispered.

"Because we might be that," Ferroki murmured.

"You don't think we're here to assist them, ma'am?"

"We were *told* we were, but I haven't noticed any of the city leaders greeting the general with open arms and thanking him for coming."

"I don't think anyone ever greets Tonovan that way."

"Rivlen then," Ferroki said.

Tezi kept herself from reiterating her comment, though she did feel it might apply to Rivlen as well. Even though Tezi had started to consider her an ally, Rivlen was always so frosty and rigid when she was in uniform and on duty that Tezi couldn't imagine anyone welcoming her with a hug. Except maybe Jak, who seemed unfazed by her frost.

Rivlen *was* beautiful, so Tezi could understand why Jak, or any male, might try to get close to her, but seeing him with Rivlen and Malek always worried Tezi. So far, he hadn't *seemed* to change in a major way, but her experience with mages led her to believe that their power inevitably corrupted them. Or at least turned them into pompous jerks. She hoped that wouldn't happen to Jak.

As they left the intersection, the spires of a great walled building came into view. A palace? An obelisk had fallen into the double gates at the front, smashing one partially open but blocking access. It had also knocked down what might have been a guard tower beside the gates.

Jak jogged toward a uniformed man lying in the street under the remains of the tower, someone who must have fallen out when the structure crumbled. Still conscious, the guard groaned when he saw their party and reached for a rifle in the rubble beside him.

Unfazed, Jak knelt and rested a hand on the man's chest.

Shikari bounded over and sat on the rifle, preventing the guard from lifting it. The man gaped at the dragonling for a second before his eyes rolled back in his head and he slumped unconscious.

"You're making people *faint*," Jak told Shikari. "Help me heal him, please. He has internal injuries."

Once again, Tonovan didn't slow the procession to wait while Jak worked on the injured person. He flicked a finger, and the battered gate flew open, and the obelisk shifted aside to clear the entrance.

Numerous roofs on the palace were smashed, and fires burned behind the windows of more than one room in its spires. The walls were charred, and smoke hugged the ground in the courtyard beyond the gates. More broken fountains spewed water onto terracotta pavers.

The tall front doors of the main building were intact, and two guards with rifles stood out front, the men uninjured and still on duty. When they spotted the approaching party, they leveled their rifles at Tonovan and Rivlen.

"Stop your group, General," one called. "Unless you have an appointment, you can't enter the palace."

"An *appointment*?" Tonovan boomed. "We *have* an appointment. Your king asked ours for our help. We're here as a *favor* to him. Why an escort wasn't waiting at the docks, I don't know, but you'll take me to your king at once."

The guard swayed and half-turned toward the door, as if to run inside, but his colleague stopped him with a hand to his arm while frowning at Tonovan. Maybe the general was using his power to try to manipulate a lesser mage.

"He doesn't know *why* these people might not be able to muster an escort, right now?" Basher grumbled. "Mages are oblivious, aren't they?"

Tezi agreed but didn't speak aloud. After her fight over the axe with Tonovan the day before, the last thing she wanted was to draw his attention. The night before, she'd slept with her arms wrapped around the weapon and had woken often, envisioning Tonovan sneaking in to rip it from her grip, then driving the blade into her skull. During their skirmish, he'd shared precisely that image with her as he'd foisted other ugly thoughts into her mind.

"The king has been injured and is being attended by a healer," one of the guards said after a moment in which he might have communicated telepathically to someone.

"So, he's not taking appointments?" Tonovan twitched an eyebrow.

"We're to escort you to a room where you can rest until he's able to see you."

"You'll take me to see him *now*," Tonovan boomed.

Once again, the weaker of the two guards started to obey, but the other stopped him with a hand and a whisper.

"Our own kingdom is also being attacked by dragons," Rivlen said in a more reasonable tone. "We can't stay for long."

Tonovan squinted at her, but he didn't berate her for daring to speak.

"We might be able to help with your injured people too." Jak had finished with the guard outside and stepped into view. "My friend here is getting good at healing humans. He's a *lot* faster than I am at fixing up wounds."

Both guards' eyes bulged when they saw Shikari, and they whipped their rifles over to point at *him*. Jak stepped in front of Shikari and raised his arms, probably raising a barrier as well, though Tezi doubted Shikari needed his protection. If he could bite Tonovan's boot off and endure all the magic the general could unleash, a couple of magelock rifles wouldn't harm him.

"You brought a *dragon*," one of the guards blurted in disbelief.

"A *friendly* one," Jak said.

"There *are* no friendly dragons. Did you see what those monsters did to our land? To our beautiful city?"

"Shikari is young and on our side. I hatched him from his egg." Jak's forehead crinkled as he questioned his word choice. "Or his egg hatched on my bed anyway. And he hasn't been infested by the parasite that makes the other dragons vile."

Tezi had heard rumors about that, but many of the mercenaries and mages from their party looked at Jak in confusion. The guards remained skeptical, with their rifles raised.

Shikari ambled forward, passing Jak and the group as he headed for the doors. One of the guards tightened his finger on the trigger, but his rifle was abruptly ripped from his grip. It flew across the courtyard and landed on the slanted roof of a spire, then tumbled down to wedge itself in a gutter.

"Did Jak do that?" Ferroki murmured.

"Rivlen, I think." Tezi nodded toward her. "It seems Shikari has more than one protector."

Tonovan shook his head and strode forward, reaching the steps alongside Shikari. "Move aside. We'll find your king ourselves."

"There are protections." One guard waved toward the door. "Visitors can't get in without an invitation."

The doors opened, startling the guards, and Shikari sashayed through.

"Is that right?" Tonovan smirked.

One of the guards lifted a hand toward him, but Tonovan jerked his own hand up and used his power to knock both men into the wall. Their remaining rifle flew out into the courtyard and landed in a fountain.

"If you attempt to impede us again," Tonovan said, "I'll kill you."

Jak gaped at him in surprise, then toward Rivlen. She only sighed and followed Tonovan inside.

"If the general *is* here to render assistance," Ferroki said, "he's not very good at it."

"I doubt anyone is grateful afterward for his assistance," Basher agreed.

As the rest of the party headed for the now-open doors, Tezi shook her head, doubting even more that Uthari's fleet was here to help these people. Jak didn't seem to have figured that out yet. He stopped to help the guards to their feet and apologize to them. The men only shook their heads and ran off to retrieve their rifles.

Tezi braced herself to have to fight once they were inside, but with pillars knocked over, people trapped under rubble, and fires filling the air with smoke, none of the residents leaped forward to defend the palace.

Though they had no guide, Tonovan turned with confidence down corridors, taking them through a marble-tiled audience hall and up wide stairs in the back. On the second floor, more guards with weapons appeared. Instead of trying to stop the party, they walked silently beside and behind them. An escort? Or were they waiting until enough of their comrades appeared to have a chance at stopping Uthari's people?

"When entering an unfamiliar den, the porcupine must be prepared to unleash its quills," Ferroki said, looking at her own people.

"In other words," Basher said, "be ready to fight?"

"I have a hunch we're not going to get out of here without doing so."

As Tezi watched Jak levitate a broken pillar off someone who'd been trapped, she couldn't help but wonder if he knew what was going on, that Tonovan had no intention of helping Temril's citizens. Even after all he'd endured these past months, Jak still seemed naive to her. Was it possible, if he knew what was going on, he could stop it? Or ask *Shikari* to?

As a mercenary, it wasn't Tezi's place to question her employers, but Thorn Company also hadn't been given a choice about attaching itself to Uthari's command. Not after Uthari's people had *killed* their last employers.

"I'm going to talk to Jak," Tezi whispered.

Ferroki lifted a hand, as if to stop her, but lowered it without speaking. Maybe she didn't want to be ordered to do something vile either and hoped Jak and Shikari could do something.

The dragonling had stopped to wait for Jak and was sitting on the marble floor as Tonovan continued toward a set of double doors. The king's private audience hall or personal suite?

"Jak," Tezi whispered, wishing she could speak telepathically with him, but only Rivlen glanced back at them, and she was too far ahead to hear. "I don't think we're here to help these people."

After moving the pillar, Jak stood up as the no-longer-trapped man stumbled away, throwing concerned glances at Shikari as he did so. "Rivlen said this is a rescue mission."

"*Rivlen* isn't in charge."

"Even Tonovan said we were here to help, just a couple of minutes ago."

"Tonovan is a liar," Tezi said. "Among other things."

Tonovan lifted his arms, and the double doors flew open. The guards pointed rifles at him, but they hesitated to fire, probably able to sense that he had powerful defenses up. Tonovan halted before he reached the open doors and frowned at what appeared to be empty air.

"There's a barrier," Rivlen said. "And booby traps, I believe."

Tonovan gave her a scathing look. "I lost my *eye*, not my senses." He considered the magical obstacle that Tezi could neither see nor sense herself. "King Temrok," he called into the chamber beyond the doors. "Per King Uthari's orders, we're here to assist your people, but you have to tell us what you want and how we can help."

The floor quaked, startling Tezi. She put a hand on a wall for support as the tiles shuddered underfoot.

"Having your engineers help mine to repair our city would be a start," came a weary baritone from inside.

Shikari made a concerned noise and sniffed one of the trembling floor tiles.

"Maybe we can offer Vinjo's help." Jak waved toward Tezi and headed toward the front of the party.

"*Jak.*" Tezi gripped his arm to stop him. "Tonovan isn't going to help these people. The captain doesn't think so, and neither do I."

Jak frowned. "That doesn't make sense. I admit Tonovan is an ass and could well be lying about any number of things, but with Uth in danger, Uthari wouldn't have sent us here without good reason. The mage kings have to set aside their differences and help each other if they're going to succeed against the dragons. Temrok probably agreed to give him aid in Uth if we came to help his people here first."

The floor shuddered again, as if earthquakes were rocking the city. But since they were floating in the air, it had to be due to problems in the infrastructure that powered everything and kept Temika aloft.

Tezi shivered as she imagined the machinery giving out, and the city plummeting. Would even the mages survive falling a thousand feet to the ground?

"And they *clearly* need help," Jak said, hurrying to the doors to join Rivlen.

"I have no doubt of that." Tezi watched his back bleakly and looked at Shikari. "But I doubt they're going to get it."

13

A POWERFUL BARRIER BLOCKED THE OPEN DOORS, AND JAK COULD sense the booby traps in the walls that Rivlen had mentioned. Shikari sat beside him and tilted his head, looking up at Jak. The dragonling shared an image that detailed exactly what the traps were and how they were meant to ensnare and cast gouts of flame at uninvited intruders, but he also showed them being dismantled by powerful magic.

Are you asking if I want you to do that? Jak asked.

The next image was one of Jak writhing on the floor with his clothes on fire and Shikari leaping on him to smother the flames.

Very noble, but you're right. I'd prefer the traps not go off in the first place.

Shikari swatted him in the back with his tail.

The guards surrounding their party stirred, eyeing each other uneasily. They all had the auras of mages and were no doubt keeping their king apprised of what was going on in the corridor. And telepathically calling for reinforcements? Tonovan, Rivlen, and their mage officers, all with barriers wrapped tightly around

them, appeared unconcerned. But if a fight started, the unpro-
tected Thorn Company women could be caught in the magical
crossfire.

Go ahead and dismantle the traps if you can, Jak told Shikari,
hoping he wasn't making a mistake. Tezi's warning floating in his
mind.

Shikari let out an agreeable squeak. Lately, he'd seemed to
understand the words Jak used to communicate with him. He
didn't need to couch his messages in images. Jak wondered if
Shikari would be able to share words of his own soon. Human
words, not dragon squeaks, screeches, and roars.

"Let us in, Your Majesty," Tonovan called to a man on a large
divan in the chamber beyond.

King Temrok? His shirt was off and medical devices rested over
bandaged wounds as a woman in silks waved her hands, healing
magic emanating from her fingers.

"I have a message for you from King Uthari," Tonovan added,
"and, as my captain pointed out, we can't dawdle here long. If you
don't want our help, we'll leave."

The king, a man with short gray hair and a beard, drew in a
shuddering breath and winced, his hand on his chest.

Jak thought about once again volunteering Shikari's healing
services, but their escort, as well as more guards inside, were all
watching Shikari as if he were a shark swimming in their midst.
Since these people's city had been ravaged by dragons, that was
understandable. Jak didn't know what more he could say to
convince them Shikari was a friend. They knew nothing about the
parasites or the differences between the infested dragons and
those that had never been afflicted.

Shikari sniffed the air in the king's direction—or toward what
looked like fried pieces of fish on a plate near the head of Temrok's
divan. It and pitchers of water and juice had survived the attacks
unscathed, or perhaps recently been brought to the injured king.

"The dragons have left," Temrok said. "Your help has come too late."

"The *dragons* are coming back," Tonovan snapped. "The two that were lurking here left to get others."

Jak eyed him, wondering if he was making that up or if he knew for certain. In the past, the dragons had shared snide telepathic messages with Jak and his group. It was possible those two had spoken to Tonovan before flying away.

"And your city is on the verge of falling out of the sky," Tonovan added. "I have an excellent engineer that I can bring in to help your people."

"Uth isn't known for cultivating engineers."

"This is someone *else's* engineer."

Temrok closed his eyes. To rest or reach out with his senses? Even though Temrok was injured, Jak sensed great power about the man, an aura equal to Uthari's or Malek's. While his wounds were being tended, he was keeping a strong barrier wrapped around his divan, encasing him and his healer.

A click came from one of the walls. Was Shikari disarming the traps? Jak could sense him doing something and wondered if he could help. But he hesitated and glanced back at Tezi, her face worried as she watched Tonovan and Rivlen.

What if Tezi was right? That Tonovan had no intention of helping Temrok and was here because... Jak didn't know why Uthari would have sent part of his fleet if not to gather allies in the battle against the dragons.

Another click sounded. Shikari's tail waved triumphantly.

Are you doing that because you want to help us get in, or you want the king's lunch? Jak asked.

All he got for a response was a tail swish, followed by a dragon expression of focus as Shikari went back for more traps.

"You have Zaruk's Lieutenant Vinjo?" Temrok asked. "His work is known to me."

"Yeah, he likes to rub bits and bobs together," Tonovan said, then muttered something about mercenaries with *damned stealth devices* under his breath.

Jak still had the stealth device that Vinjo had given him on Nargnoth, and he wondered if he should have worn it. If this escalated into a confrontation, being able to disappear might have been handy.

"But he is Zaruk's engineer," Temrok said. "Why is he with you?"

"Our company delights him," Tonovan said.

Jak couldn't keep from snorting as he thought of the times Uthari's people had tortured Vinjo and forced him to work.

Tonovan glared over at him. *Keep your mouth and your mind shut, boy. And what is your scaled pet doing?*

Disarming the booby traps so you won't be fried when you walk in. A bit of a fib, since Shikari had implied he was disarming the traps to keep *Jak* safe. Even that might not have been the whole truth since Shikari kept glancing at that plate. But Jak added, *Maybe you should kiss him and thank him for his help.*

I'd rather lick lava bursting out of an active volcano.

Shikari would probably rather you do that too.

"What are your people doing wandering around my city?" Temrok asked, suspicion lacing his voice. His eyes were still closed as he surveyed his domain with his senses.

Jak frowned. Who was wandering in the city besides their group? And why?

"Helping the injured." Silently, Tonovan added to Jak, *How many booby traps does he have left to disarm?*

Jak hesitated, wondering what Tonovan planned to do when he got inside. And also wondering what his people were *really* doing in the city. On the way in, Tonovan hadn't stopped to help a single injured person. Not all mages were healers—and Jak doubted Tonovan had ever bothered learning how to help others —but they could have at least used their magic to free people from rubble.

How many? Tonovan demanded, glowering at Jak.

I'm not sure. I'll ask.

"One group is going down into the bowels of my city. To access the infrastructure?" Temrok opened his eyes and frowned at Tonovan.

"I told you we have engineers who will help," Tonovan said. "We don't want your city to fall out of the sky while we're docked to it."

"*Vinjo* is still on one of your ships."

"*Vinjo* isn't our only engineer. As you pointed out, he's not on our payroll."

"He's your prisoner then."

"He volunteered to work for us."

Sure, after he'd been tortured.

Jak lifted a hand toward Shikari, intending to tell him to stop. He was beginning to believe Tezi had been right and that Tonovan was here for nefarious reasons, that his promise to help was a ruse. Rivlen had admitted that she didn't have all the details of this mission, that Tonovan, as her superior officer, was the one whom Uthari had filled in on everything.

Before Jak could stop Shikari, his tail swished in triumph once more, and he shared an image of all the traps being disarmed. Tonovan squinted toward the walls, as if he sensed it too.

"What are you doing?" Temrok demanded.

Tonovan pointed at Tezi. "Use your axe to pop the barrier in front of the door."

"They're here to destroy us," Temrok called, his voice ringing from the walls as he sat up with a pained lurch. "Get them. *Kill* them."

The guards in the corridor raised their rifles. Tezi hesitated to obey Tonovan. Ignoring the guards, he lunged toward her, but she sprang back, jerking the axe away from his grasp.

Jak stepped between them, raising a barrier, but Tonovan snarled, tearing it down with a blast of power that left Jak reeling. Tezi had time to back farther down the corridor and give herself room to swing the axe at Tonovan if need be.

But it didn't matter. Having completed disarming the booby traps, Shikari ambled through the doorway. With the same inherent magic that he used to pop mages' defensive barriers, he popped the one blocking the entrance to the chamber.

The guards who'd been preparing to fire at Tonovan and the others shifted their attention to Shikari, pointing a dozen mage-locks at him. Those without weapons lifted their hands to hurl fireballs and who knew what else at the dragonling.

"No!" Jak cried, surging past Tonovan and into the chamber. He recreated his shattered barrier as he added, "He's a friend. He was just—"

Weapons fired, cutting him off.

Magical charges from rifles sped toward Shikari, but they bounced off, as if they were bugs striking a porthole on a mage-ship. Two blasts streaked toward Jak. His barrier was up, but he almost panicked and dropped it. Instead, he rushed to harden it, putting more of his power into the mountain imagery that he used, great snow-capped peaks defending him from attacks. The blasts bounced off, one skipping off the floor and another smashing into the wall above the door.

Tonovan, Rivlen, and their mages ran into the chamber with their weapons drawn. Most of them engaged with the guards, but Tonovan sprinted toward the king with murder in his eyes.

The powerful barrier protecting the king remained up, and Tonovan couldn't reach him. He lifted a hand, pouring magic into it and trying to tear it down. Temrok pulled a dagger off the table by the pitchers, a dragon-steel dagger. Though he gripped his ribs with one hand, he pointed the weapon at Tonovan with the other.

"You *dare* charge into my city under the guise of helping us? And you try to *kill* me?" Temrok demanded, glancing at Shikari, who was strolling closer. "You're right that I asked Uthari for help, and I even offered my fleet's assistance if we could drive off the dragons together, but I knew I couldn't trust the bastard. Especially when he sent *you* to lead his fleet."

"What does *that* mean?" Tonovan prowled around the barrier, stabbing at it with his magic, trying to pierce it.

The healer crouched behind the divan, her eyes wide, but she'd also found a dagger, and she gripped it with shaking hands.

Get your dragon to pop this barrier too, Tonovan spoke into Jak's mind.

Jak shook his head, relieved that Shikari had stopped advancing. He was sitting, magelock charges hitting his defenses, as Rivlen and her officers engaged with the guards, forcing them to pay attention to the human intruders.

Don't take down another barrier, please, Jak told Shikari, then spoke aloud to Tonovan, "I'm not going to help you kill someone. And neither is Shikari."

Shikari was still eyeing the plate of food, but he remained on his haunches. He looked over at Jak with a perplexed expression.

Maybe he'd thought they were here to help too. Jak shook his head bleakly, not sure what to do.

"It means that your foul and dishonorable reputation precedes you, General," Temrok said coolly. He gripped the divan for support and stood as he drew several steadying breaths, a wounded man summoning his energy for a battle. "How did your boy get a dragon?"

"He's not *my* boy." Tonovan kept circling the divan as he spoke, forcing the king to turn to track him. "He's a wild one who *thinks* he's a mage."

If you get the dragon to help me, Temrok spoke into Jak's mind, *I'll give you a place in my city once we rebuild. A place in my court. You won't be a wild one here. You and your dragon will be treated with respect.*

The desperate plea rang in Jak's mind, and he sensed that the king was trying to use his power to coerce him. Whether it was a lie or not, he didn't know, but he shook his head. As much as he hated Uthari, his mother and grandfather were with him, so Jak couldn't have fled the kingdom even if he'd been enticed.

Still, he felt guilty—Tonovan wouldn't have gotten this far if Shikari hadn't disarmed the traps and barrier—and wanted to salvage this situation. Somehow.

"We need to work together," Jak yelled over the fighting, trying to will magical compulsion into his words. "Stop fighting! Please!"

Rivlen downed a guard facing her, driving her sword into the man's chest, and sent Jak an exasperated look as she sprang over him to help one of her officers against another opponent.

"The dragons are our enemies," Jak pressed on, though Temrok might not believe that when Uthari's officers were slaying his guards in his audience chamber. "Far more dangerous enemies than we are to each other. We need to lower our weapons and work together. Please, nobody wins if we kill each other."

"That's what I tried to tell Uthari, boy." Temrok kept facing Tonovan as he spoke, kept his dagger pointed at him. "You think I don't know that? He—"

A gray-haired female mage ran out of a side door, alarm splashed across her face. She raised her arms and threw a fireball at Tonovan.

He whirled, his barrier up, and deflected it.

"Sanyia, no!" Temrok barked. "Go back to our suite."

"Queen Sanyia, your *wife?*" Tonovan asked, his eyes burning with an idea even as the flames the woman had cast at him faded.

Jak sensed that the queen, though she was a mage, lacked the power of Temrok or Tonovan. And Tonovan must have sensed it too, perhaps believing he could get to the king through his wife. Weapons raised, Tonovan left the divan and charged at her.

Shikari, don't let him kill her, Jak blurted as the queen raised a barrier and faced Tonovan with fear but also determination in her eyes.

It wouldn't be enough. Jak knew that. He started to raise a barrier of his own between Tonovan and the queen, but Temrok dropped the barrier around his divan and limped out to defend his wife. At the same time, barks rang from the walls as huge dogs charged into the chamber. They ran past the fighting humans and straight for Shikari.

Shikari, who hadn't seen dogs before, rose up and bared his fangs at them. Jak's barrier faltered, and he rushed to re-form it around Shikari, instinctively wanting to protect his charge. But the dragonling's own barrier remained up, and he didn't need Jak's help. The dogs couldn't reach him. Still, they snarled and snapped their jaws, distracting Shikari. The dragonling couldn't obey Jak's request to help.

Jak funneled his own power into the queen, hoping she could defend herself from Tonovan if she had help. Right away, as Tonovan spun and sprang for Temrok, Jak realized his mistake.

Enraged by the threat to his wife, Temrok attacked Tonovan with the dagger and a swinging fist instead of calculating magic. And though Tonovan wasn't as talented a warrior as Malek, he was easily a match for the injured king. He dodged the swipe from the dagger and lunged in with his sword. The king realized his mistake and summoned his power, but he wasn't fast enough. Tonovan's weapon plunged into his chest, sliding between his ribs and into his heart.

"No!" his wife cried and leaped for him.

Tonovan yanked the dragon-steel dagger from Temrok's failing grip, roared with delight at his conquest, and whirled to face her. Jak, already crushed by his failure to realize who he truly needed to assist, formed a barrier around her, but Tonovan had that dagger now, damn it. He would tear down Jak's barrier even more easily than before.

Frustrated and furious, Jak glanced around, spotted the divan, and used the levitation skills he'd been practicing on it. The plate and glasses flew as it hurtled toward Tonovan's back. Protected by his magic, he didn't even glance back. He lunged for the queen, batting aside her magic and raising the deadly dagger.

Jak ran toward them, but he was too late. Tonovan tore aside her defenses and slashed her throat. As she tumbled to the floor, blood spurting from her arteries, Tonovan turned to face Jak, the dagger raised as he snarled more viciously than the palace dogs.

"Won't Uthari be delighted to know that his wild one changed sides today?" Tonovan attacked Jak not with the dagger but with a battering ram of magic.

Jak got his barrier up, but once again, Tonovan's power was too much for him. It knocked him backward, and he barely kept his feet as raw magic blasted into his chest like a hammer.

"We were supposed to help these people," Jak managed to gasp out.

"Those *weren't* my orders." Tonovan prowled toward Jak. "Uthari wants Temril for his own, and it's my duty to give him what he wants."

A roar came from Shikari, and the hounds tumbled away from him. They yipped and ran out of the chamber.

Shikari rushed over to stand at Jak's side against Tonovan, but having a dragon-steel weapon emboldened the general, and he only sneered at the dragonling as he continued toward Jak.

"What are you doing, Tonovan?" Rivlen demanded, striding over to them, blood on her sword, her uniform rumpled, and her bun half-falling after several fights.

"What are you doing, *General* Tonovan," he corrected her. "I'm going to kill this wild one, as Uthari should have done himself weeks ago." He pointed his sword and newly acquired dragon-steel dagger at Jak's eyes.

Most of the guards in the chamber were down now, though gongs sounded somewhere in the palace, an alarm or a plea for reinforcements.

"Guard the door," Ferroki barked to her people.

"We need to get out of here," Rivlen said, glancing from Jak to Tonovan. "More mages are coming."

"Let them come," Tonovan roared.

Shikari opened his mouth, and *he* roared.

"Your dragon won't be able to hurt me while I hold this." Tonovan waved the dagger as he stalked closer to Jak.

Jak reached for his belt, but he hadn't brought a rifle or pistol or anything besides his dagger. They were on a humanitarian mission, damn it. Once more, he created a barrier, though he knew it was pointless. Even without a dragon-steel weapon, Tonovan had the power to pop it.

But Rivlen stepped in, raising her sword between Jak and Tonovan. "Stop this. We need to deal with the rest of the natives. The very angry magic-wielding natives who are pissed that their king and queen were killed."

Shouts rolled through the corridors outside.

"You *dare* defend him?" Tonovan looked incredulously at her. "After what he's done?"

"His dragon let you in here so you could accomplish what I assume was your mission." Rivlen's mouth twisted in distaste. "Thank him, and let's get out of here."

Shikari roared again as he glared up at Tonovan. Surprisingly, Tonovan looked at him, alarm flashing in his eyes, and stopped his advance.

"I hope he's letting you know that he can take you down even when you're holding that," Jak said. "You may have noticed that even Malek has trouble killing dragons."

Invoking Malek's name wasn't a good idea, for the fury leaped back into Tonovan's eyes, the desire to murder Jak.

But Ferroki and Tezi shouted from the doorway. What looked like a platoon of uniformed defenders had shown up and were trying to get into the chamber. When Tonovan glanced toward the doorway, Shikari whirled so that his back was toward him and whipped his tail through the air. He struck Tonovan on the hand with it so hard that the dagger flew from his grip. Blood spattered the pale floor tiles as the weapon clanked and skidded across them.

Cursing, Tonovan ran after the weapon.

"Kill those defenders," Tonovan yelled at the mercenaries as he plucked up the precious dagger. He glared at Jak and Shikari, but he ran to fight the locals instead. His eye, however, promised that he would come after them later.

Jak drew his sleeve across his sweaty brow, aware of how close he'd come to death and that the repercussions from this day might yet be the end of him.

"Come on." Rivlen gripped his arm and pushed him toward the doorway, her sword in her other hand. "We have to get out of the city. He's got people setting explosives to destroy it the rest of the way."

Jak rooted his feet to the floor and stared at her. "You *knew*?"

And she'd let him believe they were here to *help* people?

"Not until he admitted it to me a minute ago." Rivlen waved at her head to indicate telepathy, then tugged on Jak's arm again.

"Come on. We don't have much time. We have to fight our way back to the ships and leave before the explosives go off."

Jak wanted to fight her—to stay and have nothing more to do with any of Uthari's people, including Rivlen—but what choice did he have? The floor quaked again, reminding him that this city might fall even without the help of more explosives.

"Come on, Shikari," Jak said numbly, walking toward the fighting at the door, wondering if all the people he'd assisted on the way in would be condemned to death. Was there any way to warn them so that they could escape? *Was* there a way to escape?

Shikari ran to the shattered plate, its contents strewn across the floor, and licked up the fish he'd been coveting. After that, he joined Jak and Rivlen.

Jak blinked away tears that wanted to form as he wished Temrok hadn't had any food in his chamber. This might have turned out much differently if such morsels hadn't been tempting a hungry dragonling.

On the deck of the *Serene Waters*, Malek sparred with multiple opponents, sweat dribbling down his bare chest as he pushed his body to the utmost. He pursued the exercise both for the sake of his training and to keep his mind occupied. Sleep had been elusive the night before, broken by dreams of Jadora being plucked out of a hole in the ship by a dragon. In his dreams, he'd failed to rescue her and had watched helplessly as the dragon tore her to pieces.

Each time, he'd awoken panting, afraid that he'd been reliving reality, that he *had* failed to get to her in time. In a panicked rush, he'd reached out with his senses. Only when he'd detected her, up late working in her lab, had he been able to relax. But only until he'd fallen asleep again and succumbed to the same dream. The knowledge that the dragons knew who she was and wanted her dead chilled him. After all they'd been through together, he couldn't stand to lose her. He didn't even want to be apart from her.

The memory of her in his bed, resting as he'd healed her wounds, kept coming to mind. He'd liked having her there in his cabin. It had felt right.

But what might he have done if her father hadn't interrupted them? If they hadn't been on Uthari's ship?

He wanted to be with her, and he'd given up on denying it. He wanted to remain at her side, to help her learn to use her power fully, and to protect her from all threats. He wanted—

"Lord Malek," came Uthari's voice from the side.

The three mage officers Malek had been sparring against broke off, bowing to him and their king.

Malek wiped sweat from his brow and reached for a towel before turning to face Uthari. Even though he'd succeeded in keeping his opponents at bay, he'd been distracted, his reflexes, not his mind, protecting him. Had Uthari noticed? His days of sword-fighting might be long past, but Uthari had reputedly been a skilled warrior at one time.

"Yes, Your Majesty?" Malek finished toweling himself off and pulled his shirt over his head. He wished Jadora had been the one on the deck watching him instead of his liege, but she was at work on Uthari's task.

"You were distracted."

"I slept poorly last night." Malek eyed the crew, not wanting to admit to any weakness, however slight, with others in earshot.

Uthari raised his eyebrows. "I trust you don't fear the battles we may soon face."

"No. I don't fear going into battle or dying. But there are others I don't want to lose."

"I'll pretend you mean me and not your professor." Uthari spoke lightly, but there was no amusement in his eyes.

"I would not care to lose either of you. But, as far as I know, the dragons are not specifically targeting you."

"It *was* startling when that one extracted her from the bowels of my yacht like a surgeon going in for a gallstone."

"A *gallstone* is not something I would liken her to, but yes."

"No doubt, you'd think of a more romantic comparison. Or would you? I've not known you to be poetical."

Malek would be more inclined to liken Jadora to a fine dragon-steel blade that one could trust with one's life, but he didn't say so. Every discussion he had with Uthari when her name came up made him uneasy.

"I don't think it requires a poetical soul to come up with a better comparison for people than a gallstone," was all he said.

"Perhaps not." The first hint of amusement lightened Uthari's expression. "Few have accused me of rivaling the word-smithing abilities of Versifero the bard." His amusement faded, and his eyes narrowed with speculation. "As we've discussed, I'm not able to read her thoughts anymore. I trust you aren't either."

Malek shook his head. "She's learned to subconsciously guard them."

"She's learned much."

"Yes."

"Thanks to a dragon."

"Yes," Malek said, worried about where Uthari was going with this. Would he again order Malek to ask Jadora to conjure up some virus or bacteria to use against the dragons?

"My understanding is that she has a great deal of knowledge that the dragons had."

"That is my understanding as well. She filled journals when we were on our way back to the portal."

"Did she? I want copies of those journals."

"Your Majesty?"

"Since she's a target, it would be wise to have the information the dragon gave her stored somewhere, everything that she wrote down and more."

"More?"

"Ask her to let down her defenses for you, Malek, to share what she learned with you. She likes you. She has no reason to mistrust you."

Malek hesitated, not certain about that. Jadora knew where his loyalties lay.

"Would it not be sufficient to have copies of her journals made?" Malek asked. "I know she was assiduous in recording her experience."

"I want that done as well. But while she's sharing what she learned with you, it will be an opportunity for you to poke around. Find out... I suppose I already *know* that I can't trust her, but will she conspire against me? When she makes my potion, will it be safe for me to drink it? She didn't sabotage my medical appliance when I gave her the opportunity, but I am not so foolish as to believe that means she's devoted to me. She may simply have seen through the trap."

Malek bristled at the memory of that test. He hadn't been there, but he was affronted on Jadora's behalf. "Your Majesty, it's not necessary to keep testing her. You already know that she has no love for you, but she'll work on your behalf to protect her son and father."

"I believed that before, but with her new power, she could think she could protect them against me no matter what she did." Uthari lowered his voice. "And she could be right."

"Your Majesty?"

"I want her thoughts, Malek, and as much of the dragon's knowledge as you can absorb. I would attempt to get it myself, but she won't lower her guard for me. She will for you." Uthari's eyes narrowed again. "I'm certain of it."

Malek wanted to protest, but Uthari pointed toward the hatch that led below, to the corridor that held Jadora's lab.

"Go to her, and get what I want."

"Yes, Your Majesty." Malek didn't want to obey, as it felt like a violation of Jadora's trust, but he headed for the hatch.

14

TONOVAN RAN BESIDE RIVLEN, LEADING THE MAGES AND mercenaries as they battled their way out of the palace and into the streets of Temika. Rivlen didn't *want* to fight side by side with him, but she preferred to keep an eye on him, and he was matching her pace, not the other way around. Maybe Tonovan believed Jak wouldn't convince his dragon to blast him to pieces if she was next to him. After they'd walked in and murdered a king and his wife, Rivlen wasn't so sure.

She hadn't been shocked by Tonovan's orders, but she had been—and still was—furious that he'd blindsided her and only told her the details at the last second. No doubt, he'd believed she would have argued. And she would have. Though if this was truly what Uthari had ordered... it wasn't her place to question it.

That bothered her. Even if Jak hadn't cast that betrayed— betrayed and *anguished*—look at her, she wouldn't have believed this had been right. Those had been mages, not terrene humans; they'd tricked and turned on their own kind. And for what? That was what she didn't understand. What value did this half-destroyed, rocky island of a kingdom hold for Uthari?

Something spiraled toward Rivlen from the window of a building, startling her. A bottle with a flaming wick, the homemade device poised to explode.

Her barrier was up, and it blew ten feet away, but she chastised herself for letting her mind wander. Once they got back to the ships and were safely away from angry mages, she could mull over the day's events, but it was her duty to make sure her party made it out of the city first.

A boom erupted from somewhere behind and below them. From under the city? Or within its infrastructure?

Tonovan swore. "Midliken is premature, that ass."

He picked up his pace, waving for everyone else to do the same.

For the last twenty minutes, the ground had been shuddering and quaking, but now it bucked violently. Something under their feet snapped and groaned. The framework for the entire city?

When two injured and soot-covered mages stepped out of an alley to hurl fireballs at Tonovan, he only sneered. His barrier was up and sufficient for deflecting their attacks. Even if it hadn't been, his newly acquired dragon-steel dagger would have protected him.

He flung a counterattack at them. Even though they'd raised barriers right after casting their fireballs, his power blew them halfway down the alley.

"Who's Midliken?" Tezi panted. She'd caught up with Rivlen and glowered at Tonovan's back as they ran, possibly fantasizing about sinking her axe between his shoulder blades.

Rivlen doubted she was the only one thinking about that. The mercenaries had an honorable streak, given that they were a bunch of sell-swords. And Jak... Rivlen couldn't bring herself to glance back at him, though she sensed him in the rear, urging Shikari along. She was monitoring him, making sure nobody jumped out and waylaid him, but she couldn't talk to him, not now. Even later, she didn't know what she would say to him.

"An engineer from one of our other ships," Rivlen said.

"Then it's true. Your people are sabotaging their city?"

"It's none of your concern," Rivlen snapped, tired of being judged by all these do-gooders.

"It might be if the city crashes while we're in it," one of the other mercenaries muttered.

An explosion landed in the middle of their group, tearing up the street and hurling rubble. Rivlen and the mages had their barriers up, but the mercenaries went flying. As Tezi tumbled past, Rivlen tried to grab her with her magic, but the axe kept her from getting a grip. Tezi hit the debris-covered ground hard and rolled toward Tonovan.

Her elbow cracked a flagstone, and she cried out, inadvertently releasing her axe. It skidded several feet, and Rivlen knew what would happen even before Tonovan's eyes lit up.

She sprinted across the quaking ground, trying to reach the axe before Tonovan did, but he was too fast. Even as Tezi scrambled to her hands and knees and lunged for the weapon, Tonovan swept it into his grip and hefted it to the sky.

"Give it back," Rivlen said, helping Tezi to her feet. Then, as if Tonovan were a reasonable man and she could use logic on him, she added, "You've already got the dagger. You don't need to steal her axe."

Tonovan laughed. "Don't be ridiculous. Like I told you yesterday, it's ludicrous for a sense-dumb monkey to carry such a precious weapon. *I'll* wield it, and I'll be competent enough to keep dragons from stealing it."

Tezi wiped blood off her lacerated palms as Ferroki and the other mercenaries gathered around her.

Rivlen glimpsed movement on a nearby rooftop—someone in black crouching up there and looking down at them. When she peered closer and stretched out with her senses, the figure was gone. Maybe it had been a shadow, her imagination.

"Please return her axe, General," Ferroki said, polite as always, though she looked like she wanted to clobber Tonovan.

The mercenaries *all* did.

"Please suck my cock, Captain." Tonovan turned his back on Thorn Company and resumed his run toward the docks.

Ferroki's disappointed look went toward Rivlen instead of Tonovan, as if *she* were his keeper. Rivlen might want to kick his ass as badly as they did, but that didn't mean she could.

The ground shuddered again, something else snapping deep within the framework of the city.

"Keep going," Rivlen ordered everyone. "We need to get back to the ship before more explosives go off. We can figure out the axe later."

Not that Rivlen believed they would be able to get it back from Tonovan. The best Tezi could hope for was that Tonovan didn't remember that she'd taken his eye and decide to have his revenge on her now that she didn't have a way to defend herself from him. Rivlen almost offered to let Tezi sleep in her cabin, but it wasn't as if she could protect her from him either, not unless Jak and Shikari slept in there as well.

She clenched her jaw, only slightly relieved when the docks and the *Star Flyer* came into view. As she urged her weary legs to greater speed, a shadow fell over her, and she sensed Shikari's aura. To her surprise, he flew past a few feet above her head, flapping his wings madly to escape... what?

Rivlen glanced back but didn't see any pursuers.

Then a building they were running past exploded. Once again, her barrier protected her, though the blinding light made her stumble. More charges went off within the infrastructure of the city, and her stomach sank as the ground shifted, dropping three feet before catching itself, then dropping again.

The crews of the mageships must have guessed—or known in advance—what was happening, for they'd unmoored from the docks. Fortunately, her crew was at the railing, and they started levitating the mercenaries into the air and toward the deck. Rivlen and the mages levitated each other. As they sailed toward the safety of their ships, the city offered a final thunderous snap and groan, then all at once plummeted downward.

Shrieks of terror from the residents pummeled Rivlen's ears as she landed in the forecastle with Tonovan, and her stomach twisted with distress. The dragons might have attacked the city and started its destruction, but her troops had finished it. No, *Tonovan's* troops. She might command the *Star Flyer,* but he commanded the fleet, and he'd set this all up. Had Uthari *truly* ordered such a villainous action?

Rivlen turned to look for Jak, worried he might not have gotten out of the city before it fell, but he and the mercenaries were together on the deck. They were all staring over the railing in horror, looking down at the wrecked city smashed on the rocks far below.

Jak dropped to his knees, hunkering low and burying his face as he gripped the back of his head with both hands. Shikari sat next to him—guarding him?

Tonovan strode to the railing to look down at the destroyed city. Rivlen doubted many of the citizens had survived that crash, and she shook her head slowly. She'd battled other mages before, military officers such as herself, but she'd never had orders like these, never had to destroy civilian targets.

"*Triumph.*" Tonovan clenched his fist and looked at Rivlen. "Do you know why Uthari likes me so much, Captain?"

"You have no scruples, and you'll do whatever he asks without question?"

"Precisely. Rulers want to be obeyed, not questioned. They want officers who exceed their expectations and who they can depend on. You'd best remember that if you want to be promoted further—" his eyes narrowed as he regarded her, "—or keep the rank you have."

"Thanks for the tip."

"Why don't you join me tonight?" Tonovan asked. "To celebrate our victory."

Victory. As if skulking into a devastated palace in a devastated city and killing an injured ruler was some great feat.

"I'll remind you what it's like to have sex with a *man*, instead of a boy." Tonovan stepped closer and reached for the side of her face, offering some loathsome caress.

Stepping back, Rivlen jerked her arm up in a block, as if he'd offered a punch instead of a caress. Both were equally unwelcome.

Using his power, he caught her arm in the air, keeping her from dropping it. Furious, she channeled more of her magic into the barrier that she always kept up when she was near him, but she couldn't drive him back. Her barrier merely clashed against his. Then he manipulated his to force hers to diminish, withering inward like a flower under a hailstorm. She didn't have the power to repel him.

Tonovan gripped her arm and stepped closer, leaning in to whisper, "You disappointed your stalwart defender today. He and his dragon are sulking with the mercenaries. You've nobody to bolster your power so you can *pretend* to be my match."

"I don't *need* him," Rivlen snarled, but she did. She hated it, but it was true. Though she tried, she couldn't draw upon enough power within herself to push him away, to force him to release her.

"What you *need* is an ally who'll tell Uthari that you performed admirably." His breath was hot and unwelcome against her cheek. "Not that you hesitated, that you've been sleeping with a conniving wild one, and that you can't be trusted to faithfully obey his orders."

"Uthari *can* trust me to obey him." And who she slept with was none of Uthari's business. Rivlen couldn't believe the old wizard would even care. "I did nothing wrong today, and you know it."

"What I know and what I tell him could be the same thing or... not. We'll see what kind of mood I'm in when we rejoin the fleet." Tonovan smiled viciously, his hand tightening around her arm. "You'll welcome me between your legs tonight if you want me to give a good report."

"Screw you, Tonovan."

"Exactly." His head tilted. "I understand your aloof father won't talk to you because you disappointed him so when you failed to be accepted into the zidarr training program. Will he be proud of you if you return home with a medal?"

Hatred for him lent Rivlen more energy—more power—and she willed it to surge up within her and knock him back. How had the bastard known about her family? Uthari knew, but she'd never told Tonovan anything, and she couldn't believe the general cared enough to research her.

A warm breeze of power whispered into her from behind. Jak.

Rivlen didn't have to look back to know he was on the deck, looking up at them. He increased the amount of power he was channeling into her, and she gathered it greedily, like water from a river after a three-day trek through the desert.

His power allowed her to strengthen her barrier, and she pulled her arm free. She also tried to thrust Tonovan back, but her magical shove passed by without disturbing him. She bared her teeth. Now that he had all that dragon steel, he was going to be even more difficult to deal with. And, judging by his snide sneer, even more insufferable.

"He showed up to help you after all," Tonovan said. "No doubt *he* wants another invitation to your bed tonight."

Rivlen doubted it. Not after the role she'd played today in helping Tonovan complete his mission.

"But you *won't* be inviting him back." Tonovan squinted as he glared into her eyes. "You saw him defy me today, Captain. I know you did. He tried to help our enemies, to *protect* them from me when I was following Uthari's orders. I command you to lock him in one of your brig cells. If he wants to continue living, he can explain himself to Uthari and beg for his life. But he's not to roam free. We don't allow enemies to wander the decks of our ships. Do you understand me, Captain?"

Rivlen stared mulishly at him, wondering if she could get away with not answering.

Tonovan turned his head toward the north. There was a dragon out there at the edge of Rivlen's senses. So far, just one, but that might change. It was in the direction the ships had to fly to leave Temril and continue on to Uth.

"I'm going over to the *Sky Warrior* to make sure we got all our engineers out of the city in time and to report to Uthari on our success and the further obstacles we may have to deal with. When I get back, that boy better be in the brig. Do you understand?"

"I understand that you're afraid to try to put him in there yourself."

Tonovan scoffed. "Please." But when he looked down at Jak, Shikari was still at his side.

Now that Tonovan had two dragon-steel weapons, Shikari might not have as much luck using magic against him, but Rivlen wagered Tonovan still didn't want to tangle with the dragonling.

"Follow your orders, Captain. As I said, I can report to Uthari that you were cooperative and competent so that he'll reward you, or I can... not."

Rivlen closed her eyes as Tonovan walked to the railing, grabbed a skyboard, and flew to the other ship. *Thanks for the help, Jak.*

You're welcome.

His words were stiff and formal, and Rivlen regretted that her actions today had likely ensured he wouldn't want to spend another night with her. Not that lovemaking was either of their primary concerns right now. Tonovan was right. She *had* witnessed Jak acting against him, and she was fairly certain Shikari had only helped them get inside because he'd wanted the king's food. Uthari might punish Jak for trying to protect their enemies. He might do *worse* than punish him.

Stay in one of the guest cabins for the rest of the journey, Jak. Rivlen couldn't bring herself to dump him in a cell, not after all the help he'd given her. *Tonovan wants you in the brig, but maybe if you stay out of his sight, he won't think to check where you are.*

There are more dragons out there. We may need to fight our way off Temril.

I know, but we'll handle it.

You don't think I can help?

I know you can, but I want you to stay out of sight and for Tonovan to forget you're even on the ship. I'm saying this for your own good.

Very well. Jak sounded hurt, but he headed obediently for the nearest hatch.

Rivlen shook her head, feeling like she'd kicked a loyal hound. But what could she do?

Sasko gripped the railing of the gateship and stared in horror as it and Uthari's three other mageships sailed away from the place where Temika had floated in the sky scant minutes earlier. Now, it lay in rubble far below, fires burning. All she'd been able to do was gape as Tonovan's party had floated back to the *Star Flyer* and explosions had ripped through the city until, with startling abruptness, it had fallen, killing all those who'd remained within.

"By Shylezar's bent tail," she whispered, "it would be less evil to be working for the dragons."

Though she'd never considered herself one to get emotional,

and she was used to death and war, this was too much. Too inhumane. Even mages shouldn't suffer such dreadful deaths.

Hands shaking—no, her entire *body* shaking—Sasko headed for the hatch. Vinjo had gone below earlier, knowing what would happen as soon as he'd seen Uthari's soldiers walking into the sky city with those backpacks. He hadn't wanted to witness the end result. Maybe Sasko should have hidden her eyes—and ears—as well, but that had seemed cowardly. If there was no one to report atrocities, how would the world know what evil had happened?

Now, she understood why Sorath had been writing a memoir. He'd seen the raw awfulness of the mages, experienced it firsthand, and he'd wanted to leave behind a warning.

Sasko climbed down the ladder, closing the hatch on the smoke that lingered even after the city had fallen, and checked on Sergeant Tinder. After the dragon battle, Dr. Fret and Jak had tended her wounds before returning to the *Star Flyer*. Sasko was thankful that they'd been allowed to do so. She'd been worried that Rivlen would be irritated by the loss of Tinder's axe and wouldn't let anyone help her.

But Rivlen wasn't the monster over there. Tonovan was. Sasko knew he'd given the orders to destroy that city.

Tinder was sitting on the edge of a bunk in the dark, her head drooping and her elbows propped on her knees. No, *slumped* on her knees. Sasko had never seen her so dejected.

"Are you mourning the loss of your axe or feeling inadequate as a warrior?" Sasko had never been the best at comforting people —and Tinder had never seemed like the kind of person to crave comfort—so she opted for humor.

As soon as Tinder lifted her head, anguish contorting her face, Sasko realized it had been the wrong choice.

"The *axe*," Tinder said, "but thanks so much for pointing out that other thing, Lieutenant."

"Sorry." Sasko tapped the mage lamp mounted on the wall to

activate it and came to sit beside Tinder. "I know you're not happy about losing it, but you shouldn't feel inadequate about failing to keep a *dragon* from getting the best of you. Be happy you're alive. Thousands of people who were ten minutes ago... aren't now."

Tinder frowned at her. "Ma'am?"

Nobody had asked the mercenaries and mages on the gateship to enter the city with Tonovan and his people, and since Tinder had been belowdecks, she must have missed everything. Sasko tersely explained.

Tinder slumped back against the wall. "We're working for monsters, and we don't even have a say in the matter."

"I know Captain Ferroki isn't happy about it. She hasn't been since Uthari's people destroyed Zaruk's ship and forced us into his employment. Who would have thought *Zaruk* would be the better of the two kings?"

"They're all monsters. All of them. I hope Jak—" Tinder glanced at Sasko and cut herself off.

"What?"

"Nothing."

"Sergeant, it's not permissible to keep secrets from your commanding officer. It's in the mercenary handbook."

"I don't believe that. Units operate on secrets. You'll have to show me the page that says otherwise."

"I think I lost my copy of the handbook in the jungle."

"I think I lost my sanity in the jungle." Tinder looked bleakly at the wall as she touched her bandaged abdomen.

Even though her healing had involved magic, the wounds would probably ache for a while.

"What do you think Jak will do to change things?" Sasko asked curiously.

"Probably nothing. I don't want to talk about it. The more of us terrene humans who know, the less likely a secret will stay secret."

"True." Sasko didn't want to put the kid at risk either. Even if he was trying to become a mage, he still seemed decent. Mostly normal. Not the kind of person to plot to destroy an entire city. "Do you want to go back over to see Fret?"

"My gouges are all right now." Tinder shifted her hand to the side.

"I meant for hugs and moral support."

"Oh. I do like those things. And I do worry about her when I'm not nearby to keep an eye on her. She's not exactly a fierce warrior, you know."

"She's fairly fierce with her knitting needles."

"I suppose."

"Given the opportunity, she might have thrust one up a dragon's nose," Sasko said.

"I can't tell you how much I'd pay to see that."

Sasko smiled, though it didn't last long. Whatever coin ended up in their hands, paid out of Uthari's coffers, would be blood coin. "I better check on Vinjo. If you want to go back to the *Star Flyer*, he can probably send you over on a skyboard or some other contraption."

"Thanks, Lieutenant."

Sasko gripped her shoulder. "We'll survive this and get back to our old lives. Don't worry."

"Sure, Lieutenant," Tinder said, though they both knew that neither of them believed the words.

Sighing, Sasko went to find Vinjo. She wouldn't have minded hugs and moral support herself, though he was probably already immersed in a project and too absorbed to provide either.

He wasn't in the navigation cabin. The ship was sailing along, flying parallel to the *Star Flyer*, apparently without anyone steering it.

A faint clinking came from the rear. From the engineering cabin? Sasko headed in that direction. On the narrow ship, with only engineering, navigation, a kitchen, and crew quarters, there weren't many places for Vinjo to be.

Surprisingly, he *wasn't* in engineering. A hatch was cracked open in the cabin next to it, and orange light spilled out.

"Vinjo?" Sasko pushed the hatch open.

He shoved something under a bunk and spun to face her, almost tripping over a toolbox on the deck.

"Whatcha doing?" she asked casually, eyeing the orange glow seeping out from under the bunk.

"Nothing."

"So, *nothing* is glowing from under the bunk?"

Vinjo shifted to the side, attempting and failing to block the glow with his legs. "That's right."

"Why is everyone keeping secrets from me today? It's quite rude." Sasko smiled, and wasn't truly irked with Tinder, but she thought she and Vinjo had a connection, so this felt like a betrayal. Granted, she hadn't originally *wanted* that connection, but he'd grown on her, and she cared for him. She hoped he wasn't doing something that would anger Captain Rivlen or the other mage officers. Two of them remained on board to keep an eye on Vinjo.

"It's not rude." Vinjo lifted his hands, almost tripping over the toolbox again as he stepped toward her. "I don't want you to get in trouble."

"Are *you* doing something that could get you in trouble?"

"Uhm."

Worried now, Sasko stepped past him and knelt to peer under the bunk. An orange crystal orb in the corner seeped light in her direction. Vinjo muttered something, and the light disappeared.

"Don't tell anyone, please," he whispered.

"Tell them what?" Sasko knelt back. "I have no idea what it is."

"Oh? Then it's... for ironing uniforms. To get the wrinkles out. You roll it over your trousers."

"You're a horrible liar, Vinjo."

He winced. "I know."

"What is it really? Or..." Sasko thought of her conversation with Tinder. "Is it better that I don't know because mages can read my mind?"

"*Yes.*"

"Fine. Don't tell me. But don't get yourself in trouble again, please."

He smiled lopsidedly at her. "I'll try, but it's hard."

"No kidding."

He melted with relief as she left his orb alone and stepped back into the corridor. Only as the hatch clanged shut did she realize where she'd seen a similar orange glow before. Those dome-jir communication devices the senior mage officers used to speak with other mages across the world.

Sasko leaned against the wall as new concerns trickled into her. It was possible Vinjo was building it simply because it was a logical thing for a ship to have, a means of communication with one's superior officers.

Except that Vinjo's superior officers weren't here. What if he'd built it because he wanted to send a message to King Zaruk? Or someone else who might like to know where he was—and what Uthari's forces were up to? Sasko remembered the blue-hulled ships they'd seen days earlier. Might they still be out there?

She rubbed her eyes. Was she obligated to tell Captain Ferroki about this? Captain *Rivlen*? If she told Rivlen, what might she do to Vinjo?

Sasko slumped against the wall, wishing she'd never gone looking for him.

15

NIGHT HAD FALLEN ONCE MORE, DARK AGAINST THE TINY PORTHOLE in the unoccupied cabin Jak had found. He stared at the ceiling, doubting he would sleep. If he did, he would have nightmares. Even lying there awake, he couldn't stop hearing the screams of the terrified people in Temika as the city crashed to the ground. Nor could he forget the anguish on the faces of the king and his wife as Tonovan had murdered them both.

It didn't surprise him that Uthari had orchestrated that and Tonovan had gleefully carried out his orders—while stealing Tezi's axe—but Jak wished Malek were there and could have seen what loathsome and detestable people he was sided with. Did he already know? It seemed he had to after decades of serving Uthari, but Jak wanted to believe that if Malek had been there, he would have been appalled, and that he would have decided it was finally time to leave his foul master.

Tears leaked from Jak's eyes, dribbling down the sides of his face. He sensed Rivlen in her cabin farther up the corridor. A part of him wanted to go to her, but she hadn't tried to stop any of that carnage. He believed that she hadn't known in advance what

Tonovan's orders were, and he knew she couldn't have overpowered Tonovan even if she had, but it was hard for Jak not to feel that he was trapped in a nest of vipers. He and the Thorn Company mercenaries.

He rolled onto his side, wishing Shikari were in the cabin with him, but the dragonling had finally grown too large to fit through hatchways and go belowdecks.

Something poked Jak in the hip. He grimaced and stuck his hand in his pocket to adjust whatever it was. His fingers brushed rounded metal edges and a needle, and he froze, his breath catching.

The kerzor.

Before obeying Rivlen's wishes to go belowdecks, Jak had grabbed his backpack, including the kerzor he'd made and the stealth device Vinjo had given him back on Nargnoth. His belongings had been mounded among those of the mercenaries, and he'd been relieved nobody had sensed the magical devices and searched his pack. On a ship filled with magic, they weren't that noticeable, but for Jak to have been caught with either might have been a death sentence, especially if Tonovan had been the one doing the catching.

He wished he'd found a way to jam it into Tonovan's skull the moment he'd made the kerzor.

But *had* he made a working kerzor? Jak wished he knew.

It was possible if not probable that he'd made a magical doohickey that did nothing. His mother's schematics had only been able to show the physical components. Vinjo had offered some advice, but he'd admitted he had no knowledge of such devices, so he'd only been making guesses.

Would Shikari know?

More than once, he'd proven that dragons had a genetic memory and he knew things that he hadn't yet experienced for himself. And hadn't Zelonsera said she'd given Shikari some of her own memories, as much knowledge as his young brain had been capable of absorbing at the time?

It was unlikely Zelonsera had known about the kerzor devices, something that humans on another world had invented, but her knowledge of magic might include how to take away another's power. And if she'd conveyed that to Shikari, *he* might know. At the least, he might be able to tell if Jak had succeeded or not.

How he would overpower Tonovan to drive the kerzor into his temple, Jak didn't know, but if he somehow succeeded only to find out the device didn't work... he would be dead. Most likely, he would die either way if he attempted it. Back on the gateship, it had taken Malek to bring down Tonovan, driving a needle full of Mother's sedative into his vein. And Malek wasn't here. Even if he were, would he defy Uthari to take down the king's loyal general? Not likely.

"Vipers," Jak whispered, swinging his feet to the floor. "All of them."

Somehow, he would have to do this himself. He could never overpower Tonovan in a fair confrontation, but maybe if he used the stealth device and sneaked into his cabin while he was sleeping...

That was his only chance. He would have to hope the dragon-steel weapons didn't warn Tonovan and that he didn't have an alarm set up to go off if an intruder entered his cabin. Jak hoped that, even if Tonovan was capable of creating such things, he would be too arrogant to believe anyone would dare strike at him in his sleep.

"Shikari first," he murmured, padding to the door.

Jak had to know if his kerzor would work before he risked his life. As he reached for the latch, a gasp of pain came from the corridor outside. A woman's gasp of pain.

Jak sensed Tonovan out there and clenched his jaw, tempted to yank open the door and spring on him right there. He wanted to free whoever he was tormenting—what if it was Tezi?

Another gasp came from farther along the corridor. Tonovan was dragging his victim off to his cabin. It didn't sound like Tezi, but that didn't make Jak feel much better. Whoever Tonovan had in his clutches didn't deserve to be pawed over by him.

Jak's grip tightened on the latch as he wrestled with emotions and rational thoughts. As much as he wanted to save the woman, he realized she might be the distraction Jak needed to go forward with his plan. Tonovan would either be busy having sex, or he would be sated and sleepy in the aftermath. That would be Jak's chance to strike.

After Tonovan disappeared into his cabin, Jak eased out of his. He hurried up to the deck, not wanting any of the people who thought he belonged in the brig to see him. Tonovan hadn't been speaking quietly when he'd given that order to Rivlen. One she would get in trouble for disobeying, especially if Jak succeeded in this. But if he succeeded... who cared? Tonovan would be powerless. Oh, he would still have the dragon-steel weapons, but maybe Jak could manage to get those away from him while he was clutching at his head and trying to figure out what was happening to him.

Jak wondered how long Tonovan would survive without his power. Dozens, if not *hundreds*, of people had to want him dead. But Jak remembered Rivlen's words, that Uthari had promised an investigation if anything happened to Tonovan on this mission.

"He won't die," Jak vowed. "He'll just be powerless."

Taking his magic from him and leaving him helpless, like the mundane humans he sneered at so often, would be a greater punishment than death.

Jak found Shikari on his belly on the deck, his tail stretched behind him and his chin between his forelegs as he gazed toward the northwest in the direction they were sailing. In the direction that Jak sensed another dragon. No, there were *two* dragons out there now. They were flying ahead of the ship and out of sight, maintaining a consistent distance. While they waited for more of their kind to show up? If they were after dragon steel, the *Star Flyer* now had more of it.

Jak knelt beside Shikari, resting a hand on his damp scales. It had been raining, and Jak's knee landed in a puddle. He was about to ask Shikari if he was worried and knew what those dragons were up to, but for the first time ever, the dragonling spoke into his mind.

I am sorry.

Jak rocked back, his jaw dropping open. He almost blurted, "You can speak?" but didn't. He'd always assumed Shikari would eventually learn to communicate as the other dragons did. He'd just expected that it would be more like human babies developing the ability to speak and starting with something like *mama* or *papa* first.

Shikari turned his yellow eyes toward him. *I am hungry all the time. I wanted the food. I did not understand that breaking the snares would start a fight. The food smelled good.*

I'm sorry you're hungry so much. You didn't come with a manual, and I have no idea how much baby dragons are supposed to eat. Why didn't you let me know?

Shikari shared an image that he'd shared with Jak before, of them hunting together in a field, and Jak sticking his head into the grass and coming up with a rat in his mouth, the tail twitching as it dangled on his chin.

"Ew, isn't that more related to you thinking *I'm* hungry?"

Shikari swatted him in the back with his tail. *You feed me enough. But I get hungry again fast. I am growing.*

Yes, I've noticed, Jak said, switching back to telepathy. The mercenaries were stretched out on their blankets, and few had fallen asleep yet. He sensed numerous sets of eyes turned in his direction.

Soon, I will be as big as the others, and then I will battle them and defeat them. Shikari surged to his feet and roared over the railing.

Uh, you better stay away from them. You understand about the parasite, right? Jak hadn't tried to explain it, but Shikari had been around for many of the conversations he'd had with his mother on the topic. And he'd been there when the motes on Vran tried to carry the parasite to him.

I understand. Shikari flopped back down to his belly.

Sorry. It's a tough time to be a young dragon.

Yes. But we will free my people. Shikari's tail slapped at the damp deck, water droplets spattering in the face—the *tail*—of his determination. *We will make them right again. And then some of them will play with me.*

You do need someone to play with you, someone without fragile, easily cut skin.

And who can fly. Longing filled Shikari's telepathic words as he gazed out at the night.

You *can barely fly, you know.*

Shikari squinted at him.

Though I did see how well you did earlier. Good job.

I will be a great flyer one day. So fast. I will plummet down from the sky and swoop up my prey.

All of the rats in Zewnath will cower in fear.

I will eat larger prey then.

Like raccoons?

That earned Jak another squint and tail whack.

I will be mighty.

I have no doubt. Jak smiled, though this wasn't what he'd come up here for. Being able to finally *talk* to Shikari was a worthwhile distraction, but he remembered the woman Tonovan had been dragging to his cabin and pulled out the kerzor.

When I'm big enough, you can ride on my back, and we can hunt together, Shikari offered.

A pang of emotion filled Jak's chest. That had been his dream for as long as he could remember, to ride a dragon and soar through the sky. Since long before he'd experienced mageships, levitation, or skyboards. And now that he had... it hadn't changed anything. He still longed to ride on a dragon.

Thank you. Jak rested a hand on Shikari's back again. *I hope to live long enough to experience that with you.*

You will live. I will protect you. When I'm mighty, that will be easier.

I'm certain you're right. Jak held out the kerzor to Shikari. *Do you remember the device you helped me remove from Malek's temple on Vran?*

A mage walking a patrol of the ship came close to them, and Jak closed his fist around the kerzor. His heart hammered in his ears, and he wished Shikari weren't too large to go below. Such discussions should be held in private.

I remember. It tasted funny.

Jak snorted, reminded that Shikari had *eaten* one of the devices. *I've tried to create another one. There's... an enemy whose magic I wish to nullify.*

Tonovan. Shikari flicked his tail.

Yeah. You've effectively nullified one of his boots, but I think the world would be a better place if he couldn't draw upon his power anymore.

Shikari gazed at Jak's closed hand—examining the device with his senses? Jak hoped he wasn't as offended by the idea of removing someone's magic as all the mages were.

Yours is not the same, Shikari said. *I do not know if it will do what you want.*

Jak's shoulders slumped in disappointment. *I don't suppose you know how to alter it so that it will?*

Jak, Rivlen spoke into his mind.

He flinched, almost throwing the kerzor overboard until he realized Rivlen was communicating with him from her cabin, not standing right behind him.

Struggling for calm, he answered, *Yes?*

I told you to stay in your cabin.

Shikari needed me, and Tonovan is occupied. Even the minor lie made Jak uneasy. Even before he'd spent the night with Rivlen, she had been good at seeing through him. Now, she probably had extra power to read him. That was how it worked with women, wasn't it?

I doubt he has the stamina to occupy himself for long. And I have a feeling the dragons aren't going to let us leave the island without a fight.

Then shouldn't I stay up here and be prepared to jump into battle against them?

Just... go to your cabin. Trust me.

Jak shifted uneasily, the deck hard under his butt. Did she know something about what revenge Tonovan planned for him? What if he intended to do something to Jak the next morning? Or that very night?

I will. I'll finish up my chat with Shikari and go below.

I'm sure that's a stimulating conversation.

You might be surprised.

Shikari had been studying the kerzor, but his head swung around on his long neck, and he focused on a tarantula sauntering out from under a lifeboat. A large fuzzy-legged stowaway from Zewnath.

Tail swishing, Shikari watched it for a moment before he lunged to his feet and pounced. It tried to skitter away, but he was too fast, and he snapped it up in his maw and swallowed it whole.

You truly are a mighty hunter, Jak told him.

Shikari returned to his spot on the deck, eyes closed halfway as he regarded Jak. *If more fearsome prey like a horned ruktar or antlered*

*moose wandered out from under the lifeboat, I also would have killed it
and chomped it down.*

I have no doubt, Jak replied, though he had a feeling a moose
could use its antlers to scoop up Shikari and fling him overboard.
Still, at the rate he was growing, he ought to be as big as a moose
in a couple more weeks. *Any thoughts on the* kerzor?

I will make it do what you want. Shikari opened his maw and
reached for Jak's hand.

Jak had to fight down the urge to jerk his arm back—Shikari's
fangs were growing impressively long. Instead, after making sure
the patrol mage wasn't nearby, he opened his palm. Expecting
Shikari to sniff it, Jak was surprised when a pink tongue shot out
and swept it into Shikari's mouth.

What are you doing? He barely managed to keep the words
silent.

Shikari wasn't going to swallow it again, was he? Even if the
needle on the back hadn't made that a dicey proposition, Jak had
wanted to put the device to use tonight, not wait for it to pass
through a dragon's digestive system.

Tasting it to compare it to the other one.

Is there a lot of magic in... taste? Jak asked dubiously.

There is magic in all things.

Shikari lifted his head and closed his eyes, holding the kerzor
in his mouth. Jak sensed a trickle of magic. Shikari *was* doing
something.

The magic of these human devices is not in my memory, Shikari
said, *but I remember them from the other world.*

Good. Jak leaned forward, daring to let himself hope this would
work.

If it did, he still had the problem of sneaking into Tonovan's
cabin and finding a way to shove it into his temple, but the stealth
device might help with that. Too bad Shikari wasn't small enough
to come with him. Would it be better to wait until Tonovan came

up on deck the next day? But then Rivlen and her entire crew of mages would also be about. If he pulled out the kerzor in front of them, Jak had little doubt they would all pounce on him the way Shikari had the tarantula.

The strands in the needle will enter his brain now and stop his magic. Shikari turned his maw back toward Jak and dropped the device in his hand.

Jak did his best not to grimace at the saliva moistening his palm. *Thank you. If I survive this, will you show me how to make more?*

Yes. But you will not need them after your mother fixes the dragons. Shikari met his gaze with imploring eyes. *We will make humans be nice to each other again.*

Dear Shylezar, I hope so.

Jak also hoped that Mother truly could *fix* the dragons. How was she doing over on the *Serene Waters*? Jak worried about her when he wasn't around to help her and watch out for her. Just because she had power now didn't mean she would be safe. He feared she wouldn't use it when it came to a fight, especially against Malek. What if Uthari found out about what Jak was doing here and punished his mother?

That thought sent an icy spear of dread into his gut, and once more he had the urge to throw the kerzor over the railing. If this didn't work, and Tonovan got the best of him, he might not only kill Jak but complain to Uthari, who could punish his mother.

Jak swallowed and closed his eyes. After what Tonovan had done today, and all the crimes he'd committed in the past, it was worth risking his life to take away the man's power. But if Mother and Grandfather became collateral damage... he would hate himself forever for that.

Something thumped across his leg. Shikari's tail.

We will fix your world, he said.

Jak forced a smile. *Because we're such mighty predators?*

Yes. Shikari showed his fangs.

Was that a tarantula leg stuck between his teeth?

Jak rubbed his face and stood up. *I'd better do this before I lose my courage.*

He was about to stick his hand in his pocket to withdraw the stealth device, but the officer on patrol looked over at him. Jak slid the kerzor in to join the other device, the needle pronging him in the thigh, and strolled toward the hatch with both hands in his pockets.

The mage watched him through slitted eyes. Was Jak radiating suspicion? He resisted the urge to break into a run, telling himself the officer was simply looking at him because there was nothing else going on. The mercenaries were sleeping, and the dragons were maintaining their distance ahead of the ship.

But the officer strode toward the hatch and cut Jak off.

"Hello," Jak said brightly. "How are you tonight? It's all right if my dragon friend eats your tarantulas, right? I assumed you didn't want them for yourself."

"You acted against us in the battle today," the man said coolly.

His rank pins marked him as a lieutenant, but Jak didn't know his name, and it took him a moment to remember him from the party that had gone into the palace.

"Just against Tonovan. I don't like him. Do you?" Jak smiled. It was, no doubt, an inane smile, but he'd used goofiness and charm before to keep people from considering him a threat. Maybe it would work now.

"Watch out for him. You may have growing power—" the officer looked him up and down, "—but I remember you from when we first caught you. You were a wild one and a runt. Tonovan will obliterate you if you irk him. And maybe if you don't."

"Yeah, he's into that. May I pass? The captain ordered me to my bed."

The officer squinted. "The rumor is she ordered you to *her* bed."

"Uhm, not tonight." And how had a rumor started about the previous night? Jak couldn't remember anyone walking past when he'd been stepping out of Rivlen's cabin. But maybe there weren't many secrets on a ship where every mage could sense every other mage's aura—and where that aura was located.

"You didn't satisfy her?"

"You'd have to ask her about that." Jak straightened his back, wishing the man weren't four inches taller than he. "Will you let me by? I need to rest in case we're attacked by dragons again."

"Will you turn on us and try to *protect* them?"

"Not unless they're innocently lying injured in their own castle as we ambush them."

Sarcasm was possibly not the right answer, for the man reached for him as he snarled.

Instinctively, Jak raised a barrier, envisioning snow-capped mountains rising up between them. The man stumbled back as Jak's *mountains* ran into him, and he bumped into the hatch. He scowled and crouched to spring, but Jak sensed Shikari behind him. The officer noticed him too. He sneered, straightened his uniform, and walked off.

It will take a lot to fix your world, Shikari said.

Tell me about it.

Jak drew a shaky breath, opened the hatch, and headed toward Tonovan's cabin. To fix the world, he would have to start with fixing one small part of it, by removing the power of someone odious and villainous.

"Let's hope this works," he whispered.

~

Malek stood in the corridor outside of Jadora's lab, aware of her inside, bent over the workbench in the back, just as she had to be aware that he was there, staring at her door. Or maybe she was too immersed in her work to notice his aura. In the minutes he'd been wrestling with indecision, she hadn't said anything.

He lifted his fist to knock, though Uthari's request made him hesitant. Had it even been a request? Or an order?

Malek grimaced, not wanting to ask Jadora to lower her barriers so that he could read her thoughts. He wasn't sure why it struck him as an intrusion of her privacy now, when he'd done it often when she'd been a terrene human. Maybe it was because Uthari essentially wanted him to ask her permission to spy on her. It was possible that Uthari cared about saving the knowledge of the dragons, but Malek was skeptical. Uthari seemed indifferent to whether or not they thwarted the parasite and changed the dragons back to their original and less aggressive state.

Has that door grown more fascinating since the last time you visited? Jadora asked telepathically.

The whorls in the oak aren't uninteresting, he replied.

Oh? Perhaps I've erred in not standing out there more often to admire them.

I believe so.

Whenever you're done, you're welcome to come in.

Malek grimaced again. Once she knew what he wanted, she might rescind that offer.

Best to get it over with. After taking a deep breath, he stepped inside.

Jadora smiled over her shoulder at him. It was such a warm and pleased smile that it made him pause to admire it. And wonder at it. Hadn't anyone ever told her that women weren't supposed to beam with pleasure at the approach of a zidarr?

"Look." Jadora stretched her hand toward three small pots under floating globes of illumination that she'd created, the light reminding him of the hazy yellowish-orange sun of Nargnoth. In two of the pots, single green sprouts with bulbous heads had risen from the soil. "They look like the little fiddleheads from our native ferns, don't they?"

"You've succeeded in propagating the Jitaruvak," Malek realized.

"Yes. Once I was able to replicate their preferred sunlight, I figured out how to use my magic to coerce them to grow more quickly than usual. By the time we reach Utharika, I might have a full-fledged fern for your king's greenhouse."

"Uthari doesn't have a greenhouse."

"Shortsighted, given his obsession. Please tell him that he must have one built. These won't grow in his windowsill."

"I will let him know." Malek smiled and walked to the workbench, the urge to hug her coming over him, but she might not appreciate his touch once he made his request. Unfortunate. Back in his cabin, when she'd been recovering from her wounds, they'd almost kissed. That wouldn't have been wise, but it would have been... desirable. "He'll be pleased."

"After all this, he'd better do cartwheels."

"He's three hundred years old. I'm not sure cartwheels are in his repertoire of physical abilities."

"Too bad. Maybe they would make him less surly. Nobody doing cartwheels has ever been surly." Jadora eyed him, perhaps wondering what had brought him to the lab. Or perhaps wondering if zidarr ever did cartwheels.

"I prefer pull-ups." Malek brushed a lock of hair away from her eyes. "Uthari sent me."

She'd started to smile at his touch, but it faltered at his last sentence.

Saddened, he lowered his hand. "He wants a copy of everything you learned from the dragon, the notes you've recorded and also... for me to convince you to lower your mental barriers so I can access your memories and try to relive that experience you had with her. I'm not sure he truly cares what you learned; I read between the lines that he wants me to saunter through your thoughts to see if you're planning anything nefarious."

Her shoulders slumped, and she looked at his jaw instead of into his eyes. So he wouldn't see the disappointment in hers?

"Did he also want you to be so honest and share his motivations with me?" she asked quietly.

"Likely not, but I feel compelled to tell you the truth."

"Ah." She didn't appear touched by his admission.

Malek wished Uthari would leave her alone and not ask him to pry. Jadora was doing what Uthari wanted. All long, she'd been doing what he wanted.

Emotion thickened his throat, and he regretted coming.

"Well," Jadora said, "I'm not planning anything nefarious, and I think it would be a good idea to make a copy of what Zelonsera shared with me and for you to grasp everything. In case anything happens to me. That knowledge shouldn't be lost."

"I won't let anything happen to you."

"I know you think you won't, but there may come a day when you have to choose whose side you'll stand by, who you'll protect."

Malek frowned. "Have you had a vision?"

She didn't carry any dragon steel, but with her new power, perhaps she'd gained some clairvoyance.

"Just a hunch," she said, still looking at his jaw instead of into his eyes.

"Uthari can take care of himself."

"Of course," she murmured, then took a deep breath and lifted her gaze. "I'm ready."

There was no fear in her eyes, no guilt or concern, and he knew before she let down her mental barriers that she wasn't hiding anything from him. He lifted his hand to her cheek, because contact made it even easier to delve into a person's mind

—and because he wanted to touch her, to let her know that he appreciated her not making this difficult. Even so, he felt like he was betraying her.

Jadora didn't hesitate to show him what she'd experienced on Nargnoth when she'd met the dragon and her human guardians— and in the days leading up to that. He relived her memories with her, her distress when he'd been stung by a death darter and afflicted with those bacteria, her fear that she wouldn't be able to find a solution to keep him from going mad, and her terror that Tonovan, Bakir, and Prolix would take over the ship and kill him. She'd been desperate to find a way to keep him alive and himself and... with her.

A tear traced her cheek, moistening his fingers. Malek blinked, her emotion threatening to bring him to tears as well.

She wiped her eyes and focused her memories on the dragon encounter, sharing with him what Zelonsera had said, what her kind hoped Jadora could do. She also shared the intense responsibility she felt to try to help them. The fear of what would happen to those eggs and the dragon heritage if she couldn't.

Jadora leaned against him, and Malek wrapped his arms around her to support her, and because the intimacy of sharing thoughts made him want to be physically close to her. Until then, he hadn't realized how alone she'd felt since she'd been given this new responsibility and the power that made her own father fear her. Even Jak looked at her with uncertainty, sometimes seeing the powerful mage instead of his mother.

Through her memories, Malek witnessed the transfer of knowledge, but it whispered by so quickly that he struggled to retain any of it. It was as if Zelonsera had inserted an entire dragon library into Jadora's mind. It was amazing that her brain had held it all.

Malek had no idea how the dragon had accomplished gifting

her with lasting power. Perhaps it was something humans couldn't grasp, that even a zidarr could never do.

"I'm glad you've been writing everything in journals," he murmured at the end. "Uthari was thinking far too highly of me if he believed I could retain any of that."

She snorted softly, leaning her face against his shoulder. "There was a lot. I'm glad you want the information though. As I said, someone besides me should know. It shouldn't be lost. Especially since... I don't know how much time I have to figure this out. Zelonsera is close to death."

"Ah." Sensing her distress, Malek stroked the back of her head, her hair soft and cool under his fingers.

Jadora wiped her eyes again and lifted her chin to look at him. "Will you do me a favor, Malek?"

He almost said *yes* automatically, because he couldn't remember her ever asking anything of him, but he made himself raise his eyebrows in inquiry. If it was something that would pit him against Uthari, he couldn't say yes.

"If I don't make it, will you try to finish my work and save the dragons?"

"I wouldn't have a chance at understanding the biology. And you'll make it. I told you. I'll be here to protect you." But he'd almost failed to protect her, hadn't he? And that had been against only one dragon. What if *more* than one dragon came after her at once?

"I know you will, but if I *don't* make it, I would hate for the dragons' hope for their species to die with me. Jak will help you. Together, you two can figure it out."

Malek looked toward the ceiling, debating if this was a promise he could make. What if Uthari forbade it? Would Malek defy his king to attempt to carry out her desire?

"I don't think you care about leaving a legacy," Jadora said softly, "but this would be the most important thing you'd ever done. Saving an entire species. After all those you've killed at Uthari's behest, it could be your gift to the future. To life."

She didn't sound judgmental when she said *after all those you've killed*, but he couldn't help but wince. He was zidarr, and sometimes that meant killing, being an assassin. It was what he'd been trained from boyhood to do. He'd never questioned it, never believed he had sins he needed to atone for, and he wasn't sure that had changed. But he *had* come to care for Jadora and what she wanted.

"You are right." Malek lowered his gaze to hers. "Zidarr aren't taught to crave anything, including leaving a legacy or gifts for anyone, but *if* something happens to you, I will do my best to carry out the mission the dragon gave you because you asked it of me."

"Thank you, Malek," she whispered, relief in her eyes.

Maybe she'd been worried about her mortality since that dragon had tried to kill her. Understandable.

He pulled her close again and buried his face in her hair, breathing in her scent, basking in her aura, smiling when a vial or something else in her pocket with a hard edge prodded him.

"I owe you a favor," he said softly, lowering his lips to the side of her neck and wishing he could invite her back to his cabin. "More than one. You keep saving me, even though you shouldn't. Prisoners aren't supposed to help their captors." Not that she'd been that to him for a long time, and he hoped she'd long since stopped thinking of him as her captor.

"Then who would nuzzle my neck?"

"I'm sure you could find a mage from a good family."

She swatted him on the shoulder and stepped back, resting a palm on his chest. "If you stay here, I'll fling myself on you, and your king won't be pleased."

He didn't want to back away from her, to step out of the influence of her aura, and almost said Uthari's pleasure be damned. But he knew she was trying to save him again, this time not from bacteria or dragon wounds but from estrangement from the king he'd long ago sworn his fealty to.

"*I* would be pleased," he said softly, even if he shouldn't have. It was true.

Her lips parted, and she leaned closer, her hand softening on his chest. He clasped his hand over hers, not minding it there, not in the least. He pressed his mouth to hers and melted against her.

Malek, Uthari spoke into his mind.

It took all of Malek's control not to telepathically growl at his king. *Yes, Your Majesty?*

Did she give you access to her thoughts?

As Jadora slid her arms around Malek's shoulders, he was positive she would give him access to all of her.

Yes, Malek replied, wanting nothing more than to end the conversation and focus on Jadora.

Come tell me what you learned, Uthari said, magical compulsion in his words.

Malek was strong enough to resist that compulsion, but if he didn't come, Uthari would know why. And he might punish Jadora for Malek's weakness. He couldn't allow that.

Reluctantly, he broke the kiss and stepped back. "I have to go."

Disappointment swam in Jadora's eyes. Her mental barriers were still down, and he glimpsed how much she wanted to be with him, that she loved him.

One day, he vowed, they *would* be together. He loved her too.

16

With Vinjo's stealth device on his wrist and activated, Jak crept toward Tonovan's cabin. He could sense the general inside but couldn't tell if he was alone—the woman he'd taken to bed hadn't been a mage with an aura—or if he was sleeping.

In the quiet corridor, Jak's heart pounded in his chest, and sweat broke out on his forehead and moistened his palms. He slipped a hand in his jacket and wrapped it around the kerzor.

Swallowing, he stopped outside Tonovan's cabin and put his ear to the door. With the stealth device activated, Tonovan *shouldn't* be able to sense him, but if the general was awake, he would see or hear the door open. And he would have time to react. If he was within five feet of the door, he would also be able to see through the stealth device's influence and spot Jak. And *kill* Jak.

Too bad Jak didn't have a dragon-steel weapon to add to his arsenal. And Tonovan *did* have such a weapon. Two of them. Would he be sleeping with the dagger or Tezi's axe? Have both close at hand?

If Jak had done this a day earlier, Tezi would still have had her axe, and he could have asked her to help. The chances of overpowering Tonovan would have been *much* better.

He shook his head. There was no point in wishing for what was not.

A few doors up, Rivlen was in her cabin. Sleeping? Making plans for upcoming dragon battles? Thinking about inviting him into her cabin to enjoy another night together?

Right. He pushed that thought out of his mind, though a part of him hoped that if he was successful and nullified her greatest enemy, she would wrap her arms around him and kiss him thoroughly. *More* than kiss him.

But he had to be successful for that to happen. It crossed his mind to ask for her help in this. She might not have a dragon-steel weapon, but she had the power to distract Tonovan.

Unfortunately, for her to attack a superior officer would be career suicide. If not *actual* suicide. If Tonovan didn't kill her, Uthari might.

No, Jak had to do this alone.

If you get into trouble, Shikari spoke into his mind, *run up on deck. I will help.*

Thank you.

Wishing once more that Shikari could fit down here and be at his side, Jak took a deep breath and gripped the door latch. Would it be locked?

It wasn't. In his arrogance, Tonovan didn't worry about keeping out intruders.

Jak's first bit of good fortune. The second was that the door didn't creak or make a sound as he eased it open.

A soft red light glowed from a table beside the bed, providing some illumination. It showed Tonovan tangled in the sheets with not one but two naked women draped across him. He lay on his back with his eyes closed, as naked as the women, his arms wrapped around them to secure them to him. One of them had her face to the wall, and Jak couldn't tell if she was awake, but he froze because the other one was looking at the door—at *him*.

He lifted a finger to his lips before realizing she wouldn't be able to see him. She had only seen the door open. That didn't mean she couldn't alert Tonovan, even if by accident.

Please don't move, Jak thought into the woman's mind. *I'm going to do something to Tonovan to keep him from hurting people anymore.*

He hoped he wasn't lying. A man could hurt a woman even if he didn't have a wizard's power.

Who's there? She lifted her head.

Tonovan's arm tightened around her. Damn it, if he woke up...

Don't move, Jak thought again. *Please. I'm here to help.*

Jak eased inside and closed the door. Tezi's axe leaned against the wall beside the bed, well within Tonovan's reach. But if Jak got a little closer, it would be within *his* reach too. He bit his lip and took a step in that direction, but the woman was still peering toward the door.

If you hurt him, he'll hurt us, the woman thought, pushing herself to one elbow, her breasts coming into view.

Tonovan grunted a protest and pulled her back down, his arm adjusting so that he could grab one of her breasts. She gasped at his grip, and anger surged into Jak. He strode forward, no longer caring if Tonovan woke up. All he needed were a couple of seconds to jam the kerzor into his temple.

"What are you doing, girl?" Tonovan demanded, his eyes opening.

Jak halted halfway to the bed. Realizing Tonovan would read the woman's mind, he attempted to shield her thoughts. Then, while Tonovan was focused on her—frowning suspiciously at her —Jak sprang.

He had a clear view of Tonovan's temple, an open line of

attack. But Tonovan saw him or sensed him or simply reacted on instinct. He pushed the woman up, using her as a shield.

The other woman jerked awake and clunked him in the sternum with her elbow. That startled Tonovan for a split second, long enough for Jak to reach the side of the bed and use his magic to push the woman—Tonovan's human shield—away. He didn't want to hurt her, but he *had* to get to the general before it was too late.

But he'd come within the range where the stealth device couldn't hide him, and Tonovan's eyes bulged.

You! he cried into Jak's mind.

Jak lunged for his temple, the needle gleaming in the reddish light. Before Jak reached him, Tonovan launched tremendous power at him. As it knocked him flying into the air, Jak lunged for the axe, fingers just curling around the haft. Tonovan's power stopped affecting him, and Jak plummeted to the floor. He managed to get his feet under him and land in a crouch.

Tonovan flung the women aside and sprang out of bed. Jak, so focused on his mission to drive the kerzor into his skull, didn't think to swing the axe. Instead, he leaped onto Tonovan, wrapping his legs around him like a monkey grabbing a tree trunk. Tonovan roared and tried another magical attack before realizing Jak was protected by the axe. As Jak lifted the kerzor toward his temple, Tonovan jerked his head forward. His forehead crunched into Jak's nose, and pain blasted him, but he hung on and whipped the device needle-first into Tonovan's temple.

It was a tiny needle, but bone crunched audibly as it drove into his skull.

Roaring in pain, Tonovan flung him back. Jak let go, though he kept the axe in hand. Or at least he tried. Tonovan might have been a bastard, but he was a trained bastard, and he lunged and gripped the handle with both hands. He kicked Jak in the knee as he twisted the weapon and tore it from his grip.

Eyes watering from his bashed nose, Jak stumbled. The women screamed—or maybe they'd already *been* screaming and Jak had been too focused to notice it.

Tonovan hefted the axe and might have cleaved Jak in two, but the cabin's ceiling wasn't that high, and the axe-head caught in it. Cursing, Tonovan yanked it free.

Jak reached for the door, but it flew open, almost striking him in the nose again.

"What's going on in here?" Captain Rivlen strode into the cabin.

Tonovan whirled toward her, pulling the axe back for a lower swing that would have cleared the ceiling without trouble.

"No," Jak yelled and sprang in front of Rivlen. It was idiotic, since she had more power than he did, but the thought of her being hurt because of his plot terrified him. "She didn't do anything."

"Tonovan, stop it." Rivlen lifted a hand toward him but frowned, realizing her magic wouldn't work as long as he held that weapon.

"Your boy sneaked into my room and *attacked* me," Tonovan snarled, the axe still poised.

Surprisingly, he didn't swing. He lifted a hand toward his temple, patting at the kerzor now embedded, and his lips rippled back in horror.

"What is *this*?" His fingers curled to yank it out.

"It'll tear your brain to pieces if you remove it," Jak warned, though he'd tried to imbue the ability to convey that warning into the device itself.

Maybe it had worked, for Tonovan froze, save for his heaving chest. As he probed the device with his fingers, fear replaced the rage in his eyes. His fingers curled, but he didn't pull it out.

"What did you *do*?" Rivlen demanded, staring at Jak.

She, who'd been on Vran with Jak and had seen those devices

everywhere, had to know exactly what he'd done. And she did. He saw it in her eyes, saw the loathing and disgust and *betrayal* there when she took two large steps back from Jak. She might have put even more space between them, but the naked women were huddled together on that side of the cabin.

"I put an end to a problem." Jak didn't regret the action, but he realized he'd been delusional when he'd envisioned Rivlen kissing him for this. She was *horrified*, and she looked at his pockets, as if he might have more of the kerzor devices squirreled away, including one for her.

"You *bastard*." Tonovan lowered his hand from his temple as he glared at Jak. "After all Uthari and Malek did for you, you would betray them? You would turn on a mage? One of your own kind?"

"Just on you." Jak would have felt braver saying that if Tonovan didn't still have that axe—and murder in his eye.

With another roar of fury, Tonovan hefted the weapon and charged at him.

Jak did the only thing he could and sprang out the open door, slamming it shut behind him. But leaving Rivlen in there with a furious axeman seemed another betrayal—what if, in his fury, Tonovan took out Rivlen and the two women?—and he paused, overriding his instincts. He couldn't leave them in there with Tonovan.

As he turned back to help, the axe-head slammed into the door so hard that two inches of it came through to the other side. Jak gaped at the blade. Tonovan wrenched it back out and yanked open the door.

No, he wasn't going to attack Rivlen; he was going to chase after Jak.

Come up on deck, Shikari spoke into his mind. *We will face him together.*

Jak sprinted for the steps, but as Tonovan ran into the corridor behind him, Jak worried that even Shikari wouldn't be able to help. The whole point of those weapons was that they let people like Sorath and Tezi hurt and even kill dragons. What if Tonovan sank the axe into Shikari's head?

The thought almost made Jak turn around to face Tonovan on his own, no matter what the repercussions, but Shikari spoke again.

Come up on the deck. This time, there was a hint of magical compulsion in the words.

Jak found that he couldn't resist it, and his legs churned, carrying him up the steps. He lunged around a corner so quickly that he clunked his wrist and the stealth device against the wall, and it emitted an offended chirp. Not pausing to check it, Jak continued through a hatchway and onto the open deck. He half-expected to run into the officer who'd questioned him earlier, but it was Thorn Company who were on their feet, the women armed and waiting as they faced the hatch. Even some of the roamers had joined them, though few of them had weapons beyond fishing spears and knives.

Shikari stood in front of their formation with Ferroki and Tezi. Tezi had acquired another axe, though it lacked the power and luster of the dragon-steel blade. She nodded at him, as if she already knew what he'd done, and hefted her weapon in preparation for a fight.

The mage officers Jak had seen earlier were still on deck, but they were only frowning in confusion at the mercenaries and also toward the hatch, as Tonovan's furious shouts preceded him.

Jak ran toward Thorn Company, whirling as he skidded to a stop next to Shikari. He might have fallen over, but he caught himself with a hand on the dragonling's back.

The rest of the mercenaries raised their weapons as Tonovan ran out, the dragon-steel axe raised. His eyes focused on Jak, and he didn't seem to see the sixty people ready to fight him. Shikari, Ferroki, Tezi, and several others sprang in front of Jak to protect him.

Unfortunately, the mage officers also stepped forward, raising their arms. To put a stop to the mercenaries?

Shikari emanated power, and whatever attack the mages tried didn't affect anyone. Further, an oar from one of the lifeboats flew over and slid between Tonovan's legs as he ran. He tripped and went down.

Jak willed the axe to fly from his hands and back into the grip of its rightful owner, but Tonovan managed to keep ahold of it. He would have rolled and jumped right back to his feet, but Shikari sprang onto his chest, all four legs coming down on him.

Tonovan tried to buck the dragonling off and swing the axe at him, but Shikari planted a taloned foot on each of his arms, talons digging in. Tonovan roared, defeated by dragon weight instead of dragon magic.

I might have been wrong, Jak thought at Shikari. *It's possible you could take down a moose now.*

Shikari turned his neck to look back at Jak and bare his teeth in a dragon version of a smile. *Obviously.*

As Tonovan tried to wriggle out from under his dragon captor, Rivlen strode out of the hatchway, gripping her shoulder with her opposite hand and scowling ferociously. The look she turned on Jak was far from grateful.

I'm sorry, he told her telepathically. *I had to do it. I should have done it a long time ago.*

Her scowl only grew more pronounced. "Get that dragon off my commanding officer!"

The command seemed to be for her crew, but Jak was the one she skewered with her glare.

Rivlen strode toward Tonovan's side and looked like she

wanted to shove Shikari away, but she might have decided that wasn't wise and instead made shooing motions at him, as if he were a bee hovering around a piece of cake. Under other circumstances, Jak might have laughed.

Shikari? Step back, please. But be ready. Tonovan still looks crabby.

An understatement. The glower Tonovan was giving Jak promised his death.

He is a very crabby human, Shikari agreed and hopped off Tonovan, but not without, judging by Tonovan's hiss and wince, sinking those talons in.

Snarling, Tonovan stopped glaring long enough to roll to his feet. He came up facing Rivlen.

"Your boy attacked me. I want him killed. And I want all the mercenaries and *dragons* who helped him put to death." The fact that he wasn't promising to handle it himself gave Jak hope. Hope that he'd succeeded, that the kerzor was working and Tonovan didn't have any power beyond what the axe lent him. If he *had* still had access to magic, he would have killed Jak himself by now.

"He took your power?" Rivlen eyed the kerzor.

"For the *moment*, maybe, but don't think for a second that I won't figure out how to remove this. I'm no idiot."

"No?" Rivlen looked around at all the mercenaries and mages, people to whom Tonovan had just admitted he was powerless. Her gaze lingered on Tezi.

"*No.*" Tonovan hefted the axe. "Kill the boy, or *I will.*"

"I'll put him in the brig until I can speak with King Uthari," Rivlen said.

Tonovan stepped closer to her, using his greater height like a weapon. "If you'd put him in the brig when I ordered you to, this wouldn't have happened. Something that *I'll* be sure to tell Uthari when *we* raise him on the dome-jir."

Rivlen clenched her jaw and didn't back away from him, but

she also didn't have an answer, and Jak grimaced, afraid he'd gotten her in deeper trouble. What if Uthari believed she'd been complicit in his attack?

Tonovan shook the axe, as if he might yet try to cleave her head off, but he stalked toward the communication cabin instead.

"Lieutenants Jayhoth and Urblon," Rivlen said to two of her men. "Put Jak in the brig and activate the wards so that neither he nor his dragon can use their power to break him out."

"Yes, ma'am." The one named Jayhoth smiled. He was the officer who'd stopped Jak earlier.

The mercenaries looked to Ferroki as the mages strode toward Jak, but she shook her head. Thorn Company might have been willing to protect him from Tonovan after his power had been nullified, but they wouldn't turn on Rivlen and her crew when they were stuck on her ship. Jak couldn't blame them. At the moment, they didn't have a single dragon-steel weapon to use against mages who pushed them around with magic.

Do you want me to bite them? Shikari asked as the mages gripped Jak's arms and patted him down.

I guess not. I don't care about irking Tonovan, but I don't want to fight Rivlen. Jak was already distressed that he'd disappointed her. Just because he'd done the right thing—he refused to believe he'd made a mistake—didn't mean she would forgive him.

Belatedly, he remembered the stealth device. It was half hanging off his wrist and must have been deactivated when he'd hit it against the wall, for nobody had trouble seeing him. He reached for it, fantasies of springing free and reactivating it coming to mind, but one of the officers got there first. The man pulled it off Jak's wrist. Jak tried to use his magic to snatch it back, but the other mage swatted him in the face with a gust of power. It struck his already battered nose, and tears sprang to Jak's eyes.

Are you sure you don't want me to bite them? Shikari asked.

No. Jak sighed and let the mages direct him toward the hatchway. *But don't. Let's just see what happens.*

Jak prayed that the wards Rivlen had mentioned weren't strong enough to defeat a dragon, but even if he escaped, what would he do and where would he go? His mother was back on the *Serene Waters* already approaching Utharika, and the *Star Flyer* was soaring a thousand feet above a ravaged Temril with dragons on the horizon.

Shoulders slumped in defeat, Jak let the mages drop him into one of the familiar oubliettes in a corridor near the engineering hold. It was the same one he and his mother had been deposited in when they'd first been taken prisoner. Sadly, she wasn't there with him to create a sticky glue for their hands to let them climb the walls.

Once at the bottom, he sank to his butt, pulled his knees up, and let his head clunk back against the wall while he wondered dully what Tonovan would say to Uthari—and what Uthari would say back.

Rivlen did her best to keep her face masked in an expression of cool professionalism as she stood in the communications cabin with her arms crossed over her chest. Her mind whirred with a confusing tangle of thoughts that included frustration toward Jak, *fear* for Jak, and guilt and disgust with herself. A full day and night earlier, she'd glimpsed that damn kerzor in Jak's thoughts, and she hadn't confronted him about it.

No, she'd been too busy enjoying having him between her legs as he stroked her hair and told her how wonderful she was. Rivlen didn't doubt that he had shared genuine feelings—he was too guileless to manipulate a woman, and she'd invited him into her quarters, not the other way around—but that hardly mattered.

She'd seen betrayal in his mind, and she hadn't done anything about it.

In addition to creating that *thing*, he'd turned against her people in Temrok's palace, siding with the king and his wife instead of helping Tonovan. Not that she hated him much for that —their actions had gone against what she believed was right, and she hadn't wanted to help Tonovan either. But the kerzor and stealing the power of a fellow mage... That was unacceptable.

If Tonovan didn't manage to kill Jak himself, Uthari would order someone else to do it. Her?

Her gut twisted at the thought. Could she kill Jak?

If Uthari ordered it and she didn't want to lose her career— and possibly her life—it would be a command she dared not disobey. She swallowed and hoped Uthari *didn't* order it, that he had some plan for Jak and considered him too valuable to lose.

A few feet away, Tonovan leaned over the dome-jir, patting it with his hand. The crystal remained dark and dull. Was Uthari sleeping and not willing to accept his communication tonight? Or had the *Serene Waters* run into trouble that kept him busy? And was it wrong for Rivlen to hope that Uthari wouldn't respond until morning? She needed time to sort through her thoughts and figure out what she should do.

"What is *wrong* with this thing?" Tonovan slapped the crystal, and it wobbled but remained dark. He eyed the axe he'd leaned against the desk, as if smashing the dome-jir with the blade might be the answer.

Rivlen blinked with realization. "You need magic to activate it."

Tonovan bared his teeth at her, but he didn't comment on the statement of the obvious. They both knew that, and they'd both forgotten. Because Tonovan had never not had magic.

"You activate it then." He jerked his hand toward it.

Though Rivlen would have preferred to wait until morning, she stepped forward and rested a hand on the dome-jir, conjuring an image of Uthari to create a link to his closest communications device. A part of her wanted to protect Jak, and pretend she couldn't get through, but this was too important not to report.

What if Jak had more of those things? He'd apologized, but that didn't mean he and his mage-hating mother didn't have plans to jam them into the heads of every magic user in the world. Rivlen shuddered at the thought of being in bed with Jak and having him stick one in *her* head while she was distracted. Though she didn't want to believe he would ever do that to her, it was hard not to let the niggling thought into her mind. The *what if.*

Uthari's head and shoulders formed in the air above the dome-jir.

Rivlen took a deep breath. "Your Majesty. I apologize for reaching out so late, but there's been an incident."

"An *incident?*" Tonovan grabbed her arm and shoved her aside.

She raised her barrier to push him away, but he'd already released her. He slammed both palms onto the desk that held the dome-jir as he leaned close to Uthari's face.

"Your *wild-one* boy stuck a device in my head to steal my magic." Tonovan jabbed a finger at his temple, turning so Uthari would see.

Always aloof, distant, and calm, Uthari didn't swear or even appear that surprised. "I ordered Malek to destroy the one they brought back from Vran. Where did Jak get that?"

"I don't know. I can't read his mind anymore."

Rivlen was off to the side, but she was still within sight of the dome-jir, and Uthari's gaze shifted toward her. He raised his white eyebrows expectantly. It worried her that he believed she would know.

She shook her head. "I don't know, Your Majesty, but the engineer Vinjo is still with us, operating the gateship."

"The boy could have made it himself," Tonovan said. "On our

mission to Nargnoth, he was talking the engineer into teaching him about tools and devices. I reported that to you, Your Majesty."

"Yes, you did. You reported everything."

Was there the faintest hint of condemnation and maybe exasperation in Uthari's tone? Rivlen hoped so, but she didn't know if it was for Tonovan or the situation.

"That boy is dangerous," Tonovan said. "I don't know why you've been coddling him or even letting him live, much less allowing his instruction. All Malek has done is make him *more* dangerous."

"Are you sure you want to question me," Uthari asked coolly, "given the situation you now find yourself in?"

Tonovan leaned back, his hand twitching toward the axe, but he didn't grab it and brandish it toward Uthari. What would he do? Threaten his monarch from a thousand miles away?

"Forgive me, Your Majesty. I'm frustrated. Rivlen won't kill the boy for his crime, and I'm—" He curled his fingers in the air near his temple and snapped them into a fist. "I would have a hard time doing it myself at the moment."

"He's not wandering the deck free after attacking an officer, is he?" Uthari looked at Rivlen.

"He's in the brig, Your Majesty. Pending the outcome of this meeting." Though she didn't want to ask it, she made herself add, "What do you wish done to him?"

Not death, she hoped. Not for this.

Even if Jak making and using a kerzor felt like a betrayal, she couldn't help but delight in the situation Tonovan found himself in. If Uthari hadn't given her that lecture about working with him and informed her that his death would be investigated, Rivlen might have finished him off herself. The axe made that more difficult than it would have been without it, but when the dragonling had been pinning him down, it wouldn't have been that hard to rush up and slice a dagger across Tonovan's throat.

"For that crime," Uthari said, "Jak must be killed."

Rivlen struggled not to let her anguish show on her face. Tonovan clenched his fist again, this time in triumph.

"Malek will be upset," Uthari continued, "but even he must admit the boy crossed a line."

"A *huge* line," Tonovan said, righteous satisfaction in his eyes. "He must be tortured extensively and killed. I will handle it personally."

Rivlen imagined Tonovan torturing Jak for days before ending his life, hearing Jak's screams as they echoed from the brig. As much as it would horrify her, maybe she should ask to kill him herself. She could make it quick and clean. But... she didn't want to do it at all. She closed her eyes, and Jak's smiling face came to mind as he burbled about how manly he was and how much chest hair he had.

"Perhaps you should get him to remove that device first," Uthari said dryly.

Tonovan's fingers twitched toward it again. "How?"

"I don't know. You might want to ask Malek for the details. I understand he underwent surgery during a dragon battle."

"I'd rather lick my own ass."

"Than speak with Malek or than undergo surgery?" Uthari sounded faintly amused.

Tonovan growled.

"If you can't bring yourself to speak with my zidarr, you'll have to get the information from the boy."

"*Gladly.*"

"I can get it from him," Rivlen heard herself volunteer. It was true. She was sure she could, but mostly she spoke up because she didn't want Uthari to give Tonovan permission to torture Jak.

"I'll *bet* you can," Tonovan said to her, then looked at Uthari again. "You know they're having sex, Your Majesty? You may want to question your loyal captain to see if she knew anything about this in advance."

Panic rose in Rivlen's chest, but she froze her face, refusing to let her fear show.

Uthari's eyes narrowed as he watched her. "Is this true, Captain?"

Normally, Uthari wouldn't ask her about who she slept with, nor would he care, she was sure, but this was a unique situation.

"I took him to my bed the night before last," she said. "I have no strong feelings for him and certainly no desire to join him in plotting against mages. He told me nothing of his plans." All true except for the part about her having no feelings for him. As much as she would prefer not to, she couldn't deny that she cared for Jak. She was glad there were so many miles between her and Uthari. This time, he couldn't ask her to lower her mental barriers and share her thoughts with him—share the full truth.

"That's fortunate, since you might have been tempted to let him strike at a certain mage if you knew about it." Uthari slanted a glance toward Tonovan.

He was far too perceptive. And it worried Rivlen that she *had* known about the kerzor. Oh, not the details or what Jak had planned to do, but if Uthari scraped through her thoughts and learned everything, would the truth be enough to save her?

Rivlen made herself lift her chin and hold his gaze. "You told me not to scheme against *certain* mages, Your Majesty, and I have not."

"Good, but you'll forgive me if I want to discuss this further when the fleet is reunited."

Once more, Rivlen fought hard to keep her panic off her face. It would be days before that happened, and a lot could occur in that time. With luck, the entire fleet would be far too busy dealing with dragons for Uthari to remember his threat.

"Of course, Your Majesty. I understand."

"I'll torture him now and learn how to have this thing removed," Tonovan said.

"I'm certain you will torture him," Uthari said, his tone turning dry again, "but let Rivlen get that information from him. If she's had sex with him, he probably *will* babble everything he knows to her. Young men tend to be grateful when beautiful women sleep with them."

"I may gag," Tonovan said.

"I'll get the information from him, Your Majesty," Rivlen said.

"Do so. I want my general operating at full capacity. If he doesn't have his power back by the next dragon battle, he won't be much good to us."

Rivlen sensed one of the very dragons they were discussing, one of the ones that had been on the perimeter of her awareness since shortly after they'd left the sky city. Earlier, it had been maintaining a steady distance, but it was coming closer now, and it was in the *Star Flyer's* flight path.

"I haven't lost everything, Your Majesty." Tonovan held up the axe. "The mercenary girl dropped it, and I claimed it for our fleet and our people. It was foolish of Malek to leave it in the hands of a mundane female whose highest purpose in life should be wiggling her boobs and writhing under a man."

Indignation flared within Rivlen, and she hoped there *was* no way for Jak to reverse what the device had done to Tonovan. As soon as the dragon threat was gone, and Uthari realized he didn't need Tonovan that badly anymore, Rivlen might be willing to help the mercenaries finish him off.

"Agreed," Uthari said.

That disappointed Rivlen—perhaps it had been in vain, but she'd hoped Uthari would be as noble as Malek and order Tonovan to return it—but she didn't say anything. She was already in water too deep to try to defend Tezi and her axe.

"Keep it safe, General," Uthari added. "You're going to need it until you resolve your other issue."

"I understand. Rivlen." Tonovan spun toward her. "We're going to the brig to question your mutinous lover."

Rivlen shook her head. "That'll have to wait."

He squinted at her. "*Why?*"

"The dragons are coming."

17

From his cell under the corridor, the grate closed high above, Jak sensed dragons in the distance. Three? Four? They kept flying in and out of range of his senses. At one point, one had headed straight toward the ship, and he'd been certain it would attack, but it had veered off and soared out to join another.

Were they wary because the last attack hadn't gone completely their way? Maybe the dragon that had lost the tip of its tail had warned the others about Tezi's axe. No, *Tonovan's* axe.

Jak grimaced, wishing he'd managed to keep his hands on it. How heroic it would have been if he could have run out on deck with it and slipped it into Tezi's grasp before Tonovan leaped out after him.

At least he'd accomplished what he'd wanted. Someone else would have to get the axe away from Tonovan. Then the general would be defenseless; if someone challenged him to a fight, he would have to resort to fisticuffs, kicking, and biting.

Jak dearly wanted to see that.

During whatever chaos the dragons brought, he hoped he would be able to escape the brig. When he and his mother had been trapped in this cell the last time, no magic had reinforced the grate. Only gravity and the bars themselves had kept them prisoners. But there had to be something that could be activated when mages were imprisoned, for he sensed a barrier up there now, stretched across the opening. It was strong enough that he wouldn't be able to get out, even if he could climb or levitate himself up there, unless someone came along and turned it off.

As time passed, Jak stretched out with his senses, searching for Rivlen and tempted to reach out to her. But what could he say? He'd tried, *I'm sorry*, and she hadn't responded.

Earlier, he'd sensed her in the communications cabin. Speaking with Uthari? What had the king said about all this?

Jak wished he could warn his mother.

"Maybe I can," he mused.

Normal mages couldn't speak telepathically from hundreds of miles away, but those with great power reputedly could. Even Jak had managed to reach out to Malek once before when he'd been at sea and Jak had been in Port Toh-drom. The *Serene Waters* was farther away now than Malek's ship had been then, but Mother had great power, so maybe that would help.

Closing his eyes, he envisioned her face and willed his mental energy in her direction. *Mother? Can you hear me?*

Long, silent seconds passed.

He tried again, though he realized it was late and she might be sleeping. *Mother? It's Jak, and I need to warn you about something I did that... might not have been wise. You better wake up.*

I was afraid you would do something unwise when you went off with Rivlen, came a distant muzzy reply. Mother *did* sound sleepy.

My unwise thing didn't involve her. His reply might have been tarter than necessary, but he didn't want any blame to go Rivlen's way. *It's about Tonovan.* Instead of sending more words, he shared an image of Tonovan with the kerzor in his temple.

Oh dear.

Shikari helped me finalize the magic so the device works. Tonovan isn't happy with me, and I'm in the brig.

You're lucky not to be dead.

I know. Especially considering Tonovan also stole Tezi's axe. Jak almost mentioned that there was plenty of time left for Tonovan to kill him, but that would only make her worry. *I'll be fine,* he assured her, *and I don't regret doing it, but I'm worried he'll whine to Uthari, and Uthari will take it out on you. Has he been by yet?*

Not yet. How long ago did this happen?

Recently. You might want to brace yourself.

I'll see if I can protect your grandfather.

Good, and protect yourself. Please. I'm not sure you can count on Malek. If he reacts the way Rivlen did, he might be pissed.

Possibly. He did not enjoy his experience with a kerzor.

I know. I hope Tonovan doesn't enjoy it equally as much.

I hope he doesn't kill you.

I won't let him. Shikari will protect me. Jak didn't point out that he was in a cell, and Shikari was on the deck, unable to come down and help. *He deserved it. Oh, Mother? Temril was awful. Uthari ordered Tonovan not to help the citizens but to take advantage of them. They'd already had their island and sky city largely destroyed by the dragons, and Tonovan killed the king and the queen.* Jak shared his memories of the events.

He's a despicable man.

Jak didn't know if she meant Tonovan or Uthari but decided the word applied to both.

Is the Star Flyer *heading back to rejoin the fleet?* Mother asked after a couple of moments of quiet as she no doubt digested what Jak had shared. *We're flying over Agorval now and may need help keeping the same thing from befalling our continent. Also, I'd prefer to have you back with me so I can keep an eye on you.* Her telepathic voice grew softer as she added, *So I can protect you.*

I'm not sure. There are dragons in our way.

Be careful.

A clang sounded, and Jak looked up toward the flickering light in the corridor, little of its orange glow penetrating the gloom of his cell. One of the mage crewmen was coming and... someone else. Jak didn't *sense* Tonovan—and wouldn't anymore, since his aura was stifled along with his magic—but he sensed the dragon-steel axe and sagged against the wall.

Boots passed over his grate, and Jak glimpsed Tonovan's red uniform and the shaft of the axe as he continued down the corridor. Metal jangled. Keys? Tools? Jak grimaced. *Torture implements?*

Tonovan returned and gazed down through the grate, the flickering orange light giving his face a demonic cast.

"Since I can't use my power, I'll have to torture you the old-fashioned way." Tonovan held up a long serrated blade made from black iron.

He must have locked up the dragon-steel dagger in his quarters, for Jak didn't sense it on him. Not that it mattered when he had the axe.

"Savage." Tonovan turned the serrated blade, admiring it. "But I think I might enjoy physically cutting you."

Jak licked his lips. "Does Rivlen know you're here?"

"Who do you think sent me?"

Jak shook his head. He didn't believe that. She hadn't been *that* angry with him... had she?

Tonovan smiled broadly and flipped a lever on the wall.

Jak stood up, wondering if this could be an opportunity to escape. He might not be able to attack Tonovan when he held that axe, but if no magical barrier blocked the exit, he could levitate himself up.

"Lower me down, and reactivate the grate," Tonovan said to someone.

"Yes, sir."

The mage crewman who'd also come in. Jak had forgotten he was there. Damn.

He'd hoped that everyone would stop following Tonovan's orders once he lost his power, but he was a general until Uthari said he wasn't. Maybe Tonovan would lose his rank if he never got his power back, but Jak didn't know. It was also possible the crew feared to act against him because they didn't know if this was a temporary state. They probably worried Tonovan would later be able to take revenge on people who crossed him.

Jak clenched a fist. He'd thought all he would have to do was embed the kerzor, and karma would handle the rest. Surely, someone was aching to drive a dagger into Tonovan's chest.

"I can't levitate you while you're holding that, sir."

"A boon and a bane," Tonovan grumbled.

"Why don't you leave it up there?" Jak called. "And we'll have our chat man to man, no magical weapons protecting anyone."

Tonovan snorted. "I'd still kick your ass, boy."

"You'd be welcome to try." Jak didn't believe for a second that he couldn't deal with someone without power.

Despite his bravado, when Tonovan swung down, grabbing the lip and lowering himself before letting go and landing in a crouch, he had the axe in hand. The speed with which he spun to face Jak suggested he wasn't positive that Jak couldn't do anything.

Jak ground his teeth, sorely tempted, but he didn't know what he could do in the empty cell. There weren't any oars or lifeboats to hurl at Tonovan.

The grate clanked back into place, the magical barrier returning. Trapping Jak down here with one of his two most hated enemies. Uthari was the other, even if the old wizard wasn't as openly nasty and menacing. Uthari willfully employed this beast, and he'd punished Malek. They both deserved a kerzor.

"Funny how well I can read your mind even without magic." Tonovan had sheathed the serrated blade for the jump down, but he pulled it out now, gripping it in one hand and the big axe in the other. "How do I remove this thing without pulling out half my brain matter?"

The image the kerzor had shared with him must have been impressive if he believed that would happen. Good.

"You don't," Jak said.

"You removed it from Malek."

"Shikari did. You'll have to ask him."

"If that's true, then there's little point in me asking you questions." Tonovan's eyes closed to slits, and he smiled. "Or keeping you alive."

"Well, Shikari likes me. If I were alive, he would be more likely to help you. If I were dead, he'd mourn terribly and definitely would not help you."

"We'll see," Tonovan said softly and prowled forward. "He'll do a lot for a few pieces of fish."

Jak sank into a crouch, though he didn't know if he meant to spring away or spring at his enemy. He doubted he could survive a physical battle with Tonovan, but there wasn't room in the cell to run.

Tonovan lunged, swinging the axe. Jak ducked under it and dove to the side. When he hit the floor, he rolled and came up with his fists raised. But the serrated blade was already slicing toward his face. He jerked his head back, but in the confining space, he cracked it on the wall. The tip of the knife slashed into his cheek.

Jak kicked up, trying to knock Tonovan's arm away, but his other arm—and that deadly axe—swung toward him. Jak squatted low to avoid both blades, but that left him open to attack. Pushing off the wall, he threw himself at Tonovan's legs, trying to tackle him to the floor.

But Tonovan cracked him on the head with the axe handle and twisted, jumping free of his grasp. Though dazed, Jak got his arm up to block the next swing, the knife whistling toward his face again. He leaped back, wishing he had more space to maneuver—and that he had a weapon of his own.

He summoned his magic to wrap a protective barrier around himself, but a swing from the axe made it pop painfully. Jak stumbled back, his shoulder blades ramming against another wall. Tonovan pressed the axe blade against his neck, and Jak froze. The edge dug in, and blood trickled down his throat.

Tonovan paused. Relishing the moment?

Rivlen? Jak called. *Is there any chance you didn't send Tonovan down here to kill me and want to help me live? Because I'd appreciate it.*

Without his power, Tonovan couldn't have heard Jak's telepathic plea, but he knew he could kill Jak, and he smiled cruelly. "I'd hoped to do this in front of your mother," he whispered, leaning the edge deeper into Jak's throat, "before I plowed my cock into her and taught her obedience."

Anger ripped through Jak, and he glanced up, willing the crewman to come down and help, to pull Tonovan off him and pummel him as mercilessly as he deserved. But he would never get past the mental defenses of a trained mage. He had to try something else.

With a roar of power like a flooding river tearing through a canyon, he willed a wave of energy to overpower the magical barrier and yank the grate from its hinges. He was too angry to doubt that it would work; he simply summoned all of his willpower and demanded that it did.

Metal wrenched and screeched, and Tonovan jerked his head up in surprise. The grate not only tore free from its hinges but it warped so that it could fit into the cell. It plummeted downward, sharp points angling toward Tonovan.

He sprang back from Jak, but there was nowhere to run. The grate slammed onto him, metal gouging into his flesh, the points barely missing Jak as he sucked in his belly.

The axe clattered as Tonovan released it. Jak took a step, but the weapon was under the grate, the same as Tonovan.

Someone jumped down from above, startling Jak. He pressed his back against the wall again.

It was the mage crewman. He landed on the grate, his sword drawn.

Jak raised his barrier, expecting an attack as Tonovan cursed from under the grate—having the man's weight on him had to make being crushed under it that much worse. But the crewman's eyes were glazed, and he didn't attack Jak. He bent and stabbed his sword between the bars, piercing Tonovan's thigh.

Tonovan screamed, and Jak gaped in confusion. Then he realized he'd asked for this when he'd tried to compel the officer to help. For a shocked moment, all he could do was stare, unable to believe he'd had the power to override the mental defenses of an experienced mage.

The officer stabbed Tonovan again, sword sinking into his abdomen. Tonovan screamed and thrashed, but with the grate on top of him and the man on top of *it*, he couldn't escape.

Jak opened his mouth and summoned his magic, knowing he should stop the man, knowing he shouldn't let him kill Tonovan, but he hesitated. After what the bastard had said about his mother and after all the evil he'd done in the world...

Jak closed his mouth and scooted to the side, then stepped onto the grate and reached through it for the axe. It clunked against the bars. There wasn't a gap wide enough to pull it through. Jak stared at the bars, walling off his heart to the screams of agony four feet away, and envisioned molten lava spewing from a volcano on the map in his mind. Several bars melted, steam wafting up around his face, and he pulled the axe free through the gap.

"What's going *on* down there?" Rivlen yelled from above.

Shame slammed into Jak like a punch, and he willed the

crewman to stop attacking Tonovan. The man straightened, his bloody sword loose in his hand, and looked blearily around.

Jak wiped at sweat—or was that blood?—in his eyes and made himself look up at Rivlen. "Tonovan came to torture me." Chagrined at what he'd let go on beside him—at what he'd willed the crewman to do—Jak blurted, "He said you told him to do it." It was more to deflect attention from himself than because he believed that and blamed her.

Rivlen swore as she looked down into the cell. "What a mess. Holkineth, what were you doing? Get up here." She flicked her finger and levitated the officer out of the cell.

"I... don't know, ma'am." His face was puzzled as he peered down at his sword before disappearing from Jak's view as he landed in the corridor.

"Get off him, Jak." Rivlen pointed at Tonovan, still pinned under the grate. He was panting in pain, still alive, though he bled copiously.

Jak didn't release the axe as he stepped off the grate and against the wall. He might be a prisoner, but he intended to make sure the blade got back to Tezi, one way or another.

With another whisper of power, Rivlen levitated the warped grate. Tonovan screamed again as a jagged piece of metal was yanked out of his shoulder.

A clatter sounded above as Rivlen tossed the destroyed grate onto the floor in the corridor. She scowled down at Tonovan, then levitated him upward as well.

"Get the medic," she said over her shoulder as Tonovan slowly rose, dripping blood onto the floor.

"Yes, ma'am," the officer said.

Tonovan soon disappeared from Jak's view until only Rivlen remained, hands on her hips as she stared down at him.

Jak watched her warily, not sure where he stood with her, especially now. Her face was hard to read as she regarded him back with a steady gaze.

Footsteps sounded in the corridor, and Jak sensed mages arriving. They lifted Tonovan and took him back the way they'd come. To the ship's sickbay, where he would no doubt be healed, left alive to torment people again.

Though Jak was ashamed that he'd stood aside and let human suffering happen—no, that he'd given the order to cause that suffering—he couldn't help but think he should have given the crewman less vague orders. *Plunge the sword into his heart.*

That was the compulsion he *should* have given. Maybe his mother and grandfather would have been ashamed of Jak when they found out, but wouldn't it have been for the best? For the good of the world? In not finishing Tonovan off tonight, he might have made a mistake that he would live to regret.

Rivlen sprang down, using her magic to lighten her landing, and faced him. "You had to destroy my cell while you were defending yourself?"

He couldn't tell if there was a hint of amusement in her tone or only exasperation. Her face said the latter, that she was exasperated with him and her mage officer and the whole situation.

"He had the dragon steel." Jak licked his lips. "I needed something to throw at him."

"So you chose my grate and my *crewman*?"

"There wasn't anything else around. If you would kindly place some decorative daggers on your cell walls, I wouldn't have to resort to vandalism." He tried a smile, though he highly doubted she would respond to it.

Rivlen glanced at the axe in his grip.

"I took it back for Tezi," Jak said, not wanting her to believe he was contemplating using it on her. He also didn't hand it to her. Even though he wanted to trust her fully, he wasn't positive she would give it back to Tezi.

"I know." Rivlen drew a kerchief from her uniform pocket and stepped closer.

She touched it to his cheek, and he almost flinched. In the heat of the battle, he hadn't felt the wounds he'd received, but he now remembered the knife cutting him. He stifled the pain and lifted his chin, not wanting to appear weak in front of Rivlen.

"Tonovan wants you dead, and Uthari agrees it's necessary, that you've become too much of a threat, but I did *not* tell Tonovan to torture you." Rivlen shifted the kerchief to dab at the wound dribbling blood into his eye. "There are dragons out there. I said we needed to deal with them before worrying about you, and that *I* would ask you how to remove the kerzor. *Without* torture."

"And then you'd kill me?" he asked softly.

Her voice had been stern, but her touch was gentle, and he longed to believe she would stand beside him, that she would help him escape before they got back to the fleet so that he wouldn't have to face Uthari's wrath.

"Holkineth isn't weak," she whispered, her face close to his as she kept dabbing at his wounds.

"Pardon?"

"The officer you compelled to attack Tonovan. He's a strong mage. Did Shikari help you?"

"No. I was just..." Jak licked his lips. "Angry."

Rivlen's gaze lowered to his lips. "I've told you how I'm drawn to powerful mages."

He meant to say something intelligent, perhaps ask her how she'd intended to get the information about the kerzor removal out of him, but she leaned against him, and all that came out was, "Yeah." He was impressed it wasn't squeaky.

She kissed him, her mouth hungry, passionate—aroused. The axe slid out of Jak's fingers and clunked to the floor. He started to lean down to pick it up again, afraid to release it for a second on this ship, but Rivlen's hand slid around to the back of his head and she leaned more fully into him.

You'll touch me, not a hunk of metal, she ordered.

"Yeah," he croaked in agreement, his lips against hers, his body awakening to the realization that whatever was going on with Uthari and Tonovan, she wanted him.

Jak wrapped his arms around her, pushing his hand up to tug her hair out of her bun so he could run his fingers through it. She nipped at his lip and rubbed against him, eliciting the fire of desire all along his nerves.

Are you going to seduce me to get what you want? He wondered if she'd told Uthari *how* she would get the information from Jak.

You are what I want.

What about the kerzor? As Jak pushed his hands under her uniform jacket, sliding them along her sleek, warm skin, he decided he should stop asking questions and simply enjoy this. Enjoy *her.*

Don't make any more of them.

And the one that's already been inserted?

I'll deny it if you tell anyone, but I like it where it is. I'm sorry I didn't come a minute later and that my duty compelled me to stop you— no, that my fear of losing my career did. She unfastened his belt.

I wouldn't tell anyone. He unfastened *her* belt. *I don't want you to lose your career. I want to support you.*

I know you do. And that arouses me almost as much as your power. And how you're going to use it on me. She slid images into his mind of her writhing under his touch, physical and magical.

You're a demanding woman, he thought as he complied, thankful she seemed to be on his side. At least for the moment.

He couldn't expect her to stand up to Uthari for him, but maybe she would help him escape his wrath. Though as she groaned against his mouth, he wasn't even sure he cared about the future. Right now, all he wanted was to be with her.

I'm the captain. Take me, Jak.
Yes, ma'am.

As rain fell from gray clouds above, the *Serene Waters* reached the kingdom of Uth. Home.

Jadora sensed the land and the cities and the people below, and she took a break from her plants and parasites to head up to the deck. She wanted to see her homeland with her own eyes. She wished she could also see her *son* with her own eyes. The last she'd heard from Jak, he was in the brig on the *Star Flyer*, his fate up in the air.

If only she were there to help. The idea of Jak in danger a thousand miles away filled her with anxiety.

Even more anxiety washed over her when she stepped out into the rain only to have Uthari walk out of his suite a moment later.

"Let's take a walk, Professor," he said, his eyes cooler than usual.

He'd heard about the kerzor. She knew it before he said a word.

"Off the plank?" Jadora couldn't manage a smile to go with the joke. Perhaps because it might not be a joke.

"Not while I still need you." Uthari didn't deny that it might be an option after she finished her work.

She thought about mentioning that the Jitaruvak had sprouted. It was the only good news she had, but Malek had likely already relayed that information to Uthari.

More motes had appeared in the dishes, and she'd had no luck destroying them or the parasites growing underneath them. She'd also lost her option to hurl the dishes over the railing and into the ocean. That might not have been a solution, as they could have floated until they washed ashore somewhere. She doubted dumping the parasites from a great height would kill them. Not when intense fire and other types of magic couldn't. And then they would be here in Uth, waiting for a possible host to come along. She still didn't know if dragons were the only hosts the parasites would take or if lesser beings might serve for a time. Lesser beings like humans.

"I do miss the days when I could read your thoughts," Uthari said, watching her face.

"They're grim. I don't think you'd enjoy them."

"No? I thought they might be of my shirtless zidarr."

Jadora wished Malek was present, shirtless or not, but she sensed him belowdecks in the yacht's kitchen. Apparently, he didn't order the staff to bring meals to him in his suite.

"Do women often scowl with worried looks in their eyes as they ponder him?" Jadora was positive she hadn't had a pleasant expression on her face.

"Enemies sometimes." Uthari's eyes narrowed. "It would be a shame for him to become such to you."

Jadora had thought Uthari was past contemplating ordering Malek to kill her, but after Jak's actions, perhaps not. She hoped Malek cared too much about her to follow such a command, but she wouldn't know for certain until Uthari gave that order and he disobeyed. Or didn't.

"Yes," was all she said.

Uthari walked to the railing and gazed down at the forests and farmlands below, leaves on deciduous trees starting to turn color. As they'd flown north, a crispness had entered the air, and the scents of fall foliage wafted to them. A wave of homesickness came over Jadora as she remembered walks through the trees on campus, on her way from one office to the next, or to join her late husband for a picnic lunch in the grass at the park as geese strutted around on the bank of the pond.

She shook her head at the memory, though she couldn't help

but miss him—and wonder if Malek would ever deign to join her for something as lowly as a picnic lunch. He probably would if the world ever allowed them that peace.

"We're going over to the *Soaring Eagle*." Uthari pointed to the mageship that held the portal, the great dragon-steel artifact strapped down on its deck. "I want you to try something."

"Speaking with it?" she guessed.

Since Jak wasn't here, and the portal had zapped Uthari the last time he'd given it a command, he might want to know if someone else could access it. The idea of commanding it to send lightning bolts into the hearts of enemies chilled her, but perhaps she could do it if those enemies were dragons that were destroying her world. Earlier, when that dragon had been carrying her away, it had occurred to her to try.

"Getting it to attack with lightning," Uthari said, using his magic to sweep her over the railing.

He followed after her, levitating himself without need for a skyboard. As they floated over, he watched her, and she wondered if he was contemplating letting her drop. If he did, she could levitate herself, as long as a dragon tail didn't hit her in the head.

She reached out with her senses, wondering if they were nearing dragons now. Why else would Uthari be asking this unless a daunting battle lay ahead of them?

It amazed her how far she could sense, feeling the auras of the mages on all the ships around them and far to the north, a few in garrisons on the ground and then far more in the sky—that had to be Utharika. Unfortunately, she sensed dragons as well. A couple of them were in the Sawtooth Mountains east of Utharika, and others flew around the city, as if assessing it for weaknesses. Or were they waiting for even more dragons to join them?

Jadora wondered if that chest of dragon steel had been taken to Utharika. She knew Uthari had sent it, and the blacksmith mage who'd learned to use her acid to work it, ahead of the fleet. If it was in the city, the dragons had likely been contemplating an attack for a while. Maybe they'd already tested its defenses and found they needed more firepower.

Uthari set her down next to the portal. The dragons weren't close enough to be an immediate threat, so Jadora let herself focus on him and the artifact.

"It may not respond to me." Jadora recalled how it had clearly preferred Jak when they'd been studying it early on. It had given him visions of friendly dragons frolicking in the sky. It had given *her* warnings.

"We'll see." Uthari extended his hand toward the portal, suggesting she try, but he also spoke further. "You know what he did?"

"He?"

"Your son."

"He's updated me on his current placement in a brig cell."

"He deserves *death*," Uthari said, "and if we knew how to get that kerzor out of Tonovan's head without him and his pet dragon, he would be dead already."

Jadora rested her palm on the cool dragon steel, more for support than to communicate with it. But what would happen if she asked it to attack Uthari?

Numerous officers were on deck, some watching the route ahead for threats but others watching her and Uthari. They would attack her if she convinced the portal to strike at him. She had no doubt of that. And he had survived being struck by its lightning not once but twice, so he might survive again.

"Your face is easier to read this time," Uthari said.

"You did put thoughts of Malek in my mind," Jadora said, hoping he would believe that was who she'd been contemplating.

His cool gaze said he didn't.

She looked toward the *Serene Waters*, hoping to spot Malek out on the deck, but he wasn't there. Should she reach out to him in the yacht's kitchen?

"If you try to kill me, he'll be no protection for you," Uthari said. "And I've already extracted a promise from him about what to do with you if you turn against us."

"Force me into exile on another world," she stated.

"If he won't kill you, yes. Check the portal, Professor. See if you can rouse it to use against our *enemies*."

You are my enemy, she thought but didn't say aloud or telepathically.

Before she made an effort to bestir the portal with her power, it pulsed with warmth and blue light. Uthari took a wary step back, and she sensed him wrapping more layers of protection around himself. The portal, however, focused on her, sending images into her mind, along with a sense of hope. The images were of the jungle and the pool where it had been erected, where it could operate.

You want to go back there? Jadora wondered.

Given all the deadly creatures, including the dragons, that had come through the portal, it was hard to imagine anyone vying for that. Unless the portal *wanted* humanity to fall.

It shared images of blue-scaled dragons with her, the majestic creatures flying over the jungle, some of the younger ones playing with each other. It was an ambiguous response, because it didn't show humans at all, but she guessed it represented the portal's longing for a return to the old days, to before the parasite had ravaged the dragons.

It pulsed again. An affirmative?

Next, it showed her a dark underwater place she hadn't seen before, one where orbs glowed on pedestals. The Orbs of Wisdom? They had to be.

They also pulsed, as if with a promise. To share the answers she needed? To cure the dragons?

I am not in control of your fate, and I've been told we need to deal with the dragons here—the threat to humanity—before we can return you to Zewnath. Even *after* they dealt with the dragons, if they could, Jadora wondered if Uthari and the other rulers would allow the portal to be placed where it might be opened again. Even she didn't think that was a good idea. *I'm trying to find a solution that doesn't require visiting another world.* One where the portal and the orbs were underwater. That would make accessing them difficult, if not impossible.

How deep were those orbs? Judging by the darkness of the vision, they were nowhere near the surface and sunlight.

The portal showed her an image of Uthari standing on the deck, watching it and watching her. A question seemed to accompany the image, along with a disgruntled feeling.

Did it want to know if he was the one who'd ordered the portal moved? Or maybe it already knew. It certainly knew that Uthari had been calling upon ancient magic to force it to work for him. And it resented him.

As long as it didn't resent *her.* Jadora worried the portal would be disappointed if she couldn't do what it wanted. Since Zelonsera had given her power, the portal might expect her to use it.

"What's it saying?" Uthari asked after another pulse of light.

"It doesn't speak. It's sharing images, and you have to interpret the meaning. I gather it wants to be returned to the pool in Zewnath though. There's a place it wants us to go to try to find answers about how to remove the parasites and heal the dragons."

Uthari's lip curled. "As I've told you, you can work on that *after* you synthesize my drug and we've dealt with the threat to Torvil. Utharika and the cities of Uth, including your own Sprungtown, are being attacked as we speak. There's no time to try to solve a ten-thousand-year-old problem."

"I understand," she said, though she planned to keep working on it.

With the parasites in her dish growing, and more motes popping up, she had a feeling time was of the essence. If she was forced to discard the samples, she would have to start again with new samples that could only be acquired from an infested dragon.

"Do you?" Uthari squinted at her and stepped closer. "From what I've seen of the lab, you haven't even *started* trying to synthesize the drug."

"As I told you and Malek, I need better equipment for that. I've made sure we can grow more of the Jitaruvak here on Torvil. That's progress." Jadora sensed Malek on the *Serene Waters*. He was coming up on deck, perhaps wondering what she and Uthari were doing.

"Any farmer can grow the plant. I need a formula."

"Any farmer can*not* grow the plant. It has particular requirements, including special light that replicates the natural sunlight on Nargnoth. The suns are different on each world we've visited."

"Uh huh. It appears to *me* that you're dawdling." Uthari squinted and probed her defenses.

She reinforced the barrier she'd subconsciously had up. Would he test himself against her? As she'd so often seen Tonovan do against Malek? Searching for a weakness, thinking about attacking if one could be found?

Even though she didn't want to use the power she'd been given to hurt anyone, and certainly not to *attack* anyone, the thought formed in her mind that she might be able to teach Uthari a lesson. If she proved stronger than he, she could pay him back for having hurt Malek and so many others over the years, for having allowed the despicable Tonovan to lead his forces and torment people.

A pulse of power came from the portal, not a simple flash of light this time, but energy that it directed at Uthari. His barrier didn't falter, but he stumbled back from Jadora and shot a furious, incredulous look at it.

"You told it to attack me," he said.

"No, I didn't." Jadora hoped that was true, that it hadn't read her thoughts and that she hadn't subconsciously urged it to harm him.

Malek reached the deck of the yacht, jogged for the railing, and jumped on and sprang from it. His powerful legs and a whisper of magic sent him the fifty feet between the ships, and he landed in a crouch next to Jadora and Uthari.

He started to step toward Jadora, as if to protect her, but Uthari turned his furious expression on him.

Malek stepped between them and raised his hands in a peace-making gesture. "There are dragons ahead, between us and Utharika."

"I'm aware." Uthari stood straighter and regained his calm. "The professor is *supposed* to be finding out if the portal will obey her if she commands it to attack those dragons. She's not supposed to be ordering it to attack *me*."

Malek looked at Jadora, his face difficult to read. Did he believe she'd done that? He ought to know better—know *her* better—by now.

"I believe I may be able to *request* that it help us," Jadora said, "but attacking the dragons isn't what it wants. It wants me to find a way to fix the dragons so they won't be enemies anymore."

"It understands what happened to them?" Malek asked.

"I think so."

"Just make sure it wants to protect you the next time a dragon swoops down and plucks you up." Uthari frowned at the portal. "She's the only one who might be able to help you, so you better keep her, and all of those who are protecting her, alive." He sprang onto the railing to head back to his yacht. "See me in an hour, Malek," he called over his shoulder.

Jadora almost pointed out that Uthari and his officers had

done very little to protect her, but was that true? Uthari *had* ordered Malek to keep her alive.

"It would be beneficial if it would help us against the dragons," Malek said.

"Yes. I think it might, but we might have to promise to do what *it* wants in return."

"Set it up and seek out the orbs?"

Jadora nodded.

"You don't believe you can find a way to kill the parasite without visiting them?"

"I don't know. I'm trying a lot of things. When we reach Utharika, it would be a good idea to set up a laboratory that can be completely sealed off from the rest of the castle and city. A place where I can experiment without worrying about the parasites escaping."

"I'll arrange it."

"And I'll need a full set of chemistry equipment to make Uthari's drug."

"I'll arrange that too." Malek lifted a hand toward her but hesitated and lowered it, clasping his hands behind his back instead. "I sensed the power you were gathering. Were you going to strike at Uthari?" His tone was calm and without judgment, but he watched her intently.

As she could never allow herself to forget, his first loyalty was to his king.

"I didn't want to," she said, though she remembered that brief contemplation she'd had, "but he seemed to be getting ready to attack *me*. I need to live long enough to finish this mission for the dragons. I promised them I'd do my best."

"You're a threat to him now. He knows he needs you, but he's frustrated and furious with Jak." Malek shook his head. "Uthari just lost General Tonovan, and that's the second powerful magic user in his command this month. He also lost Yidar."

"Lost?" Jadora rested her palm on the portal for support. "Tonovan is dead?"

"Not dead but powerless. As far as Uthari is concerned, he might as well be dead, unless Jak can remove that thing from his head." Malek arched his eyebrows.

"I'm sure he and Shikari can," Jadora said, though she wondered if Jak would agree to do so. Even if they threatened to kill him, he might think it was worth dying to make sure Tonovan remained impotent. The thought of losing her son terrified her.

Jadora rubbed her face with both hands. She'd been the one to suggest Jak stay on the *Star Flyer* so that Shikari wouldn't be threatened by the parasite. If she hadn't done that, Jak would still be here with her and wouldn't be in trouble. *Worse* than in trouble.

The portal pulsed. It didn't share an image, so Jadora had no idea what the pulse meant, but she hoped its message was that it would help defend Jak if Uthari tried to kill him.

"What does it want now?" Malek asked.

"I don't know."

"Be careful, Jadora," he said softly, stepping closer. "Don't threaten Uthari in any way. Please."

"What if he threatens my son?" She couldn't stand back and let the man kill Jak.

"Hopefully, it won't come to that."

"And if it does?" Jadora looked at him.

Malek couldn't expect her to stand back and do nothing, could he? He cared about Jak to some extent. She was sure of it. She'd seen them together as mentor and mentee. Sometimes, they'd almost been like father and son.

"We'll figure something out," Malek said quietly, then lifted his arms and hugged her.

She hoped he spoke the truth, that he would help her find a way to protect Jak, but if Uthari ordered Malek to kill her son, would he truly disobey?

18

"MA'AM?" CAME AN UNCERTAIN CALL FROM THE CORRIDOR ABOVE the cell where Rivlen had unwisely been giving into her passion. "Two dragons are heading toward us, and there's a druid on the dome-jir who wants to talk to you about an alliance."

"I'll be right there." Rivlen eased out of Jak's grip and grabbed the pieces of her uniform that she'd torn off for their fervent dalliance. Her heel clipped a piece of metal that had fallen off the grate. They'd had sex against the wall due to wreckage strewn about and because... it had been arousing. "What am I supposed to do with you?" she asked him.

His hair was tousled from her fingers, the cuts on his face were in need of a healer's touch, and his clothing was rumpled and torn —that which wasn't on the floor—but he grinned lopsidedly at her. "That thing you were doing five minutes ago was great."

"How can you have the aura of a man and the goofy grin of a boy?"

"I'm young at heart."

"You're young all over." Rivlen tugged her boots and trousers on, hardly able to believe the feelings she'd developed for him.

But he'd defeated Tonovan, even with the general lugging that giant axe around, and he'd halfway enslaved her lieutenant, probably not even realizing what he was doing. She hadn't taught Jak how to compel people, and she doubted Malek had either.

"But still sexy and alluring, right?"

"Maybe a little." Rivlen let herself smile at him, even though she worried about the future—about what Tonovan would tell Uthari and about what Uthari would say about her role in all this.

She'd hurried down as soon as Jak had called out for help, but a part of her wished she'd delayed. If she'd known he had gotten the situation under control and had been about to kill Tonovan through her officer... Oh, how she wished the general were dead and not simply injured. But Uthari's promise of an investigation came to mind again. Rivlen dared not let Tonovan be killed on her ship.

Besides, did she need to arrange his death when he had no power? It wasn't as if he would get it back anytime soon. She'd been there for Malek's brain surgery and knew Shikari had been responsible, that Jak had only been guiding the young dragon. And Shikari did not like Tonovan. Besides Uthari, nobody did. She wasn't even that sure about Uthari.

"You need to stay here." Rivlen glanced at the top of the oubliette with its missing grate. She would have to see if the device that controlled the magical barrier had also been destroyed.

"When dragons are coming?" Jak gripped her arm and radiated power as he said, "Let me help. You know I can."

All trace of the boy was gone, and he was the man, the mage, again. All power and confidence. *That* was the side of him that made her long for him.

"You're not trying to coerce *me* now, are you?" Rivlen asked, feeling a trace of it in his voice, though she doubted he realized he'd done it.

"Not with magic, no. Just logic." His forehead creased, and he lowered his hand. "I *wasn't* using magic, was I?"

"Yes, but I'm too powerful to be manipulated like that."

"I'm sorry. I didn't mean to try. When I urged your officer to help me, I was desperate."

"Don't apologize for using your power, Jak." Rivlen gripped his shirt and looked fiercely into his eyes, willing him to understand that his power was a useful tool, not something to shy away from, and that he could grow into a great mage, if not a wizard, if he embraced it. "The stronger you become, the less you'll have to worry about people like Tonovan."

There was uncertainty and hesitation in his eyes, but he nodded and repeated, "Let me help you with the dragons. I don't want to lose Thorn Company or *you* because I'm down here useless. I don't want to lose Shikari either."

"I doubt they'll target him. It's the dragon steel they've wanted." Rivlen, reminded that they had little time—and what did a *druid* on the dome-jir want?—crouched and used her magic to spring out of the cell and land in the corridor.

"They've shown interest in him in the past, in wanting to turn him into one of them. And if they get close and infect him with that parasite, they could do exactly that."

Rivlen looked down at Jak, debating on reactivating the barrier and trapping him down there, per Uthari's wishes, or bringing him up to the deck for the fight. She knew he was right and that he could help. Among other things, he could share his power with her to amplify her effectiveness, and she valued that. A lot. If she explained the situation to Uthari, he would understand, wouldn't he?

"Rivlen?" Jak could have jumped up and joined her as she wrestled with indecision, but he merely raised his hand toward her, waiting.

She could sense the dragons flying closer.

Shaking her head and certain she would regret it, she waved for him to join her in the corridor. "When he finds out, Uthari is going to throw me in the cell next to yours."

"Will he relieve you of your command?" Jak winced. He might not like Uthari, but she knew he didn't want her to be punished.

Unfortunately, his actions had ensured she would be. She just didn't yet know to what extent.

"I don't know."

Jak hesitated, but he clearly didn't want to stay in that cell. He tossed the axe up, then used his magic to leap out after it.

As he plucked it up, Rivlen strode for the steps that led to the deck and the communications cabin. With the dragons flying closer, she was tempted to ignore the druid, but they'd never contacted her before—she didn't think they'd contacted *any* of the mages before. This had to be important. Maybe she would get lucky, and the druids wanted to share secret knowledge about how to defeat dragons.

"Wishful thinking," she muttered.

As she walked across the deck, leading Jak, several of her officers looked at them with curiosity. Some were openly startled. The word had gotten around about Tonovan, she trusted.

Jak detoured to the Thorn Company women. They and the other mercenaries were at the railing, ready to fight, but Tezi saw him carrying her axe, and her eyes grew round. As he held it out for her, she ran forward, almost impaling herself as she hugged him.

Rivlen wasn't positive Tezi was the best wielder for that weapon, but she didn't object to its return. Tonovan had acted like a thief when he'd acquired it, a mugger in an alley biding his time for an ambush. She wouldn't admit to her feelings where any mage loyal to Uthari could hear her, but Tonovan had gotten what he deserved.

"Two dragons are ten miles out," an officer called.

"Be ready to fight." Rivlen made a note to hunt for the dagger Tonovan had also stolen on Temika. Having another dragon-steel weapon for the battle would be useful. "I'll return shortly."

When she stepped into the communications cabin, the dome-jir still glowed orange on the desk, with the head and shoulders of a familiar green-haired woman floating above it. Rivlen felt no warmth at seeing Kywatha, but at least she spoke Dhoran.

"What do you want?" Rivlen asked.

"We are flying across Temril in your direction."

"Then you're a long way from your jungle."

"As you are a long way from your kingdom."

"We came to help these people." Rivlen hated lying about that, but she also wouldn't give free intelligence to an enemy. "Unfortunately, we were too late."

"Yes, mages are known for rushing to the aid of those in opposing kingdoms."

Rivlen kept her face neutral, not giving anything away. It sounded like Kywatha already knew what had happened in Temika. Maybe the druids had a spy there.

Even if they knew the truth, it didn't matter. It wasn't the druids' right to question Uthari and his choices. Sadly, it wasn't Rivlen's right either, not if she wanted to climb the ranks to the culmination of her career that she'd dreamed of for years. Even if she had her doubts about Uthari's decisions lately... what other choice did she have? To leave the kingdom? To bring shame on her family? She would *not* do that.

"I'm very busy," Rivlen said. "I repeat: what do you want?"

"Though it will be difficult for both our peoples, I propose that we work together to defeat the dragons you are about to face. We can bring our ship in and try to flank them while you unleash your power on them from the front."

"You have a ship?"

"We did not ride here on the backs of dolphins."

"No? That sounds like a druidly thing to do."

"Do you want our help or not, Captain?" Kywatha asked. "Thus far, *we* are not being targeted by the dragons. *You* are."

No kidding.

"Fine. Come help if you can. I don't know what my commander or my king will say, but they're not here." Technically, Tonovan *was* there, but his injuries should keep him out of the battle and prevent him from giving commands—she hoped. He'd had a sword jabbed into him numerous times. Even with magical healing, he shouldn't be mobile until the next day. Assuming they all *survived* until the next day.

"Your generosity will be remembered, Captain."

As the dome-jir went dark, Rivlen asked, "Was that druid sarcasm?"

There was nobody in the cabin to answer. Jak had remained on deck with the mercenaries.

"I'm positive it *was* druid sarcasm," she grumbled as she headed out.

She hoped the dragons noticed the druids, found them obnoxious, and spread their hatred among all of the ships. Especially since Rivlen sensed another dragon angling toward her little fleet.

"Three at a time should be a delight." She tried not to think about what they would do if even more showed up.

"I'm going to try to get close enough to the dragon to strike it with my axe," Tezi said, addressing two dozen Thorn Company women, including the new recruits that Ferroki had accepted into the company on a trial basis. "Chances are, I'll only be able to clip it, like when I got the tip of its tail, but if I get the axe close enough, the dragon's defenses will drop. This *kills* magic." She hefted the weapon.

Most of the mercenaries already knew that, but she hadn't noticed many of them taking advantage during the brief moment the last dragon's magical defenses had dropped. They might not have realized the ramifications of her getting through with the axe.

"I'll try to yell and let you know when I get through," Tezi continued, "but you have to be ready, the same as when the mages raise and lower their defenses of the ship. When the dragon's defenses are down, you fire. It might be hard for normal swords and black-powder weapons to get through its scales, but a mage-lock rifle might do some damage. And if any of you have lesser-dragon-steel blades, I've seen those slip between scales." She wished Malek or Sorath were along to fight with her. It seemed suicidal for mercenaries with only mundane weapons to get within a hundred miles of a dragon, but what choice did they have?

"Sure," Basher said around her cigar, "I keep my lesser-dragon-steel knife collection right next to my jewelry box full of diamond rings."

Someone in the back snorted. "You're even less likely to have a jewelry box than Sergeant Tinder."

"That's not true. I like the pretty sparklies."

"I wouldn't mind a diamond-encrusted sword," someone else said.

"Nah, you don't want weapons like that," Basher said. "Messes up the balance of the blade. Stick with diamond rings."

"Where do I get those? My purse is short on the funds for their acquisition."

Tezi cleared her throat. She felt presumptuous overriding the more experienced and higher-ranking mercenaries, but... "The dragons will be here any moment. Are you ready? Do you have any questions about the plan?"

She didn't know whether or not to hope the new dragons would be like the last ones and come close enough to try to steal her axe. That would mean they were within striking distance for the mercenaries, but it would also mean the mercenaries would be in striking distance of *them*.

"Yeah," someone said. "Which one of us gets your axe if a dragon eats you?"

"If I go down its gullet, I'm taking the axe with me to carve my way out from the inside."

Basher laughed. "You would, girl."

"That's *corporal*," Ferroki said quietly, coming up behind Tezi.

Basher waved indifferently. "Sure, Captain."

"I hope you don't mind me talking to the company, Captain." Tezi hadn't realized Ferroki had been watching.

Would she think it presumptuous for a newly appointed corporal to take charge? As a rookie, her duty had been to speak little and take orders without complaint. Hypothetically, she should have more responsibility as a corporal, but it wasn't as if she'd been given a squad to command. The Thorn Company squads already *had* leaders.

"I don't." Ferroki drew her away from the group to speak privately. "You're practically an expert on fighting dragons these days."

"Not quite, ma'am. The only reason I had some luck last time was because Sorath was there, invisible and helping out."

"I know. I saw." Ferroki smiled. "Or *didn't* see."

"I wish he was still with us, ma'am." Tezi liked Thorn Company and thought the all-woman mercenary group did fine without male help, but Sorath had been almost like a father figure. Or maybe he'd been exactly what he was. An older veteran soldier who called everyone *killer* and made them believe they had it in them to battle impossible odds.

"So do I. I also wish we had a few more axes." Ferroki nodded at Tezi's blade, meaning *dragon-steel* axes, not the weapons in general. "Tinder is recovering from her wounds, but she's upset that the dragon got hers."

"Yes, ma'am." Tezi hoped she could keep the new dragons from making off with hers. When Jak had given the axe to her, she'd been surprised but relieved. After losing it to Tonovan, she'd felt like a failure and had thought about giving back her rank pins and declining her promotion.

She glanced to where Jak stood at the railing, peering out into the night in the same direction as the mage officers. Tezi assumed that was where the dragons would come from.

"Do you know what happened, ma'am?" Tezi asked. "How Jak got my axe back from Tonovan?"

"No, but there's a rumor spreading that Tonovan is in sickbay being treated for some bad injuries."

Tezi licked her lips, half tempted to visit him in sickbay. With her axe. "You know what that metal disc embedded in his temple means, right?"

The mages hadn't told the mercenaries anything about it, and Tonovan certainly hadn't chatted with them, but Tezi had rocked back in understanding when the general had stomped past earlier in the evening. She'd seen hundreds of discs like that on Vran.

"Tonovan admitted in front of all of us that he doesn't have access to his magic," Ferroki said. "I assume it has something to do with that little device and that he can't remove it without harming himself further."

"That's right. It's a kerzor. Jak must have brought it back from Vran. Or maybe Jadora did. At one point, the group had a couple of them."

"If so, Jak picked a good target for it, but there will be repercussions."

Tezi hesitated. "Do you think there would still be repercussions if Tonovan... didn't make it through the night?"

Ferroki gazed at her. Was that sadness in her eyes? Or *disappointment*?

Tezi tried not to wince or blurt anything defensive. The captain hadn't had the run-ins with Tonovan that Tezi had. She might not realize how awful he was, how much better off everyone would be if he were gone.

"To defeat an enemy in battle is honorable," Ferroki said. "To slit his throat while he recovers in bed is not."

"Sometimes, you have to do things that aren't honorable to make the world a better place, ma'am. Better for one person to live with dishonor so that others may live in peace."

"That's a wobbly line of reasoning. I will suggest that if he's meant to die, we're on a dangerous mission, and the gods themselves might take him from this world."

Tezi prayed to Thanok rather than any vague *gods*, and *The Teachings* said Thanok helped those who worked hard to help themselves and their families. But she didn't want to argue with the captain. The mages were warning that the dragons would arrive within five minutes, so there wasn't time to sneak down to slit Tonovan's throat even if Tezi decided it was the right thing to do.

If she hadn't feared losing the axe again, she might have been tempted to run down and slide it under his bed. The image of a dragon maw crashing through the hull and into his sickbay cabin to snap him up whole flashed through her mind. Alas, if she did that, the dragon would get him *and* the axe.

"You're wearing the scheming expression of the hare plotting an incursion into the farmer's garden to steal carrots," Ferroki observed.

Tezi shook her head. "It was a *wistful* expression, ma'am, not a scheming one. Maybe I was fantasizing a bit, but I won't act on it."

"Good. Assuming we all survive the night, I'm giving you some troops to teach, lead, and mold."

"Mold, ma'am? Troops?"

Ferroki pointed to the three women who'd volunteered to join Thorn Company, the women Tezi still wasn't sure they could trust. Had Ferroki already decided they could?

"Yes. You'll turn them into good fighters and solid soldiers."

"Since they came from another mercenary company, shouldn't they already know the basics?" Only after Tezi spoke did she realize what the captain was offering. Command, in a small sense. A squad of three for Tezi to lead. It would be a chance for her to train and help the new women as she herself learned how to be a corporal.

"We strive to be *more* than basic."

"Yes, ma'am. I understand."

Corporal Tezi, Rivlen spoke into her mind.

She'd come out of the communications cabin and was heading into the forecastle. This time, Tonovan wasn't beside her, but Jak walked over to stand beside her.

She crooked a finger toward Tezi. *Bring your axe and join us.*

"Captain Rivlen wants me, ma'am," Tezi said.

"She probably wants that axe right next to her so she can make sure the dragons don't get it."

"You don't think she wants me up there because I'm a skilled soldier who's death to dragon tails?"

"I'm sure that's part of it." Ferroki gripped her shoulder and looked into her eyes. "Be careful, Corporal."

"Yes, ma'am."

As Tezi headed up to join Jak and Rivlen, the first two dragons came into view.

19

FLASHES OF YELLOW AND ORANGE LIGHT CAME FROM THE NIGHT SKY ahead, signs of a battle engaged. The druids had warned everyone that they were getting close to dragons.

In the front of the raft, Sorath rose to his feet. Behind him, roamers milled, clanking their weapons together in anticipation of battle. Too bad the seer with her lesser-dragon-steel-tipped staff was the only one of them with a weapon that could damage dragon scales. Even that seemed unlikely. What would she do? Thump her staff on a dragon's talons?

Most of the roamers didn't even have magelock weapons. They waved swords and black-powder muskets and rifles.

Though Sorath doubted those would do any good, he turned and made himself address them. For whatever reason, they believed he would successfully lead them into the battle.

"I've fought dragons before," Sorath called to them, "and survived. My advice is to wait and let those with magic do the fighting from a distance, but if the dragons come in close and I'm able to use this dagger on one—" he held it aloft to show them, "—its defenses should drop, at least for a couple of seconds."

More lights flashed in the sky behind him, reflecting in the eyes of dozens—maybe *hundreds*—of people looking at him. Even some of the druids were listening. Sorath wished he had some great wisdom that he could share, wisdom he'd gleaned from his battle with the dragon he'd helped kill, but all he'd done was dart in while it had been focusing on Uthari, the portal, and Tezi.

"There are mercenaries on the ships up ahead," Sorath continued, hoping he was correct and that they were sailing closer to the *Star Flyer* and Thorn Company, as well as the dragons, "who have axes made from dragon steel. If any of those weapons get close, they'll also pop the dragons' magical defenses briefly. That's when you unleash everything you have at them. Until you see one of those blades get close, don't waste your ammunition. If anyone has explosives, those can help distract a dragon, but don't expect them to do a lot of damage. Do you understand? Are you ready?"

A collective roar of agreement came from the roamers. They'd stared down in horror as the raft had passed over the wrecked villages along the coast, places where they and their kin wintered. One had also grimly pointed out wrecked ships in the reefs, roamer ships that hadn't made it.

Grunk weaved through the crowd to join Sorath and pat him on the back. *Good talk.*

Oh? Do you feel emboldened, heartened, and ready to leap into battle?

Always. Grunk showed his pointed teeth in a garish smile. *Do you think the girl will be out there? The girl with the axe? Tezi?*

She'd better be. Sorath watched the sky ahead as they communicated, and when light flashed again, he glimpsed the first dragon. And were those the lights of Uthari's ships? *We need her axe.*

I like her. She came to rescue me.

Yes, she did.

I didn't get to thank her. Do you think she likes crazy druids? Grunk jumped, spun a full turn, and landed in a crouch with a couple of his daggers out.

I don't know. She hates mages—with good reason. I guess druids are a little different, but I don't know if she's that interested in men.

If Tezi had been, Sorath suspected she would have gone for a nice boy like Jak, rather than a crazy druid. Sorath didn't mind Grunk—any good fighter who took directions well in battle was all right in his eyes—but most women weren't into blood-licking knife fighters.

She reminds me of my people. Back north. Before Vorsha's mages enslaved me and made me fight. I'm not sure I want a woman in a physical way, on account of Vorsha making me hate that, but I miss... home. When I was a boy, pretty girls like her worked in the bakery and the shops, and when they went to the well in the morning for water, they giggled at my jokes.

Vorsha didn't drag you off to her bedroom, did she? Sorath wondered if that was why the kid had hated her so much.

I'm a good fighter. Agile. Exotic. Grunk wasn't bragging; his lip curled back in disgust, and he shook his head.

Sorath had a feeling he was quoting someone. Vorsha?

I was supposed to be honored. But she was creepy and mean and made me hate... Grunk's face twisted even more, and without releasing his knives, he pressed the heels of his hands against his temples and sank into a crouch.

She's dead now, Grunk. Sorath leaned over to rest a hand on his shoulder. *She can't bother you anymore unless you let her.*

Unfortunately, Sorath knew how difficult it was to keep one's memories from haunting oneself. Just because someone was dead didn't mean they couldn't keep on damaging a person.

It's hard.

I know.

I used to be called... Erkanor. Not Grunk.

Do you want me to call you that?

Grunk hesitated, then lowered his hands and stood. *No. Erkanor is dead.*

Too bad. He had the kind of noble name that women like.

Grunk arched his eyebrows. *Like Tezi?*

You'll have to ask her. Maybe Sorath shouldn't have said that. He didn't want to give Grunk false hope, and he might be doing a disservice to Tezi for not squelching his interest.

I'll just thank her. Grunk is too broken for a pretty girl who goes to the well for water in the mornings.

The last time Sorath had seen Tezi, she'd been driving an axe into the back of a dragon. Once, she might have been the kind of girl Grunk remembered from his village, but she wasn't anymore. If Ferroki and Thorn Company hadn't promoted Tezi yet, Sorath would recommend it. If he got a chance to talk to Ferroki again. He sighed. Would he?

"As soon as we deal with these dragons," Sorath whispered, counting two now in the sky. Someone had mentioned sensing a third flying in as well. "Good luck to us all in this battle."

He gripped the dagger as the raft sailed closer. The dragons were harrying four mageships—he recognized the *Star Flyer,* two others of similar size, and the long and narrow gateship that Vinjo had built.

Why was that vessel in the thick of things? It hadn't been built for combat, and it appeared too fragile to stand up to dragons. It also floated to the side of the other three ships, looking like a vulnerable target. Surprisingly, the dragons were ignoring it in favor of the *Star Flyer.*

"Of course. That's where the dragon-steel axes are." Sorath leaned forward, willing the raft to fly faster so he could get there in time to help.

In the forecastle of the *Star Flyer,* Captain Rivlen and Jak were visible. Though he didn't wear a red uniform, it was almost as if he'd joined her crew. They worked together, casting walls of fire that roared toward the dragons circling their ship. Tezi was also with them, her axe in hand, but she couldn't do anything unless their enemies flew in close.

The rest of the mercenaries were on deck, pointing magelock pistols and waiting for the opportunity to shoot. Sorath searched for Ferroki among them. There. She was still alive.

He tightened his fist around the hilt of his dagger, telling himself that his reward for defeating the dragons would be getting to see her again.

I cannot sense that vessel. Grunk pointed at the gateship. *I see it but don't feel its magic. Or anything about it.*

"Did Vinjo build some magical camouflage into it?" Sorath wondered. Since he'd left camp before the gateship had been completed, he didn't know anything about it, but he glanced at the stealth device on his wrist, aware of what Vinjo could do. "And if so, why aren't Tezi and Tinder and their axes flying on *that* ship?"

Grunk only shrugged.

From the center of the raft, Kywatha gave a command. Druids lifted their arms and sent their versions of fireballs—spinning green globes of energy—toward the dragons.

With no range weapon of his own, at least not one that would do anything, Sorath could only watch and wait. He doubted the dragons would leave the *Star Flyer* to attack the raft, but if they did, he was ready. He even waved the dragon-steel dagger in the air, in case it might catch their attention. If the dragons noticed the raft, the blade would be the reason.

You use my dagger for bait? Grunk asked.

I can't thrust it into a dragon's eye unless one comes close.

True.

The roamers must have interpreted Sorath's wave as a challenge, for they loosed battle cries, also waving their weapons and beckoning to the dragons. They shouted insults, telling them they were pompous, overdeveloped geckos who mated with whales and had the tiny penises of gorillas.

"Somehow, I doubt that's going to get their attention," Sorath murmured. Besides, as reptiles, dragons wouldn't even know what penises were.

It got his *attention.* Grunk pointed, not toward the two dragons attacking the *Star Flyer* but toward the third one the druids had sensed.

It was visible now, flying in from the south as it headed toward the raft instead of the mageships. Even though night's darkness made it hard to see details, Sorath somehow knew that it had a crazy gleam in its single yellow eye.

Human warrior, it cried into their minds—or just Sorath's mind? *I will take that little blade this time.*

Bring your single working eye close, Sorath replied. *You know how much I want to give it to you.*

You will fail to harm even one of my magnificent scales before I tear you into a thousand pieces.

Uh huh. Where's your gong? I thought you'd be wearing it around your neck on a chain like a choke collar. You'd look good in a choke collar.

I delivered it for the mission. As I will deliver your little knife.

Delivered it where?

To the south. Past the jungle to our new lair!

New lair? That sounded ominous, like the dragons were planning to take up permanent residence in this world.

You're not delivering anything, and I'm going to cut your tail off at the root. Sorath had no ability to telepathically convey visions, but since the dragon was already in his head, he attempted to share an image of himself sawing through the base of the dragon's tail, then flinging it into the ocean.

With that tiny toothpick? Even one of your axes wouldn't be a match for my wondrous tail.

Sorath had no idea why this dragon liked to single him out to trade insults, nor why he was going along with it. But with a lurch of realization, it occurred to him that a chatty enemy could be a weakness to its allies. Usually, a pretty woman was sent in to seduce a soldier to get information, but if he, for some reason, had the ability to draw out intelligence from this dragon...

What mission are you on for your new lair, dragon? Why do beings so powerful as you need dragon steel?

I see what you seek to do, human foe. To steal intelligence from me! Do you think I'm a fool?

Sorath would have suspected the dragon of reading his thoughts, but shouldn't the dagger have protected him from that? Maybe it was smart enough to guess what he was doing. He reminded himself not to underestimate the intelligence of the dragons.

No, but you like to chat. I thought you might like to fill me in.

I will fill you with fangs! Prepare to die, mouthy human!

The dragon's wings flapped faster.

"That one is coming for us!" someone warned, pointing a weapon at it.

"Keep an eye on the others," Kywatha called, "but brace yourselves for this one. We're raising our barriers."

I'm ready for you, One-Eye. Sorath strode into the center of the raft so he would have room to maneuver without risk of falling off.

One-Eye? came the indignant reply. *I am Yoshartov, slayer of enemies, winner of races, he who has beauty more magnificent than the stars!*

That's a long name. Does it all go on the tombstone? Sorath doubted dragons used tombstones, but he trusted it—*Yoshartov*—would know what he meant.

Who are you, little human? He who doesn't tremble and quake at the approach of our kind?

Sorath debated if it mattered if the dragon knew his name. He was surprised this Yoshartov cared. *Colonel Sorath. Soldier.*

That is a short name. What a meager tombstone you'll have.

Yoshartov furled his wings so he could dive toward the raft. By the green light of druid lightning that crackled toward the dragon's head, Sorath could see that its single eye *did* have a gleam in it. Whether that gleam announced delight in battle or anticipation of its enemy's death, Sorath didn't know, but as the dragon streaked toward him, he had little doubt that he was the target.

"I'm ready for you," he whispered and did his best to stare fearlessly back at the dragon.

Yoshartov dove faster than gravity, undeterred by the attacks the druids hurled at him. Sorath crouched, aware of the roamers firing their weapons, even though he'd told them to wait. Someone hurled an explosive that blew up in front of Yoshartov's eye. It half-blinded Sorath and did nothing to the dragon. As Yoshartov flew through the smoke, talons outstretched, Sorath dove to the left.

But the dragon anticipated his movement, and one of those talons lashed sideways. It clawed Sorath's ribs, raising fiery pain. Instinctively, he slashed with the dagger. As fast as the dragon was, Sorath almost missed, but the blade sliced through its barrier and clipped one of its talons as it withdrew them.

Had that been the only blow Yoshartov suffered, Sorath would have come out far worse in the confrontation, but the druids hammered the dragon with their power. Yoshartov's defenses were only down for seconds, but it gave Sorath time to roll away and jump to his feet. They even managed to knock Yoshartov off the raft. Seeing the dragon tumble over the side was almost startling, and when Yoshartov didn't reappear, Sorath hoped it had been more hurt than he would have guessed and had plummeted into the sea.

"Brace yourselves," Kywatha yelled, then repeated something similar in her own language.

The raft shuddered so hard under Sorath's feet that he almost fell. Many people did, tumbling sideways and into each other.

"It's hanging onto the logs underneath us," Kywatha yelled. "Like a tick."

The raft shook as Yoshartov roared. *I will tear your bundle of sticks apart, and you'll all fall. After you drown, I'll take the dragon steel for myself.*

It's a bundle of logs, you dolt, Sorath thought. *Aren't dragons supposed to be intelligent?*

You dare insult me! The raft quaked again.

Kywatha lifted her arms as she yelled something to her people, orders to use their magic to hold the raft together, Sorath hoped.

You know I dare. Get up here and face me like an honorable opponent. Sorath glanced at the holes in his tunic, blood saturating the fabric. He doubted he would survive facing the dragon honorably, but better he die than the raft be torn apart and *everyone* die.

The logs jolted. Had Yoshartov let go?

"He's coming back up." Kywatha pointed toward the front of the raft, the other dragon battle only a couple hundred yards away now.

Sorath jumped over two people getting to their feet and sprinted for the bow. Yoshartov came into view, the dragon's winged form dark against the water below. It flapped its wings, turning to come up close to the raft. Sorath crouched, timing the dragon's approach, then jumped.

His heart leaped into his throat when Yoshartov adjusted his ascent at the last second and Sorath landed on the back of a wing instead of astride its spine. The flaps halted as his weight startled the dragon. Using his pickaxe and dagger like mountain climbing tools, Sorath scrambled toward its back before Yoshartov could shake the wing to dislodge him.

As it had done before, the dragon rolled in the air. With a mighty blow, Sorath drove the dagger between two scales. It sank in to the hilt, but as Yoshartov spun, gravity threatened to pitch Sorath to his death. The dragon's tail whipped up and thunked him in the back, almost knocking him free.

One-handedly, and with all the determination he could manage, Sorath held on to the hilt of the dagger, hoping he'd wedged it in so deeply that it wouldn't slide out. He tried to drive his pickaxe between two other scales, but the metal wasn't strong enough to pierce the dragon's defenses.

Had Yoshartov flown upside down for a few seconds, the dagger would have slid out, and Sorath would have fallen, but the dragon kept spinning, corkscrewing through the air, as if it were trying to make Sorath throw up instead of fall. Sorath wished he *could* vomit all over his obnoxious foe.

Green lightning streaked through the air, and Sorath glimpsed the raft. It was below him now, at least for the second. If he yanked the dagger out and dropped, he might land on it and be safe. But he'd jumped onto the dragon to kill it, not merely for a ride.

When Yoshartov's back rotated skyward again, Sorath jerked his wrist and yanked the dagger free. As he'd done before, he hurried to the dragon's neck. Yoshartov started to spin again, and Sorath wrapped as much of his arm around its long neck as he could, but it was thicker than a tree trunk. Once more, he had to drive the dagger between two scales and hang on.

His back burned where the tail had struck him, as if Yoshartov were a scorpion and had delivered venom.

The dragon roared, its head twisting back, but it couldn't reach the base of its neck where Sorath clung. The snapping jaws came close, and Sorath thought he might have to yank out the dagger and slash at them, but a magelock charge blasted into Yoshartov's lone eye and startled the dragon. More attacks struck it, some hitting its scales so close to Sorath that he would have been knocked free—or killed outright—if he hadn't had the blade. One brilliant green ball of energy blasted into the top of the dragon's neck, the light half-blinding him, and he barely kept from flinching away and falling.

Yoshartov's wingbeats grew erratic, and Sorath glanced down, but they weren't over the raft anymore. If the dragon fell from the sky, he would too.

"So be it." Sorath pulled out the dagger and climbed higher, certain he needed to reach the head to deliver a mortal blow.

Yoshartov snapped for him once more—no, for the dagger. The dragon seemed more focused on getting it than on killing Sorath.

But Sorath had climbed too high for his opponent to reach. As he had in their last battle, he made it to the top of the dragon's head and hooked an arm around a horn. Magical attacks whispered toward him but didn't affect him. He kept the dagger firmly in hand for its protection.

Once more, Yoshartov rolled, shaking his head and trying to throw Sorath free. He tightened his grip on the horn and hung on, even as his legs flew out, knocked away by gravity.

Get it in the eye! Grunk cried into his mind. *You're close. You can do it.*

"Kill it!" came a chant from the roamers. "Kill it!"

As soon as gravity allowed it, Sorath crouched on Yoshartov's head. Instead of going for the eye, something that would require him to release his grip on the horn, he lifted one arm and plunged the dagger downward, hoping to break through the dragon's skull.

The tip started to dive in, piercing between two scales, but Yoshartov shook his head so hard that Sorath couldn't hang on to the horn any longer. His pickaxe clanked against it as he tried to readjust his slipping grip, but he flew free with a roar of frustration.

Wind railed at him as he tumbled through the air. Sorath

hoped one of the druids would be able to grip him and levitate him to safety, but with a jolt of horror, he realized they couldn't. Not while he held the dagger. But if he released the weapon, the dragon could swoop down and catch it.

Did that matter? If Sorath hit the sea at a hundred miles per hour and died, Yoshartov would get the blade anyway.

His moment of indecision only lasted a second. He wouldn't give in, even if it meant his death. As he tumbled, he sheathed the dagger. Whatever his fate, he wouldn't throw it away.

He landed with bone-breaking force, not on the water far below but on the edge of the raft. His head cracked on one of the logs, and he nearly passed out. He wished he had, for bones *did* break, and pain assaulted him from every part of his body.

Grunk ran over and knelt beside him. *You didn't kill it, but you hurt it!*

Sorath could only groan in response.

All around him, the roamers were pointing at the sky. The dragon had flown off to the side and was batting at its skull with one of its wings, as if that would help the puncture wound in its head. Sorath only wished he'd been able to sink the dagger in deeper, to pierce the dragon's skull and brain.

Kywatha crouched on Sorath's other side, though she kept her eyes toward the sky—toward Yoshartov and the other dragon battle, one Sorath was now powerless to help with. "We'll heal you when there's time."

"I look forward to it," Sorath rasped, wincing as the words caused more pain. He feared his ribs had broken and were piercing his organs.

"We moved the raft to catch you," Kywatha said, "but we couldn't soften your landing."

Not wanting to speak until it didn't hurt so much, he merely lifted two fingers in acknowledgement while hoping Yoshartov wouldn't return. If the dragon did, Sorath wouldn't be able to do a thing to keep it from getting the dagger.

Sweat beaded on Jak's forehead as he alternated between funneling power into Rivlen to give her fire attacks more strength and into the barrier to protect the ship. He happened to be looking toward the strange raft that had shown up, surprisingly full of roamers as well as druids, when Colonel Sorath tumbled free of the dragon he'd been fighting. The raft had lurched to the side to catch him, but Jak couldn't tell if he was alive. Hitting a log at top speed wasn't much better than falling a thousand feet into the sea.

"We need to let them get close." Tezi crouched with her axe as she tracked the two dragons, two dragons focusing exclusively on the *Star Flyer* while ignoring the gateship and the other mageships. "I can't do anything to them from down here."

"They can't do anything to you either." Rivlen touched a dagger sheathed on her hip—the dragon-steel weapon that Tonovan had stolen from King Temrok. She must have found wherever he'd stashed it. "Better to keep our barrier up while the other ships attack them. We're the bait." She grimaced as she spoke, and Jak knew she would also prefer to attack rather than defending.

A dragon roared as it flew close, scraping at the barrier with its talons. Its cold yellow eyes locked onto Tezi and her axe. Maybe the larger weapon was more enticing than Rivlen's new dagger.

"Where are they putting the dragon steel after they find it?" Jak wondered.

Tezi glanced at him.

"That's the same one that attacked before, I think," he said. "That got Tinder's axe."

"Pockets?" Tezi suggested.

Rivlen gave her a scathing look, then power surged from within her as she poured more energy into the barrier. Those talons had almost gotten through.

Shikari sat between Jak and Rivlen, sharing his power with them, but he shifted uneasily from foot to foot. *They speak to me,* he told Jak. *Threats. They are promising to make me one of them.*

Lovely. Can you ask them why they're gathering dragon steel?

Fireballs from the other nearby ships struck the attacking dragon in the flanks, and it wheeled away. But the second one replaced it, diving for the ship and making an attempt of its own.

They only threaten me, Shikari said. *They will not give me information. They say that if I want to learn things, I must join them. But I will not.*

Good.

"Jak," Tezi blurted, her face contorting as if she were in pain.

"What?" He looked her up and down—had the dragons found some mental attack that could strike her through the axe's protection?

Tezi thrust the shaft of the weapon toward him. "Vision."

"Now?" Jak glanced up as the dragon lashed out at the barrier —Rivlen wobbled on her feet before bracing her knees and finding even more power to use on their defenses—then touched Tezi's axe. He didn't expect anything to happen, not thinking it would share its insight with two people, but her vision swept over him with startling clarity.

Startling and *confusing* clarity, for all it offered was a view of the ship and the current battle with the mages and mercenaries poised to attack the dragons if they broke through the barrier.

But then the view dove belowdecks to the interior of the ship. It showed a hooded man in black hiding his face in shadow as he crept through the corridors, a sword and a dagger in his hands. Lesser-dragon-steel weapons, their blue hue promised, and the man moved with the agility of a well-trained assassin. Or a zidarr?

Could someone have sneaked aboard while they'd been docked in Temika? Or even before? Early on in the journey, Zaruk's ships had been shadowing Uthari's. Maybe someone had flown across on a skyboard and stowed away then.

"Rivlen," Jak blurted before he realized he had no idea if this was happening now or it might happen in the future.

"What?" Rivlen demanded without looking at them. "I could use some more of your power."

Sweat dampened her hair and gleamed on her face, and she lifted her sleeve to dash it out of her eyes.

The ship shuddered as a dragon flew past, slamming its tail against the barrier and causing the *Star Flyer* to lurch to the side. In the vision, the corridors also lurched. This was happening now.

"We've got an intruder," Jak said. "The axe is warning us. It might be a zidarr."

"On my ship?"

Jak nodded. "I can't tell which corridor, but if he's heading for the engineering area..."

Rivlen looked toward her lieutenants on the deck and opened her mouth, as if to send them, but she cursed and turned toward Tezi. "No, you go check. With your axe. Jak, go with her to help her." She dug into her pocket and pulled out the stealth device her officer had taken from him and thrust it into his hand. "If it *is* a zidarr, let me know. We'll have to combine forces to deal with—" She broke off as a dragon soared past, sending a huge wall of fire toward the forecastle.

Jak channeled more power into the barrier and into Rivlen, parting his streams of magic in an attempt to strengthen them both.

"We can't take much more of this," someone on the deck cried.

"Ma'am, are you sure?" Tezi held the axe up again, her eyes toward the dragon.

The barrier held, and Rivlen nodded. "If someone destroys the engines, we'll crash and the dragon won't matter."

"Come on." Jak touched Tezi's shoulder and pointed toward the nearest hatch. Even though the idea of facing a zidarr scared him as much as facing a dragon, the thought of the ship crashing and everyone aboard dying scared him even more. With the rest of the fleet engaged in battle, they might not be able to help the *Star Flyer*—or the crew—if it went down.

Tezi hesitated, but Rivlen barked, "*Go!*" and she obeyed.

Jak slipped the stealth device onto his wrist, then leaped down from the forecastle, bypassing the steps, and ran toward the hatch leading to the engine area. At least on this ship, it was a large chamber, and its openness meant that no walls would offer hiding spots. If someone was down there, Jak ought to be able to see him. Unless the zidarr had a stealth device. But as far as Jak knew, Vinjo was the only one who made those. Hopefully, no enemy could have acquired one.

If you find enemies, Shikari spoke into Jak's mind, *lead them back to me, and I will assist you with them. Together, we are mighty.*

Yes, we are. Jak smiled briefly, though he doubted he would be able to coax an assassin out onto the open deck.

He ran through the hatchway ahead of Tezi and peered left and right as he reached the stairs leading into engineering and hurried down them. The power supply pulsed from the bottom of the chamber, glowing tendrils stretching away and disappearing through walls toward various sections of the ship. A single mage officer stood guard near the power supply and squinted suspiciously toward them.

"Have you seen a man in black?" Jak asked.

"No." The suspicious squint didn't change.

"Keep an eye out. There's an intruder down here. Maybe a zidarr."

"I would have sensed anyone with such a powerful aura."

"He may have a way to squelch it." Jak remembered Malek camouflaging himself—and even an entire ship—before, but the officer shook his head.

"Civilians and mercenaries aren't allowed in this area. Get out before I call the captain."

"The captain *sent* us," Tezi said as she peered into the shadows in the corners of the chamber.

"Come on. We'll check the steering compartment and the lift generator." Since his lessons with Vinjo, Jak knew more about how the mageships worked—and what might be sabotaged to bring one down.

Leaving the officer to scowl after them, Jak and Tezi jogged into a corridor that ran parallel to the one with the cells. He had no interest in checking *that* area. Besides, he'd been the only prisoner. Unless the man was looking for him, he wouldn't go there.

The *Star Flyer* shuddered, and the mage lamps mounted on the walls flickered. Jak sensed the two dragons still out there, flying about the ship and attacking. How much could it withstand?

"Whoever's in here," he whispered as they continued down the corridor, "they timed their skulking perfectly."

"What's the plan if we find a zidarr?" Tezi whispered back.

"You sink your axe into his back while I distract him."

"How are you going to do that?"

"I'll let you know when I figure it out." Jak pushed open the door to the steering compartment.

It was small, with a couple of devices emanating power and light. There were deep shadows in the corners, but Jak didn't see or sense anyone crouched in them. He ran into those corners, just in case someone *was* camouflaged, but nothing stirred as he passed through.

"You should use Vinjo's device." Tezi waved to his wrist. "Then when he's looking at me, *you* can stab him in the back."

Jak glanced at the utility knife sheathed on his belt, wishing he'd thought to grab a magelock. Still, if he had an opening, the simple weapon would do to kill a man who wasn't paying attention.

"Or give the stealth device to me, and *I'll* cleave his head off when he's looking at you."

"Good idea." Jak slid the gizmo off his wrist. "You'd be a lot more deadly sneaking up from behind someone."

He held it out to her as he headed for the door. They would have to go down to the bottom level to check the lift generator. Since he'd never been invited on a tour of the ship, Jak wasn't positive exactly where the generator was, but he could sense it, as he sensed the other devices that powered the mageship.

Tezi seemed startled and didn't accept his offering.

"Take it." Jak thrust the stealth device at her. "I think magic that you're activating yourself works fine with the axe, just not stuff thrown at you by others."

"It does." Tezi accepted the device, looping it over her wrist and activating it. "Thanks. I didn't think you'd give it up."

"Well, I want it back," he said dryly as they ran for a ladder heading down.

"Against a zidarr, you should want it *now*."

"True, but I trust you." Jak lowered his voice. "We'd better stop talking in case he's down here."

As they ran through a corridor in the bowels of the ship, a scream came from one of the levels above. Jak halted. It had been a man, the voice somewhat familiar, but it was hard to tell from down below. All he knew was that whoever it was, the man was in pain.

"Is that the engineer?" Jak whispered, torn between checking the lift generator and running back up to help whoever had screamed.

It was possible there were two saboteurs, one creating distractions while the other cut into crucial power systems.

"I think it was Tonovan," Tezi said, her voice seeming to come from empty air in the corridor behind him.

"Tonovan? Why would *he* be a target? Maybe he woke up in pain. I don't know if the mages had time to treat him."

"Anyone who's met him would happily target him," Tezi grumbled.

The ship shuddered again, and a crack came from the frame. Only one dragon was attacking, but one could do plenty of damage.

Jak hesitated. What if Rivlen needed help with the defenses?

Another scream sounded, the cry of a man in fresh, *new* pain. Jak bit his lip. "He's the general and commander of the fleet. It's possible he *is* the target."

He turned and started back toward the ladder they'd descended, but Tezi came into view as he drew closer to her. She wasn't moving.

With her jaw set, she pointed past him. "Let's check the lift generator."

"But Tonovan—"

"Deserves whatever he's getting." Usually, Tezi was warm and friendly, but as she spoke now, her eyes and her face were carved from ice.

"I don't doubt that, but he could be the first in a long *list* of people this zidarr is targeting. What if he goes after Rivlen next? Or Captain Ferroki?"

Tezi's face twisted with skepticism.

Jak admitted it was unlikely a zidarr would be sent to assassinate a mundane mercenary captain, but Rivlen was a real possibility, and fear jolted him as he realized she would be an easy target while she was focused on defending the ship.

"Step aside." Jak squeezed past Tezi to run to the ladder.

Fortunately, she didn't try to stop him. But, as he climbed toward the higher levels and ran toward sickbay, he also didn't know if she was following him. With the stealth device around her wrist, she might have stayed in the lower level, and he wouldn't know until he needed her... and she wasn't there.

Though the thought almost made him pause, fear for Rivlen drove him on.

Everything all right up there? Jak asked her telepathically.

Dandy, came her terse reply. *Who screamed?*

I'm about to find out.

Before opening the closed hatch to sickbay, Jak threw all of his power into creating what he hoped was a diamond-hard barrier around himself. The screams had halted, and Jak had no idea what he would find inside.

As he pushed open the door, he wished he'd kept the stealth device for himself. His heart hammered against his ribs as he crouched, expecting someone with deadly speed and power to leap out at him.

But it was dark and quiet in the sickbay, and nothing stirred. On the walls, the mage lamps had been broken, and night pressed against the portholes. The only light entered from the corridor behind him, and Jak realized he was outlined by it. A clear target.

He tried to funnel even more power into his barrier as he eased inside and stepped out of the light. There were three bunks, and the outline of a man was barely visible on the one farthest from the hatchway. Tonovan.

Focused on that form and listening hard for the sound of someone inside with him, Jak almost tripped over something on the floor. No *someone* on the floor. Someone who didn't stir when his boot thumped against the body.

Jak wanted to conjure a light for a better look, but he couldn't do that and maintain his barrier, and his instincts told him he had better not lower his defenses, not even for a sliver of a heartbeat. Fortunately, his eyes adjusted to the dimness enough to make out the person on the floor. It was the ship's healer. It *had* been the ship's healer. Jak couldn't tell if her throat had been cut, but if she'd been alive, he would have sensed her aura.

He stepped over her and headed toward Tonovan's bed. For a moment, he wondered if *Tonovan* might have woken up, furious at having been hurt and losing his power and killed the healer. No, the axe had shown Jak a vision of an intruder. That was who had to be responsible.

As he reached Tonovan's bed, one of the dragons outside blasted the side of the ship with fire. Orange light poured through the window, illuminating Tonovan's face—and his dead vacant eye. Multiple stabs wounds in his gut leaked blood, and more ran from a cut that had sliced the arteries in his neck. The kerzor gleamed, reflecting the orange light before it faded and shadows returned to sickbay.

Before full darkness came, Jak glimpsed movement beside the hatchway. The man in black, both of his blades drawn, exactly as the vision had shown him.

"The captain sent a *boy* to check on her commanding officer?" the man—the zidarr?—asked.

He was cloaking his aura somehow, making it so Jak couldn't sense him, and when darkness returned, Jak could barely see him. But something told him that was a zidarr. A dangerous and powerful opponent.

"Are you even in her fleet?" the zidarr asked.

A chill ran through Jak. The man meant Rivlen. He'd wanted Rivlen to walk in so he could kill her as well as Tonovan.

"I'm kind of a guest." Jak, realizing this man would kill anyone allied with Uthari's officers, tried to change his answer. "Technically, I'm a prisoner. Had you visited a few hours ago, you would have found me in one of the cells, fighting Tonovan. I'm the one who made it so he had to come to sickbay where you could easily prey on him. You're welcome."

"*You*?" The zidarr scoffed and stepped closer. "You're a boy. You have power, but it would have been no match for his."

"I stole his power with that device." Jak pointed at the kerzor without taking his eyes from the zidarr. "Again, you're welcome. Why don't you run along now and leave me be? Whoever you are, I doubt I'm your enemy."

"I am Drakmur zen Temrok, zidarr of my now-dead king. And you were there with Uthari's treacherous party. I saw you."

"I didn't attack him, and I didn't want to go along." Jak resisted the urge to glance toward the corridor. If Tezi was out there, he wouldn't see her, and he didn't want to make the zidarr believe he had an ally.

Besides, he wasn't positive that he *did* have an ally. Had Tezi followed Jak to sickbay or not?

The ship quaked under another attack, and the zidarr strode forward. "I don't believe you."

Power preceded the man and railed at Jak's defenses, trying to tear his barrier away so that the sword would have no trouble piercing his heart.

Need some help, Rivlen, Jak called telepathically as he lifted his hands, willing the mountains around him to stay strong. Why hadn't he asked to borrow her dagger? *Zidarr in sickbay. He got Tonovan, and he's about to get me.*

Shit. Buy time. We're—

The *Star Flyer* quaked again, and Jak sensed the barrier around it falling. Because the mages intended to combine forces and attack the dragon? Or because they simply couldn't hold it anymore?

Another attack tore at his defenses. The zidarr was too power-ful, too strong for him. His magic shredded Jak's and left him defenseless.

Jak drew his knife, but it was a futile gesture, and he knew it.

Far better armed and trained, the zidarr crouched and was about to spring when he detected a threat behind him. Tezi? Jak couldn't see her, but the zidarr whirled about, a strong barrier around him.

Jak threw the knife at the man's back, afraid Tezi wouldn't have time to get close for an attack. His throw was off, but it didn't matter. The hilt bounced off the zidarr's defenses. Still, maybe it distracted him for a fraction of a second, for he didn't get his sword up in time to deflect the axe whistling toward him. Or maybe he believed that his magical defenses would protect him and that he needn't worry. But the dragon-steel axe cleaved through his barrier and lodged in his chest.

Afraid the man would survive that blow, Jak shifted all the power he'd been channeling into a barrier into making fire. Terror lent him strength, and he hurled the largest fireball he'd ever made at the zidarr. It engulfed him, charring him in its inferno of heat and power.

"Jak!" Tezi yelled, her form just close enough to be visible as she hurled herself between two bunks.

Only then did it occur to Jak that having thrown the axe, she wasn't protected from his magic. He released his power, and the fire disappeared.

The charred body of the zidarr thudded to the deck, weapons clinking as they fell from his dead hands. The axe was still embedded in his chest.

"Sorry," Jak rasped. "Are you all right?"

Shaking, Tezi rose from between the beds, her cheeks red from the close call with the fire. "Just... warn a person before you throw a fireball at them."

"I will. I'm sorry."

As she pulled the axe from the man's chest, it occurred to Jak to wonder why it hadn't protected him from his fire. He'd been touching it, after all. Maybe dragon steel could tell the difference between being held and being lodged in an enemy's body and shared its protective power accordingly.

Tezi glanced at Tonovan as she wiped off her blade. "Please tell me he's dead."

"He is."

"Well, that's one good thing that came out of the day. Here." Tezi thrust his stealth device back at him, then ran out of sickbay. Eager to get back to the battle?

Jak was less eager, but he couldn't leave Rivlen to face those dragons without his help.

When they reached the deck, however, the dragons were no longer near the *Star Flyer*. They were still in the area—they'd joined the dragon the druids had been facing, but all three had flown a few hundred yards away from the ships. Here and there, mages continued to throw attacks at them, but they did no damage. The dragons might have paused to lick their wounds, but they all had barriers up.

As Jak hurried back up to the forecastle to join Rivlen and Shikari, he sensed a fourth dragon flying in from the west. He groaned at the thought of another powerful enemy. Were the three they'd been fighting waiting for their buddy before starting Round Two?

"What happened down there?" Rivlen asked Jak and Tezi when they reached her.

"The zidarr is dead, thanks to Tezi and her axe," Jak said. "But he killed Tonovan first. He said he was King Temrok's man."

"Was he all in black?"

"Yes, with some magic camouflaging his aura."

Rivlen cursed. "I saw him on a rooftop in the city as we were leaving. Tonovan was flapping his tongue and stealing Tezi's axe, and I forgot. He must have found an opportunity to sneak aboard as we flew away."

"Your healer is dead too," Jak said, wishing he didn't have to deliver bad news. "And I don't know how many more. Sorry."

Rivlen appeared too tired to do more than offer another curse as she wiped sweat out of her eyes. "I'm going to be blamed for Tonovan's death, if not for this whole mess."

"Uthari can't blame you for a zidarr assassin getting him," Jak protested.

Rivlen gave him a frank look. "Would that assassin have succeeded if Tonovan hadn't lost his power? And he hadn't been injured and vulnerable?"

"Maybe." Jak didn't care if he took the blame for Tonovan's death—it wasn't as if Uthari liked him anyway—but *Rivlen* shouldn't get in trouble for it, for any of this.

"I knew about the kerzor, Jak," Rivlen admitted quietly. "Before you did it. I knew, and I didn't do anything about it. Uthari will find out."

"How could you have known?" Jak asked, though he'd wondered if she'd glimpsed his thoughts when they'd slept together.

"You let your guard down in bed, and I saw it in your mind. I didn't take it from you and punish you for making it. I... let this happen. Uthari will see everything, and he'll punish me. Or worse." Face bleak and more anguished than Jak had ever seen it, Rivlen looked toward the west, almost as if she hoped the new dragon would arrive, destroy the ship, and end her career and her life before everything could be stripped from her.

"Rivlen..." Jak extended a hand toward her, wanting to comfort her.

Without looking at it—or him—she stepped away.

His shoulders slumped as the fear came over him that she might not talk to him again. She definitely wouldn't kiss him again. She believed she'd made a mistake.

He wanted to shout out that she hadn't, that they'd done the world a favor. She *hated* Tonovan. Surely, she had to understand that Jak had done the right thing. Besides, he hadn't even been the one to kill the general. One of his own enemies had, someone who'd watched Tonovan kill his king. It had been revenge, pure and simple. The only shocking thing was that it hadn't happened to Tonovan earlier in his career.

Jak wasn't trying to hide his whirring thoughts, but Rivlen put her back to him and didn't comment on them. Maybe she'd stopped listening, stopped caring what he thought.

He blinked at moisture forming in his eyes, not wanting to break into tears with Tezi standing beside him and dragons flying around nearby. They were in the middle of a battle. Who cried during a battle, damn it?

That fourth dragon flew into view against the dark cloudy sky, and Jak inhaled deeply, ordering himself to get it together. Whether Rivlen wanted him anymore or not, she would need his help to battle four dragons at once. She would need *everyone's* help and that of the gods as well.

But the dragon was flying erratically, as if injured. No, not injured. It gripped something huge and heavy in its talons. An... obelisk?

"What is that?" Tezi pointed.

"Whatever it is, it's magical," Rivlen said. "Oh, it's made from dragon steel."

Yes, Jak sensed that too. It was made from a *lot* of dragon steel. Maybe as much as was in the portal.

The other three dragons flew around the mageships, staying at the edge of their attack range, and headed toward their buddy. If they spoke, Jak didn't hear their words, but he imagined the new one blurting something like, "Look at what I found, guys!"

One of the dragons flew close to the porter, and they rearranged the dark obelisk so that they each gripped one end. Jak was surprised they didn't batter each other with their wings, but through their magic, they made it work. The other two dragons flew beside them, as if to guard the porters while they toted their prize.

"Why were they worrying about my axe and Sorath's dagger if they could find something like *that*?" Tezi wondered.

"Maybe they just discovered it?" Jak squinted, wishing there were more light. There was something familiar about that obelisk, something that nagged at the back of his mind. He was positive he'd never sensed or seen it before, but... "Oh."

Tezi looked at him.

"I think that's the pillar from Agathar Island in the Tarnished Sea. That dragon must have found it and torn it out of the ground. It's an archaeological monument that's stood for thousands of years. Or it was."

"Now it's a prize for dragons," Rivlen muttered, watching them with her hands raised in case the dragons attacked.

But they avoided the ships as they flew past again, this time heading south. All four of them flapped their wings hard, and they sped away.

"What are they going to do with it?" Rivlen asked. "With *everything* they're taking?"

Jak shook his head. As far as he'd heard, nobody knew why the dragons wanted the dragon steel, and he didn't have any idea either. Back on Vran, the ziggurat had helped him and Shikari attack and *kill* two of the mottled dragons. And the portal on Nargnoth had deliberately thwarted their attempt to fly to Torvil. He had been under the impression that the dragon steel had been crafted long ago by the unaltered blue dragons and didn't like the tainted dragons.

An officer climbed into the forecastle and cleared his throat. "Ma'am? The dome-jir activated."

Rivlen grimaced. Would it be Uthari contacting the ship? He couldn't know about Tonovan's death already, could he?

Jak didn't know, but as Rivlen followed the officer toward the communications cabin, she looked like a woman going to the gallows.

20

RIVLEN MENTALLY BRACED HERSELF AS SHE STEPPED INTO THE communications cabin and closed the door behind her. She expected to find Uthari's face floating over the dome-jir, that he'd somehow sensed from across the world that his faithful general had been killed. And that her failures these past couple of days had led to the events that had allowed it to happen.

But the face of the druid woman Kywatha hovered in the air. No sense of relief filled Rivlen. She would have to speak with Uthari eventually, not to mention the captains of the other ships. She wasn't the senior-ranking officer left in their little fleet. Based on time-in-rank, Captain Hevlor would be in charge now. Once she told him about Tonovan's death.

"What do you want, Kywatha?" Maybe Rivlen should have thanked the woman for showing up, but the druids hadn't done anything to help against the two dragons that had been after the *Star Flyer*. They'd had their own dragon to deal with, one that had seemed far more interested in their floating logjam.

"To share in your joy that the three dragons who were

attacking our ships have been driven off." Kywatha arched her eyebrows.

"Joy, right."

"We're alive. Is that not a victory?"

"I suppose. Do your people know why our winged tormentors are collecting dragon steel?"

"No, but we recognized that monument they tore up."

"The pillar from Agathar Island?" Rivlen had been numb and barely paying attention when Jak had been speaking, but she'd caught that.

"Yes. And we have an idea where they're going. That's what I wanted to tell you."

"Oh?"

"The one that keeps attacking Sorath traded banter with him and let something slip."

"*Banter*? I didn't know dragons knew how to do anything except deliver threats."

"I gather there were plenty of those too. The one-eyed dragon is out to get him—or at least the dragon-steel dagger he's now carrying."

Sorath had found another dragon-steel weapon? As if that man needed any more advantages. Rivlen would be happy never to see him again, but she did want whatever information he'd gleaned. Maybe if she could offer up something crucial to Uthari, the rest of what she had to tell him wouldn't seem quite so detrimental in his eyes. So... career killing.

"Where are they taking the dragon steel?" Rivlen asked.

"Past the jungle to the south is what the dragon told him."

"I was hoping for something less vague."

"Our continent of Zewnath is presumably the *jungle*. Unless the dragons are going to drop their prizes in the ocean, only the Glacier Islands are beyond that."

"I hear they're lovely."

"Not particularly, but they are remote. If someone were up to something, they could work on it there for a long time without being noticed."

"What could the dragons possibly be working on with a bunch of metal?" Rivlen asked.

"It's more than mere metal. You must know that by now."

Rivlen sighed, aware of the visions the dragon steel could share and the magical protection it offered. It could be turned into wonderful weapons, but she didn't understand why dragons *needed* weapons. They were already more powerful than a hundred humans. With the might of four ships' worth of magic users, her fleet had only succeeded in driving off their attackers, not in killing them.

"I have a hypothesis about what they're doing," Kywatha said. "No proof, mind you, and I wouldn't mind speaking with one of those two archaeologists, if either is with you."

"Jak is." Rivlen barely kept from grimacing as she said his name. If it was possible to care about and appreciate someone and also wish they weren't anywhere around, that was what she felt toward him. She wished Jak hadn't been sent along on her mission, even if he had been the one to learn about the zidarr intruder and deal with him. "But why do you need—"

Rivlen rocked back as certainty about what the dragons were doing struck her like a boulder. "Do you think they're making another portal?"

"That's my guess," Kywatha said. "The stories say that they or their ancestors made the original ones, so they ought to know how. Uthari removed the one in Zewnath, trapping them in our world and keeping them from bringing in more allies. But if they make another one..."

"You think gathering all the dragon steel for that is less work than attacking Uthari's fleet and taking back the portal?" Rivlen asked.

Kywatha shrugged. "I don't know. Malek has killed their kind, and the portal has *attacked* their kind. Maybe they have the power to make one that likes them."

The last time Uthari had tried to make that portal work for him, it had zapped him. But did the dragons know that? Rivlen closed her eyes, trying to remember the order of events the night of that battle. She was fairly certain the other dragons had been gone and Tezi and Sorath had fought and killed the one at the portal before Uthari had been zapped.

"That sounds like a tall order," Rivlen said, "but I see your point."

Kywatha lifted her chin. "As the defenders of our homeland, we feel compelled to go investigate. To those of you from north of the equator, the Glacier Islands are distant, but if the dragons set up camp there, they would be neighbors to our continent."

"Given how fast they fly, they're neighbors to all of us."

"True. Will you send some of your fleet with us to the south? We don't often leave our homeland, and this is the only ship we have."

Rivlen resisted the urge to scoff at the notion of that oversized *raft* being worthy of the name ship. This wasn't the time for insults. Kywatha wanted help; she wanted an alliance. It seemed crazy, given that they'd been fighting against each other for weeks, but if the dragons were working to create another portal and perhaps bring even *more* dragons—and who knew what else—into the world, mages and druids would have to combine forces to keep that from happening. Every human on Torvil might have to combine forces.

"I'm inclined to agree that we need to work together and make sure they're not making a portal," Rivlen said, "but I'm only one captain in command of one ship. I need to report this information to my king and see what his orders are."

"We'd have taken even one ship." Kywatha smiled faintly.

"I understand, but I can't go flying off on my own." Unfortunately. What did it say about Rivlen that she would rather go spy on deadly dragons than reach out to Uthari and explain the night's events to him? "Our gateship would actually be the best vessel to send to investigate. There's some camouflage on it that makes dragons less likely to see it, at least from a distance."

Kywatha narrowed her eyes. "I have noticed that."

"But I also can't send it off without orders from above."

"Will you contact your superiors soon? We shouldn't delay leaving for long. The dragons already have a head start on putting their plan into place."

"Yes. I'll report in now."

"Thank you, Captain. I'm glad there are some reasonable officers among Uthari's fleet."

Rivlen wanted to snap that *most* of the officers were reasonable, but she remembered Tonovan killing Temrok in his own throne room while his engineers set explosives in the sky city, and she didn't know if she believed that. There were *some* reasonable officers, but many others seemed willing to mindlessly follow orders, even vile ones.

Would she have planted explosives if Tonovan had ordered it? Or if Uthari had? She liked to think not, but she didn't know. She was glad they hadn't told her anything about their plans.

"One way or another," Rivlen said, "I'll let you know what King Uthari says."

"Thank you." Kywatha inclined her head and faded from view.

Rivlen wiped palms that had gone sweaty and rested one on top of the dome-jir. As much as she wanted to put this off, she couldn't. She envisioned Uthari's face and ordered the device to reach out to the dome-jir on the *Serene Waters*.

A part of her hoped Uthari was deep in sleep and that one of his young officers responded, but she would have to ask for him regardless. This was too important to put off.

Though it was late, he was the one to answer. "Captain Rivlen. I've been expecting an update from Tonovan regarding his questioning of the boy and his problem."

"I'm sure he would have liked to give you one, Your Majesty, but a zidarr assassin stowed away on the ship. Tonovan is dead."

Uthari's eyebrows didn't fly up in surprise. No, his eyes narrowed to slits as he stared at her.

"Explain," was all he said.

After taking a deep breath, Rivlen did so. She wanted to confess to everything, but she left out the hint of forewarning she'd had when she'd seen the kerzor in Jak's mind. Maybe later, Uthari would force her to her knees in front of him and use his superior power to tear down her mental barriers and sift through her every thought, but he couldn't do that from a thousand miles away. She told him *most* of the truth, as she knew it, and didn't speculate on anything she hadn't witnessed directly.

"I need to go look at the zidarr's body to verify his identity, but I heard it was one of Temrok's men." Rivlen left out that she'd glimpsed him in the city when they'd been leaving. Another failure on her part.

"And Jak and that mercenary girl dispatched him?" Uthari asked, oozing skepticism.

"She has that axe." Rivlen shrugged, though she now wished she'd gone to sickbay to investigate herself before contacting Uthari. But time might be of the essence. "And it's not unprecedented. She killed Yidar too."

Anger flashed in Uthari's eyes, and Rivlen wished she hadn't reminded him of that.

"Yidar, who arrived with Zaruk's men and seemed to be betraying you," Rivlen added.

"I know what he *seemed* to be doing."

"I have more to report, Your Majesty." Rivlen hurried to share what Kywatha had told her, leaving out that *Sorath* had been the one to glean that intelligence. Maybe she shouldn't have— keeping things from her king wasn't a good idea—but Uthari might dismiss the information if he knew it came from the merce- nary he hated more than any other. And Rivlen, having seen the dragons heading south with that giant pillar, believed the message.

Uthari leaned back in his chair. "Is there anything else you'd like to report, Captain?" he said, not saying whether he believed the dragons might be making a portal or not. "I trust you under- stand that there *will* be a full investigation later."

"Yes, Your Majesty. You made that clear."

"And even so, you couldn't keep one general from dying on your ship."

"One general with a lot of enemies and no power with which to protect himself."

A muscle ticked in Uthari's temple. Something else she shouldn't have reminded him of...

"Because of that boy, that boy who's cheerfully making devices to rob mages of their power and their ability to defend themselves. Who robbed *my general*." A thud sounded as Uthari slapped his hand down on his desk.

Rivlen, who'd seen him deliver threats but never lose his temper, clasped her hands behind her back and struggled to keep her features calm, but a bead of sweat ran down her spine. Why was facing this man more daunting than battling dragons? Because she'd always believed that if she could prove herself to her king, it would be enough to prove herself to her father?

Damn it, why did her father's good opinion even matter anymore? She was a grown woman. She should want to succeed solely because it was what *she* wished.

Perfectly reasonable and rational words. Too bad emotions were rarely reasonable and rational, and her father's stern disap- proving face never lingered far from her thoughts, reminding her that when she'd failed the test to be taken on for zidarr training, she'd failed the family.

"Vinjo taught him to make it, I assume," Uthari said when he regained his composure.

"I don't know, Your Majesty. Vinjo has been on the gateship, and I haven't interacted with him." Rivlen almost said that Jak had been aboard the *Star Flyer* the whole time, but that wasn't true. Before they'd slept together, he'd been on the gateship. No doubt working on that damn thing with the engineer.

"Tonovan told me about Vinjo's interest in teaching Jak on Nargnoth. I've had enough of that boy—*and* that engineer. I thought when he made that ship so quickly that he might be worth suborning and putting to work on future projects, but he's conspired against us from the beginning. I have orders for you, Captain."

His face was so cool that Rivlen was sure his first order would be for her to execute Vinjo. She didn't want to carry out an execution, but whatever orders Uthari gave, she dared not question them.

"Yes, Your Majesty?"

"Put Jak and Vinjo on the gateship and send it to my castle in Utharika. I will deal with those two myself."

Fear for Jak rose up in Rivlen, along with the urge to stand in front of him and protect him from Uthari's ire, but she couldn't do that. He'd brought this on himself. Besides, it would be better for her career if he weren't on the *Star Flyer*, his imploring gazes and goofy smiles leading her astray from her mission. He was a distraction, a bad influence, and he was without a doubt the reason Tonovan was dead.

Rivlen would never mourn the general's death—one day, she would even rejoice it—but this hadn't been the right time for it. Not when her fate had been linked to his, when her career, maybe even her life, rested on the blade's edge.

"Yes, Your Majesty," she heard herself say, though she had a strange sensation of not being fully in her body, as if viewing this conversation from the outside.

"Send some loyal and *powerful* officers along to make sure those two don't try to make off with that ship," Uthari said.

"Yes, Your Majesty."

"I will contact Captain Hevlor. He will be in charge of your remaining three ships, and you'll head south to find out what the dragons are up to. If they are indeed constructing a portal of their own, you'll need to sabotage it before it can be completed."

She needed to? Herself? He wasn't even putting her in command.

"I understand, Your Majesty," she made herself say though this sounded like a suicide mission.

Hell, maybe it was. Uthari's eyes were still narrowed, and he radiated displeasure. Was he intentionally sending her to die?

"Good," he said.

"The druids have a ship and have volunteered to help." Once again, Rivlen didn't mention Sorath. "They're worried about the dragons taking up residence next to their continent."

"Yes, *now* they're worried. Where were they the night dragons were streaming out of the portal?"

Rivlen spread a hand. "Do you object to us working with them?"

"No. If you're smart, you'll send their ship in first and use them as cannon fodder."

"I will keep that suggestion in mind, Your Majesty."

"Good. Don't forget to send the boy to me before you fly into danger. And his pet engineer. I'd hate for anything to happen to them before we get to have a long chat."

That fear for Jak returned, but Rivlen had no choice but to obey. Uthari would likely share these orders with Captain Hevlor to ensure they were carried out. For Jak's sake, Rivlen would hope that Uthari still needed him and his mother and wouldn't hurt him too badly. He'd already had to endure Tonovan's attempt to interrogate him—or whatever that had been.

"Yes, Your Majesty."

"Don't disappoint me, Rivlen. It seems there'll be an opening in my command structure. I'll have to decide who will fill it."

She almost rocked back again, surprised that he would suggest it was possible she could receive a promotion. After all her failures, would he truly consider it? Before, he'd said she was too young, that Tonovan's position wouldn't be available even if he died. But now...

"I'll deal with the dragons for you, Your Majesty," Rivlen said, though it sounded ludicrous. They hadn't dealt with even *one* dragon yet, and if all of them were in the Glacier Islands working together, how would she get close? Especially if she had to send away the one ship with magical camouflage.

"Do so, Captain." Uthari cut communications first, his image vanishing.

Rivlen rested her palms to either side of the dark dome-jir and let her head droop. She had to send Jak away, likely to be punished in Uthari's castle. Punished and *more*. She might never see him alive again.

While it might have been better for her career if he hadn't come along, she couldn't deny that he'd helped her. Not only did she hate the idea of him suffering at Uthari's vengeful hands, she didn't like the idea of sailing into trouble without him at her side.

"Damn it, Jak," she whispered to the empty cabin. "Why couldn't you have left things alone?"

If he hadn't made that kerzor, they might have been sailing to the Glacier Islands to face the dragons together.

On the druid raft, "sickbay" was a log slightly flatter than the others with bedding stretched along it. At least, as a druid healer treated him, Sorath didn't have to be too removed from the action to follow along. With the open sky above and soft drizzle falling on his face, he would be sure to see if the dragons returned.

Fortunately, the last couple of hours as night waned and dawn approached had been quiet. The dragons, content with their prize —at least for the time being—hadn't made a reappearance.

Something told Sorath that they would be back eventually, though it was silly to risk one's life for a dagger when one could have an entire *pillar* of dragon steel. It was possible, however, that they needed every shred they could gather. As he knew from his archaeological texts—that hobby seemed so far in the past now— dragon steel wasn't abundant on Torvil. The ore that it was made from didn't exist here, and what was in their world had been brought through the portal long ago.

Kywatha knelt at his side, her eyes weary, her green hair tangled and damp around her shoulders. "Are you recovering under Daritha's touch, Colonel?"

"My back and ribs don't hurt as much, so hopefully. I wouldn't recommend falling a hundred feet onto a log raft though, no matter who'll be touching you afterward."

"It was only thirty."

"And yet, I still can't recommend the experience." It had felt like an eternity when he'd been falling, terror slowing down time to etch every fraction of a second in his mind.

"You could have died, so you should be pleased."

Sorath snorted. "That fate is inevitable. It's just a matter of time."

"True. Especially since we're flying south after the dragons."

"That's the plan?"

"To figure out what they're up to, yes. And to come up with a plan to stop them. Captain Rivlen has contacted her king, and he's agreed to send their three mageships along with us. Their small, narrow ship won't be coming, since it's been tasked with delivering someone back to their king, but it isn't a warship anyway."

No, but it *was* a camouflaged ship. That would have made it ideal for a stealthy incursion into a dragon camp.

"I'm glad the *Star Flyer* will be coming with us." It saddened Sorath that he was flying so close to Ferroki but hadn't been able to exchange a single word with her yet. As long as they were on different ships, he might not get a chance at all. "Who's being sent back on the gateship?" Sorath hoped it wasn't anyone from Thorn Company. He was positive that most of the mercenaries were of no interest to Uthari, but Tezi's *axe* was of interest to everyone.

"Captain Rivlen didn't confide that in me. I don't think she likes me much." Kywatha smiled faintly.

"I imagine that has to do with all the attempts you and your people made to steal the portal."

Her smile vanished. "It was not *theft*. The portal did not belong to them in the first place, and they had no right to erect it in the middle of our homeland. It was an invitation for exactly *this* to happen." Kywatha flung an arm out wide to indicate the dragons, though none remained in the nearby night sky.

"I know. Is the gateship still here? Maybe you could ask Vinjo to camouflage your raft before it leaves."

"We do not need any mages to assist us when it comes to magic," Kywatha said stiffly.

"Then I suggest camouflaging it yourselves so the dragons don't sense us coming."

She hesitated. "I'll see what we can do."

Sorath let his head clunk back onto the log. He wondered what they would find when they caught up with the dragons. What *were* they doing with all that dragon steel?

"Oh," he said, realization coming to him. "I bet they're making another portal."

The druids must have already reached that conclusion, for Kywatha only nodded.

"Though the pillar alone ought to be enough for that. They wouldn't need to make more than one for some reason, would they?"

"I hope not." Kywatha wiped raindrops from her face and frowned toward one side of the raft. "Captain Rivlen and some of Uthari's other officers are coming over on skyboards. Will you stand with us, Colonel?"

"Oh, yes. Captain Rivlen would be disappointed if I didn't join her meeting." Sorath turned his head to squint into the drizzle. His heart lifted, for he spotted Ferroki riding behind one of the mages, her legs spread for balance as the oval-shaped skyboard sailed over empty air.

With his heart lighter, Sorath thanked the healer for her work and pushed himself to his feet. His back twinged and his ribs hurt if he breathed too deeply, so he hoped he would be able to get more magical treatment later. At least his bones had knitted.

One of the other mageship captains was coming over with Rivlen—Hevlor, he believed the man's name was—and Sorath wondered who was in charge. Several rows of roamers were lined up by the railing of the *Star Flyer*, as if waiting for something. Once Rivlen landed on the raft, she turned and used her power to start levitating the people over.

Kywatha ran up to question her, though the roamer pirates on the raft were cheering and waving in invitation, wanting to be reunited with their kin.

"I wonder what the maximum weight capacity of this raft is," Sorath muttered.

He'd only taken a few steps when something tapped him on the arm. A staff capped in lesser dragon steel.

"What can I do for you, Jary?" Sorath asked the seer, though

Ferroki was about to land, and *she* was the woman he wanted to speak with.

"It is good that you did not slay that dragon."

"Oh? Why is that?"

"It had one eye. One day, you will ride a one-eyed dragon and lead our people to a free and prosperous future."

"Uh, if that's true, I'm positive it won't be *that* dragon."

"I have not seen others with one eye."

Sorath almost asked how she could have *seen* any of them when she was blind, but it would be cruel to tease her about her lost vision. "Didn't you say that it would be a *blue* dragon that I rode?" Not that Sorath believed he would ride any dragon, unless it was to climb its back to land a killing blow with his dagger. "That one is an ugly brown-and-gray. They all are except for Jak's Shikari."

"Perhaps there will one day be more blue dragons."

"And more one-eyed dragons. After I get done with them, there could be a *lot* more." Sorath gripped the hilt of his dagger with determination, though his aching injuries didn't make him feel like a mighty dragon slayer.

Jary smiled knowingly, her blindness not giving her any trouble seeing through his bravado.

Captain Ferroki broke away from the mages and druids—and dozens of arriving roamers—and headed toward Sorath. He stepped away from Jary and lifted his arms, wanting to greet her with a kiss, but she was a reserved woman and might not want that in front of so many witnesses. Alas, a log raft offered little in the way of privacy. She accepted his hug, kissed him on the cheek, and gripped him back for several long moments.

"Has it been bad?" Sorath asked quietly, aware of Rivlen frowning over at them—or, more likely, *him*.

"No worse than usual."

"So moderately awful?"

"Yes." Her dark eyes were bleak as she lifted her chin to meet his gaze. "Thorn Company wasn't ordered to commit any atrocities, but atrocities were done."

"Captain Rivlen ordered them?"

"No, Uthari, and through him Tonovan. Though... he's dead now."

"Tonovan is dead?" Sorath asked for clarification. As awful as the general was—had been?—Uthari was the true criminal.

"Yes. I understand one of Temrok's zidarr got him in the end. Fitting."

"I'm surprised even a zidarr could take down that man."

"Jak stuck a device in his head that stole his magic."

Sorath blinked. During the brief time he'd gotten to work with Tezi, she'd mentioned seeing such devices on the world she'd visited, but nothing about the conversation had led him to believe that they would appear on Torvil.

"If he's dead, is the device available to be reused?" Sorath would have no problem plucking something that valuable out of a dead man's head. "Or are there others?"

"Jak would be the one to ask, but he may be back in the brig."

So much had taken place since Sorath had parted ways with Thorn Company and the *Star Flyer*. "I wish I could return with you to ask you for more details. And... just because."

Ferroki managed a quick smile, but the bleakness didn't leave her eyes as she looked over the roamers. "Your place may be here with the druids and with them."

"I'm not interested in kissing *them*."

"Not even that blind woman who kept nudging you with her staff? She looked interesting." Ferroki smiled a little longer.

"Not in the least. She wants me to ride a dragon. I can tell you from experience that dragon riding is *not* a healthy pastime. Never take advice from blind seers to do crazy things."

Ferroki's brow furrowed, and Sorath would have explained further, but Kywatha waved for them to come over.

"It's crossed my mind to activate Vinjo's stealth device," Sorath murmured as he and Ferroki headed toward the group, "and join you on the *Star Flyer*, whether Rivlen wants me there or not."

"Do you have a skyboard as well as a stealth device?"

"No, but I'm a pretty good jumper."

Ferroki eyed the hundred-yard-gap between the raft and the mageship. "Are you sure it's the *seer* inspiring you to do crazy things?"

"My ardor and passion to be with you might also prompt unwise decisions."

She snorted. "Well, don't let it. After the dragons are gone and the mages no longer need us..."

"Sure," he said, though he didn't manage to hide his disappointment.

He would have preferred it if Ferroki, moved by ardor and passion of her own, had suggested sneaking aboard would be a good idea and that she had room for him under her blankets. Further, he worried the dragons might never be gone and the mages would continue to need mercenaries to throw away as fodder. Would they both survive the month? The year?

Though she didn't speak again, Ferroki clasped his hand and didn't let go as they stopped next to Rivlen, Hevlor, Kywatha, and two elder druids.

Rivlen frowned, not at their handclasp but at Sorath. "Colonel, it is to my king's consternation that you continue to show up alive."

"Your king's consternation can lick my hairy—"

Ferroki squeezed his hand, much as she had back in Uthari's suite to try to keep him from getting himself killed.

"—arm," he finished.

"Won't that be appealing?" Rivlen muttered, then looked back toward the druids.

"Per Colonel Sorath's suggestions," Kywatha said, "one of our elders is studying the magic that is subtly camouflaging your gate-ship and keeps the dragons from developing much interest in it."

Rivlen and several others looked at the narrow craft, and Sorath wondered when it would leave. And would it take Thorn Company personnel with it? He spotted Lieutenant Sasko on its deck in between a couple of red-uniformed mages. Had they all been ordered to guard it? Or guard *Vinjo* to keep him from sailing off in it? Maybe he was the one being sent to Uthari.

"We believe we may be able to place such magic on our own ship," Kywatha added.

"You're calling this piece of flotsam a *ship*?" Hevlor pointed at the logs. "It looks like something beavers made and left to clog a river."

Kywatha frowned at him before addressing Rivlen. "I was going to offer to fly ahead and scout and report back what we see when we find the dragons, but perhaps we should volunteer your mouthy colleague to fly ahead."

"We would appreciate it if you went ahead." Rivlen lifted a hand to keep the other captain from offending the druids further. "Especially if you're able to camouflage your craft from dragons. Perhaps we should spread out our ships so that we can sense dragons across a wider area. Just because we *think* they're going to the Glacier Islands doesn't mean they are. Colonel, you have only the word of a dragon about that, correct?"

"That's right." Sorath was surprised Kywatha had shared that information with Rivlen, but since he'd been the one urging the druids to work together with the mages, he couldn't object. "He said it smugly. Like they've got something planned."

"Aren't all dragons smug?" Rivlen asked. "Even Jak's dragonling seems so." She winced, glancing toward the *Star Flyer*.

Was Jak truly in the brig? And, if so, had she placed him there?

"This one is extra smug," Sorath said.

"If we find something that we must deal with," Kywatha said, "or even if the dragons are only congregating in the area, we will need more than this handful of ships. Is your king prepared to send the rest of his fleet?"

Rivlen shrugged. "I would guess it depends on how many are harrying Uth right now. You might be better off asking for ships from other nations, though if we find something dire... I would hope that everyone would join in."

"*I* might be better off?" Kywatha arched her eyebrows. "The mages detest the druids and me in particular."

"They also detest each other. Uthari is especially unloved at the moment, so I don't think I'd have any luck talking mages from other kingdoms into helping."

"I see," Kywatha said. "Perhaps we should see what's waiting to the south first."

"Agreed," Rivlen said.

"You are not in command of the fleet," Captain Hevlor whispered to her. "Stop making decisions and leading this conversation."

"Do you think we should do something else?" Rivlen didn't bother to whisper as she replied.

"Not at the moment, but Uthari placed *me* in charge."

"Congratulations."

Hevlor glared at her, grabbed a skyboard, and flew back to his ship.

Since the meeting was breaking up, Sorath drew Ferroki aside. He feared Rivlen would float her back to the *Star Flyer* soon and that he only had a moment.

"Tinder lost the second axe," Ferroki admitted. "Tezi still has hers."

"Tell her to watch it carefully. Even though the dragons got that huge pillar, they might yet want more dragon steel."

"What do you think they're doing with it all?" Ferroki leaned against him. "Keeping us from using it or more?"

"More. Building another portal, maybe."

"So that more dragons can come through into our world?"

Sorath sighed. "I hope not."

He hoped not, but that was exactly what he feared.

"Come, Captain," Rivlen called, pointing to Ferroki and then the *Star Flyer*. "Your people need you, and the colonel... A lot of people want him dead."

"That's distressing," Ferroki murmured, patting Sorath on the chest before stepping away.

"And yet, not new information," Sorath said. "At least *she* doesn't seem to be targeting me."

"She will if Uthari remembers you're in her range and orders it. Be careful."

"I'm always careful."

"Two hours ago, you were dangling from a dragon's horn while it spun circles in the sky."

"Yes, but I was dangling *carefully*." Sorath smiled, touched that she'd been watching even though she'd had her own battle to worry about. He hoped he'd managed to look strong and agile while he'd been dangling, not helpless and in over his head.

"If you think that, you need to look up the definition of that word."

"I will. Perhaps I can use it in my memoir."

"That memoir will have a lot more to go in it after this."

If he survived, it would. He hugged Ferroki again before reluctantly releasing her to go back to the *Star Flyer* with Rivlen.

21

Jak sat with Tezi and Thorn Company as the *Star Flyer* turned not toward Uth and home but toward the south. Back toward Zewnath? To follow the dragons that had ripped that pillar out of the earth?

Neither Rivlen nor anyone else was keeping Jak apprised. At least Rivlen hadn't thrown him back into the brig after the battle. He was attempting to lie low and not attract attention, but Shikari kept galloping around the mercenaries, trying to convince them to share food with him.

If we return to Zewnath, there will be many bugs and animals for you to hunt, Jak promised him.

Earlier, he'd given Shikari most of his breakfast, but the growing dragon had a bottomless stomach.

We are not going to Zewnath. Shikari wandered toward Jak but paused in front of Dr. Fret, who'd finished tending her people's wounds and had pulled out a knitting project. Shikari startled her by sniffing at her bag and poking his snout inside.

Do you know where we're going?

This ship is going after the dragons to see what they are doing. I do not think we are going with them.

Where else would we go? Jak peered toward the railing.

Your mate will tell you. Shikari flicked his tail, then lifted his snout, a ball of red yarn between his teeth, and looked toward where Rivlen was speaking with several of her officers.

Jak blushed. *She's not my mate.*

You mated with her.

We had sex, and it didn't mean... Jak stopped himself from saying *anything.* That would be a lie. It had meant a lot, at least to him. *It doesn't mean we're mates.*

You will not produce offspring together?

Jak nearly fell over. *No. I'm sure Rivlen doesn't want that. She's... a captain. She has other responsibilities besides motherhood.* Not to mention that Jak couldn't imagine having children yet. What would his mother say to being a grandmother at such a young age?

You also have other responsibilities.

Such as saving the world, ending mage rule, and healing your parasite-infested people? That latter was more a task for his mother, but Jak felt compelled to offer whatever assistance he could.

Such as taking care of me. I need more food.

Can't you use your magic to levitate fish up from the sea below to fill your gullet?

That is unsporting. I prefer to fly and dive and capture them with my fangs.

You can do that too. How's your flying come along?

I don't know if I can fly up a thousand feet yet. Shikari flicked his snout, and the yarn ball flew into the air.

Dr. Fret lifted a hand, as if she would object, but the mercenary next to her flattened her arm to her side and shook her head. When the ball came down, Shikari batted it with his nose. Unraveling as it went, it flew through the air and bounced on the deck at Rivlen's feet. Shikari galloped after it, but Rivlen picked it up first, frowned at him, and then frowned at Jak.

Gathering yarn as she walked, she headed toward him.

"Kid's about to end up back in the brig," one of the mercenaries muttered.

"Maybe not. There are rumors that he's been warming the captain's toes in bed."

Jak stood up, wishing he'd sat somewhere else. Sadly, he didn't have many friends here, especially when Rivlen wasn't talking to him. He missed his mother. Both for her company and because he wanted to be there to protect her from Uthari's machinations. Was Malek taking care of her? Or was he too busy doing his master's bidding? Jak hoped Mother wasn't afraid to use her power to defend herself against the king.

"Gather your gear, Jak," Rivlen said as she approached. "And your dragon."

"Am I going somewhere more appealing than the brig?"

Maybe Shikari had been right.

"You're going to Utharika. Uthari wants you."

Jak grimaced. "So, the answer is *no*, I'm not going somewhere more appealing than the brig."

He supposed this would give him an opportunity to check on his mother, but he worried he would only end up on his knees before Uthari, being used as a lever against her.

"Sorry," Rivlen said, thrusting the half-unraveled ball of yarn at him. "You shouldn't have made the kerzor."

Jak couldn't bring himself to apologize for that, even though he now wondered if it had been necessary. Might an assassin have killed Tonovan even if he'd had his power?

"How will I get there?" Jak waved toward their southward direction.

"You're going on the gateship with Vinjo. Uthari wants to see *him* too."

Rivlen didn't brush her hands together to indicate she was glad to get rid of them, but Jak couldn't help but get that impression. There was an aloofness—a *distance*—to her that made him believe she thought she'd made a mistake in having a relationship with him. That saddened him, since developing feelings for her was one of the few things he didn't regret.

"I'm to send a number of powerful mage guards to make sure you two don't conspire and decide *not* to take the ship to Utharika. If it had a brig, I think Uthari would have ordered you two to ride in it."

"I see. What are you and the rest of this fleet going to be doing?" Jak pointed at the other two mageships.

"Going with the druids to see what the dragons are up to."

"Is that wise?"

Rivlen shrugged. "We have to know. Gather your gear."

She turned and walked toward the navigation cabin. Jak watched the back of her head sadly, wishing she'd drawn him aside and said goodbye with a kiss and a promise that when this was all over, they could spend more time together. But he feared that wouldn't happen. Whatever Uthari wanted, Jak was sure it would involve more than *seeing* him. Would the vengeful old wizard kill him for presuming to have made the kerzor? Or punish him the way he'd punished Malek?

Jak didn't have much gear to collect, so it didn't take long. After collecting as much of the yarn as he could, including extracting pieces from Shikari's fangs, he apologetically handed the tangled mess back to Dr. Fret.

When he walked to the railing nearest the gateship, four mage officers wearing packs, weapons, and sour expressions joined him. One thrust a skyboard at him.

Were these the powerful guards Rivlen had mentioned? They

didn't *seem* that powerful, at least judging by their auras and ranks. Most didn't look much older than he, and one was the officer whom Jak had compelled to attack Tonovan. Maybe he was being sent as punishment for failing to resist Jak's manipulation.

Or maybe... Jak's jaw dropped as a thought occurred to him.

Had Rivlen picked these people because they *weren't* powerful? Because Vinjo and Jak might overcome them, lock them up, and take control of the gateship?

He sensed Rivlen's aura in the navigation cabin and looked over to find her standing in the hatchway and watching him. Her face was masked, but he thought he sensed concern from her. And that she cared.

He didn't say it, Rivlen spoke into his mind, *but Uthari may be planning to kill you and Vinjo. He still needs your mother, but he doesn't need your knowledge anymore, and he said it had been a mistake to let Malek train you. It may be in your best interest if the gateship is lost at sea along the way to Utharika.*

Thank you, Rivlen, but... won't you get in trouble for this?

I'm hoping he'll be too busy in the near future to question the choice I made about who to send along.

And if he isn't? Jak remembered her concern about the promised investigation into Tonovan's death. Somehow, he doubted Uthari was ever too busy to punish officers who went astray.

Don't worry about it, Jak. Just disappear, and stay out of trouble. Rivlen stepped back into the cabin and shut the hatch.

Jak didn't know if she truly expected him to *stay out of trouble* when the whole world was at risk, but he would do his best not to let himself be deposited on Uthari's doorstep.

～

The *Serene Waters* and the rest of the fleet were less than fifty miles from Utharika when Malek sensed the dragons around the city. He'd heard from reports that the mage defenders were fighting them off thus far but that they needed help. The fleet had already passed over numerous terrene cities and mage watchtowers on the ground that were smoking, people having fled into the forests to escape their winged assailants.

Not only the cities had been targeted. Croplands that had been ripe with vegetables and grains almost ready to be harvested had been devastated, only smoldering black fields remaining. The dragons knew exactly what they were doing, what would bring the human civilization to its knees.

As Malek headed across the deck to Uthari's suite, he spotted the wreckage of a mageship below. It wasn't only the farms and cities of terrene humans that the dragons were threatening.

Uthari was in his office, finishing up a meeting with King Jutok, when Malek entered. He clasped his hands behind his back to wait, listening to the last words of a conversation that ended with Jutok saying that nobody trusted Uthari now and that his people were on their own. There would be no alliances. Besides, Jutok and the other rulers were too busy defending against dragons in their own kingdoms. Few continents had been spared from their ravages.

Malek tried not to judge Uthari for his actions, as it wasn't his place to do so. Besides, some of the mistrust from others came because Vorsha had died in Uthari's bedroom and the other rulers believed he'd been responsible. Still, Uthari's choice to have King Temrok killed... Malek hadn't believed that wise. Everyone in the world should have been focused on the dragons and not on taking advantage of each other.

Malek looked toward the north, longing to get out there and fight, to do his part against these terrible enemies.

The dome-jir went dark, and Uthari folded his hands on his

desk as he regarded him. "I always thought *you* would be the one to kill Tonovan when the day came that he pushed you too far."

"Even if I'd been tempted, I would not have chosen this time to do so. He was powerful, and we need power against the dragons."

"Indeed. I've lost Tonovan *and* Yidar in the last couple of weeks. I'm not pleased."

Malek nodded.

"I'm not pleased with *Jak*."

"He had nothing to do with Yidar's death," Malek said, though he doubted that would matter to Uthari. To have raised a hand against a mage at all was a crime.

"He made a kerzor after I forbade it. And I'm positive he lured that engineer into helping him do it. I've ordered Rivlen to have both of them sent to my castle. I'll be disappointed if a dragon destroys their ship along the way, because I want to wring their necks myself."

Malek didn't move, didn't breathe. He'd feared this, that Uthari would kill Jak. Not only would that devastate Jadora, but... Malek didn't want to lose Jak either. All along, he'd been teaching the boy, hoping Jak would be willing to serve Uthari one day. But perhaps it had been foolish to believe Jak's bond with Malek would make Jak willing to obey Uthari.

"I assume you care little about the engineer," Uthari said.

"Vinjo? I've not interacted with him much, and he is an enemy soldier from Zar, so, no."

"But much about the boy."

Malek let out a slow exhale, though he was careful to keep his face neutral.

"He's become too dangerous. They both have. We were foolish to believe Jak could be turned to our side and become loyal to me." Uthari squinted at him, watching his face. "Will you defy me in this?"

"In executing him?"

"Yes."

Malek closed his eyes, seeking an answer that would be neither a lie nor a statement that would sever his relationship with Uthari forever. "Is there no alternative?"

"What? Exile? For him and his mother?"

"You have contemplated that."

"Since then, it's occurred to me that for them, the portals might be willing to operate without a key."

True. Malek had seen Jak open the portal on Nargnoth without using a key. The dragons didn't use keys. For those whom the portals approved of, or who simply had a great deal of power, they weren't needed.

"That is possible," Malek said, "but it's also possible they would obey our wishes and not return to Torvil. Not if the alternative is death."

"I don't particularly want them on another world, building an army and warehouses full of those kerzor either. All it would take is someone like Colonel Sorath to get through the portal to visit them, take what they've made, and return to attack us. After we deal with the dragons, we'll already be weakened. Our people, since we are the ones who can fight them, will suffer most in this war."

After seeing the cities and croplands destroyed, Malek doubted that was true. Everyone was suffering, mage and terrene human alike.

"So, you want them dead," he said woodenly.

"I want the boy dead. I know you care for the professor, and she's not the hothead that he is. I think if he's gone, she could be permitted to live."

Malek didn't know if that was true at all. After losing her husband, Jadora had been driven to give up her career and devote all her time and resources to traveling around the world and searching for the portal. If she lost Jak, she might be driven to much more. She might join with Sorath in working to overthrow the mages. And now she had the power to make a difference.

Further, Malek didn't say it, but he also cared about Jak. Even as he stood in front of Uthari, he ran through options in his mind, trying to come up with a way to save him.

If he smuggled Jak and Jadora out of Uth and to another world, Uthari might leave them there. He would punish Malek, but Malek had been punished before. It wouldn't be as bad as if he openly defied Uthari and stood with Jak and Jadora against him. Malek did not want to do that. He owed his life and his training and everything to Uthari. And if Uthari was forced to, he might have the power to kill Malek. Malek was always prepared to die in battle, and accepted it as inevitable, but he didn't want to betray his king and be forced into *that* battle. Whether he failed or was victorious, he would lose.

"I suggest you wait until after we deal with the dragons," Malek said, not because it was the wisest course of action for Uthari, but because he needed time to mull over his limited options. "He can be useful against the dragons."

"He's still just a boy."

"One the portals like."

"They like Jadora now too." Uthari smiled thinly. "I checked."

Malek opened his mouth but paused before replying. When Uthari had tested Jadora while they stood next to the portal, Malek had assumed it was because Uthari was frustrated and had lost his temper, but maybe he'd been far more calculating than that. Maybe he'd wanted to see if the portal would defend her. And he'd gotten his answer. It would. Therefore, they didn't need Jak.

"We're about to fly into battle," Uthari said. "Take the professor to the portal and have her rouse its power. I want every dragon attacking my city zapped by its lightning."

"Yes, Your Majesty." Malek headed for the door.

"Malek?"

He paused and turned. "Yes?"

"I have a request for you, an appeal to your honor. If you decide to turn on me, don't do what Yidar did and try to distract me and strike me down while I'm protecting our people."

"I won't turn on you, Your Majesty." Malek hoped he was telling the truth, that Uthari wouldn't push him to a point where he had no choice but to choose between Uthari and Jadora, and that he wouldn't... let his emotions propel him to do something his logical mind would later regret. Just because he questioned Uthari's choices didn't mean he wanted to throw away decades of his life and turn on the man who'd been as a father to him.

"Good." Uthari smiled. "Your loss would mean a great deal more to me than Tonovan's."

As Malek walked away, he considered whether that had been a threat. An assumption that if they did battle, Uthari would win, and he would have to kill Malek.

He shook his head and left the suite to head to Jadora's lab. As he walked across the deck, the smell of smoke tainted the air. Numerous crewmen were pointing to the north, though the sky city and the dragons weren't yet in view. As mages, they could sense both, as Malek could.

After knocking on Jadora's door, he stepped inside. She looked up from her books and the young plants growing under the special lights, and her pockets clanked faintly as she turned.

Was she still carrying around vials of acid to throw at handsy mages? Or containers to take sample specimens? He didn't know, but an ache started in his soul as he gazed at her and thought about how she would feel if Uthari succeeded in killing her only son. His throat tightened with emotion, and he wanted to pull her into a hug and tell her Jak would be fine, that Uthari wouldn't hurt him, but he couldn't promise that.

"Uthari wants you by the portal as we fly into battle," Malek said. "To order it to use its power against the dragons threatening Utharika."

"I can *request* that it do so."

"As long as it obeys those requests, that's fine."

"And if it doesn't?"

"Then we do it the hard way." Malek touched the hilt of his sword. "I suspect the hard way will be required regardless."

"Probably. I haven't noticed that dragons strive to make our lives easy."

"No." Malek extended an arm toward her and tilted his head toward the corridor.

Jadora squared her shoulders and walked forward, though he noticed moisture in her eyes. Had she been thinking about Jak? About how in previous battles *he'd* been the one to make requests of the portal?

When she drew even with Malek, she paused. The determined set of her chin relaxed, a quaver to it as she closed her eyes and swallowed.

"Malek..." she whispered and wobbled.

He wrapped an arm around her, only to support her, he told himself, but he ended up pulling her into a hug.

"He plans to kill Jak." She collapsed against him, pressing her face into his shoulder. "And if I try to stop him, he'll consider it a threat, an *attack*. And maybe it will have to be one in order to save my son. But then you..." Her throat tightened, and she didn't get any more words out.

Malek squeezed her gently, distressed by her distress and upset at the thought of having to fight her. As if she were an enemy instead of the woman he cared about, the woman he loved.

Her emotions wrapped around him as well as the aura of her power. It was still strange to sense her with power, and he struggled not to be affected by it, by the desire to mingle his power with hers, to be with her magically, emotionally, and physically.

I won't let him hurt you. Malek switched to telepathy, aware of other mages nearby, getting the ship ready for battle, and not wanting them to overhear what some might consider blasphemous words. What *Uthari* might consider blasphemous words if someone reported them to him. He leaned his forehead against her soft hair, though he ached to lower his lips to hers, to kiss her and make the world a safe place for her.

What about Jak?

We'll figure something out. I don't want you to lose your son. I don't want to lose him either.

She leaned her head back and met his gaze, her eyes brimming with unshed tears and warmth. Warmth for him? *I believe you. Thank you.*

Her mixture of power and vulnerability filled him with warmth for *her*. Warmth and desire.

Maybe this wasn't the time, but he shifted her out of the doorway and shut the door so they had privacy. He kissed her, and as he kissed her and she kissed him back, he realized he was making a decision. He might not be willing to turn on Uthari, the way Yidar had, but he wouldn't let him kill Jadora or her son. She meant too much to him. She'd *done* so much for him, saving his life several times, even when she shouldn't have, when they'd clearly been enemies and she should have taken the opportunity to slit his throat. She'd never even considered it. She'd been loyal to him, and he would be a horrible betrayer if he wasn't the same to her.

If he tries to kill Jak, I'll stop it, Malek said, realizing his answer about figuring things out had been vague. Jadora deserved more than vagueness. She deserved a promise that she could count on, a reason to go into battle at his side and trust him fully.

She responded by kissing him more deeply and sliding her hands under his tunic, her warm fingers running over muscles that quivered under her touch. They needed to prepare for battle, and he knew that, but his words had intensified her desire for him, and her emotions washed over him along with her power.

That filled *him* with desire. Before he knew what he was doing, he'd unbuttoned her dress so that he could run his hands over her, seeing and touching parts of her he'd only seen once before, in that cell in Vran. He very much wanted to see her again, *all* of her. And to finish what they'd started back on Vran.

To do this on Uthari's ship and under his nose would be foolish, but Malek realized that with one choice, he'd made others, whether he should have or not. He wanted Jadora, to reward her for the loyalty and love she'd shown him and... to reward himself. Maybe he didn't deserve happiness, but he wanted it anyway. He wanted to be with her.

Her hands slid down to his trousers, but she hesitated. Even as they kissed, longing emanating from her, she asked, *Malek? I hate that old man, and I love you and want to be with you, but I don't want to ruin your life. I don't want you to regret this or resent me. I...*

Tears leaked from her eyes, running down her cheeks to her lips, and he tasted them as they kissed. She started to pull back, but he growled, refusing to let her go. He reached down and unfastened his own trousers before turning around to lean her back against the wall. If he later regretted this choice, so be it.

He used his magic to stroke her body and arouse pleasure even more thoroughly than he could with his hands. Determined that she wouldn't walk away from him, and she would cry out with pleasure, not worry or concern or fear, he slipped off the rest of her clothing. She gasped and squirmed under his touch, welcoming it. Welcoming *him*. Her hands tightened on his shoulders, and she pulled him closer instead of pushing him away.

Malek couldn't bring himself to voice the seditious words that he would choose her over Uthari and stand with her against him to save her son, but at that moment, he knew they were true. Jadora didn't deserve the cruelty of an ambitious wizard who cared nothing for her. She deserved all the admiration and devotion and pleasure that Malek could give to her.

More, she deserved his heart and his soul and his loyalty. And as he gave her his body, he vowed to himself she would have the rest. Always.

22

Sasko woke from a doze, an uneasy feeling in the pit of her stomach, along with the certainty that something bad was about to happen. It was morning, but most people aboard the gateship were sleeping after being up during the night battling dragons. A couple of hours earlier, the ship had left the fleet and turned north again. Heading toward Uth.

Trying to determine what had woken her, Sasko lay still as she stared up at the bunk above hers. It was now occupied by Tinder, since her cabin had been given to two of the mages Rivlen had sent over to guard Jak and Vinjo. Tinder was breathing evenly, still sleeping.

Sasko listened for the sound of boots on the ladder rungs or a warning call from the mage on watch on the deck. All was quiet, however, with only the faint hum of the engines emanating through the deck. Still, she couldn't shake the feeling that something was wrong.

Moving quietly, so she wouldn't wake Tinder, Sasko grabbed her weapons and eased out of her cabin. There weren't any portholes in the corridor, but lamps on the walls kept it lit well enough that she could see that everyone's hatches were closed. The navigation hatch was also closed. Odd. That one was usually open. Was something going on in there? Some secret meeting between Vinjo and... who? Jak? They'd muttered nothing more than muted hellos when Jak and the guards had come on board.

Sasko crept to the hatch and pressed her ear against it. It was too thick for her to hear much, but she *thought* she caught someone speaking. Maybe there *was* a secret meeting. Or maybe —her stomach twisted as she remembered Vinjo sneakily making that communication device—Vinjo was reaching out to someone.

If he was, Sasko highly doubted it was to Uthari or anyone Uthari would approve of. What if the mages that had been sent along found out?

She gripped the latch, thinking of thrusting the hatch open to catch him in the act, but instead, she eased it open an inch and listened. The male voice she now heard more clearly didn't belong to Vinjo, Jak, or anyone else she recognized.

"...where are you?" the person was asking.

"Over the sea between Temril and Agorval," Vinjo replied, whispering, as if he expected to be caught at any second.

Sasko could imagine him nervously kneading the hem of his tunic.

"We've been ordered to go to Utharika. I think Uthari plans to kill me." Vinjo's voice grew louder and more bitter as he added, "I haven't been the perfect little turncoat slave he wanted."

"That you've done anything for him at *all* is deplorable."

"I didn't have a choice."

"You could have let them kill you. Or you could have killed *yourself*. Better that than to make things for that snake. I can't believe you made him a *ship*."

"I don't want to die," Vinjo snapped. "Are you going to help me or not?"

"You'll have to give me more precise coordinates than *over the sea.* It'll be harder for us to get close to you once you're in Uth. Their ships are all over the place."

"I thought you were following along with the fleet."

"The main fleet and at a distance. We didn't even realize you were with those ships that veered off to Temril. Whatever you did when you built that vessel, it's hard to detect. Why didn't you contact me sooner? We could have gotten to you before those people assassinated King Temrok."

"I had to build a dome-jir first."

"You built an entire ship in two days. Don't pretend you couldn't have prioritized that and done it sooner."

"The ship took a week," Vinjo said, "and I could work on it while their mages were watching me, because they ordered it. I had to build the dome-jir on the sly."

A long moment passed with neither man speaking, and Sasko wondered if Vinjo had noticed the hatch. She hadn't dared push it further open, not enough to see anything inside, but that didn't mean he couldn't have glanced back and spotted it ajar.

"Tell me where you're going to come ashore or if you'll fly over an island or someplace where we can more easily find you. Right now, I can barely sense that ship even when it's in sight. I need to know where to meet you." The man lowered his voice, and Sasko almost missed the rest. "Our family is being punished. Zaruk knows you've been working for Uthari."

"Not voluntarily."

"It doesn't matter. It's shameful. *You're* shameful."

"Then come rescue me, so we can go home. I'll... I'll bring this ship. It has new magical technology that I invented, and I can show it to our king. I can weave my camouflaging spell around the ships in Zaruk's fleet. I can be even more useful to him than I was to Uthari. Just come get me before the ship gets to Utharika. Please, Veejar."

"Don't call me that."

"Fine. *Please*, Night Wrath. I know Zaruk might have ordered you to... do away with me, but I can be useful. You'll see. Just get me out of here. I want to fix things for our parents too. I don't want shame or punishment to come to our family."

"I need a landmark, somewhere to direct our fleet to."

Sasko grimaced at the idea of numerous blue-hulled ships lying in wait to ambush them. She had no interest in visiting Utharika, but she hated that Vinjo was speaking with his brother. As a powerful and well-trained zidarr, Night Wrath might be a match for everyone on the ship, and she didn't believe he wanted to help his brother. Hadn't the man tried to *kill* him in the past? Why would Vinjo trust him now? Was he that desperate to avoid Uthari's wrath?

Sasko admitted that was a legitimate thing to want to avoid. That probably *was* his reason for doing this. She worried, however, that it was a bad idea. If all of Zaruk's ships—the very ones that had been shadowing the fleet earlier in the week— showed up with hundreds of mages and a zidarr, the gateship would be taken and everyone on board except Vinjo might be killed. Hell, he might be killed too.

She thought of Tinder and Jak and even his dragonling Shikari. They were as much prisoners as Vinjo and didn't deserve to be killed simply for riding along on this ship, for having no choice but to do so.

"The Twin Dragon Horns on Uth's southern shoreline," Vinjo said. "I'm flying the ship, and I can navigate us toward that spot."

Night Wrath made an exasperated noise. "If you're flying the ship, point it toward where we are."

"I can't. There are four mages onboard to guard us—to make sure I don't deviate. One is on watch on the deck right now. He'll notice if the ship makes a turn, but as long as I'm heading north on a believable route, he shouldn't doubt my choice to angle for the Horns."

"How powerful are the mages? And is there anyone else on board that we need to worry about?"

"They're surprisingly not powerful, actually," Vinjo said.

Sasko winced as he gave away all this free intelligence and agreed to a meeting spot. The urge to burst in and throw a towel over the dome-jir came over her. Or to shatter it with a blade. But for all she knew, the magical device would explode and kill them both.

"They're stronger than I am," Vinjo added, "at least when it comes to throwing fireballs—"

"Who isn't?" his brother said in a snide tone.

"—but I'm not sure they're more powerful than Jak and definitely not than his dragon."

"Than who and *what* dragon?"

Sasko intentionally clunked her arm against the wall. She stepped back a couple of feet and called, "Vinjo? Are you up there?"

She had to stop him from sharing any more intelligence about who was on the ship. Maybe she should have jumped in and not worried about whether Night Wrath saw her, but if the zidarr believed someone had overheard everything, he might alter his plans. Better that she know what those plans were than not.

"I have to go," Vinjo whispered. "The Twin Horns."

By the time Sasko opened the door, the face that must have floated over the dome-jir was gone, and its orange inner glow was fading.

Vinjo leaped from the pilot's chair and spun, throwing up his arms and smiling nervously. "Sasko! Was your nap refreshing? It's a delight to see you."

"I'm sure." She pointed at the dome-jir. "Look, Vinjo. I can understand you not wanting to deliver yourself to Uthari's castle— trust me—but your brother tried to *kill* you less than a month ago. This is a bad idea."

He bit his lip. "How much did you hear?"

"Enough to tell you to avoid the Twin Dragon Horns at all costs."

Vinjo surged forward, gripped her wrists, and pulled her inside while glancing into the corridor. For the moment, it was empty. He pushed the hatch shut anyway.

"Please, don't tell Uthari's people," he whispered, lifting a finger to his lips. Then to *her* lips.

Sasko scowled at him. "I won't, but you have to change your plans. Delivering yourself into your brother's hands could be as deadly for you as walking into Uthari's castle."

"He promised me when I first contacted him that he won't kill me. And I told him I had some information for him. Did you hear that part?"

"No, but I don't trust him."

"He's my brother."

"And he's an ass to you."

"Well, yes, but he cares about our family, the same as I do. We want the same thing. He'll take me to Zaruk instead of killing me. I'm sure of it." Why did he sound like he was trying to convince himself?

"Why do we have to go to either of those places?"

"What do you mean?"

Sasko pointed toward the porthole in the front of the cabin. "Turn left. Or right. You're the one navigating. Take this boat off to somewhere remote until everything is settled and it's safe to return to Zar."

Whenever that would be. Sasko didn't know, and she felt a little derelict of duty for suggesting that they run, since that would mean her disobeying Rivlen and, through her, Thorn Company. But she believed Captain Ferroki would understand. When they could, Sasko and Tinder would rejoin the unit.

"I can't. The mage guard." Vinjo pointed in the direction of the deck.

"It sounds like you think you and Jak and Shikari could overpower him. Shikari is up there now. We can ask him to whack the man with his tail and send him over the railing."

"I don't think the dragonling would obey us. I'm not even sure he obeys Jak."

Sasko admitted that was true. From what she'd seen, Jak was as likely to be catching bugs or fetching other food for the dragon. *He might be the one taking orders from Shikari.*

"If you were sneaky, you could overpower them even without help." Sasko waved to a stealth device on Vinjo's wrist. She hadn't seen him use it since she'd come on board, but she had no doubt that it worked. "If you need me to, I'll be happy to crack them over the head for you."

"And push them overboard to their deaths?" Vinjo shook his head. "They're probably talented enough to levitate themselves back up."

"We could lock them up."

"This ship doesn't have a brig that could hold mages. Or a brig at all."

"Then make some more of those kerzor." She'd only heard part of the story on those, but before they'd parted ways with the *Star Flyer*, Tezi had told her Tonovan was dead because Jak had made one. Sasko assumed Vinjo had been teaching him how to do so the night that Jak had been aboard the gateship. "I'll help you jab them into their temples."

"Sasko." Vinjo released her wrists and rubbed both hands over his face, the backs splotched with grease. "I appreciate that you want to help me—I really, *really* do—but I have to go home. I have to straighten things out with the king so that my family isn't in danger."

"Then go home. I'm from Zar too, you know. I won't object to that. But go of your own accord. Don't you think it'll look better if you fly to Zarlesh in your own ship, not as a prisoner in your brother's brig with your ship being towed along behind his? Besides, your people might kill Jak and Shikari and anyone else who opposes them." Not to mention Vinjo himself...

Vinjo lowered his hands and gazed at her. "You would go home with me?"

The distress that had been twisting his face faded, he smiled hopefully at her.

"Back to Zar? Yes. I couldn't stay indefinitely, as I'd have to find my way back to the company, but..." Something about the adoring expression he'd locked on her made Sasko want to forget the rest, to simply say that, yes, she would go home with him. The vision she'd received from that druid device came to mind, of her having two children and living in some cozy home in Perchver with Vinjo. She hadn't thought she'd wanted that, or seen a way it could come to pass even if she did, but if the alternative was for Vinjo to die at his brother's hands, or at Uthari's hands... "Yes, I'd come back with you."

"See, *this* is why I want to live." Vinjo managed to smile at her and glower at the dome-jir at the same time. "So I can kiss you and do things with you."

Before she could ask what *things* he had in mind, Vinjo grasped her waist with his hands and leaned in to kiss her.

Her first thought was that she should finish talking him out of this course of action before giving in to any tender moments with him, but warmth flowed from his fingers, his magic seeping pleasure into her body. She found herself stepping closer and returning his kiss. Maybe if she showed him how much he could enjoy living and being a free man, he would realize that going to see *either* of those kings was a bad idea. Far better for them to take the ship somewhere remote and see how events played out in the world. It could save his life, Jak's life, *her* life, and—

She gasped as more of his magic flowed into her, sending fire along her nerves and exciting her in a way she wouldn't have believed a goofy engineer with grease on his hands ever could.

"Vinjo," she groaned, all of her whirring thoughts fading from her mind, all save one that involved taking him to find a bunk.

Sasko, he whispered telepathically, his lips too busy for speaking. *You care about me. You, a strong warrior woman with irreverent thoughts, care for me. It's wonderful, and I want to be with you.*

He shared thoughts of them entwined on the navigation console, and she realized they didn't *need* to use a bunk. That instrument panel didn't look that comfortable, but the idea started to intrigue her as their kisses grew more heated, as Vinjo unbuttoned her uniform and pushed the jacket back from her shoulders. It fell to the deck, and she pushed his tunic open, running her hands over his chest.

"Vinjo..." she breathed.

But he jerked his head back and stepped away from her.

"What? Don't stop." She reached for him, but he spun toward the hatch as it burst open.

The mage who'd been on guard on the deck stood there, scowling at Vinjo, though his expression turned to shock when he saw Sasko inside with him. He gaped at her bare breasts, and she snatched up her uniform jacket.

"I sensed someone using power in here," the man said, turning his scowl on Vinjo again.

Whether by accident or design, he had his back to the dome-jir, blocking it from the mage's view.

"Yes," Vinjo said. "That was me."

"It *felt* like the aura of a communications device being activated."

Vinjo tilted his head in apparent confusion. "That's not it at all. I was using my power on, uhm." He looked at Sasko.

Technically, he *had* been doing that, and Sasko couldn't keep from blushing, though she was aware of Vinjo fumbling behind his back, trying to open a drawer when the mage wasn't looking. So he could slip the dome-jir inside. Would that be sufficient to hide it from another mage?

"Does she *want* you to use your power on her?" the mage asked skeptically.

"Of course," Vinjo said. "I'm sexy and appealing to mercenaries."

"Uh huh." Surprisingly, the mage waved for Sasko to step outside, as if he wanted to save her from Vinjo's odious attention. Maybe he had a chivalrous streak and did, though such traits were rare in mages.

Sasko stepped toward him, more so he wouldn't see what Vinjo was doing than because she wanted to be saved.

The mage took her wrist and pulled her out of navigation. Judging by the soft clunk that Sasko heard, that gave Vinjo time to hide the device. Maybe he'd used some magic on that drawer, and it could camouflage items that he tucked inside. For his sake, Sasko hoped so.

"That idiot wasn't bothering you, was he?" the mage asked, though any thoughts she had of him being chivalrous disappeared when he looked down at her chest.

She'd covered herself with her jacket but hadn't had an opportunity to put it on yet.

"It's fine," she said. "I can take care of myself."

He snorted. "Not against someone with magic. But magic doesn't have to be used to *force* women to have sex. It can give women a good time. You've got great tits, you know." He smiled, his gaze shifting from her chest to her mouth as he planted a hand on the wall behind her. "I thought this mission would be boring, but maybe it won't be."

He leaned in, groping her with his magic. What had been pleasurable from Vinjo was appalling from this jerk, and Sasko whipped her dagger out and pointed it at his throat, the tip brushing skin. She was surprised she was able to get it that close to him, since she didn't have a dragon-steel blade, but he must have been focusing his magic on her instead of on keeping a barrier up.

"Look here, mercenary woman," he growled. "You're here to—"

A hatch opened, and Jak stuck his head out. "What's going on?"

With his hair tousled from sleep and his shirt rumpled, he looked as if he'd innocently and accidentally walked out at that moment, but Sasko wasn't so sure. The mage jerked back, his shoulder blades bumping the opposite wall, and he turned and frowned at Jak. Long seconds passed as they glared at each other. Testing each other's magical defenses?

"Nothing," the mage finally said, and stalked into the ship's little kitchen.

"You all right?" Jak whispered.

Sasko sheathed her dagger. "Fine."

"Good. I'm being told someone needs assistance with fishing from a thousand feet up." Jak offered a lopsided smile and headed for the ladder.

"A most important mission."

"So I'm told."

After he climbed up the ladder, Sasko returned to her cabin, regretting that any tryst she might have wanted to have with Vinjo would have to wait. Her encounter with the horny mage guard had put her out of the mood anyway.

Thank you, came a grateful message from Vinjo as she sat on her bunk. *I got it hidden.*

Good. Hopefully, he's too stupid to realize the magic you were using on me wasn't the same magic that your communication thing uses. I assume they feel different.

They do. And he is stupid. And was distracted by your, uhm.

Great tits. I know.

He said that? Indignation came along with Vinjo's words.

Yeah, but don't worry about it.

I liked your idea. I wonder if Jak is interested in making more kerzor devices. A lot *more.*

I don't know, but first make sure to alter the path of the ship so that it doesn't go over those Horns. I don't want you to have to stick one of those things in your brother's head. That was the truth, but Sasko did suspect the personalities of all zidarr would be much improved if they received such treatment. *Much better for us to direct our own fate, right?*

She didn't know if Vinjo was monitoring her thoughts beyond listening to her words, but she tried to share the image of their gateship flying leisurely across the sea, unmolested by mages or dragons, while she and Vinjo finished what they'd started in the navigation cabin.

You're promising to sleep with me if I change course?

Sasko couldn't tell if he sounded amused or intrigued. He definitely wasn't offended, and she almost said yes. But...

I don't want to bribe you with sex.

I wouldn't mind at all.

Just... alter the course, Vinjo. We can do this without your brother.

All right, Sasko. Uhm, I love you.

Maybe she should have said it back—that was polite, wasn't it? —but what came out was, *Good.* She hesitated, decided that sounded callous, and added, *I care about you too, Vinjo.*

I know. You're amazing.

She just hoped she'd gotten through to him. It was too easy for her to envision Night Wrath thrusting a dagger into Vinjo's chest, then killing everybody aboard and taking the gateship back to his master as a prize.

~

When Jadora followed Malek up on deck and levitated over to the *Soaring Eagle* with him, it was all she could do not to clasp his hand—or maybe his butt—and steal kisses. She struggled to keep her face masked, though she wanted to grin, to bask in the memory of the passion they'd shared in her lab, the passion she'd wanted to share with him for so long. She still feared Malek would regret it—that Uthari would *make* him regret it—but when she'd given him the chance to come to his senses and back away from her... he hadn't.

For whatever reason, he'd finally decided he wanted her and didn't care if Uthari and his Zidarr Code forbade it or not. She was worried for him, but it was hard to feel any regret. She'd enjoyed being with him and longed to join him again that night, and every night thereafter.

But dragons and Utharika were visible in the sky ahead, flames burning on the docks outside of the wall, and she made herself focus on the moment. She had to help Uthari defend his city, both to save those who lived within and so she could get back to the research she needed to do to save the dragons.

After she and Malek landed next to the portal on the deck of the *Soaring Eagle*, he drew his weapons. "Unless Uthari calls me away, I'll stand next to you. Once the dragons realize that you're responsible for the lightning shooting from the portal, they'll try to get to you."

Yes, they might also try to get her *before* that.

Malek looked at her, his eyes intense as they met hers. "I won't let them succeed."

He almost growled the words, and a shiver went through her, her entire body tightening in response. The memory of him promising not to let Jak be killed came to mind, and appreciation welled up within her once more.

After they'd had sex, she'd thought her desire for him would slacken for a time, but her treacherous mind shared an image with him of them naked and writhing together on the portal. Since she could now unconsciously protect her thoughts from other mages, she didn't expect Malek to catch the fantasy, but she must have accidentally shared it, for a wolfish smile curved his lips. He whispered a promise of, *Later*, into her mind.

She swallowed and nodded and would have smiled back, but she sensed Uthari stepping out of his suite on the yacht. He looked toward her and Malek, standing close to each other, and watched them for a long moment.

Jadora strengthened her barrier and turned toward the dragons ahead. She had few delusions that Uthari wouldn't find out—knowing Malek, he would feel compelled to confess his sins —but she didn't want to flaunt their relationship. She hoped that with the distraction of the battle, Uthari might not notice that anything had changed between them.

Though Jadora did her best to ignore Uthari, Malek looked over his shoulder and held his king's gaze for several long seconds. Certain they were exchanging words, Jadora willed the ships to fly faster so they could engage in battle sooner. It was only *partially* for the sake of the sky city and those in it, though Utharika clearly needed help.

Whatever Malek and Uthari said, it was brief, and it didn't cause Malek to step away from her. With his weapons still in hand, he stood at her side and faced the threat ahead. Four dragons. It was the most Jadora had seen at once, and she feared they would zero in on her and the portal, just as Malek had suggested. She was glad he would stand beside her, but would it be enough? As deadly as Malek was, he couldn't fight so many.

She reminded herself that *she* had power now too, and she could help him. At least she *hoped* she could. Even with all that Zelonsera had given her, it wasn't the equal of one dragon, much less four.

"Trust in yourself," Malek said softly, as if he were still able to read her mind, as if he knew her every doubt. Maybe her fears were written plainly on her face. "And don't be afraid to throw a vial of acid if all else fails."

"I'm *never* afraid to do that."

"I know." He looked at her, and she sensed that he wanted to kiss her, but with Uthari at their backs, he didn't. He merely nodded at her and smiled.

It was enough.

"Lower your barrier, *Soaring Eagle*," Uthari called, "so the portal can attack."

"We'll be vulnerable to the *dragons'* attacks, Your Majesty," the captain of the ship called back.

"I'm aware. Do it anyway."

The captain glanced at Malek, Jadora, and the portal, skepticism twisting his face, but he obediently called back, "Yes, Your Majesty."

There was a part of Jadora that wondered if Uthari hoped she would fail and that the dragons would kill her. If he did... to the Slavemasters' hell with him.

As the mages in the lead ships launched the first fireballs at the dragons wheeling and diving around the city, Jadora stepped forward and rested her hands on the side of the portal. She couldn't and wouldn't try to force it to attack, but she implored it to strike against the dragons, to protect the city that had the lab equipment she needed to study the parasite more thoroughly. If only for that reason, the portal should want to see them victorious.

Marshaling all the power she'd been given, Jadora promised to lend it to the portal, to give it everything it needed to strike at their deadly enemies.

As she drew upon her power, Malek looked over at her, his eyes widening slightly. It couldn't be with surprise, since he knew what she was capable of now. His lips parted slightly as he watched, and he sheathed one of his blades so he could step closer and rest a hand on her shoulder.

Everything all right? Jadora asked, not certain what the gesture meant, though she liked having Malek close.

Maybe it wasn't wise with Uthari watching, but she found herself inching close to him, drawn by his touch, by him.

Just hoping we're successful in this battle and get the opportunity to enact that thought you shared with me. He squeezed her shoulder and shared a similar version of the image with her, of them entwined on the portal, of her back arched as she cried out with desire.

Her cheeks heated, both because she hadn't *meant* to share her thought and because his version had her writhing a lot more wildly. She couldn't bring herself to object to the idea though, not when she knew she'd lost all of her control in the lab. They hadn't even had a bed, nor had she cared, simply clinging to him as they used the wall, like wild animals against a tree in the forest.

Maybe she inadvertently shared *that* thought with him as well, for his grin widened, but only for a moment. The dragons had noticed the mageships attacking, and two of them broke away from the city to fly toward the fleet.

Jadora focused on the portal, willing it to attack them and hoping it could. She also hoped it hadn't caught the images she and Malek had been sharing or, if it had, that it wasn't offended by the idea of people using it for a bed.

Amusement trickled into her mind, along with a fresh image, this one from the portal instead of Malek. It was of itself, standing by the spring in the jungle, with two blue-scaled dragons perched atop it while they... oh dear. Jadora's cheeks heated again. Previously, she'd never wondered how dragons procreated, simply assuming it was similar to geckos or other lizards, but apparently there was some vigorous sexual activity.

She wiped her face, hoping her embarrassment didn't show.

Lightning, please, she told the portal as it completed the vision by showing the dragons finishing and diving into the pool to relax in the aftermath of their lovemaking.

Fortunately, the portal heeded her request. Two branches of thick red lightning shot toward the approaching threat.

The magical attack struck their barriers hard enough to knock the dragons back in the air. They screeched in surprise, then roared in fury. Fury and determination. They flapped their wings hard and kept coming. Before, they'd been angling for two different ships, but now they both flew at the *Soaring Eagle.*

Jadora willed the portal to shoot more lightning, lending her own power, though the dragon-steel artifact had great power of its own and didn't likely need her help. Still, she found herself wanting to mingle her power with its to better direct the attacks. She sent a streak of lightning toward one dragon's eye. At first, its barrier protected it, but the portal poured more and more power into the attack, and the lightning slipped through, zapping the creature's slitted yellow eye.

Screeching, the dragon veered away.

Fireballs from the mages slammed into the other one, battering at its barrier. The dragon's protection remained up until the portal sent more lightning bolts toward it, striking it repeatedly from the flank to the back to the snout. One of Uthari's massive fire balls slammed into its head, and the smell of scorching scales tainted the air.

As the dragon roared, a red branch of lightning arced into its maw, bouncing between its teeth and highlighting its gullet. It snapped its jaws shut as it shook its head, its wingbeats faltering.

That didn't keep its cold eyes from focusing on Jadora. The dragon brushed aside its pain and flew straight at her, picking up speed as it came.

With both weapons in hand again, Malek sprang onto the portal to put himself between the dragon and Jadora. She willed the lightning to shift and strike at its wings. One bolt got through its barrier and burned into its bones. The dragon faltered, lost altitude, and crashed into the hull of the *Soaring Eagle*.

That sent everyone on the deck stumbling backward, Jadora included, and she lost her contact with the portal. But it knew what she wanted, and it kept striking at their attackers, even sending branches of lightning at the two that remained near Utharika. Fireballs also flew from the city and the castle walls, but it was the portal's lightning that deterred the dragons. Soon, all four had enough, and they wheeled and turned toward the south. The portal went dark and stopped sending out bolts.

"Keep going!" Uthari cried from his yacht. "Finish them! Kill them so they can't heal their injuries and return to attack us again."

The words might have been directed at everyone, but he was looking at Jadora.

Though reluctant to be merciless, especially if the portal didn't wish it, Uthari had a point. If the dragons returned the next day, perhaps with more allies, it would mean another battle. Perhaps a more deadly battle.

Jadora rested her hand on the cool dragon steel again. *Will you keep attacking? So they can't threaten us again?*

Sadness swept over her, along with great reluctance. The portal shared an image of blue dragons again, the same pair as before, now flapping their wings as they floated in the pool, playfully swatting each other with their tails.

"Make it keep attacking!" Uthari yelled, startling Jadora for he was on the deck right behind her now.

"It doesn't want to finish them off." Jadora accepted the portal's decision and stepped back, lowering her hands. "It knows those used to be its allies, and it hopes they will be again."

"They're *not* allies, not to humans. Look at what they've done to my city, my land!" He flung out his arm toward the burning docks.

"*You* did that to your kingdom," Jadora said, "by not listening to all the people who told you to take down the portal so that dragons couldn't fly through."

Rage incensed Uthari, and he strode forward, his power crackling in the air around him. Fear shot through Jadora, and she funneled her own power into a barrier, afraid she was about to find out if Zelonsera had given her enough strength to match a wizard.

But Malek sprang down from the portal to stand in front of Jadora, his weapons still drawn as he faced Uthari.

Uthari halted, disbelief stealing his rage as he gaped at Malek.

Malek didn't threaten him, but he didn't back away either. "The city is safe for the moment, Your Majesty. I suggest we hurry to perform repairs, reinforce the barriers, and find a laboratory sufficient for the professor to work in."

That last bit was to remind Uthari of Jadora's worth to him. She had no doubt.

Uthari clenched his jaw, glaring past Malek to her.

You had better do all that you've promised you can do in that lab, Uthari told her. *Since you've cost me my general and my zidarr.*

Malek is still loyal to you, she hurried to respond, hoping Uthari didn't truly believe he'd lost Malek.

If he did, he might decide to strike out, to arrange Malek's death.

I'm not the one he was screwing when the rest of the fleet was preparing for battle. Uthari looked at her in disgust, then sprang into the air and levitated back to his own ship.

A tremor went through Jadora. Whether it was weariness from drawing upon so much power, fear for Malek, or fear for Jak and herself, she didn't know. Maybe it was everything. The events of the past months weighed on her like a mountain.

When Malek sheathed his weapons, he returned to her side and rested his hand on her shoulder again. He sent warm healing magic through her, and she appreciated it, but she feared what it meant for the future. She hadn't wanted to make Malek choose between her and Uthari, and she wasn't positive that he had—he'd simply been trying to stop a fight, damn it—but if Uthari *believed* he had, that was as bad. And didn't bode well for either of their futures.

23

"I THINK YOU'RE SUPPOSED TO USE SOME OF YOUR MAGIC WHEN YOU fly," Jak called to Shikari from the railing on the deck of the gateship. His charge bobbed about like a bumblebee as he flapped his wings, making ungainly circles around the ship, reminding Jak little of the majestic adult dragons. "Your body mass is too large to do this on pure physics. It'd be like putting wings on a whale and expecting *it* to fly."

Shikari flapped heroically to reach the deck again, and when Jak received a whack to the head from a wingtip, he was positive it wasn't accidental.

"I'm just giving you the academic perspective," he said as Shikari landed, talons clacking on the wood.

The mage guard on duty, his arms crossed over his chest as he watched them with bored eyes, did not comment as Shikari flopped over on his back, legs crooking in the air, wings flapping to the deck. On the narrow gateship, his wings stretched from railing to railing. An adult dragon wouldn't have fit on the craft at all.

"See how tired you're getting? You need to use your magic." Jak stirred a gust of wind to tickle Shikari's wings, though he wasn't positive that was the type of magic dragons used to help with flying, or even if they needed such assistance. They had lighter bodies than whales, so it was possible they could fly without using their power. He just deemed it unlikely.

"When is that dragon going to get scary and intimidating?" the guard asked.

"Didn't you see what he did to Tonovan's boot?" Jak asked before remembering the general was dead and that his loyal officers might not appreciate the reminder.

The mage curled his lip.

Shikari hissed at him. If he hadn't been on his back, like a dog lounging in the grass with his head upside-down, the hiss might have been *scary and intimidating*.

Jak wished the mage would go away and that Vinjo would come up on deck. When Jak had knocked on his hatch earlier, Vinjo's mussed hair had promised he'd been napping. Given that he'd been piloting the craft since they'd left the others, that was understandable, but Jak needed to talk to him. If they were going to do something other than directing this ship straight into the dock in front of Uthari's castle, they needed to come up with a plan. And soon. He expected to see the southern edge of Agorval on the horizon soon.

He thought about reaching out and trying to contact his mother. Twice that afternoon, he'd attempted to do so, but he hadn't gotten a response from her either time. Since he'd managed to contact her from farther away, he felt he should have been able to do so again. Maybe *she* was napping.

He hoped it wasn't anything more ominous than that. Ever since she'd mentioned the motes, he'd worried. A part of him *didn't* want to do anything to divert the ship so that he could rejoin her and make sure nothing bad was happening to her, but Rivlen's words haunted him. He had no trouble believing that Uthari intended to kill him, perhaps at his mother's feet. Would she have the power to stop it? Jak didn't know. It would be better if he could avoid her needing to test herself against Uthari. He also didn't want her to have to watch him die.

Besides, Jak was haunted by the memory of those dragons flying off with the pillar. Rivlen might not appreciate it if he and Vinjo showed up on her scouting mission, but he wanted to see for himself what the dragons were up to.

A hint of dizziness came over him, catching him by surprise. Jak turned his back on Shikari, who'd risen and was preparing for another flying attempt, and gripped the railing.

A vision of the jungle—of *Zewnath?*—came to him, as if another mage were inserting imagery into his mind, but it wasn't coming from the guard. If he'd had a dragon-steel weapon, Jak would have believed he was receiving a vision from it, but there wasn't any dragon steel on the ship. Besides, the touch didn't seem to be coming from the ship but from somewhere to the north. And there was something familiar about it.

Portal? Jak envisioned it on the deck of one of Uthari's mage-ships, though he didn't know if it was still en route. By now, the main fleet could have arrived in Utharika. *If* they hadn't been attacked along the way. *Is that you?*

The Torvil portal had never spoken to him—only the portal on Nargnoth had done so and only once—but he had communicated with it through imagery enough times to recognize its magical signature.

A pulse in his mind seemed to represent a *yes*.

Are you in Utharika again? How can I help?

This time, the pulse emphasized the jungle vision. In it, the trees blurred past, as if he were seeing them from above, then parted to reveal the familiar pool and the remains of the merce-nary camp. With the tents gone, he had a clear view of the charred and torn land and the ripped-up trees. The attacks from various powerful enemies had destroyed most of the foliage in a half-mile radius of the pool, but that didn't seem to be what the portal was emphasizing.

The vision shifted, showing the portal back by the pool, standing upright with stars glowing inside. It was active, a passageway to another world open in invitation.

You want to go back and be used again?

An affirmative pulse.

We can't set you up. More dragons might come through. Evil dragons, not like the ones who built you. We still have to figure out how to heal the mottled dragons. He didn't know if the portal understood about the parasite or knew of the meeting Jak and Mother had shared with Zelonsera and her human guardians, but it might. The portal on Nargnoth had known a lot.

Still gripped by the vision, Jak grew dizzy again as the viewpoint blurred, traveling from above the trees to the portal and through it. Stars whizzed past, as if he were actually traveling through the magical gateway, and then he popped out into what looked like the bottom of a lake. Or an ocean? All he could tell was that he was underwater and it was dark, save for the glow coming from the active portal behind him.

The vision focused on one of the symbols on its inner ring. It was highlighted, a constellation to a world Jak and the others hadn't yet visited. And *couldn't* if it was underwater. This reminded Jak of the vision Shikari had shared with him days earlier.

You want me to go there? Jak asked. Seeing that this particular portal was underwater made him think this ought to be a warning, a suggestion that they *not* go there, else they would die.

But the portal gave him another agreeable pulse.

Humans can't breathe underwater. Jak glanced at Shikari, wondering if dragons could, or if they could hold their breath for a long time.

Once more, the vision shifted, whisking him around boulders and coral and finally into a maze of ruins that rose up from the lake or sea floor. Again, he grew dizzy and now a little nauseated as the vision moved left and right to go around pillars and ancient temples. Whatever that place had been, it was now covered in algae and seaweed and other organisms Jak couldn't name. He had a feeling the ruins had been underwater for a long time.

Yellow light came from up ahead, pushing back the murky darkness. Beyond a few more ruins, three pedestals rose up. Atop each one rested a glowing yellow sphere.

Jak's grip tightened on the railing. A sphere or an *orb*?

Are those the Orbs of Wisdom?

Another affirmative pulse.

Have you shared this vision with my mother?

The portal sent another pulse, but this one seemed tinged with frustration. Because it had shown Mother, and she hadn't understood? Or she had understood but hadn't been able to do anything about it? If she was stuck slaving in a lab for Uthari, she wouldn't be able to escape to do what the portal wished.

For that matter, could *Jak* do what it wished? If he wasn't mistaken, the portal wanted him to kidnap it, take it all the way back to Zewnath, activate it, and travel to a world where he would be dead in two minutes because he couldn't breathe.

There's no way we can go there.

That earned him another frustrated pulse.

Even if we could breathe underwater, we couldn't risk opening the portal again. What if more dragons come through? If my entire world is enslaved, we won't be able to find a cure for your kind.

The next pulse contained as much disappointment as frustration.

Look, let me think, Jak told it. *Maybe there's a way. Especially if you think the answers are there. That those orbs have them.*

A more cheerful response came from the portal.

Wait, Jak thought. *If your kind have known about these orbs all along, why didn't you seek them out for the answers you need?*

Dragons can't breathe underwater either, someone nearby spoke into his mind. Shikari.

Was he witnessing this vision too?

After sharing one more insistent image of the portal operating in Zewnath, the vision faded. Once more, Jak grew aware of the world around him—and Shikari crouched at his side. The dragonling wasn't looking up at him but down at the sea.

Are you saying it's because those Orbs of Wisdom are underwater that your people haven't visited them for answers? Jak asked, but he had a hard time believing dragons couldn't use their magic to swim underwater for extended periods if need be. Couldn't they make a bubble of air around themselves?

I do not know, but that may be part of it. My memory... Shikari was still focused on the water far below, but he shared an image with Jak. *This is what my people remember from long ago.*

The image was of a sunlit valley, lush green grass waving in the wind around temples and a marketplace. Blue-scaled dragons lounged on the flat surfaces, reminding Jak of cats lying on sunny windowsills, and humans in togas and sandals walked about, trading coins for goods. Occasionally, one walked up and interacted with a dragon, but the humans seemed almost oblivious to their presence, as if dragons were such a common thing that one need not pay much attention to them.

In the sky overhead, young blue dragons wheeled and played. Nostalgia and longing for a time long past, a time Shikari had never known, emanated from him. Or maybe he simply wished he were there and could play with other young dragons.

Jak was about to ask why Shikari was showing him this particular image, but then he saw the orbs resting on sunlit pedestals, and he realized the significance.

That's what that place looked like before it flooded? Jak asked.

Yes.

What happened? Did it rain too much, and the valley flooded? Or did glaciers melt and sea levels rise?

I wasn't there. Shikari shared an image of an egg.

Jak snorted.

Zelonsera didn't know either. Because of the war between the tainted and untainted, dragons were distracted and didn't visit that world for many years. That is all I know.

But you believe answers may be there.

They may not, but they may be.

Vague.

Dragons are a cryptic and inscrutable species. Shikari squinted, and something flew up from below. A fish.

It startled Jak as it sailed over his head to land on the deck with a splat. A dozen more followed, dripping water on Jak as they passed, then landed beside the first.

"What's all that?" the guard demanded.

"Lunch, I think," Jak said.

Once he was done levitating his meal aboard, Shikari sprang upon the pile of floundering fish. He chomped down on the first, devouring it whole.

"You're not *that* inscrutable," Jak muttered.

Shikari's long neck turned so that he could look at Jak with half a fish sticking out of his maw. He slurped, and it disappeared down his gullet.

"I guess it's easier than flying down to get them yourself," Jak said as the hatch opened.

A fish that had landed on it tumbled off. Shikari sprang to pounce on it.

Vinjo shrieked, ducked back into the ladder well, and tugged the hatch shut. Shikari landed on the fish and devoured it.

What is your dragon doing? Vinjo asked Jak telepathically.

Having lunch.

His method of doing so is alarming.

Especially if you're a fish. You can come up.

I need to talk to you. But not with a mage guard right there.

He might find it suspicious if we skulk off to engineering and close the door. Also, you might want to wipe the dragon spittle off your hatch.

Why? It's not corrosive, is it? The hatch opened again, and Vinjo stuck his head out, craning his neck to peer at Shikari, who was munching on his last three fish. He'd eaten the others, bones, scales, innards, and all.

As Jak knew from past experience, dragons had amazing digestive systems. *I don't think so, but you'd have to ask my mother. She's the one who tested it.*

For corrosive potential?

Parasites, actually. Jak waved for Vinjo to join him at the railing, though after what the portal had shown him, he didn't know what to say. He'd intended to plot with Vinjo against the mages to take over the gateship and alter course, but now? Now, it seemed like he needed to go to Utharika, figure out a way to get the portal, take it back to Zewnath, and determine how they could go through it without needing air to breathe. Imagining everything involved gave him a headache.

"A lovely day out here, isn't it?" Vinjo smiled up at the clouds as he joined Jak at the railing.

Rain started pattering on the deck, and the mage scowled over at him.

Good job not arousing suspicions, Jak thought, careful to pinpoint his telepathy so only Vinjo would hear.

Thanks.

A second mage climbed out on deck, the lieutenant that Jak had magically coerced when he'd been in the brig on the *Star Flyer.* The man scowled at him before joining the other mage. The uniformed pair didn't even pretend to be looking toward the route ahead. They watched Jak and Vinjo, no doubt attempting to pick up on their telepathic conversation.

I'm glad you wanted to talk, Vinjo told Jak, ignoring the men, though hopefully also using pinpoint telepathy. *It's possible I made a mistake.*

Oh?

I made a dome-jir and contacted Night Wrath. My zidarr brother who's on one of Zaruk's ships and not far away. In fact, he should be heading toward the Twin Dragon Horns.

Are we heading toward the Twin Dragon Horns? Without any landmarks visible, Jak had only the sun and stars by which to navigate, but they weren't visible now.

That was the plan, but Sasko convinced me it would be better for me to return to Zar of my own volition, not being dragged by my brother, who may have orders to kill me.

Uthari wants to kill me. *I was hoping to convince you to help me subdue these guards and turn the ship in another direction, but Zar isn't where I had in mind.*

Why not? It's my home. The sun and the dry desert air are fabulous. I miss both.

If it's like the rest of the world, it's being ravaged by dragons. We need to take care of them before going to anyone's home.

We? Vinjo touched his chest. *If you're thinking of making more kerzor devices, they won't work on dragons.*

I know, and I'm not, at least not for dragons. If Jak could figure out a way to get close enough to Uthari to drive one into his skull, he would cheerfully do so. *Also, the one we made wasn't quite right. Shikari adjusted it so it worked.*

Shikari? Your toddler of a dragon knew how to fix it? Are you *sure it wasn't right?* Vinjo cast an indignant frown toward Shikari, who, his meal complete, was back to lounging on his back with his legs crooked in the air. His tail swished back and forth as raindrops fell on his belly scales.

He said it wasn't and did something to it. He had intimate knowledge of one of the originals, so I trust it was necessary. Really *intimate.*

Jak touched his stomach, though Vinjo was still frowning at Shikari. *Can I convince you to turn this ship not toward Zar but toward Utharika while taking a roundabout way there to avoid the Horns?*

Vinjo focused on him again. *I thought we were going to try not to go there, on account of Uthari wanting to kill us both.*

I need to borrow the portal for an extended period of time and take it back to Zewnath. Would you be willing to help with that? Also, is there any possibility that this ship is waterproof and airproof and could journey underwater?

Vinjo's jaw sagged.

Which part has you confused? Jak asked after several silent moments passed.

All of the parts.

Jak did his best to share the imagery the portal had shown him of the underwater valley and the orbs on pedestals. *We need to go there. Through the portal.*

Why?

To learn what's necessary to solve the dragon problem. To turn these evil brown-and-gray mottled dragons into fun and friendly-to-humans blue dragons like Shikari.

A belch came from behind them. It wasn't either of the mages.

Is that possible? Vinjo asked.

I hope so. Jak remembered his mother's warning that the dragons, even if the parasites were killed, might not return to what they'd been thousands of years ago, before they'd been infested. It was possible that they'd been hosts to the parasites for too long. But even if they died or simply lost all of their aggressiveness, wouldn't that be enough? *We need to get the portal and go through it to visit those orbs.*

I... Vinjo ran a hand along his railing. *Watertight and airtight are possible. With some sealant around the hatches and portholes, the ship could be those things now. But to travel underwater would take a lot of tinkering.*

You like tinkering.

We'd need to add some kind of... ballast tanks. A way to weigh the ship down so that it sank, but you'd also want it to be able to float back to the surface again. Vinjo scratched his jaw. *I've read papers positing hypothetical ways to make ships that travel underwater, but I'm not aware of anyone who's actually crafted them.*

You could be the first. Jak smiled. *You'd be famous.*

This argument seemed to sway him slightly. At least Vinjo arched his eyebrows in speculation. *I wonder if that would bring honor to my family. Mages across the world haven't been that delighted by my other inventions.*

Thorn Company likes them.

They are not mages.

Thankfully.

Propulsion wouldn't be that difficult, but how far underwater would you need the ship to go? When you dive down, the pressure rises rapidly, and this vessel is made out of wood. Think of an egg. Vinjo opened his palm, then made a fist to simulate crushing something.

I'm not sure. The portal neglected to show me the depth of the orbs.

Probably because a hunk of metal doesn't care about pressure. It's essentially a dragon-steel brick. We humans are a lot more fragile.

Couldn't magic be used to reinforce the ship? Jak asked.

I suppose. I need to think about it.

Good. You think about that, and I'll think about our other challenge.

Sneaking into Uthari's heavily guarded city, stealing his even more heavily guarded portal, and making it all the way to Zewnath with his very angry mages chasing you?

That's the challenge, yes. The portal does like me, so that could be helpful.

What happens if you succeed in setting it up in Zewnath again, but more dragons fly into the world while you're gone?

Let's worry about one challenge at a time, Jak said, though they had a lot more than *one* challenge to overcome.

Aware that they would have to deal with their mage guards before they tried to sneak anywhere, Jak looked back to consider them. To his surprise, they weren't there. Only Shikari remained on deck with them. With his meal complete, he'd gone from burping to snoring.

Jak swept over the ship with his senses, wanting to make sure the mages weren't up to anything fishy. Was it possible they'd caught some of what Jak and Vinjo had been discussing?

They had gone into one of the cabins, as if they'd simply gotten bored watching Jak and Vinjo and had abandoned the task.

Jak hoped that was all it was, but he doubted they would be that lucky.

When Jadora had arrived in Uthari's castle, she'd found a new laboratory with everything she had said she needed. Chemistry equipment stretched from wall to wall, with plenty of counter space for creating formulas. And mages had come in and built the special room she'd asked for to safely contain the parasites, technology and magic combining to seal it off from the rest of the compound. Her samples were now inside, waiting for her to return to them.

In the meantime, she added more of the plant extract she'd made to the food dishes of a pair of aged mice a servant had captured and brought for her. She'd already given the extract to some typically short-lived fruit flies, and they hadn't died yet, so that was promising. It was early, however, to presume that her extract worked.

Still, she believed it would. Unlike with the parasite, knowledge of how to turn the Jitaruvak plant into an extract that could extend human life had been deposited into her memory, courtesy of Zelonsera.

It was common knowledge to dragon kind, as they'd long ago given it to their human allies to extend their lives. Jadora might have been able to make it on the yacht, but it was easier here, with the proper equipment. Besides, she worried that as soon as she successfully made it, Uthari would try to kill her. She might have power now, but that didn't mean she could defend herself every moment of the day. She had to sleep, after all.

She supposed she could sleep out in the courtyard in the center of the portal, as Jak had once done. It had been set down in the same spot it had once occupied in the castle. Would it defend her if someone attacked her?

Jadora sensed Malek approaching, walking with someone else with a powerful aura, though she didn't recognize the person. As long as it wasn't Uthari. He hadn't said anything to her since the battle outside of the city. Malek had said he was busy overseeing repairs of Utharika, but Jadora had no trouble envisioning him scheming as he sulked in his suite, convinced she'd ruined Malek for him.

She took a sip from a tea mug, smiling into her beverage as she thought of exactly how she'd ruined him. Twice, now. Perhaps a third time later that night? She hoped so.

She'd worried he would come to believe he'd made a mistake, as he had in the past when he'd let himself grow close, and that he would distance himself from her. But he hadn't yet. He wasn't flaunting his feelings for her to Uthari or in front of anyone else, but he also wasn't that quick to step away from her if someone walked in. A couple of times, she'd even caught him glowering at a male mage in the process of checking her out.

That male attention continued to bewilder her, and she was glad she'd gotten to know Malek, and vice versa, before Zelonsera had infused her with power. She knew he liked her independent of the enticing aura that she apparently now radiated into the world. Admittedly, she'd wondered if *it,* rather than any natural appeal she had, had pushed Malek from restraint to... *not* restraint, but she couldn't bring herself to object. She liked unrestrained Malek.

Come in, Jadora thought to him before he lifted a hand to knock. *I was thinking of you.*

Writhing atop the portal again?

She blushed as the door opened, revealing Malek and a man in black who reminded her of Yidar. It took her a moment to remember that she'd seen him the last time she'd been a prisoner in Uthari's castle. It was Gorsith, the king's other remaining zidarr.

No. They hadn't *done* that. Even if they'd wanted to, the portal was always out in the open with mages guarding it. *I find beds suitably stimulating.*

I don't object to beds, though the wall was invigorating.

To someone with the stamina to hold a woman up for an extended period of time.

You know zidarr have excellent stamina. Malek smiled across the room at her. *Of course, the lab bench was acceptable as well.*

Perhaps we could try a bed tonight. For variety.

It sounds sedate, but I'm amenable to experimentation.

Gorsith looked at him and raised his eyebrows. Malek dropped a mask over his smile, but the twinkle of humor didn't quite leave his eyes.

He was so different from the aloof and superior zidarr Jadora had first met. Could someone like Gorsith, who hadn't seen him for months, see the change? She knew Uthari did—and feared he would do something about it. Though he must not have forbidden Malek from having sex with her, or Malek wouldn't be making plans with her now.

"Professor Jadora Freedar." Malek extended a hand toward her as he spoke to Gorsith. "You'll guard her with your life while I'm gone. She's refining something extremely important for the king." He looked curiously at the bottle of extract in her hand.

Jadora nodded at him. *I'm testing it on insects and animals, but I believe I've succeeded in making it.*

Excellent. You are a talented and amazing chemist. Malek bowed toward her.

The words pleased her far more than praise about her looks or her ability to wield magic ever would, but she felt compelled toward modesty. *It's easy to be amazing when a dragon dumps an encyclopedia's worth of knowledge into your brain and it somehow sticks.*

You would have been able to create the compound even if that had never happened.

It was relatively simple once we acquired the plant. But perhaps I'm premature. We should wait and see how these terminally ill mice fare.

So, it'll take some time before you know of its efficacy for certain?

Yes. I hope the dragons will give us that time.

As do I.

"Guard her with my life?" Gorsith had been scrutinizing her, both with his eyes as well as his mage senses. Fortunately, unlike with some of the other men lately, that hadn't involved ogling her chest. He appeared to be assessing her more as a possible opponent. Funny how she preferred that. "She doesn't seem to need guarding. Wasn't this woman here before and *not* powerful? Not *anything*?"

"She was *something*," Malek said coolly.

Gorsith made a chopping motion with his hand. "But not a mage."

"That's a recent development."

"How?"

"A dragon granted her power so that she might do a task for it."

Gorsith blinked. "That's possible?"

"Apparently."

"I'd do a task for a dragon for more power. Is there someplace I can sign up for this?"

Malek snorted. "Your power is fine."

"It could be finer."

"Best to hit the training hall then."

"Or snuggle up to a dragon-steel weapon?" Gorsith raised his brows again. "We've been getting some interesting rumors back here about what you've discovered on other worlds."

"That might work over time," Malek said, "but thanks to the kleptomaniac tendencies of the dragons that came through the portal, there isn't much dragon steel around."

"Well, she should be easy to guard." Gorsith waved at Jadora.

"Let's hope. Stand outside for a moment, Gorsith. I need to talk to her before I leave."

The zidarr shrugged and stepped into the hallway, closing the door behind him. Maybe it was early to judge him, but Jadora didn't think he had the edge of frustration and bitterness that had cloaked Yidar.

"Leave?" she asked.

"For a short time. Uthari received a vision from his lesser-dragon-steel dagger. I've told you that we sometimes get those from our weapons, right?"

"Yes, and that the last time Uthari had a vision, it was of us kissing under the gladiator arena." Jadora grimaced, imagining Uthari's dagger showing him her and Malek again. What kind of perverted weapon shared the intimate moments of others with its wielder?

"There have probably been others since then, but yes. He says he saw Jak and Vinjo on the gateship and in trouble. They were being attacked by blue-hulled ships even though they were flying over Uth and toward Utharika. In case that's happening, or about to happen, he wants me to take a ship or two to help."

"He wants to help Jak and Vinjo?" Jadora struggled to keep the skepticism out of her tone even as she worried that her son was in fresh trouble. "I thought he wanted to kill both of them anyway." She might have managed to hide the skepticism, but she didn't bother when it came to her bitterness toward Uthari.

"He's not pleased with them, but he doesn't want to lose that ship. And if Zaruk has presumed to send ships into our land when we're busy battling dragons, Uthari wants them destroyed and a strong message sent to his rival."

Jadora wished the wizard rulers could set aside their differences and combine forces to fight the dragons, but it seemed that was too much to ask. She couldn't, however, object to Malek going to help Jak. Assuming that was truly what Uthari wanted him to do. What if all Uthari cared about was getting the ship, and he told Malek to shove Jak and Vinjo over the edge and to their deaths?

She took a shaky breath, telling herself that Malek wouldn't do that. Even if Uthari asked him to, Malek had told her he wouldn't let anyone kill Jak, and she believed him.

"I understand," she said. "I hope the vision was wrong and that they're not in danger, but if they are, I'm positive you'll be successful in helping them. And I thank you for going."

"Of course."

"I guess the bed experimentation will have to wait."

Malek stepped forward, clasped her hands, and kissed her on the cheek, his lips lingering. "Not for long." He looked at the extract. "Wait until I'm back to report that it's ready for Uthari."

"Do you think he'll find a way to get rid of me once he has it?"

"Now that you've proven you can get the portal to attack and defend the city, I hope not, but... he's being curt with me. I know he's not pleased."

"I'm sorry." And she was. Not because she cared one whit about Uthari's feelings but because she cared about Malek's. She struggled to fully understand the devotion he felt toward the cruel wizard, but she wouldn't judge him for it. Nobody was perfect, herself included.

"After we deal with the dragons, we'll figure something out. Some way to go forward without death." Malek grimaced.

"I'm not sure that's possible, but I'll hope so."

"Will you make me one promise?"

"Likely so," she said, "but you'll have to ask it before I commit to it."

He smiled slightly. "You're not one to fall head-over-heels over a man and be willing to do anything he wishes, are you?"

"I don't think anyone my age is. Maybe if you'd seduced me at eighteen, my hormones would have prompted such foolishness."

"I was busy training to be a loyal zidarr then."

"Aren't you still doing that?"

"I suppose." Malek released her hands so he could rest his on her shoulders and gaze steadily into her eyes. "I meant what I said about keeping anyone from killing Jak."

She almost corrected him, saying it wasn't *anyone* but Uthari specifically who was the problem, but his somber face didn't invite interjection, so she only nodded.

"But," Malek said, "will you promise me that you won't let him make any more kerzor?"

"I..." If she wanted to do that, *could* she? Jak might not obey her wishes.

"I'd prefer none at all, but at the least, none that he will use against Uthari. Or me." Malek winced, no doubt remembering what it had been like for him not to have his power.

"He would never try to put one in your head."

"I'm not sure that's true, but nonetheless, if I... go against Uthari's wishes and save Jak's life, I don't want—I could not *live* with myself if he later found a way to jam one into his head and Uthari was killed because he lost his powers. I can't mourn Tonovan's death, but Uthari has been..."

"A father to you. I know."

"One day, he will likely die." Malek glanced at the extract. "But do you understand why it can't be at my hand? Or why I can't facilitate it, even inadvertently?"

"I do," Jadora said, though she didn't want to make this promise. And not only because she didn't have control over Jak. She might *influence* him, but he was long past the age when he obeyed her without question. "But I haven't been able to reach Jak for two days." She touched her temple to indicate telepathically.

"Most mages can't reach people that far away and must use dome-jir."

"I was able to when he was back on the *Star Flyer,* and it was over Temril. If he's heading this way, he should be closer now."

"It could have something to do with the camouflaging magic Vinjo put on that ship."

"Ah." Jadora riffled through the memories that Zelonsera had shared with her and did find information to support that hypothesis, that such magic could have a dampening effect. It would be similar to what the druids placed above their tunnels to keep mages from detecting them and their magic.

"Promise me, Jadora?" Malek opened his mouth to add more but shut it again. Because he didn't want to say he would be forced to change his mind about helping Jak if she couldn't give him this promise? *Would* he change his mind?

She hoped he wouldn't go back on his word, but she didn't want to risk it. Or force him into a position of choosing between old loyalties and new loyalties.

"I can't control what Jak does, but if he comes up with that plot, I'll do my best to keep him from enacting it." Jadora took a deep breath and held his gaze. "You have my word."

"Thank you."

He smiled and kissed her again, on the mouth this time. His lips lingered and had her already longing for his return.

As he walked out, saying a few words to Gorsith before leaving, she wondered if there was any way that she, Jak, and Malek could find happiness, or even be safe, as long as Uthari lived and breathed. But could she wish for his death? If it came about as a result of her or Jak's actions, Malek might never forgive them. He might never forgive *her*.

More than ever, she hated the idea of losing Malek.

24

"I WASN'T EXPECTING TO BE PUT IN A LITTLE *GIRL'S* SQUAD," YELOTTA, one of the new recruits, whispered to Mursa, one of the others.

"She helped kill a dragon," Mursa whispered back.

"I heard Colonel Sorath was invisible and did all the work."

Tezi, who was a few feet away and critiquing the form of the third recruit, clenched her jaw and debated whether to respond to their comments or not. They were whispering to each other, but the women weren't trying to keep Tezi from hearing them. They probably wanted Captain Ferroki to hear them as well and assign them to someone else. Someone older and more experienced.

Ferroki, who was sparring with Corporal Basher, glanced at Tezi but didn't say anything or give so much as an eye widening that might have suggested a preferred solution. Meaning Tezi was supposed to figure this out herself. Over the months, she'd proven herself to the Thorn Company women, but it seemed she now had to do it all over again with these new recruits, soldiers several years more experienced than she.

"Keep your elbow in closer when you guard yourself," Tezi said. "Right now, you're leaving your ribs open."

"Maybe, but I like more time to react and to keep them farther away from me." Hevlina thrust her sword out to demonstrate. "I've been in battle before. I know what I'm doing."

"Let's spar then. We'll see if your method works."

"When you've got a giant axe that'll cut my sword in half? That's hardly fair."

"I'll use a practice blade." And Tezi would aim for her *ribs,* not her sword. She bared her teeth as she headed for the practice weapons.

After the departure of the gateship with Tinder, Sasko, Jak, and Vinjo, the *Star Flyer* had sailed south all day with the two other mageships as well as the strange druid raft. Once again, they were flying over the jungle continent of Zewnath, a place Tezi hadn't wanted to see again any time soon.

"She thinks she's a sword master because she accidentally got a magical weapon," Yelotta whispered.

"She *has* managed to keep it," Mursa replied. "She must know a thing or two."

"*Please*. I heard she tripped, and that general took it from her. The boy with the dragon had to get it back for her."

Tripped? Who'd said that? Tezi had been hurled twenty feet by an explosive detonating behind her.

With embarrassment scorching her cheeks, she picked up a practice blade. She almost wished it were a *real* blade with the sides sharpened to a razor's edge. But Yelotta was a Thorn Company mercenary now, or she would be if the three women passed their trial period and Ferroki accepted them permanently into the unit. As much as Tezi wanted to clobber them, she knew the captain expected her to help them pass muster. And to earn their respect.

Sighing, Tezi wondered how long she would have to be a soldier, and how many battles she would have to survive, before people respected her because they could tell she was competent at a glance. The way everyone did when they looked at Colonel Sorath. Would she have to lose a hand before she looked like an experienced veteran?

"Corporal Tezi?" a mage officer asked, walking up. "Captain Rivlen wants to see you in her cabin."

"Oh?" Tezi looked at Ferroki, who'd heard but only shrugged.

Tezi traded the practice blade for her axe. By now, she trusted Rivlen, inasmuch as one could a mage working for a king who thought terrene humans should all be slaves, but she preferred that even ally mages not be able to read her mind.

The officer's eyebrows rose, but she didn't object to Tezi taking the axe, nor did she escort Tezi to Rivlen's cabin. After weeks on the *Star Flyer*, maybe Thorn Company was trusted enough to walk around the ship. Or maybe the officer didn't think Rivlen had anything to worry about from Tezi.

"Probably true," she muttered.

When she'd first acquired the axe, Tezi had sparred with Rivlen and knew she was a solid fighter as well as a powerful mage. Further, Rivlen knew the capabilities of dragon steel and would hurl objects at someone wielding such a weapon, rather than foolishly wasting time with straightforward magical attacks.

As Tezi walked down the corridor to Rivlen's cabin, she reminded herself that she hadn't done anything wrong and shouldn't have to worry about attacks from Rivlen. Rivlen hadn't even attacked Sorath when she'd gone over to the druid raft with Ferroki. Tezi had watched the meeting from the *Star Flyer*, concerned for the colonel, especially since he'd been injured in the battle.

"Come in," came Rivlen's voice through the door before Tezi knocked.

"Yes, ma'am," Tezi said as she stepped inside.

Surprisingly, Rivlen sat on her bunk, slouching against the wall, and wore only her sleeveless undershirt instead of her full uniform. She held a glass loosely in her hand, and a bottle of amber alcohol rested on the table next to her. Her hair, which was *always* pulled back in a tight bun, hung around her shoulders, and she looked at Tezi with bloodshot eyes.

Tezi glanced toward the porthole and the sun streaming in from the west. It was early in the day for drinking, especially considering she'd never seen Rivlen take so much as a sip of alcohol. She was always the epitome of military professionalism.

"Come have a drink with me." Rivlen waved her hand at an empty glass next to the bottle. Her words weren't slurred, and her eyes weren't bleary, so maybe she'd just started drinking. Her eyes could be bloodshot for another reason.

Such as that she'd been crying? That seemed as out of character for the strong woman as the drinking.

"I'm supposed to be training some new recruits, ma'am."

"Take a break. We have to celebrate."

"Celebrate?" All that Tezi could imagine celebrating with Rivlen was Tonovan's death, something she would admittedly raise a glass to, but Rivlen didn't appear to be in a celebratory mood. She looked like she'd lost her best friend.

"He's dead." Rivlen grabbed the bottle, filled the empty glass with what smelled like whiskey, then offered it to Tezi. "I borrowed this from Lieutenant Dustmok, who hates to be called Dustmop, so I suggest you don't do that."

"No, ma'am." Tezi didn't even know who that was.

"I suppose it's not *borrowing* if I drink it all. He warned me not to since I've got an inexperienced liver. I told him my organs are all strong and resilient, like me, and I'll be fine."

As Tezi accepted the glass, she decided Rivlen might have been drinking for a while after all. Maybe she'd gotten to the point where she didn't want to be alone. Tezi didn't have a lot of experience with alcohol and taking a sip of the stringent stuff didn't convince her that she'd missed out on anything.

"To the death of an odious ass of a man." Rivlen lifted her glass.

Tezi clinked hers against it, then sat in the desk chair. Rivlen's simple cabin didn't have a lot of furnishings.

"Since I'm going to get in all kinds of trouble for it, I have to admit I wish I'd done it myself." Rivlen sipped from her glass, then made a face as it doubtless burned its way down her throat. "It was somewhat enjoyable knowing Jak suborned one of Tonovan's own officers to stab him a few times, but I feel cheated that an enemy assassin was the one who finished him off. *I* should have finished him off instead of helping him to sickbay, the bastard. Or I should have walked him past your unit, and *you* could have finished him off. I'm sad we didn't get to enact our plan."

"Yes, ma'am." Tezi suspected all Rivlen wanted was someone to rant to. Someone who'd also suffered at Tonovan's hands. She well remembered standing in that arena suite with Rivlen and saying she would help her kill Tonovan if the opportunity arose.

"But I knew Uthari would find out, either from my crew or by questioning me." Rivlen pointed her glass toward her temple. "And I didn't want to risk annoying him. Which is silly, because he's beyond annoyed with me. He'll be even *more* annoyed with me if Jak escapes."

Rivlen let her head thunk back against the wall and closed her eyes, but not before Tezi glimpsed moisture in them. She *had* been crying and was on the verge of doing it again.

"I think he's going to kill Jak," Rivlen said softly. "If he doesn't run away. But I have this feeling in my gut that he won't. I tried to make it so he could, but Uthari has his mother and his grandfather. That old wizard holds all of our fates in his hands."

Tezi couldn't disagree. Uthari wasn't even her king, and somehow her fate had ended up entwined with Rivlen's and Sorath's and Jak's and everyone else's.

"I hope Jak doesn't try to make another kerzor and attack

Uthari. Even if his little dragon helps him, that wouldn't go well. Uthari's too wily and experienced to be caught off guard with two women in his bed." Rivlen sipped from the glass again. "I suppose Sorath caught Uthari off guard, but I don't know. *Vorsha* is the one who died that night. I don't know what happened, but Uthari walked out of that without his hair so much as mussed. Maybe he even planned for Vorsha to be killed by an assassin. Who knows? He's not one I'd want to cross." Her grimace implied she feared she already had.

"So we shouldn't make a pact to take him out if we get a chance?" Tezi asked.

She meant it as a joke, but the concerned look that Rivlen gave her made her wish she hadn't uttered the words. Apparently, it was all right to plot against one's general but not one's king.

"Stay away from him, Tezi. Pray to whichever god you favor that he doesn't take notice of you, any more than he already has because of that." Rivlen waved at the axe.

"Yes, ma'am."

"I wish I'd given that advice to Jak, not that he would have heeded it. He's got strange notions in his head for someone who was a powerless terrene boy this time last year." Rivlen shook her head, but a hint of a smile touched her lips.

"You care for him, ma'am?" Tezi had heard rumors about Jak spending the night with Rivlen, but she didn't know what to think about them, or if Jak spending the night in Rivlen's cabin necessarily meant they'd had sex. She could easily imagine him staying up all night drawing her maps.

"Yeah." Rivlen opened the drawer under the bottle and pulled out a metal sphere. "He made me this."

She tapped her thumb against it, and the sphere opened and created an illusion in the air above it. A map of Uth.

"Guess I need to change that to Zewnath, since we're currently flying over it," Rivlen said, and the floating map shifted to the jungle continent. "Or maybe the Glacier Islands."

It shifted again, showing the island chain between Zewnath and the South Pole, ice caps floating in the real-looking dark blue water between the white landmasses.

"It looks like a useful tool," Tezi said.

"Yes." Rivlen set it on the table, leaving the map activated. "*He's* useful."

Tezi nodded. "I hope he survives seeing Uthari."

"Me too. I... feel like I sent him to his death. He doesn't deserve that. He—" Rivlen's throat seemed to tighten, and she closed her mouth on whatever else she'd intended to say.

Maybe she and Jak *had* slept together, and she genuinely cared about him.

"I've been with a lot of men," Rivlen said. "Not *a lot*, but a decent number. Other officers. Mostly recreationally, since I'm too busy to have relationships, and I'm certainly not interested in getting emotional and distracted from my work, Shylezar forbid." She shuddered. "None of them really supported me. I didn't think I even wanted that. I didn't realize until I had it that..." She took another sip. "It's nice."

"I imagine so." Tezi, who'd contributed little to the conversation, felt she should say something more intelligent. "It's why I like Thorn Company. They tease you and give you a hard time sometimes, but they've got your back in a fight."

"Yeah. Exactly. Jak didn't even tease me, not really. The first time we met, he accepted that I was capable and didn't challenge me or assume that because he's a man, he must be superior." Rivlen rolled her eyes.

Tezi nodded, having gotten her share of that from the male mercenaries that had shared the camp with Thorn Company. She took another sip of the drink. The burn wasn't as bad the second time, and a warmth spread through her, tempting her to drink more. It would be nice to relax, to not have to *prove herself* for a while.

"He didn't assume that because I'm a woman, I must have *slept* my way into my captaincy." Rivlen sighed. "And he didn't wish I was a man."

Tezi, who'd been following along and nodding, didn't quite know what to make of the last comment. "I think he prefers that you're not. Especially, if, uhm." Tezi waved at the bed and decided to drop it.

"My father always wanted a boy. I think I've told you that before."

"Ah."

"Your parents are dead, aren't they?"

"Yes."

"Lucky you."

Tezi shook her head. She'd loved her parents and her brother, and she missed them. If she could have brought her parents back, she would have given her life to do so.

"You can't disappoint the dead," Rivlen mused, her focus more on her glass than Tezi.

"I'm not sure that's true, ma'am. The dead can haunt you as much as the living."

"Maybe that's so. I refuse to let Tonovan haunt me though." Rivlen met her gaze. "You don't let him haunt *you* either, all right?"

"I won't."

Tezi smiled, though she wondered if she'd spoken the truth. These past weeks, she'd been too busy to dwell much on Tonovan's attempted and nearly completed rape of her, but every time they'd crossed paths and he'd looked at her, the memory had sprung vividly into her mind. Somehow, he'd been worse than the mage who'd done the same after killing her parents. But at least she'd gotten her revenge on that man by taking his life. With Tonovan, she'd only been able to take his eye.

Would that, and knowing he was dead, be enough to give her peace in the future and let her carry on? Or would she forever fear being caught in that same situation again?

She was glad the axe had been returned to her. She didn't know if the answer to what haunted her was to forever go around armed, but in this world, it was necessary. Maybe Jak and his mother would figure out a way to put an end to mage rule, to mage cruelty, and it wouldn't always be that way, but it was hard for her to see a future like that. She wanted to be optimistic, but the world made it hard. How many times could one be beaten down and still hope for a better future?

"He's not haunting you right *now*, is he?" Rivlen asked, sober enough to notice her troubled expression.

"Not him. Not exactly." Tezi shrugged, not sure how to articulate her thoughts or even if she could to a mage. "It's fine. You wouldn't understand. You've always been powerful."

"If the rumors about the dragon steel are true, you'll be powerful one day too. As long as you keep sleeping with that axe."

"I've... heard that. That after enough time, you start to develop the ability to use magic."

"That's what Jak's mother thinks."

"I hope Thorn Company won't look at me like I'm weird if I do." Tezi wasn't sure she wanted magical power. The axe was enough. Though if she had power *and* the axe, maybe she could take on a dragon. And protect the company against enemies with magic. That notion had some appeal.

"Don't they look at you like that *now*?" Rivlen smirked.

"Not as much as they used to. Except for the new recruits. They think I'm a little girl who accidentally found a magical weapon."

"Didn't you?" Rivlen's eyes crinkled.

"It wasn't an accident. I *looked* for it." Tezi grimaced, wishing she'd won the axe in battle, not found it lying next to a suit of armor after *Malek* vanquished their enemy.

"I'm teasing you. It doesn't matter if you get lucky and find something. It's what you do after you have it, and you're doing fine."

"Thank you, ma'am."

"Club anyone who believes otherwise on the side of the head."

"I think Captain Ferroki would prefer I earn their respect by proving myself capable in battle in front of them."

Rivlen's gaze slid to the glacier islands floating above the table. "I have a feeling you're going to get a chance to do that soon."

Some time after Malek left on a fast ship heading south, Uthari visited Jadora in her laboratory. She'd sensed him coming as soon as he'd left his suite, descended the stairs, and walked toward this hallway. She'd kept hoping he would detour, heading off to check on the portal or the repairs of his city or on some other errand, but his feet brought him to her.

She turned and faced the doorway as he entered without knocking. Gorsith had been standing in the hallway earlier, acting as the bodyguard Malek had requested, but Uthari might have told him to go away, for she now sensed his aura on the far side of the castle.

Uthari smiled as he walked in, though the gesture didn't reach his eyes. She was fairly certain he'd never given her a sincere smile.

"I understand you've made progress on synthesizing a drug."

"Yes." That morning, she'd been experimenting on the parasite in what she was optimistically calling the *safe room*, but she'd first checked on her fruit flies and mice and found them all hale. Even more promising, the graying around the muzzles of the mice had faded, the browner fur of their youth filling back in so rapidly that only magic—or an inherently magical plant—could account for it.

"And that you're experimenting." Uthari walked toward the mice and clasped his hands behind his back as he peered into their cage.

That gesture with his hands was so familiar to the way Malek often stood that it startled her. Had Malek gotten the habit from Uthari?

She shook her head, telling herself that it didn't matter, though it did. Uthari and Malek's long history together mattered a lot.

"What are the results thus far?" Uthari looked at her intently.

Though Malek had warned her not to tell him about it until he returned, Jadora didn't have much choice with Uthari standing in front of her and asking about it. She summed up how she'd made the extract and how much she'd used on the insects and mice. "It would be wise to do a number of trials on animals before moving to human testing, but if you're eager, I can give you some. It's not as if I've made this from scratch as an entirely new drug. The knowledge of the dragons is in my mind and has guided me. Their kind have used the Jitaruvak for millennia to help their favored humans."

"Yes, once one has a good and well-trained slave, one hates to lose him or her."

Jadora clenched her jaw. It was possible some of the dragons had taken humans from their home world in order to make them slaves, but the relationship she'd seen between Zelonsera and her long-lived human guardians on Nargnoth had made it seem symbiotic, one in which both got something out of the deal. The entire mythology of the god Shylezar and his followers suggested a benevolent leader and a satisfied congregation.

"The same can be said of kings and their zidarr," Uthari said.

"You haven't lost him."

"No?"

"He's loyal to you."

"And to you."

"It's not a competition."

"Everything, dear professor, is a competition, and in all things, there can be only one winner."

"We're not running a race with Malek as the prize."

"Let's hope not." Uthari picked up the bottle of extract and examined it with his senses. "I learned long ago to tie together the shoelaces of the other competitors to ensure victory."

"Is that how you got your kingdom?"

"It is. One doesn't win a kingdom by fighting fair." Uthari held the bottle out to her. "Take a sip."

Jadora blinked. "Pardon?"

"I can't read your thoughts anymore. If it were poison, I wouldn't see the truth in your mind. Thus, I must revert to the old-fashioned way of determining the safety of a substance. Court tasters."

She rolled her eyes, accepted the bottle, and removed the cap. When she hesitated, it wasn't because she worried about the safety of her extract but because she questioned if she wanted what it offered. Longevity. Whether it granted immortality, she didn't know—she doubted it. But a longer than natural life. Was that what she wished? To live three hundred years, like Uthari, and forget what it was to be human, to stop being able to identify with the common man, to view herself as something beyond and above?

She snorted and sipped from the bottle, the cool liquid burning as it went down, but it was more like brandy than poison. It was unlikely it would grant her more than an extra year or two if she only consumed it once. From what she understood, it wouldn't require the frequent treatments of Uthari's chair and the concoction his doctor pumped into his veins every week, but one dose also wouldn't grant immortality.

"I didn't sabotage your chair when it crossed my mind." Jadora capped the bottle and set it on the counter between them.

Uthari offered another insincere smile. "But you admit it crossed your mind."

"Can you blame me?"

"An idea may cross a person's mind several times before she finally decides to act on it."

That was true, but she didn't nod or give any indication that she agreed. Let the old bastard test her. What she'd made wouldn't kill her.

As he watched her—waiting to see if she grabbed her neck and pitched to the floor?—the burning in her throat faded. Did she feel more invigorated? It was hard to tell, but her senses grew aware of something within her, a hint of magic seeping through the lining of her stomach without passing through her digestive system. It flowed into her bloodstream, soon finding its way to every toe and fingertip and to her brain. She drew a deep and refreshing breath. She *did* feel invigorated.

"Very good." Uthari picked up the bottle. "What is the optimal dose?"

The answer was in Zelonsera's memories. "Half an ounce twice a year."

"I'll need you to make more and write down the recipe."

"Of course."

At which point, he wouldn't need her anymore. His eyes narrowed, as if he were thinking exactly that, and he kept his gaze on her as he sipped his half ounce.

"A part of me wants to slit your throat for suborning my zidarr," Uthari said with startling bluntness. "A part of me wants to let him have you so that he'll be happy. He's served me loyally for three decades. He deserves to be happy."

"Doesn't the Zidarr Code forbid that?" she muttered, though

she didn't want to be too sarcastic, not if there was a chance Uthari was seriously considering the second option.

"Excelling at one's duty is supposed to provide the necessary satisfaction to make a zidarr happy. It's in all the old books."

"Books written by kings rather than zidarr, I'll wager."

Uthari smiled faintly. "Scribes working for kings, but essentially." He considered the bottle. "It burns going down, but I feel... something. A tingling through my body from my feet to my scalp."

"If those mice are an indicator, your hair may regain its original color."

"A natural result of scalp tingling?"

"Apparently."

Uthari set the bottle down. "You've figured out how to grow the plant here so that more can be made, correct?"

"Yes. I can instruct some of your mages on creating the appropriate type of light so the plants can thrive here. Greenhouses would be ideal so the environment can be controlled. Perhaps in multiple places so humanity won't lose Jitaruvak a second time if one greenhouse is destroyed."

Uthari grimaced. "The dragons might target them specifically if they learn of our ambitions."

"It's possible."

"Start making more of the extract so I can distribute it to worthy people whose longevity would be a boon for the world."

"Worthy mages?"

"Of course. Terrene humans are a tax on the world, not a boon. If you don't see that yet, you will soon. Now that you're one of us."

Jadora dearly hoped that wasn't true.

Uthari looked toward the steel magically-vacuum-sealed door that was the sole entrance to the safe room. Little was in there except for a counter and the dishes of parasites. "Show me your work in there."

A tendril of unease wound through her gut. "Why?"

His eyes narrowed as he looked at her. "Because I wish it."

"You've realized that killing the parasite that infests the dragons is the best way to ensure they won't keep attacking and destroying our world?"

"Professor, you may believe that your new power gives you more rights in this world, and that is perhaps true, but it does *not* give you the right to question a king."

Jadora stared bleakly at him. Whatever he wanted in there, she doubted it was to see her progress on finding a solution. She wondered if he even wanted the dragons cured. After all, the blue-scaled untainted dragons of old had reputedly been friends to humans and might not like the power dichotomy that existed on Torvil. If they returned, they might do as Jak had longed for them to do from the beginning—overthrow the wizard rulers and give terrene humans the freedom to create governments and nations of their own.

Uthari grunted and strode toward the door, using magic to break the vacuum seal that Jadora had carefully created.

"Don't go through the second door before resealing the first," she blurted, hurrying to follow him.

She was tempted to use her power to try to stop him completely, but she didn't know if she was his equal. Even if Zelonsera had granted her more power than most mages and wizards on Torvil, Uthari was far more experienced at using his.

"What happens if these parasites escape?" Uthari waited for her to join him in the small vestibule, then resealed the door behind them and faced the second metal door.

Jadora lifted a hand while she used her senses to scan the little chamber to make sure there weren't any parasites inside. They *should* still be confined to their dishes, but with each day, she grew more uneasy about that, believing they might find a way out.

"They would be able to enter a host and from there, spread all over Torvil," she said, hoping to impart how dangerous they were.

"A *dragon* host, right?"

"They seem to prefer dragons, but we don't know for certain that they can't use humans or other creatures as hosts. Especially if there aren't any dragons around for them to hop into."

Uthari considered that, not yet applying his magic to the inner door. "Malek's report said that when you were on Vran, he destroyed the parasites and the motes they were riding on with fire."

Jadora nodded. "He did, but I've attempted to replicate that on the strains I've been growing."

"And it didn't work?"

"Nothing has worked. I believe it's possible that the parasites on Vran were weakened by the death of their host and more susceptible to being destroyed by heat. It's also possible there was something special about that dragon-steel ziggurat or even the valley there that made it easier to kill them."

"Perhaps your fire magic isn't as refined as Malek's."

"My fire magic burns as hot as his, but you're welcome to try to destroy the parasites in one of the dishes, if you wish."

"Show me."

Sighing, Jadora unsealed the inner door. Maybe having Uthari interested wasn't that bad of a thing. If she could convince him of the importance of finding a way to eradicate the parasite, he could bring in more resources to help. After all, it wasn't as if unicellular flagellate eukaryotes were her specialty. She'd tried dozens if not hundreds of chemical and herbal substances on them, but she wasn't a biologist. Academics in other fields might have more ideas.

They stepped into the windowless laboratory, which had been a storage closet before the conversion. It was dark, and Uthari conjured a light before she could. He floated it over the four sealed glass dishes on the counter, each further enclosed by all the magic she'd been able to summon with her new knowledge.

Uthari gripped his chin as he looked down at the dishes. Without a microscope, the parasites weren't visible, but the motes were. They glowed softly, some dishes holding as many as twenty now. Twenty magical motes that could float through the air to infect dragons.

"Your son deserves death for what he did," Uthari said without looking at her.

Startled, Jadora pressed a hand to the wall for support. It wasn't that she hadn't known Uthari's feelings on the matter—Malek had warned her—but she hadn't expected him to bring it up.

"Tonovan was a vile, cruel, and disgusting man," she said. "*He* was the one who deserved death."

"I don't believe for a second that the boy will stop at Tonovan's death," Uthari said, without responding to her statement. "Now that he knows how to create those devices, he'll make more." He looked coolly over his shoulder at her. "I was foolish to let Malek talk me into sparing his life and training him. I should have known better. Age doesn't always bring wisdom."

"Jak won't be a threat to you. I've already told Malek—" Jadora paused, not wanting to share their private conversation with Uthari. But wasn't it possible that if he knew about her promise, he wouldn't kill Jak? "I'll keep Jak from making more of the kerzor."

"Of course. Young men are so quick to obey their mothers."

"I'm more powerful than he is now," she reminded him.

"And thus, you'll crush any devices he attempts to make?"

"To save his life? Yes."

"You might believe you can stop him, but he's already proven himself dangerous. I must be *certain* that he won't act against me or any more of my officers."

"You don't have to *kill* him." Jadora thought about sealing the door and challenging Uthari to a fight right there, finding out if her magic was more powerful than his. But even if she'd believed she had a chance against him, hurling magic around in the room where the parasites were stored would be idiotic. A fight might not only break the dishes but tear down the walls and let the contents escape. She'd seen how destructive magic was.

"Perhaps not," Uthari said, as she was raking through her mind for ways to get rid of him, to eliminate the threat to Jak. "Perhaps, as I did with you, I need only make sure he's suitably motivated to do my bidding."

The speculation in his eyes made her unease return. On the way to the sky city, she'd talked Malek into helping her take her father down to Sprungtown, finally returning him home, but that didn't mean he was beyond Uthari's reach.

"How?" Jadora mouthed, though she was afraid to find out.

Uthari turned back to the dishes. "He cares a great deal about his young dragon, doesn't he?"

Jadora didn't nod. She didn't have to. Uthari had seen enough of Jak and Shikari together to know it was true.

"I imagine he would find it most distressing if his faithful blue-scaled friend turned into one of the mottled monsters taking great pleasure in killing people." Uthari rested a hand on one of the dishes.

"No." Jadora stepped forward, realizing what he meant to do.

But a wall of power formed, separating her from Uthari. He lifted the dish and faced her again, holding it in the air, the motes inside stirring, as if they sensed an opportunity to escape might be coming.

"I expect Malek to return with Jak and his dragonling soon." Uthari slipped the dish into an inside pocket in his tunic, nestling the thing right next to his heart. "If Jak isn't willing to swear his allegiance to me and do everything I wish..." He flicked his empty fingers, as if he were throwing a glass dish to the floor.

It would take more than a drop to break the magically reinforced container, but Uthari was capable of stripping away all the protection she'd added.

"Doing that could endanger *you* as well," Jadora said. "If they can infest humans, that longevity potion isn't going to protect you from those parasites. The dragons that have been infested have lived very long lives. As monsters."

"You've told me yourself that the parasites prefer dragons. If Jak's pet dragonling is in the room, we both know where they'll go." Uthari lowered his arm and headed for the door. "I must see to the repairs of my city. Good day, Professor."

Jadora slumped against the wall, then banged her fists against it in frustration. She wished Jak had saved the kerzor he'd made for Tonovan and used it on Uthari instead. Tonovan had been a petty villain in comparison to Uthari.

25

MALEK KNELT ON A THIN MEDITATION MAT IN THE CABIN HE'D BEEN given on the *Current Darter*, a fast vessel that could cross Uth in hours, as long as it knew where to go. Aware that the gateship had camouflage that would make it difficult to detect, Malek reached out with his senses and searched for clues that would point him to it. The vessel *should* have been on a direct course from Temril to Utharika, but it was possible that Jak and Vinjo hadn't obeyed Rivlen's wishes—*Uthari's* wishes—to head to the sky city.

His lesser-dragon-steel dagger and sword lay on the deck in front of the mat, and the flash of a vision came to him. In it, the gateship was flying through the night over the southern forests of Uth, but pursuers were hurling fire and cannonballs at it. Pursuers in blue-hulled ships.

Uthari had warned him he'd seen those ships, but fresh indignation flared within Malek. Zaruk *dared* send his troops directly into their kingdom? What did he want? There was no dragon steel on the gateship, and Jak wasn't that valuable. Zaruk might want the dragonling for himself... or maybe he was after Vinjo.

Either way, when the vision faded, Malek knew which way to

fly. He sent a telepathic command to the captain of the ship to alter course slightly so they would intercept the gateship—*and* its pursuers. It was still daylight, so Malek hoped that meant they had time, that his weapons had shown him the future rather than what was happening now. Or what had already happened.

That thought made him grimace as he imagined Jak lying in wreckage that had fallen from the sky, his body broken and his eyes frozen open in death. It would be a shame for him to die so young, when he'd only begun learning about his powers, when Malek had only begun teaching him.

Something that Uthari wouldn't allow anymore, Malek admitted with a frown. He didn't care about turning Jak into a super-powerful mage—and he doubted Jak cared about becoming one—but he'd enjoyed having someone to mentor, someone who looked up to him and whom he'd come to care about.

Malek sighed and pushed himself to his feet, realizing he would have had a hard time killing Jak even if Jadora and her feelings weren't a factor. What was he going to do when he returned to Utharika with their wayward young mage and stood before his king? Place himself in front of Jak to block any attacks Uthari sent at him? Since Malek didn't know if he was a match for Uthari's power, he had better come up with a better plan than that.

Lord Malek? the captain spoke into his mind. *I've altered course.*

Good. Continue at best possible speed.

Yes, my lord. King Uthari has reached out via our dome-jir and wishes to speak with you.

A hint of dread crept into Malek's belly. It hadn't been that long since he'd left. Uthari couldn't have learned about his plans to defy him when it came to Jak, could he? He couldn't read Jadora's thoughts anymore, so she couldn't have given it away, unless she'd spoken up for some reason. But he couldn't imagine she would do that. Unless she were forced to. But she ought to be able to protect herself from such force, and Malek had tasked Gorsith with watching her. Not that Gorsith would stand against Uthari if *he* were the one who showed up to question her.

I'll be there in a moment. If Malek delayed, Uthari would only find it suspicious.

He sheathed his weapons and strode to the ship's communications cabin, where Uthari's head and shoulders floated over the dome-jir.

"Yes, Your Majesty?" Malek ensured his features were neutral, that his wariness didn't show. He missed the days when he hadn't had to feel wary around Uthari.

"I have been considering a few things since you left."

Malek clasped his hands behind his back and waited.

"You have given me a conundrum," Uthari said. "As you well know, the Zidarr Code forbids a zidarr from having a romantic relationship with a woman or anyone else."

"Yes, Your Majesty."

"And it is also not permitted to take on students and mentor them. There should be no relationships that might create conflict between a zidarr and his king."

"I know, Your Majesty." Malek didn't make any excuses, for he had known. It wasn't as if he hadn't known all along that the feelings he'd been developing for Jadora and her son were forbidden.

"If you were anyone else, I would have punished you for disobeying the Code, but I admit that I was tempted into leniency because you have served me loyally for so long. And I must take some of the blame for first suggesting you woo Professor Freedar as a way to earn her trust."

Malek silently agreed, but he didn't say anything or even nod.

"And when I found out that you'd taught the boy..." Uthari grimaced. "It was my mistake for not foreseeing what he could become and forbidding that. No, I *did* foresee this, but against my better judgment, I let myself believe his feelings for you might lead him to be loyal to the kingdom and the crown. To me."

Malek remained silent, not certain where Uthari was going with this. It sounded like he had regrets about what he'd allowed. Did that mean he wanted to remedy his mistakes now? What if he decided that Jadora *and* Jak needed to die, for the safety of the kingdom? He'd once proposed exiling Jadora. Malek hadn't liked that idea, but he would far prefer that solution to her death.

"As I said," Uthari continued, "I now find myself in a conundrum. I'll be honest and say that, now that I have my Jitaruvak extract, I would prefer the two Freedars disappear forever and vex my kingdom no more."

Malek stopped breathing. But. Was there to be a *but*? There had better be.

"But I am not blind. I would lose you if I ordered that."

Malek closed his eyes, not sure whether to be relieved or not. Uthari had to be setting him up for something. "As I promised, Your Majesty, I would not turn on you."

"You might not drive a dagger into my heart, but what we would be after they were killed is not the same as we have been. I would be a fool not to see that. You would either leave forever, or... you would decide you don't want to continue on in this life. The Code forbids suicide, but to fling oneself into an unwinnable battle and die fighting valiantly... that is very zidarr."

At first, Malek shook his head, but he couldn't manage to voice words of denial. He'd never considered suicide, but would losing Jak and Jadora change that? Before he'd met them, before he'd fallen in love with Jadora, he hadn't realized how empty his life was. How all-consuming his work and his duty had been, never granting him the freedom to partake in friendships or hobbies or anything except his zealous devotion to his king.

For a long time, that had been enough for him. Having lived always in the dark and never seeing the light, he hadn't known he was missing anything. But now...

"I suppose that's true," he finally said, aware of Uthari watching him. Waiting for disagreement? Or a confirmation?

Uthari sighed, as if that wasn't the answer he'd wanted. "I value you, Malek, and I don't want to lose you, body or heart."

Malek lifted his eyebrows. Dare he hope...?

"But I also can't let that boy roam free and continue to plot against our kind. He may not have driven the dagger into Tonovan's chest, but he was responsible for Tonovan's death. I have no doubt. And now that he's brought down one powerful mage, he'll know he has the means to kill others."

"Jak isn't a killer. If he *was* responsible for Tonovan's death, Tonovan brought it upon himself with his cruelty."

Uthari lifted a hand. "Save your defense of the boy, and please don't be naive about what he's capable of and what his ambitions are. You're too smart for that."

Malek resisted the urge to argue further. It sounded like Uthari was trying to find a solution that didn't involve killing Jak—or Malek being forced to fight Uthari if he tried. Malek needed to guide his thinking along those lines, not argue. "Yes, Your Majesty."

"I've decided that it may be acceptable to let him live... *if* I have a handle on him."

"You have his mother in your castle," Malek said flatly, not liking where this was going, though it was a very Uthari thing to do. He'd done it with Jadora, after all.

"His now extremely powerful mother whom I'm not sure I could best in a battle." Uthari's lips twisted with distaste. "At the least, I would have a hard time getting through her defenses."

Malek said nothing, well aware that Jadora hadn't asked for and didn't want that power, but *he* wasn't displeased that she had it now.

"Jak is fond of the dragon," Uthari said.

Malek blinked. "Shikari? Yes."

It took a moment for the ramifications of Uthari's words to sink in.

"What do you plan to do to him?" Malek asked, not hiding his wariness this time.

"If Jak cooperates and serves us loyally? Nothing."

"And if he defies you?"

Uthari smiled thinly. "Jak will find out at our meeting what I will do to his young dragonling if he defies me."

Uthari's eyes weren't exactly smug, but he looked pleased with himself for having come up with a solution to his problem. Since Shikari had sashayed through Tonovan's defenses often enough, it was possible he could do the same with Uthari's, and Uthari might find that even a young and inexperienced dragon would be difficult to kill. Maybe he wanted to—

The answer came to Malek like a brick to the side of the head.

"You took a sample of the parasite," he said with certainty.

"I did. And if Jak doesn't want his faithful companion to turn into one of those monsters, he will do exactly what I wish."

"For how long?"

The parasite was a potential threat to Shikari until Jadora found a way to eradicate it, and Uthari hadn't been that accommodating in giving her the time and resources to do that. All he'd wanted all along was his longevity potion. Now that he had it, would he let her do the research she'd promised Zelonsera?

"Until the dragon problem on Torvil is resolved and until I'm certain Jak won't be a threat to me," Uthari said. "Given his hatred for mages, that may require him relocating to another world. Permanently."

So, they were back to the exile plan. Malek didn't agree with that, but if this new idea meant Uthari wouldn't kill Jak the instant he stepped off the gateship, that was something. Malek wouldn't have to choose between saving Jak and defying Uthari. At least not today.

"I understand," he said.

"Make sure the dragonling comes to the castle with Jak."

"That shouldn't be a problem."

"To ensure it's not, and that the boy doesn't come up with some creative way to avoid his fate, I've had Blacksmith Homgor construct something for you. You'll find it in a chest in the hold."

"I don't think that's necessary, Your Majesty."

"And yet I insist that you use it. Humor me. I've made mistakes these past months, Malek. I don't want to make any more. Now that I have the longevity potion, I plan to live many more centuries, and I have much left that I want to accomplish."

"Very well, Your Majesty."

"I will have some of that potion for you, as well, my son. Together, *we* will ensure Torvil becomes a better place for our kind, and we will leave a mark that history will never erase."

The dome-jir went dark before Malek had to think up a reply for that. That was fortunate because leaving a mark on history wasn't something he'd ever desired. Of late, he'd wondered what it would be like to have a family and spend time with them instead of flying all over the world, springing into battles and taking out Uthari's enemies. It wasn't that he didn't enjoy testing himself or like serving, but lately... he'd realized he wanted something more.

Malek reached out with his senses toward the hold, certain that whatever Uthari had sent was magical. And if Homgor had made it, it had likely been from the stash of dragon steel they'd brought back from Vran.

Yes, there it was. A surprisingly large amount of dragon steel. It seemed to be formed into an anchor and a chain and...

His heart sank.

A collar. Uthari wanted him to bind Shikari.

For the first time, Malek realized that in order to save Jak's life, he would have to betray him. After this, Jak might not want anything to do with him. Thanok forbid, he might even start plotting to build a kerzor to stick in Malek's head.

A quote from an Egarath the Eternal play came to mind. *Dear Tybara, sometimes the only way to save a man from himself is to steal his freedom.*

Twilight found the gateship flying over the southern end of Agorval. On its deck, Sasko lowered her sword to look down at a city that hadn't been destroyed by dragons, at least not yet. Nearby croplands and silos burned.

Sasko didn't think they were near the Twin Dragon Horns, but they also weren't heading east toward Zar. Hadn't that been Vinjo's plan? All day, she'd been waiting for him to call her for help subduing the mage guards, but the red-uniformed men were still wandering about the ship.

Outside of the city, watchtowers were visible, uniformed men standing on the crenellated rooftops and looking toward the sky. Could they see the gateship skimming past under the clouds? Or was it camouflaged to their senses?

Shikari lay on his belly, peering under the railing at the burning ground far below. Was it Sasko's imagination that he seemed saddened by what he saw? Could dragonlings experience such feelings?

"Getting tired?" Tinder lowered the sword she'd gone back to after losing her axe. They'd been on the deck sparring, but the dimming daylight made it dicey.

"Getting concerned," Sasko said.

"You're *just now* getting concerned?"

"About our destination."

"It's Utharika, isn't it?" Tinder, as someone who wasn't on the list of people Uthari wanted to kill that week, didn't seem worried about that.

"I thought there might be some changes along the way."

Tinder frowned toward a forested stretch of land well beyond the watchtowers. "Changes like attacks from enemy ships?"

Sasko spun to look. A dark mageship lurked on the horizon. It wasn't one of Uthari's.

Shikari sat up and roared.

"That's a blue hull, isn't it?" Sasko asked, dread creeping into her stomach.

How had Vinjo's brother found them? The gateship was supposed to be camouflaged.

"One of Zaruk's ships," Tinder said. "I bet it's one of the ones that was spying on the fleet days ago."

"I didn't think they would have the audacity to fly over Uthari's kingdom."

"Maybe they think Uthari's people are suitably distracted." Tinder pointed back toward the city.

Moments earlier, it had been undisturbed, but now plumes of smoke wafted from it, and was that a dragon flying above the towers and buildings?

Shikari issued a softer and less certain roar.

A second mageship flew into view, drawing up beside the first.

Sasko opened the hatch in the deck and called below. "We have trouble coming."

"We see it," someone else called back.

A moment later, the four mages climbed up the ladder to join Sasko and Tinder. All along, Sasko had been thinking of them as annoying nannies, but as the two mageships sauntered in their direction, she wished there were more of them.

"The engineer thinks the camouflage of the ship will make it hard for Zaruk's people to spot us," one mage said, gripping the railing and eyeing Zaruk's big vessels.

"Isn't the *engineer* the one we think contacted them to tell them where we are?" the other mage asked.

Sasko exchanged looks with Tinder, knowing full well that Vinjo had done exactly that. She hadn't realized Uthari's people had figured it out, and she had the urge to run below to check on him. But when she stepped toward that hatch, one of the mages scowled at her and pointed at the deck.

"You two mercenaries be ready. If they plan to rescue their engineer, they'll try to disable this ship, then board us. You're going to have to fight with us."

"Too bad that one gave her axe away," the other mage grumbled, scowling at Tinder. "They'll be little use in a fight now, especially against so many."

"Let's hope our fleet shows up soon."

"How long ago did you reach out to them?"

"Only a couple of hours ago. I had to find where the engineer hid his dome-jir first." The mage shook his head in disgust. "He camouflages *everything*."

"He should have camouflaged himself. I'd have killed him already if I didn't think we might need him to barter with."

The hatch creaked open, and Jak climbed out. Shikari galloped over and leaned against him. Jak patted him on the head, a head that rose nearly as high as his chest now. If Shikari leaned any harder against him, Jak would end up pitching over the railing or back through the hatchway.

"Is that dragon a match for two enemy mageships, kid?" one of the mages asked.

"I don't know, but he can help us keep our barrier up. Maybe we can sail through."

A cannon fired from one of Zaruk's ships, magic making the ball glow red as it flew in their direction. It blasted past fifty feet in front of the ship before plummeting and splashing down in a pond far below.

"Can't they see us with their eyes?" the mage asked.

"It's getting dark."

"I'm sure they'll zero in. Barrier up, everyone." The mage looked pointedly at Jak and Shikari.

Jak gripped the railing, his eyes glazing as he contributed his power to their defenses. Sasko, with only her sword and magelock rifle, had little to contribute. Once all the mages appeared to be focused on creating a barrier, she headed for the ladder again. This time, nobody stopped her.

She found Vinjo in navigation, his hair damp with sweat as he stared out the porthole. From inside, the mageships weren't visible yet, but she had no doubt Vinjo knew they were there.

"What happened?" Sasko rested a hand on his shoulder. "We didn't fly over the Twin Dragon Horns, right?"

"I'm guessing they realized we weren't going to make our meeting and flew in the direction they believed we were going. I haven't contacted my brother again since the first time." Vinjo looked earnestly back at her. "I promise."

"I believe you."

Another red-glowing cannonball sailed over them, only thirty feet ahead of the ship this time.

"They're supposed to *rescue* us, not take us down," Vinjo said.

"Rescue you, maybe. I'm sure they'd like to kill the rest of us." Sasko wasn't that positive they wanted to rescue even Vinjo. As she'd pointed out to him earlier, Night Wrath might want to rid their family of its most embarrassing member rather than return him safely home.

"Maybe there's someone else we can reach out to for help. We're flying over Uth now. Uthari's people ought to object to interlopers in their kingdom." Vinjo opened the drawer where he'd stored the dome-jir, then swore. "It's *gone*."

"That's what I came down to tell you," Sasko said, not mentioning that she'd also been worried for his life. "One of

Uthari's mages said he found where you hid it and contacted his fleet."

Vinjo looked in other drawers and cabinets, under a map on the console, and finally under his seat. "What did he do with it *then*?"

"Put it in a pocket?"

The ship shuddered, and Sasko had a feeling one of the cannonballs had found them. The barrier must have repelled it, but if the crews of the mageships knew their location now, they would unload everything they had on them.

"It's too big for that." Vinjo stood and attempted to pace, but there wasn't room in the small navigation cabin, and he ended up thumping his fists on the back of the co-pilot's seat instead.

Fireballs streaked toward the ship. Through the porthole, Sasko could only see a few of them, but that was enough. She knew without being up on deck that they were being pounded.

"I'm sorry." Vinjo gripped her hand. "This is my fault. If I hadn't reached out…"

"You would be on your unimpeded way to Utharika, where he's waiting to wring your neck."

"That's what Jak wants."

"Your neck to be wrung?"

"No. For us to go to Utharika and steal the portal."

"How were you going to do that when it's probably sitting in Uthari's courtyard now?"

Vinjo shook his head bleakly. "I don't know. We hadn't finalized our plan."

Sasko rubbed her face, wishing Vinjo had spoken to her about their discussion. She would have told him that Jak was an idealist, and there was no way they could steal the portal from a well-defended sky city full of powerful mages.

"We should have gone to Zar." Sasko tried to give him a reassuring smile but couldn't manage it.

If they somehow made it to Utharika, she doubted Uthari would kill *her*, but she would be powerless to keep Vinjo alive. And now that she'd come to care about him, that distressed her almost as much as the thought of her own death.

"I'm afraid you're right." Vinjo straightened his back. "I better help the others with the barrier. As long as it's up, and we're still flying north, there's a chance that some of Uthari's mageships will arrive in time to help us. Or at least come to flay Zaruk's people for their impudence."

"Better do your best to keep that barrier up then." Sasko squeezed his hand.

As fireballs splashed off the barrier, yellow light blinding outside of the porthole, she couldn't help but think it unlikely that anyone would show up in time to do anything. They might go down in this forsaken kingdom, everyone dying in the crash, or in the aftermath, when Night Wrath stalked through the wreckage, using his power to kill them all.

26

A BEAD OF SWEAT RAN DOWN JAK'S SPINE AS HE KEPT CHANNELING his power into the barrier the four mages had formed around the gateship. Shikari sat beside him on the deck, also funneling power into their defenses. Without him, the barrier would already have failed. Dozens of mages and a zidarr stood on the decks of the two blue-hulled mageships, firing upon them as they flew closer.

Early on, they might have struggled to see and target it, but that had changed. They knew exactly where the gateship was now.

Underfoot, the deck rumbled as Vinjo urged the craft to fly as fast as possible, but he'd designed it to fit through the portal, not win races. It couldn't outpace the powerful engines of the big mageships.

I'm sorry, Jak, Vinjo spoke into his mind from the navigation cabin. *Like I said before, I'm the one who contacted them. I was terrified to be taken to Uthari and thought my brother would come rescue me.*

I know. It's understandable. And it was, but Jak couldn't bring himself to say he forgave Vinjo.

After all they'd been through together, he wished the engineer would have checked with him before reaching out to enemies. Even if Zaruk's people had been willing to rescue *Vinjo*, Jak knew they would have captured or killed him and the mercenaries.

And what of poor Shikari? After the suffering the world was enduring from the ravaging dragons, Zaruk's people might kill him outright, not caring enough to learn that he was different from the others.

Jak glanced at the four officers on deck with him, their faces twisted as they strained to keep the barrier up. Regret swarmed through him. Rivlen had given him weaker mages as guards so that he could *escape*. The vision from the portal had thrown a wrench into that plan, but maybe he'd been foolish not to try to subdue the mages somehow and take over the ship when they'd been at sea. Then he could have controlled their flight path. But it might not have mattered, not if Vinjo had been sending secret messages to Zaruk's people.

"There's another ship up ahead," one of the mages blurted, his face as beaded with sweat as Jak's.

"Focus on our barrier," one of his comrades berated him.

"Wait," Jak blurted. "If it's one of yours, we need to reach out to them so they'll sense where we are. Shikari, keep the barrier up, please." He patted the dragonling as he shifted his own focus from defense to stretching out with his senses. The other ship wasn't yet visible on the horizon, so he didn't know if it was one of Uthari's, but this deep into his kingdom, the odds were good. Jak just had to convince the captain to come help them...

A round of fireballs pounded against the gateship's barrier, and one of the mages grunted and dropped to one knee. "Get your magic back in here, kid. We need you."

"Who would have thought the kid had that much power to share?" one of the others muttered, knuckles white as he gripped the railing.

"Hold on for one more minute." Jak didn't recognize the mageship out there, but he detected a familiar aura among the crew. "It's Malek," he blurted in relief.

But was his ship close enough to make it in time?

Malek? Jak reached out, hoping the telepathic communication would help Malek pinpoint the gateship's location. *Do you know where we are?*

Presumably the center of where all those fireballs are landing.

Ah, yes. We could use some help.

I gathered. Malek's telepathic tone was dry instead of worried.

Jak hoped that meant he believed he had things under control and that they could handle the threat, but the gateship's barrier wavered under the onslaught, and Jak worried Malek wouldn't arrive in time. Taking a deep breath, he once more channeled all his power into their defenses. The barrier strengthened slightly, but how long would it last?

Shikari rose to all fours and roared in the direction of Zaruk's ships.

I don't think that's going to scare them, buddy, Jak thought.

They are foolish to challenge the might of a dragon! Shikari roared again.

The sound *had* grown more fearsome these past few weeks, but Jak didn't know if the crews of the other ships heard it over the booms of their cannons.

Fortunately, more fireballs soon streaked through the sky, and they weren't targeting the gateship this time. They came from the black-hulled mageship that Malek rode on. Shikari roared again, as if he'd caused it to arrive in a timely manner.

Jak snorted and wiped his brow. A surge of power came from Shikari, startling him. He'd stopped reinforcing their defenses and launched an attack at one of Zaruk's ships, somehow sending his magic through their own barrier.

"Their barrier is down!" one of the mages said.

It was in time for the fireballs that Malek and his crew had been casting to land. With nothing to oppose them, the magical attacks tore into the other ship, blowing holes in its hull. The forecastle exploded, the mages up there flying off into the night.

Did you do that? Jak asked Shikari.

His next roar sounded smug, and his tail thumped the deck.

A black-wearing zidarr with a powerful aura jumped into the forecastle of the ship that hadn't yet been damaged. Was that Vinjo's brother? Night Wrath?

The zidarr lifted his arms, ordering his crew to lower their barrier so he could attack, and sent a wall of fire toward Malek's ship. The red-uniformed mages had a strong barrier up, and the fire didn't penetrate it.

Malek climbed into the forecastle of his ship and faced Night Wrath across the distance, hundreds of yards separating them. He must have ordered his own crew to lower their barrier, for he sent an attack of his own toward his counterpart. Pure energy roiled from him, the night air shivering as it passed. It targeted Night Wrath rather than his entire ship. A barrier formed around the zidarr, but he stepped back, as if overwhelmed by the power.

And a great deal of power it was. Even from a distance, Jak had no trouble sensing it. Shikari cocked his head and watched.

Once the assault faded, Night Wrath launched another attack, a fireball instead of a wall of flames this time. It crackled as it roared across the night toward Malek, who raised a barrier to defend against it. The two zidarr seemed to have agreed to a duel.

"Let's target the other ship while they're doing that," Jak said.

"Don't do anything, kid," one of the mages said. "They're not attacking us now. I like it that way."

"If we don't help, it'll be two ships against one." Jak pointed at Malek's vessel. From what he could see and sense, it had come alone.

"Malek likes those odds."

Jak didn't. He silently asked Shikari to help him target the engines and power supplies on the ship that had already been damaged. Right now, it was still a threat, but if they could crash it...

If Malek wins, Vinjo spoke into his mind, *we end up in Uthari's court, being punished for having a role in that general's death.*

I think I'll end up there one way or another anyway. His mother was there, and the portal was calling to him. Where else could he go?

When I say punished, I mean killed, *Jak.*

I won't say you had anything to do with the kerzor. Remember, I told you I wouldn't when you first started teaching me.

It won't matter. Uthari will rip away your mental defenses and see the truth in your mind.

Malek might protect me, Jak said, though he admitted that Malek might not. If it meant defying Uthari, would Malek act?

More likely, he'll help Uthari tear down your defenses. Don't think that because you've been on some missions together that he's loyal to you. He's Uthari's man through and through.

Malek sent a wave of power at Night Wrath that tore down the other zidarr's defenses. Night Wrath pitched to the deck, clutching his chest, as if Malek were using his power like a vise to squeeze his heart. Maybe he was.

As Malek stood in the forecastle, radiating zidarr power, Jak saw him as the great warrior he was. The great warrior loyal to Uthari and a threat to anything or anyone who stood in his king's way.

After Night Wrath dropped, Malek sent more power toward the ship. Its mage crew scrambled, realizing their zidarr had lost the fight and they had to reestablish their barrier, but Malek's attack struck first. It blew a massive hole in the side of the ship.

The sound of screaming men, splintering wood, and wrenching metal tore through the night air.

As the damaged mageship lost altitude, heading for the ground far below, the other craft turned to fly away. But Malek, joined now by his crew of mages, blasted it with attacks. The vessel barely made it a hundred yards before one of its power supplies exploded. Pieces of the hull blew outward, and the remains of the ship descended toward the ground. Both craft gathered speed as they dropped out of control, the crews unable to slow their fall. Before they crashed, Jak knew they would be no more trouble.

"I guess he didn't need our help," Jak whispered to Shikari.

Malek looked over at him, the wind flapping his jacket and riffling through his dark hair. Across the distance, his face was hard to read.

Earlier, he hadn't sounded angry with Jak, but what if he'd heard all about the kerzor and Tonovan's death and knew that Jak had ultimately been responsible? Malek had suffered the indignity of having one of those devices stuck in his head and knew what it was like to lose his power. He might hate Jak for having created another one.

Uthari's mageship turned and flew toward them.

"We're saved!" one of the mages cried, arms aloft.

Jak hoped that was true, but as Malek approached, he couldn't help but think about Vinjo's words.

Sorath held his breath as Captain Ferroki floated through the air between the *Star Flyer* and the druid raft, not exhaling until she landed on a log next to him. Originally, he'd asked Kywatha to levitate him over to *her* ship, but she'd pointed out that she couldn't unless he left the dragon-steel dagger behind. Given that they could run into dragons at any time, that hadn't sounded like a good idea. Instead, Kywatha had reached out telepathically to Ferroki, asking her if she wanted to come visit. Sorath had tried to give the stealth device to Kywatha, so she could float it over to Ferroki, and none of Rivlen's mages would notice her leaving, but Kywatha had thought that would be more suspicious than Ferroki simply coming over to the raft.

Not positive that had been true, Sorath had watched the officers on the *Star Flyer*'s deck with concern as Ferroki left the mageship. But the mages seemed indifferent to the comings and goings of the mercenaries. Maybe they even believed it made sense for the Thorn Company captain to join the roamers and make plans for the inevitable dragon battle.

Sorath would have preferred sharing octli with Ferroki and speaking of nothing of importance, perhaps while kissing and trying to find privacy on the raft, but with the Glacier Islands less than a day away, he didn't know if she would be game for such frivolity.

Still, Ferroki greeted him with a kiss.

Kywatha raised her eyebrows. "Did I just arrange a tryst?"

"A meeting between mercenary leaders," Sorath said, though he'd admittedly requested it more because he wanted a chance to visit with Ferroki than because he thought they could come up with an effective plan of attack against dragons.

"Are lips usually involved in mercenary meetings?"

"For those without telepathic powers, it's hard to have a meeting without them."

"Interesting." Kywatha left, giving them what privacy could be found on the raft.

"I do want to talk with you," Ferroki said quietly as she frowned around the raft, the druids and roamers and their gear leaving little room.

"I assumed. As magnificent as my lips are, I doubt they alone are worth risking the ire of mages for sneaking away from one's assigned ship."

"They're worth it." Ferroki smiled. "I shouldn't stay long though. I want to, and... something tells me maybe I should, but... Lieutenant Sasko left with the gateship, so the sergeants are running the show."

"A recipe for chaos." Sorath smiled, but her pauses puzzled him. What wasn't she telling him?

He guided her to the spot he was sharing with Grunk. Thanks to the kid's quirks, he warranted an entire portion of a log to himself.

"Do you have a plan?" Ferroki asked as they settled against a couple of packs—the closest thing to backrests aboard the raft. "For when we inevitably encounter more dragons?"

"Besides trying to spring onto their backs, climb up their necks, and stab them in the eyes? No. You?"

"Tezi's style involves hoping for a tail to get close and lopping off the tip."

"I trust that irritates them but doesn't incapacitate them."

"Not that I've noticed," Ferroki said. "If they're like lizards, they can grow back their tails."

"I've been battling with a one-eyed dragon who doesn't seem capable of growing back his mangled orb. Unless he just likes the look. There's nothing like missing body parts to attract the ladies." Sorath raised his pickaxe appendage.

"Is that so?"

"Clearly, since you're here." He patted her on the shoulder with his hand—even the most fearless mercenary woman might flinch at a pickaxe waving near her head.

"It was one thing when Thorn Company and the other mercenaries were being called upon to defend the portal against the druids and others who might want it," Ferroki said, "but we have no effective way to battle dragons. We're even out of explosives. We can recharge our magelock rifles aboard the ship, but Rivlen doesn't have any grenades to share with us. It's been weeks since we purchased provisions in Perchver. Even if we *did* have explosives..."

"I know. I'm out of pop-bangs and in a similar situation. At least when Professor Freedar was traveling with us, she could make me explosives from her never-ending supply of chemicals and compounds."

"Uthari kept her lab well-stocked."

"Yes."

"All I've got is a doctor with a never-ending supply of yarn."

"I *have* wondered how she keeps finding more out here."

"She trades. It's important that her hands have something to do when the company is going into battle, and she's worried about us. Or when Sergeant Tinder has been sent off on another ship, one being delivered to the gallows on Utharika." Ferroki grimaced.

"I wondered how many of your people were on it when it left."

"I don't know for certain that Tinder and Sasko are in danger, but Rivlen didn't let me call them back to the *Star Flyer*, and that concerns me. Jak and Vinjo were both, if the rumors can be believed, involved in Tonovan's death. There will be reprisal."

"Poor kid."

"Which one?"

"Both."

"Vinjo is in his thirties," Ferroki pointed out.

"That became a *kid* for me a while ago, and for you too, I believe."

"If you're calling me old, that's not the best way to get me in your bedroll."

"I assumed that wasn't an option while on a raft with hundreds of unwashed druids and roamers." Sorath sniffed his own armpit. "And mercenaries."

"I did wonder about the toilet facilities here."

"The less you know the better."

"Everyone isn't just going over the edge, are they?" Ferroki peered toward the side with an appalled expression. She might have been a mercenary with thirty years of experience, plenty of it in the field, but she was still a lady.

"No. There's a lean-to thing in the back of that navigation and engineering cabin. I didn't ask for details, but there are different kinds of vines in there that are, uh, magically absorbent."

Ferroki's expression didn't grow any less appalled.

"Never mind," Sorath said. "As to the plan, you got the gist of it when you were here before. The last I heard, Kywatha and her fellow druids are, as we speak, working to apply some of the same camouflaging magic to this raft that Vinjo did to his gateship. Something that makes the vessel difficult for magic users, and even dragons, to sense."

"What about the mageships? Will Rivlen's people also be able to figure out how to do that?"

"I don't know, but we volunteered to go in first and scout." *Sorath* hadn't volunteered, but if it was possible he and the druids could get in and out without alerting the dragons, he approved of the mission. And if they couldn't, but they could take the brunt of the dragons' ire while Ferroki and Thorn Company escaped... he approved of that as well. "I suspect the raft will part from the mageships soon."

That knowledge was part of what had prompted his request to Kywatha to bring Ferroki over. If things went poorly, he might not see her again, and he wanted a chance to say goodbye.

"I doubt we'll end up that far behind," Ferroki said. "Captain Rivlen isn't one to hide."

"I suppose not."

Sorath frowned toward the horizon, wondering how much longer it would be until they sailed over the southern end of

Zewnath and across an ocean he'd never before visited. Not many people visited the Glacier Islands or the South Pole. There were few natural resources down there and little reason to go beyond a desire to explore.

It occurred to him that the dearth of humans in the area was probably why the dragons had chosen that spot. Had Yoshartov not blabbed, months might have passed before anyone from Torvil thought to check on the Glacier Islands.

"I'm concerned about what we'll find out there," he admitted.

"Dragons building another portal?"

"Maybe. But I've wondered why they would have had to go so far to do that. Why leave Zewnath at all? If the other portal had to be set up on that continent to work, a second one presumably would be too."

"Are we *sure* it had to be placed there?"

"I believe so. Jak or his mother would be the ones to ask, but I seem to remember them saying something about the constellations in the sky being crucial. There's one that has to be visible from where the portal is placed." Sorath lifted his gaze toward the stars, the Dragon's Tail in the night sky ahead of them. That was the one they'd mentioned, wasn't it?

He wished he'd spent more time with Jak and Jadora. Since archeology had long been an interest of his, he would have enjoyed learning more.

Too bad he'd been busy dodging irate wizards with a grudge. Not for the first time, he wished he'd shoved Rivlen out of the way the night of the battle and sunk that axe into Uthari's chest. He'd had one of the dragon-steel weapons at the time. As powerful as Rivlen was, she wouldn't have been able to stop him, at least not easily.

"Lost opportunities," he whispered.

Ferroki looked at him, but he only shook his head.

She leaned against his shoulder. "If we somehow survive this, and rid the world of the dragon threat, what will you do afterward? Go back to writing your memoir?"

"I wouldn't mind a moderately sedate pastime after all this," Sorath said, "but I lost my shop and most of my savings. I'm not even on anyone's payroll at the moment. Retirement is going to be harder this time, unless Uthari's people are paying you well, and you're willing to support me in my old age."

"The pay has been steady, if not extravagant, given how often we've been dragged into battle."

"No combat bonuses?"

"I'm afraid not."

"I guess I'll have to find another wealthy matron to support me in my retirement years."

Ferroki looked wryly at him. "Do you get a lot of offers?"

"Not as many as you'd think, given my rugged appeal. Perhaps after I finish my memoir, that'll change. Women love a scribe."

"Yes, bards have written countless songs about the appeal of nearsighted men with ink-stained fingers."

"My sight is fine."

She arched an eyebrow.

"*Maybe* I wear spectacles to write, but they only add to my appeal."

"Your rugged appeal."

"Rugged *and* sophisticated."

She leaned over and hugged him, so he forgave her for the teasing. But she paused, touching a rip in the back of his tunic. After all he'd been through, neither druid nor mage offering him fresh clothing along the way, he was surprised it was the only one. When the dragon had smacked him there, it had left a bruise as well as a rip. A *rugged* bruise.

"Did you know that your back is glowing?"

"*Glowing?*" Sorath craned his neck, but he couldn't see the spot.

When he'd been whacked by Yoshartov's tail, his back had burned, and he remembered wondering if the dragon had injected venom, but after he'd broken his ribs, he'd forgotten all about the lesser wound. He'd assumed the healer had tended to it, along with his other injuries.

Ferroki shifted the ripped fabric aside. "I can't see it all. Take off your shirt."

"Words I've dreamed of you saying, though not while sitting on a log with hundreds of druids and roamers around."

"You don't think they want to admire your shirtless, rugged sophistication?"

Sorath untied the tunic's laces. "I'm sure they do, but I don't let just anyone see that."

Despite his time with the healer, his body still ached, so he lifted his tunic gingerly. Ferroki helped, her fingers brushing his skin. He supposed it was only in his imagination that her touch was particularly tender.

"Interesting," she said when his tunic hung around his neck, and his back was on display.

"The word I always envisioned you using was *magnificent*."

"To describe your back or the glowing bruise?"

"Glowing bruises didn't figure in my visions." Sorath craned his neck again. Though he still couldn't see the spot, it was dark enough that he *could* make out a faint silver glow emanating from his skin. "Did that bastard *mark* me? Like a dog pissing on a tree?"

"You think the dragon was claiming you as his territory?" Ferroki asked skeptically.

"I don't know, but I haven't heard of anyone else glowing after battling a dragon."

"True, and I've seen others be struck by them. Lord Malek and Corporal Tezi would also be glowing if it were a common side effect of contact with their scales. Not to mention Jak. His dragonling thumps him regularly."

"He better watch out for the day when that thing is full grown."

"It seems like affectionate thumping." Ferroki rested her palm gently on his bruise.

"That doesn't mean it couldn't hurl him off the side of a building—or a mageship."

"This is a little warm to the touch, but I suppose skin usually is when it's inflamed. I should get Dr. Fret over here."

"I doubt she has a tincture for dragon glow."

"No, but we should make sure it's not the start of some kind of infection."

"I'll ask the druid healer about it later. I'm more worried about what the dragons are up to." Sorath pulled his tunic down and rose, walking to the edge of the log raft.

"Nothing good," Ferroki said, following him.

Far below, the dark sea was visible now, and they were flying away from the southern shoreline of Zewnath. They wouldn't see land again until they reached the ice-covered Glacier Islands.

"Is that a logical hunch, or do you know something the rest of us don't?" Sorath waved at the druids and roamers.

Ferroki hesitated. "Sasko lent me a magical rock—I think she called it a future stone—that one of the druids gave her back on Zewnath. Apparently, it showed her a couple of visions of possible futures. I've held it a few times, and it warms in my hand, but it's only shown me one future."

"Not either of us dying, I hope. I'd like there to be a lot more back fondling before that happens." He smiled, but her eyes were grave, and she didn't return it.

Instead, she slipped an egg-shaped stone out of her pocket. "We *are* together in it, but..."

"Not fondling each other?"

"Dangling from the talons of a dragon."

"Together? That's romantic."

She shook her head. "Injured and being carried off over the sea toward something dark on the horizon. That's where the vision ends. I almost didn't come over here tonight, because..." She looked down at the sea, then shrugged. "It seems like we're approaching the point where that vision takes place. I was torn between my duty to lead the company and being afraid that if I didn't come, you would be taken and stuck somewhere alone."

"It sounds like a scenario that could only end in my death. If I'm destined to die, I'd rather not take you with me."

"You shouldn't die alone."

Sorath shook his head and looked around for Kywatha, figuring he should send Ferroki back before it was too late. But while they'd been talking, the trio of mageships had fallen back. He sucked in a startled breath. Were they too far away now for Kywatha to levitate Ferroki back to the *Star Flyer*? Sorath hadn't intended to separate her from her company.

"Let's talk to the druid healer." Ferroki was eyeing his back again, more concerned about his glow than the receding fleet. "I think it would be better to get her opinion now than wait."

"I suppose." Sorath sighed. "Remember the good old days when we only fought other terrene soldiers?"

"I remember there were usually mages in the mix."

"But not dragons."

"Not dragons," she agreed and leaned against him.

Sorath wrapped an arm around her shoulders, but she pulled back.

"The healer?"

"Right."

But before Sorath could find the druid woman, Kywatha called out a warning from across the raft.

"There are dragons ahead."

LINDSAY BUROKER

Sorath blew out a slow breath, wondering how effective the camouflage they'd put on the raft would be.

"A *lot* of dragons," Kywatha added. "And I sense something else. The dragon steel, I think."

Sorath closed his eyes and tried not to think about Ferroki's vision.

27

Jak sat alone in a cabin on what he'd learned was the *Current Darter*, a mageship that had never gone to Zewnath, instead remaining in Uth, defending the kingdom in Uthari's absence. It had a similar layout to the *Star Flyer*, and might have felt comfortably familiar to Jak, but the officers were all strangers who'd eyed him with suspicion if not outright distaste.

Had they heard about his exploits? He didn't know, but he wished he had someone friendly to talk to.

Vinjo, Tinder, and Sasko had been left aboard the gateship with the four mages Rivlen had sent along, and only Jak and Shikari had been taken aboard this ship, escorted by stone-faced officers who hadn't spoken, other than to point Shikari to a corner of the deck and direct Jak to a cabin.

At first, it had looked like they might take Jak to the brig, but he'd ended up in a section of crew quarters with a guard stationed outside his door. The guard worried him. Why had Malek felt that was necessary? Or was he not in charge of the ship? Maybe there was a fleet officer who'd issued the command.

As of yet, Jak hadn't seen Malek, and that also worried him. He started to wonder if he was right, if Malek *was* angry with him.

It was possible that Malek was busy reporting to Uthari that he'd found Jak and the gateship, but how long could that take? The *Current Darter* hadn't been the recipient of much damage during the battle, so Malek couldn't be overseeing repairs. What was keeping him?

"Maybe he just doesn't want to talk to me." The thought depressed Jak, and his shoulders slumped as he sat on the edge of the hard bunk.

He reached out to Shikari to assure himself that the dragonling was all right. When he'd flown over to the *Current Darter* and landed on the deck, the crew had eyed him warily and kept their distance. Since this ship had never been to Zewnath, they hadn't met Shikari before. It was possible, however, that they'd encountered and had to fight against the tainted dragons.

A sense of confusion and uncertainty came from Shikari.

What's wrong? Jak asked.

He chained me.

Jak blinked. *Chained you?*

He imagined a dog linked to a tree. But what kind of chain could keep a dragon from flying away?

Shikari shared an image of a thick collar around his neck attached to a chain that ran to a heavy anchor hooked to the deck. All of the items were made from dragon steel.

I was confused. I let him do it because I did not understand. I thought he was an ally. Shikari shared an image of Malek.

Dread sank into Jak's stomach like that anchor. An anchor that was too heavy for Shikari to lift if he tried to fly away? An adult dragon might be able to, but Shikari couldn't fly that well yet.

Malek is *an ally,* Jak said, not willing to believe that had changed. *I'll talk to him. His king must have ordered him to do that. Malek wouldn't be that mean.* Or that foolish. Dragon steel wouldn't stop Shikari from using his power. Jak was positive of that. If he wanted to, he could incinerate the entire ship around that anchor.

Of course, the anchor would then fall through the incinerated ship to the ground, and if Shikari couldn't fly with it attached, he might end up dying when it landed.

A sense of disgruntlement roiled from Shikari as he scratched his neck around the collar.

Don't do anything right now, please, Jak said. *I'll find out what's going on. Malek shouldn't have done that.*

No. I am a good ally.

You are.

Jak rubbed the back of his neck, wondering where Malek had found an anchor and chain made from dragon steel, but then he remembered the blacksmith, who, thanks to Jak's help, had a chest of dragon steel to work with. Jak shook his head in disgust. How had Uthari kept that from being stolen by the dragons?

Finally, Jak sensed Malek's approach and stood to face the door. His palms were sweaty, and he wiped them on his trousers, realizing how nervous he was.

Maybe it was strange, but he was more afraid of losing Malek's good opinion of him than whatever Uthari planned to do to him. It was possible that if the portal was inside Uthari's castle when Jak arrived, it would protect him from harm, as it had done in the past. But it couldn't protect him from Malek feeling betrayed and distancing himself from Jak.

A soft knock sounded.

"Come in, Lord Malek," Jak said, compelled to formality, both because he didn't know how Malek felt and because he himself felt betrayed. After all they'd been through, Jak couldn't believe Malek had chained Shikari.

Malek stepped inside and shut the door behind him.

"Why did you chain him?" Jak blurted, unable to wait for

Malek to speak first. "He helped us against Zaruk's people. He *always* helps us."

"I know, Jak." Malek sighed and sat on the edge of another bunk in the cabin, facing him. "Uthari sent the chain along and ordered it."

"But *why*?"

"He wants you, Vinjo, *and* Shikari in his court as soon as possible."

"Where did he think Shikari would go? He's my charge, my friend. He goes everywhere with me. You've seen that. Even on Nargnoth, when that chief tried to lure him away with food, he came with us. With *me*." Jak couldn't keep the hurt out of his voice. He had no trouble believing Uthari would do something stupid like ordering Shikari locked up, but why would Malek think it was a good idea? Or follow Uthari blindly when there was no need?

"Uthari said to protect you from Zaruk's people and retrieve you and Shikari." Malek hesitated. "I believe he suspected you might not come otherwise."

"We were *on* the way. You can tell from the direction of the ship."

"That's good, then. Uthari checked on the mages that Rivlen sent along to guard you and make sure you didn't deviate from your route, and he wasn't pleased with the selection."

Fresh fear crept into Jak, not for himself or Shikari but for Rivlen. Had Uthari figured out that she'd set things up so Jak could escape?

He slumped back down on his bunk. Why hadn't he been smart enough to use that opportunity? He and Shikari could have overpowered those four and taken the ship... somewhere. But where? The portal was in Utharika and wanted him, and his mother might be in danger.

Jak sat up straight. "Is Mother all right? She hasn't reached out to me for days."

Dear Shylezar, what if Uthari had killed her? What if she'd finished making his potion, and he'd decided he had no more use for her?

"She's fine. I believe she tried to communicate with you but struggled because of the camouflage protecting the gateship. Vinjo's magic is effective."

"Oh." Jak hadn't thought of that. He should have spent more time up on the deck, though he didn't know if that would have made a difference. "Is Rivlen going to be all right? Or will she be... punished?"

"I don't know. Uthari isn't pleased with her either. He wants to question you about her, the kerzor, and Tonovan's death." Malek's tone was frosty when he said the word kerzor. Far frostier than it had been for *Tonovan's death.*

Jak slumped again. "Question me or kill me?"

Malek sighed again. "I told your mother I wouldn't let anyone kill you. I hope I can fulfill that promise."

Anyone wasn't the problem. Uthari was, and they both knew it.

"Can I tell you what happened?" Jak asked quietly.

"I've received the reports."

"Not everything was in those reports, I'm sure. Like that Tonovan murdered the king and queen and stole Tezi's axe and was a jerk to Rivlen and tried to kill me in the brig."

"It won't matter to Uthari."

"I don't *care* about Uthari. I care about—" Jak extended a hand toward Malek. "I want you to know the truth."

Malek gazed at him, and Jak worried he would say that *he* didn't care about Jak's truth either, or that it didn't matter. But he nodded. "Go ahead."

Jak told him everything that had happened since they'd parted ways. Maybe it wouldn't matter, and maybe it wouldn't change anything, but he needed Malek to know that he had done the right thing. And Jak believed he had. Malek had to see it. Just because he hated what a kerzor had done to him didn't mean Jak had been wrong to use it on Tonovan.

And Tonovan wouldn't have even died if he hadn't been a total ass and murdered King Temrok. After that, Temrok's assassin would have been after him regardless of kerzor status. Jak admitted Tonovan might have been able to fight off the zidarr if he hadn't been injured and without his powers, but Jak didn't know that for sure. The zidarr were among the most powerful mages in the world and had all that combat ability as well. Would Tonovan have been able to best *Malek* if he'd been the assassin? Jak highly doubted it.

"I don't know if it will make a difference to Uthari, Jak," Malek said quietly in the end.

"Does it make a difference to you?" Jak whispered.

Malek closed his eyes. "I'm not angry with you. I'm just in a difficult situation."

"Because you agree I'm a great student, a loyal friend, and deserve to live?" Jak smiled hopefully.

"Yes, but others won't see it that way."

"*Uthari* won't see it that way."

"Uthari and other mages. Creating those devices... Jak, you saw how they were used to enslave the people of Vran. People who *should* have been powerful and capable mages. And they were turned into slaves in that society."

"Anyone who acts like Tonovan deserves some time as someone else's slave. To see what it's like. Then people like that wouldn't be such complete bastards the rest of the time."

Malek stood up. "Get some rest, Jak. It won't take us long to get back to Utharika, and then... I don't know what will happen."

"Except that you'll try to keep me alive?"

"As I promised your mother."

"Thank you, Malek." Jak wanted to hug him, for not being

angry and for listening, but he hesitated. Malek had also chained Shikari, and that worried Jak.

When the time came and Uthari decided to kill Jak, would Malek truly act against his master of more than three decades?

Malek walked out without another word.

Sasko had seen sky cities before, but there was something especially ominous about Utharika, with a fleet of black-hulled ships flying patrol around it and countless guards in the towers along its walls. She lowered the spyglass she was looking through and offered it to Tinder. Without it, the sky city was still a distant speck more than ten miles off.

Sasko wished it were even *more* distant. And she hoped Jak was all right. After the *Current Darter* had driven off Zaruk's ships, Malek had levitated Jak and his dragon over to the deck and taken him below.

"I don't want to see that place," Tinder muttered, waving away the offer of the spyglass.

"We're not getting the option. We're going to get a close-up look at the docks."

"As long as that's *all* we have to see." Tinder looked toward the hatch as it opened, and Vinjo stuck his head out.

Sasko was relieved but surprised that Malek hadn't grabbed him along with Jak and thrust him in a brig cell. "I don't think Uthari has any reason to want to see or torment us personally," Sasko said. "We're not very important."

"Thank Thanok."

"I'm not important either," Vinjo said, joining them, "but people keep wanting to torment me."

"Because you build useful things and give them to their enemies."

"I can't help it. I love building." He lovingly patted a wrench sticking out of the waist of his grass pants.

Sasko wondered if he would ever have an opportunity to find real trousers again. At the least, he had to miss pockets.

"Do you think he's going to torture me?" Vinjo asked.

"Uthari? I don't know. I get the feeling from *that*—" Sasko pointed toward the deck of the *Current Darter*, to where Shikari was now chained to a dragon-steel anchor, "—that Jak has more to fear from him."

"Poor kid. When he first asked me about making those devices, I told him he would get caught." Vinjo grimaced. "And that he would be questioned and someone would figure out that *I* taught him. As long as we're stuck here, it's only a matter of time until Uthari thinks about me and comes for me." He twisted something on his wrist—one of his stealth devices.

"Maybe he won't find you," Sasko said.

Vinjo glanced at the device. "This ship is small, and anyone within five feet can see me even with this. I might be able to sneak off and hide in his city, a city full of mages loyal to him, but that doesn't sound that appealing either. I'd be stuck there indefinitely, and you..." Vinjo turned his gaze to Sasko. "Where will you go?"

"Where we're ordered to, I suppose."

"I want to go home. Maybe not by way of Zaruk's court, but I miss the desert and the dry heat and being almost entirely forgotten about by the world."

"There's something to be said for that." A part of Sasko was tempted to tell him about the vision she'd received from that druid stone, but it had also given her one of Ferroki dying horribly in a dragon battle, and she feared that one was more likely to come true. It bothered her that she wasn't with Thorn Company and had no idea what was befalling them.

"It seems cowardly though." Vinjo rotated the device on its strap around his wrist. "My brother has always been the brave one, fearless and courageous and knowing just how to use his power to excel at everything. I've always been afraid. You're from Perchver, so you know about tarantulas, right?"

"Intimately."

"I was scared of them as a boy. The first thing I ever used my magic to build was a tarantula catcher. It was this wheeled box that rolled over them, opened a hole in the bottom, dropped down, closed the hole, then took its hairy-legged prisoner outside to dump in the yard."

"That's very humane," Sasko said, wondering why he was telling her this story. "I'm surprised you didn't squash them."

"My brother suggested that, but I didn't want to get my box dirty. It wasn't as if *he* would clean out the bug guts."

"Ah."

"My point is that sometimes... I get tired of being afraid of everything." Vinjo bit his lip as he gazed at the sky city on the horizon. "I have this stealth device, and it's crossed my mind... Well, it's ominous that Shikari is now chained up over there, and Jak might be in the brig. Malek looked frosty when he came and got him."

"Malek always looks like that. It's a zidarr job requirement."

"Jak is a good kid. He doesn't deserve to be tortured."

His words and the determined set to his chin gave Sasko the first inkling about what he might be considering. "Don't try to be a hero, Vinjo."

"No?" He raised his eyebrows. "I thought you might find it sexy if I valiantly sneaked into the enemy city to rescue a boy, a dragon, and his mother. If I could get them back to this ship, we might be able to slip away. The camouflage..." Vinjo grimaced. "I just realized it might not be as good as I believed since Malek found us."

"One of those mages probably *told* him where to find us with the dome-jir that went missing. But look, Vinjo." Sasko held up a finger. "If you were going to rescue him, it should have been before Malek showed up and we ended up being towed by his ship."

Vinjo's shoulders slumped. "I know. I was worrying about rescuing myself, and I'm not even sure my people—my *brother*— were ever willing to do that. I made a mistake and feel like I need to make up for it."

"No, you don't. You should turn that on." Sasko pointed at his device. "Then hide under a console and hope Uthari forgets about you."

Tinder hadn't said anything during this conversation, but she nodded in agreement. "Mercenaries don't get paid enough to be heroes. It's about doing the job, surviving another day, and hoping you live long enough and make enough to retire."

"But I'm not a mercenary," Vinjo said.

"I believe engineers have a similar philosophy," Sasko said. "Or they *should*."

"It's not an *unwise* philosophy in a normal world," Vinjo said, "but since the dragons came, our world hasn't been normal."

Sasko almost said that since mages had taken control of Torvil centuries before, it hadn't been normal, but she reminded herself that Vinjo was a mage.

"You weren't on Nargnoth," Vinjo said, "so you don't know everything that transpired with the dragon there, but I have a hunch that if we don't keep Jak and Jadora alive, the entire world may regret it."

Jak appeared on the deck of the *Current Darter* with four red-uniformed mage guards surrounding him. He looked at Shikari, who lifted his head, appearing confused by his collar and chain, and Jak could only shrug sadly at him.

Sasko hoped Vinjo was wrong, because she didn't think the kid was going to survive the day.

〜

Sorath and Ferroki were still standing at the edge of the raft, leaning against each other as they watched the night sky, when the first dragons came into view. Two were flying lazily ahead, as if they were on a boring patrol route. Maybe they were. They might have been tasked with guarding... whatever the dragons were doing to the south. Sorath couldn't yet see any white glaciers on the horizon.

"The one-eyed dragon is among them," Jary the seer said, as if she'd known. Perhaps she had.

"Yoshartov," Sorath muttered, wondering what snarky comments the dragon would make to him this time.

For the dozenth time, Ferroki looked backward, regret and uncertainty in her dark eyes. The mageships were no longer in sight. *Thorn Company* was no longer in sight.

"I'm sorry," Sorath said. It was his fault that she was stuck here.

Ferroki opened her mouth but paused when the raft started to descend.

Kywatha came over to join them. "We're going to try to fly low to the sea and under those two dragons. We believe the camouflaging magic will only work if we don't get close."

Sorath nodded, lifting his wrist and the stealth device. "That's how Vinjo's tools seem to work."

"There are many more dragons farther ahead." Kywatha pointed to the south. "We should be getting close to the Glacier Islands."

Sorath hoped the mageships were far enough back that the dragons couldn't detect them. If they did, it wouldn't matter if the raft was partially hidden.

"*Many* more?" he asked. "I was hoping a lot of them would be out collecting dragon steel and that we could sneak in unnoticed."

"If we hug the waves and they don't sense us, it's possible we still can."

"Sorath was marked by one of the dragons." Ferroki pointed to the rip in his tunic. "He's glowing, and I've wondered if it'll sense him if he gets close."

Kywatha grimaced and probed his bruise. "I don't know. It doesn't emit a lot of magic or seem like a beacon to me, but dragons are reputedly far more sensitive."

"If that one-eyed bastard comes after me again, I've got something for him." Sorath pulled out his dagger.

"What if he brings friends?" Ferroki asked.

"Did you see that in your vision?" Sorath asked.

"No, but it didn't show what was around the dragon or even much of it. I mostly saw us hanging from talons."

"Unless we push you off the raft," Kywatha said, "we can't do anything even if it *is* a beacon. I wish I'd known earlier. I would have given you to Rivlen."

"So I could draw dragons to *her* ships?" Sorath asked.

"They weren't camouflaged anyway." Kywatha patted him on the shoulder. "Let's hope the camouflage magic overrides whatever that mark is and that they don't sense you. We—" She turned her gaze upward.

The raft now skimmed along twenty feet above the waves, a few icebergs bobbing here and there, the air chilly. The dragons on patrol were above them, but to the south something else was in the air, something besides dragons.

It was darker than a storm cloud and more angular, reminding Sorath of the sky cities, except that the bottom wasn't flat with buildings on top. There were protrusions from top and bottom, some blunt and wide, some narrow and spiky. A long sinuous one hung down from the center, reminiscent of a dragon's tail.

Distance made it hard to tell how large the floating structure was. A half a mile wide? A mile? It levitated perhaps five hundred feet above the first of the Glacier Islands, starkly dark against its paleness below. A moon was out, but the structure seemed to swallow light instead of reflecting it.

"It's made from dragon steel," Kywatha breathed. "They weren't building a portal but an entire floating lair."

"More like a fortress," Ferroki murmured.

Jary groaned and touched her head. "The power it emanates. It's painful."

"Yes." Kywatha frowned. "I don't know how close we dare get. There are dragons nesting on it—and maybe *in* it—and all it would take is a shout, or a roar, for them all to leap out and attack."

"There are people in there too," Jary said. "Enslaved people."

Kywatha looked sharply at her. "How can you tell? The auras of the structure and the dragons are so overpowering that even if there were mages, I don't think I could sense them."

"I can *see* them," Jary said, turning her blind eyes toward them.

A shiver went through Sorath, and he gripped the hilt of the dagger, but what could such a tiny weapon do against such a great structure? And all the dragons guarding it?

A screech came from the sky above them.

He is here! a familiar voice cried telepathically. *The one I marked has come. He sneaks, but we will find him. No humans shall enter our territory.*

Sorath swore. "Yoshartov sensed me."

Kywatha was already running to the navigation cabin, no doubt giving telepathic instructions to her people. The raft turned around, ponderously in comparison to the sleek and agile dragons.

"We're going to have to fight," Ferroki said grimly, then ran to get her magelock rifle.

The weapon would do less than even Sorath's dagger. He wished she had a dragon-steel axe or that she'd brought Tezi over to the raft with her. Would Rivlen keep flying this way with the mageships once she sensed the dragons engaged in battle?

Yoshartov issued more screeches. Sorath didn't need magic to sense dragons rising up from their fortress, wakened by the cries.

Get down, Kywatha warned, switching to telepathy and speaking to everyone. *And be quiet. There's a chance they can't sense exactly where we are.*

The raft lurched as it increased speed, heading back to the north and toward Zewnath. Sorath and Ferroki dropped to their hands and knees along with everyone else. He doubted the raft would be able to outrun the dragons, but if they made it back to the fleet, maybe together, the mages and druids would have the power to make a stand.

But as he looked back at all the winged shapes taking to the sky, his heart sank. Thus far, they'd only battled two or three dragons at a time, but there had to be twenty launching from the fortress. Not to mention Yoshartov and his buddy flying downward toward the raft. They weren't on a direct course, so maybe the camouflage was helping, but Sorath's back itched as he envisioned the mark drawing Yoshartov to him.

An abrupt realization came to him. "I have to get off the raft."

Ferroki gaped at him. "What?"

"They're using me to find it. *He* is."

Though the logs shuddered unsteadily as the raft flew at its top speed, Sorath pushed himself to his feet.

"We're in the middle of the ocean." Ferroki grabbed his leg. "If you jump in here, sharks will get you."

"No, *dragons* will get me." Sorath smiled sadly. "But if it means the raft can get away, it's worth it."

He shifted, trying to extract his leg from her grasp, but Ferroki didn't let him go. She stood up and switched her grip to his arm.

"I'll go with you," she said. "I can fire my rifle and distract them while you attack with the dagger."

"No. You'd be committing suicide."

"*You're* trying to commit suicide."

"So everyone else has a chance to get away." Sorath looked

over at Jary and found her white eyes turned toward him.

She nodded slowly.

Sorath strode toward the edge of the raft. "You stay with the druids," he said as Ferroki, still gripping his arm, walked with him. "Let's not let your vision come true. There's no point in you dying as well."

He looked up as the dragons descended, Yoshartov drawing closer to them. And the dragons who'd woken in the fortress were flying in their direction as well.

"Damn it, Sorath." Ferroki didn't say it, but she knew he was right, and her grip loosened.

"Survive this, Ferroki. I have to believe there's an end worth living for, and I want you to see it." He kissed her and tasted her salty tears on her lips. Or maybe those were his tears.

She kissed him back, and he wished they'd had an opportunity for more. But there wasn't time.

Dagger in hand, he inhaled deeply and bent his knees to spring off the raft and into the water below.

But an attack preceded the dragons, coming not from them but from the fortress they'd built. A thick red beam of energy lanced out from that tail hanging down from the bottom, and it blasted into the druids' vessel.

Their barrier wavered, not strong enough to entirely deflect the blow, and the raft bucked. Since he was on the edge already, Sorath let it tilt him off. But to his horror, Ferroki lost her balance and fell right after him.

"No!" he cried, as he plummeted toward the dark water, but it was too late. Though it wobbled, the raft continued on, speeding to the north.

Sorath cut his cry as he landed, the icy water such a shock that he almost dropped his dagger. He tightened his grip around it and willed strength into his body as he clawed his way back toward the surface. The dragons were coming, and he had to protect Ferroki.

28

In her lab in Uthari's castle, Jadora finally succeeded in reaching Jak telepathically. Engrossed in several new attempts to destroy the parasites, she hadn't tried for a few hours. In that time, he must have left the gateship and joined Malek on his mageship.

Are you all right, Jak? she asked, sensing that he was no longer that far away. Perhaps even within a hundred miles of Utharika. Her emotions vacillated as she shifted between wanting to see him and crush him in a hug and wishing she could send him far away, where he wouldn't be in any danger. Though where in the world that might be, she didn't know.

For the moment, yes.

I'm glad to be able to reach you again. I didn't realize we wouldn't be able to talk once you were on the gateship.

I didn't either. It's being towed behind us. I'm with Malek on the Current Darter. *But, Mother—* Anguish came through along with his telepathic words. *Uthari had a dragon-steel anchor and chain and collar made, and Malek's put it on Shikari so he can't escape. Shikari didn't even* want *to escape. He would have come with me. This wasn't necessary.*

Jadora closed her eyes. She hadn't known about that, but she wasn't surprised, not after her meeting with Uthari. What good would those parasites be for delivering threats if he couldn't get close to Shikari?

I'm sure Uthari was the one who ordered it. Jadora hated the idea of Jak blaming Malek for this. She knew Malek wouldn't have wanted to do it. He'd probably seen it as the only way to keep Uthari from killing Jak. Maybe that vile man had even posited it as such.

I know he was. I hate him.

Wariness slid down her spine. *You haven't built any more kerzor, have you?*

Not since the one I used on Tonovan. I thought about it, but I didn't want to do anything—anything else—that could result in you or Grandfather or anyone else being hurt.

Good. Jadora slumped against her workbench in relief. *I know I'm the one who brought back the schematics and originally asked Vinjo to make them, but...* She hesitated, hating to admit that she'd subconsciously been willing to risk Vinjo's life, but it was true. Everything had changed when *Jak* had been the one making them. *I promised Malek that if he kept Uthari from killing you that you wouldn't make another one to use it on Uthari.*

Someone *should make one and use it on him,* Jak grumbled.

But not you. Please. It was the bargain I had to make. Uthari planned to kill you.

But he's changed his mind, right? He must have, or why chain Shikari? He wants to threaten him if I don't cooperate.

I know.

Well, he'll find that Shikari is growing up and has gotten more powerful. If he tries to hurt him, Shikari will gnaw his leg off.

Jadora realized he hadn't yet figured out what Uthari intended, and she hated to tell him, to worry him, but Jak would find out sooner or later, and she would prefer he not be blindsided by Uthari.

He won't threaten Shikari with magic, she said. *He took one of my dishes of the parasites. I wasn't able to stop him.*

A long moment passed before Jak issued a soft, *Oh.*

I'm sorry.

Are you sure *I shouldn't make a kerzor to jam into his brain?* Fresh anger accompanied Jak's words. *There might be time.*

We can't risk it.

Mother? Has the portal communicated with you at all? It reached out to me, and it wants to go home—back to Zewnath—and for us to go see those Orbs of Wisdom.

I know what it wants, but I don't see how we can escape Utharika with the ship and the portal. There was a dragon attack recently, and the castle and city are well guarded. There's also a zidarr outside my laboratory door. Malek supposedly left him to protect me, but I suspect he's my prison guard as well.

We would need Malek's help to get the portal. And a ship.

He's not going to defy Uthari. He's too loyal to him, and he's already risking much by trying to keep us alive.

Especially me, Jak said glumly. *I'm sorry, Mother, but I can't regret shoving that thing in Tonovan's head. He was so vile. He hurt so many.*

I know, Jak. I don't think you did the wrong thing, but right things can come with as many consequences as wrong things. Especially in this world.

We have to get the portal and go to that other world, Mother. It's the only way to fix the dragons. It's the only way to save Torvil and make things better.

Jak... Jadora chose her words carefully, terrified that he would make another kerzor and end up getting himself killed, despite her and Malek's attempts to keep him alive. *As I said, I know what the portal wants, and Zelonsera* did *recommend visiting the Orbs of Wisdom, but the very fact that she knew about that resource means it's not enough. If the answers were there, the dragons would have found them long ago. I think it's just a library of sorts.*

If the portal wants us to go there, it must be important, Jak insisted.

The portals have the souls of dragons within them, she said, having that knowledge now, *those who'd been infested with parasites and gave up their physical bodies before they could succumb to the parasites' changes. They embedded their thoughts and memories into the portal system, but they're no wiser than the other dragons who lived at the time. Zelonsera is probably the wisest of them all since she outlived them and searched for millennia for answers.*

That doesn't mean we shouldn't go, that we shouldn't check every possible resource. With your knowledge of chemistry and herbs, it's possible you'll find something in the dragon's library that they didn't know was important.

I don't disagree, but we have to be careful. I think we're going to have to continue to work with Uthari and try not to alienate him or Malek for the time being.

I hate that plan.

Your professors at the university must have found your bluntness refreshing.

They didn't.

Odd.

Can't you talk to Malek, Mother? Get him to release Shikari? I want to tell him to fly away. To leave before we reach Utharika.

So he can be infested by one of the other dragons flying around the world?

He might be, but he might not. He's smart. He can avoid them. More easily than he can avoid Uthari if he's dragged into his castle behind me.

I'll talk to Malek, Jak, but no kerzor, all right?

If he turns Shikari into a monster, I'm going to make one, and I don't care if I die figuring out how to get close enough to insert it.

Jak... Jadora thunked her forehead on the table.

Then promise me you'll kill him, all right? If he kills me, you have to kill him. I don't want to die and for him to live.

No kerzor, Jak. Right now, he's not pointing his bow at you. Please don't do anything to change that. I'll talk to Malek and Uthari. I'll do my best to convince them to let us take the portal and the gateship to another world, all right?

Jak's long silence worried her. All she could do was hope that he didn't have the resources on that mageship to make a kerzor even if he wanted to. And that he hadn't already thought to make more back when he *did* have the resources.

If he tries to hurt Shikari, Jak finally said, *I'm going to try to convince the portal to stop him. I can't walk in there without a plan, Mother.*

I understand.

More worried than ever, she released her link to Jak. Maybe *she* should talk to the portal. Maybe she was being foolish to stay here and do Uthari's bidding.

She'd figured out how to grow his plants for him, and she'd made an extract and written down the recipe. She'd fulfilled the promise she'd made—however he'd strong-armed her into making it.

If she disappeared now, would Uthari come after her? Surely, he had to stay and guard his city. The dragons had been driven off once, but they would be back. What if she slipped away, found Jak, and they made it to the gateship? If Vinjo was still on it, she had a feeling he would gladly pilot them away from the kingdom.

"And why not snatch the portal too?" Jadora snorted at herself, having no idea how she might get the portal *or* Jak and the gateship. With her power, she might be able to walk out of the castle without being killed, but they would soon know what she was doing, and the combined might of Uthari's forces would have no trouble stopping her. "Too bad I let Uthari take that stealth device," she mumbled.

Had he destroyed it? Or might he have tossed it in a drawer in his office and forgotten about it?

Jak might still have the one Vinjo had given him. Maybe Jadora could distract Uthari's men while Jak sneaked off to the gateship and found a way to pluck up the portal. If he and Vinjo could go to the Orbs of Wisdom, might they find what was needed to destroy the parasites? Jak didn't have her training though and might not recognize clues. She had to go with them. One way or another.

The portal was the key. It wanted to leave this place, so it ought to help them. They were going to need its help to have a chance at escape.

Jadora straightened, wishing she'd thought of all this earlier. Time was limited now. She needed to have a chat with the portal, but she found herself reaching out to someone else first.

On the one hand, she didn't want to ask Malek to do anything else that would pit him against Uthari. But on the other hand, it was hard to imagine succeeding without his assistance. Maybe *he* could distract Uthari and the mages here while Jadora and Jak fled with the portal and the gateship.

Malek? Jadora reached out to him, though she realized she couldn't say much. If he knew what she was thinking, he would feel compelled to warn Uthari.

Jadora. He sent warmth along with her name.

She closed her eyes, wanting to bask in that warmth, and wishing things could be easier between them. *I spoke to Jak.*

Ah.

Was it necessary to chain Shikari?

Uthari commanded it.

Do you know what he wants to do?

I know what he will threaten to do.

Oh. She couldn't hide her disappointment. She could understand why Malek would choose to sacrifice Shikari to save Jak, and she would make the same choice herself if she had to, but she hated the idea of him betraying Jak in any way. Jak loved him as a coach and a mentor. That had to make this much worse for Jak.

I have to obey him, Jadora. I know what you promised, and I thank you, but I also know Jak is a man now, and men don't always do what their mothers wish.

Can't you just search him to make sure he doesn't have a kerzor? There's no need for anything to do with Shikari. Jak isn't a threat to Uthari.

He could be hiding it in his dragon. It wouldn't be the first time.

Despite the dire situation, Jadora managed a smile at the thought of twenty kerzor lined up inside Shikari's digestive system. *He had to break off the needle to do that,* she reminded Malek. *Otherwise, that would be quite the uncomfortable passage.*

Dragons are hale.

I'm sure there aren't any kerzor smuggled inside of Shikari.

I doubt it too, but I've already pushed Uthari as far as I dare. Malek shared a memory of them together, making love in her lab. *I have to obey him in this. To save Jak. And to save you.*

Jadora stared bleakly at the wall, wondering if Uthari had threatened to kill her. Why not? She'd given Uthari what he wanted. She'd completed his potion. He had no use for her now.

I understand, she made herself say, though the realization that her hours might be numbered if she stayed gave her the resolve to go out and communicate with the portal before Malek and Jak returned. *I love you, Malek,* she said in case she didn't get another chance.

I love you too.

Tears welled in her eyes. She'd known of his feelings, but it was the first time he'd told her. That made the fact that she was plotting against him, or at least against his master, all the worse.

But it didn't keep her from walking into the safe room, carefully inspecting the dishes, and tucking them into her backpack. She sensed Gorsith in the corridor outside her lab and debated how to get past him. She could also sense the *Current Darter* fast approaching and knew she didn't have much time until Jak's arrival. Once again, she lamented the loss of the stealth device. She should have done a better job of hiding it.

Reminded that she didn't need to touch the portal to speak with it, she stood in her lab and reached out toward the courtyard where it rested. Only to frown in confusion. She could sense the dragon steel but barely. Something about it was wrong. It was as if it had gone back into a dormant state, but not even a day ago, it had been sending her requests to take it to Zewnath.

She eyed her lab's sole window, but it didn't look toward the courtyard. She might be able to climb out and down, but Gorsith would sense her departure. Now that she had the magical aura of a sun, everyone in the castle would feel her moving around.

"Jadora," she said quietly, facing the door, "you're a powerful mage now. You can go where you wish."

She wrapped a defensive barrier around herself and opened the door. Gorsith faced her, his hands resting on his weapons, but he didn't have dragon steel or even lesser-dragon-steel blades. He shouldn't be able to breach her barrier.

"I'm going for a walk to mull over my problems," Jadora said firmly.

"Yes, ma'am," he surprised her by saying.

Maybe she wasn't as much of a prisoner as she'd believed. But as she headed down the corridor toward the courtyard, Gorsith followed after her.

She probed the portal with her senses, trying to determine why it felt dormant.

Portal? Jadora asked telepathically. *Can you hear me?*

It didn't respond. As she walked toward the doors that led into the courtyard, she sensed someone *else's* presence. Uthari didn't say anything to her, but he was also walking toward the courtyard from a different corridor.

If Gorsith hadn't been trailing her, she might have turned around. But what would she say? She'd walked sufficiently? He'd probably told Uthari as soon as she'd left the lab.

When she stepped out into the courtyard, the walls repaired since the battle that had taken place months earlier, Uthari was waiting. He stood in his silks, his wispy white hair stirring in a breeze, and leaned against the portal. It did nothing to object to his familiarity, and when she tried again to wake it, she sensed nothing.

Uthari patted something on the side and smiled.

Back on the *Star Flyer*, when Vinjo and his brother had sneaked aboard the ship to sabotage the engine and nullify the portal, she hadn't seen the device he'd used on the artifact, but she well remembered Jak's story about how he hadn't been able to wake the portal. That had been the day he'd ended up almost dying with a spear thrust into his abdomen.

"Good evening, Professor," Uthari said. "You're going for a walk with all of your gear?"

"Yes. For fitness purposes. I've been terribly lax with my exercise regimen lately." She looked at his hand, at the blue-black lump now attached to the side of the portal. Was it the same device and he'd thought to order it saved? Or maybe he'd had an engineer replicate Vinjo's work.

"Convenient that you've shown up for the arrival of Malek and the *Current Darter*." Uthari tilted his head toward the south, and she sensed the mageship less than five miles from the city.

Jadora had missed her opportunity to rebel, to take matters into her own hands, and chagrin filled her. If Jak had been here, he would have prompted her into action earlier. Academics more than forty years old couldn't be blamed for not thinking first of stealing artifacts and ships and fleeing hordes of angry wizards. Even now, she wondered if she could have possibly managed such a feat.

"I expect you'll want to be present for his questioning," Uthari added, his smile in place but his eyes cold.

"Of course." And she would step in front of Jak to keep Uthari from hurting him.

"I imagine you can understand why I didn't want the portal acting up to *assist* him in some manner. I do hate to have my questioning sessions interrupted."

"What questions do you have for him? Perhaps I can answer them."

"Doubtful, Professor. Your obsession with seeking a solution for the dragons makes you rather predictable, so I haven't been worried about insurrection or trouble from *you*, but teenage boys are another matter."

"He isn't planning insurrection."

"Just to steal the magic from every mage he doesn't approve of?" Uthari's smile disappeared, all pretense of cordiality gone.

"Tonovan was a monster, and you know it. It's shameful that you didn't deal with him yourself."

"'Ware your sanctimonious tongue, Professor. You may be powerful now, but you are alone here, without allies."

Jadora sensed the mageship gliding into dock, Malek on the deck, and wanted to say that she *did* have an ally, but she kept her mouth shut. Though he'd done much for her, protecting her from threats many times, and he'd said he loved her, she had never put that love to the test against his loyalty to Uthari. She hadn't wanted to because she'd long feared that she wouldn't like the result of that test.

I can't sense the portal, Mother, Jak spoke into his mind.

He was also on the deck of the ship, standing next to Shikari. The *chained* Shikari. Would Malek lead him in on a leash?

Uthari put Vinjo's device on it to force it into dormancy. How did you remove it last time?

With magic and frustration. I can try when I get inside the castle.

It may be difficult. Uthari is standing right next to it.

And he didn't budge. He merely folded his arms over his chest as he continued to lean against the portal. Jadora groped for something to do, but she feared she'd waited too long and it was too late.

Soon, Malek walked into the courtyard, leading Shikari by a blue-black dragon-steel chain linked to a collar around his neck. Jak walked beside him, though not as close as he might have if their relationship hadn't been strained. There was a resentful twist to his lips as he glanced at Shikari.

Aside from the chain, the dragonling seemed fine, and Jadora wondered if he could have escaped if he'd truly wanted. Though Malek, as long as he gripped the chain, would be protected from magic. And Jadora doubted Shikari was strong enough to fly away with the chain and Malek dangling from his neck. One day, he would be, but he wasn't yet a powerful adult dragon.

Too bad.

Jadora looked for Vinjo but didn't see him. Had he been permitted to remain on the gateship? Maybe he was also chained, a problem Uthari would deal with later, after he'd *questioned* Jak.

Is Vinjo on the gateship? she asked her son.

I think so. I can't sense who's on it, but he and Sasko and Tinder weren't brought aboard the mageship.

So they're alone on the gateship and have control of it?

Not alone. Rivlen sent four mages along to guard it—to guard Vinjo and me. It's possible Vinjo could come up with a way to sneak off. If he's smart, he will.

I was thinking more of the rest of us grabbing the portal and sneaking on.

Jak raised his eyebrows, noticing her pack for the first time, but he spotted Uthari, and the fledgling hope in his eyes died shortly after it sparked. Still, he asked, *Do you have a new plan about how to make that happen?*

I have magic and vials of acid in my pockets.

So, the usual plan. Jak smiled, but it didn't reach his eyes.

"Come." Uthari lifted a hand, and Jadora sensed him sending a tendril of power to wrap around Jak.

Jak got a barrier up so that it didn't harm him, but it didn't force the magic to release him. Uthari had him on a leash as surely as Malek had Shikari.

Furiously, Jadora lashed out and snapped that leash. Uthari's only reaction was to narrow his eyes as he looked over at her. Malek also looked at her, a hint of wariness in his eyes.

We're not enemies, Jadora wanted to yell at him while pointing at Uthari. *He* was the enemy.

But to Malek, he wasn't. And Jadora kept her thoughts quiet.

"This way," Uthari said, leading them toward his chambers in the castle.

A dozen guards walked behind Jak and Shikari, ensuring they would follow. Jak tried to sidestep toward the portal, no doubt thinking of removing that device, but two guards stepped into his path to block him. Jadora thought of knocking them back, but Uthari had all the advantages here. She would have to pick a moment when her power could make a difference. She just hoped she got that moment.

Rivlen stood in the forecastle, chill wind tugging at her bun, a lingering headache from her experimentation with alcohol. At the time, it had been appealing, drinking to forget about Jak and the death she might have condemned him to by sending him away. She'd also been trying to forget about her equally condemned career. Once Uthari had time to sort through everything, he would realize that she'd failed him.

Grimly, as the *Star Flyer* sailed high over the dark ocean, she wondered if her family would be proud if she died valiantly in battle. Probably not unless she achieved something before her death. She had to live long enough to rid the world of these dragons. Maybe then her transgressions would be forgiven.

Tezi climbed up to join her in the forecastle, and they both watched the horizon to the south. They'd let the druid raft fly ahead, and it had been out of sight for the last couple of hours. Rivlen hadn't heard from Kywatha yet. Had they found the dragons? Was their camouflage working?

She thought she sensed something in the distance, but it didn't feel like the dragons. It reminded her more of dragon steel. Could it be the portal that some people believed the dragons were making?

If so, that was surprising. Rivlen didn't think they were close to the northernmost Glacier Island yet, and she typically couldn't sense the portal from more than a dozen miles away. Was it possible the dragons had created something larger? With a greater aura? A giant portal? Or... something else?

"It's getting colder," Tezi observed.

She didn't sound hungover, but she hadn't swilled as much booze. She'd merely humored Rivlen by taking a few sips. That was fine. It had been better to have company than not, and there were few aboard whom Rivlen could confide in. Few who understood how much she'd loathed Tonovan and been glad to see him go, few who were haunted by memories of the past and fears of the future.

"That happens when you fly toward the poles," Rivlen said.

The temperature had been cooling noticeably even before they'd left land, with the southern end of Zewnath more temperate forests than tropical jungles.

Captain Rivlen, a voice sounded in her mind. Kywatha.

Yes? Rivlen answered.

The dragons spotted us and are attacking. They and their fortress

LINDSAY BUROKER

are attacking. Kywatha shared imagery of what she'd seen, including a great blue-black floating base in the sky—a *dragon-steel* base, Rivlen realized, her jaw dangling open at the size of the thing. By Thanok and Shylezar, what power would a structure made from that much dragon steel have? More than the portal, and the portal already had a *lot.*

Sorath and Ferroki threw themselves into the water as a sacrifice, and a couple of dragons are going after them, but the rest of them are chasing us. Our camouflage is only partially working. They know roughly where we are.

We'll increase speed and come help you.

No. Save yourselves, and report this to your king. To all the kings. *We'll never make it back to land, but maybe you still can.*

Rivlen bared her teeth at the thought of fleeing from a battle. Then Kywatha shared more imagery, this time of her people struggling to keep their barrier up and defend against the attacks of numerous dragons. More than that, red beams of pure magical energy shot out from the fortress. A million times stronger than blasts from magelock rifles, the beams slammed into the raft, annihilating the druids' barrier... *and* the raft itself.

Logs blasted apart, hurling roamers and druids into the air. Kywatha went flying, disjointed and dizzying imagery reaching Rivlen before Kywatha lost her concentration—or her consciousness?—and the telepathic communication ended.

Rivlen gripped the railing. *Kywatha? Did you survive that?*

As she stared out at the ocean, the silence was thunderous in her mind. She warred between the desire to go help, to thrust herself into battle and prove herself to the world, and the reluctant acceptance that they needed to turn around and hope they could get away. *Far* away.

There were no cities on the southern end of Zewnath, no mages or druids who could help against such an onslaught of dragons. Kywatha had spent what might have been her last moments telling Rivlen to flee and warn the rest of the world. She had to do exactly that.

"Something wrong, ma'am?" Tezi asked. "Are they coming?"

"The dragons have built a huge floating fortress out of dragon steel. It has weapons that make the green beams from the monuments look puny. The druids' sky raft has been destroyed. Sorath and Ferroki are likely dead. They all are. I have to report to Uthari and every other king in the world. We're going to need help. A lot of it." Rivlen shivered at the memory of that huge red beam. It would take far more than a fleet of mageships to defeat what the dragons had built.

She ran to the dome-jir, intending to reach out to Uthari and anyone else who would listen.

Sorath struggled to swim and reach Ferroki as icy waves carried him on their swells, then dunked him down in their troughs. He'd seen Ferroki fall but not where she landed. Now, he shouted her name, trying to find her. He spotted the druid raft first—what remained of it.

Hundreds of yards from him, burning logs floated, people grabbing them. Some of the druids managed to hurl attacks at the dragons circling above while others could only duck underwater and try not to be snatched up.

"Sorath!" came a gargled cry from his left.

Ferroki.

Sorath paddled toward her, kicking hard as saltwater washed into his mouth and eyes. Holding the dagger made swimming difficult, but he dared not release it.

There is my prey that I marked, the crazy voice of the one-eyed dragon sounded in Sorath's head.

Go suck a whale, Yoshartov. Sorath kept swimming, not looking up, though he was sure the dark figure blotting out the stars was his dragon nemesis.

You remember me! Excellent. Perhaps I will make you my servant instead of eating you.

Eating me would be less punishment, you crazy bastard. "Here, Ferroki!"

The waves surged against his chest, threatening to push him farther away from her. Sorath paddled harder as she stroked toward him.

Then you shall most certainly serve me. You will bring me tasty morsels, stroke my belly, and rub my horns.

Sounds like you need a mate, not a servant. The water swirled under Sorath, almost hurling him into Ferroki.

But he'd finally reached her. They grabbed each other, clinging together as they kicked to stay afloat, their clothing, boots, and weapons battling the buoyancy of the saltwater and threatening to drag them under.

"The raft was destroyed," Ferroki gasped, water splashing in her face.

"I know." Sorath stroked in that direction anyway, pulling her along with him.

When he'd believed he might help the others get away, he had been willing to drown out here—or be killed by a shark or dragon —but now that the raft was destroyed and everyone was in distress, they had to work together.

"Look out!" Ferroki raised her rifle past his shoulder, struggling to aim it with one hand as she treaded water with the other.

A black-powder weapon wouldn't have worked when wet, but the magelock rifle fired. Even so, the bolt of energy it sent aloft seemed weaker than usual. Or maybe it was that her target was so large and powerful.

Yoshartov swept toward them, talons outstretched.

Though this was what had been predicted in Ferroki's vision,

Sorath couldn't keep from fighting against their fate. When her charge bounced harmlessly off the dragon's barrier, he shouted, "Down!"

He took a breath and pulled Ferroki under the surface with him.

But there was no escape. Talons wrapped around his shoulder, piercing his back and chest, and he couldn't keep from screaming, bubbles of air streaming from his mouth.

I have you, Colonel! Yoshartov cried in triumph.

I know! I can feel your daggers of talons shredding me, you idiot. Despite the terrible pain, Sorath wrapped his arms around Ferroki, refusing to leave her to die, though he feared their fate with Yoshartov wouldn't be any better. Especially if he kept insulting the dragon. Struggling to be rational, even as he was hefted out of the water and held up by the talons piercing his torso, he added, *I can't serve you if I'm perforated.*

You will serve me wonderfully, and all will see that I captured the human warrior who defied me. And his mate. Yoshartov's talons also wrapped around Ferroki's torso, sinking into her flesh and eliciting cries of pain that tore at Sorath's heart.

"I'm sorry, I'm sorry," he told her as Yoshartov carried them aloft.

Why hadn't he told her to go back to the *Star Flyer*? Why had he called her over to start with?

Because he'd been selfish. He'd wanted her company.

Look at my prizes! It wasn't clear if Yoshartov was speaking to the other dragons or Sorath and Ferroki, but Sorath didn't care.

He lifted his dagger and swiped at the dragon's talons, but he could barely use his arm with them piercing his body, and he almost lost the weapon as pain streaked through him.

Yoshartov snapped his head down, trying to take the dagger from him. Furious and almost blind with pain, Sorath slashed at the dragon's maw. The blade barely grazed the scales, but it was enough to make Yoshartov jerk his head back and shake his talons.

The pain intensified, and Sorath almost blacked out. He wished Yoshartov would fling him away, but that would mean his death as surely as being eviscerated by a dragon's maw.

My servant continues to fight. It will be a challenge to break him. I love a challenge!

"This is... an odd... dragon," Ferroki said between pained gasps of air.

"Tell me about it."

The dragon roared—or was that a cackle?—and flew higher with Sorath and Ferroki dangling from separate sets of talons. The flames of the burning logs grew visible below, dragons swooping down to slay druids and roamers—or pluck them up. Were they also seeking servants?

Yoshartov left the wreckage and flew toward the Glacier Islands and the ominous dark fortress.

"I'm sorry, Ferroki," Sorath whispered, knowing he'd doomed her to death, eternal servitude, or something worse.

"The rabbit... who steals berries... from the wolf's den... chooses her own fate." She managed a smile, though there were tears of pain in her eyes.

If only they were being taken to a wolf's den. They might escape that. But as Yoshartov flew closer and the dragon fortress loomed larger, Sorath doubted there would be any escape for them.

29

The last time Jak had been in Uthari's castle, he hadn't known anything about his power, hadn't known how to defend himself from magical attacks, and hadn't even been able to keep mages from reading his mind. That had all changed, and he had a young dragon walking at his side, talons clicking on the marble floors, and his now-powerful mother on his other side. Even so, he felt helpless.

The castle guards escorting them didn't worry him that much, and if he could get to the portal, he believed he could remove that device in a few seconds. He wasn't even that scared of Uthari, though maybe he should have been. What scared him was that Uthari would unleash that parasite, causing it to infest Shikari, and that Jak would lose his dragon friend. His dragon friend who'd just learned how to speak, who could barely fly, and who was nice and fun and didn't deserve to be turned into a monster.

It was bad enough fighting those mottled dragons, knowing they'd once been benevolent dragons and friends to humanity. He hadn't ever *known* them. But he'd known Shikari since he hatched. The dragonling had ridden on his shoulder, saved Malek's life—if not *all* of their lives—back on Vran, and it was perhaps only because of Shikari that the guardians on Nargnoth had agreed to waken Zelonsera, who'd given Mother her power.

The thought of losing Shikari after all they'd been through was too painful to imagine. It would be even worse if he changed before their eyes, and they had to *fight* him.

Jak's chin quivered as tears threatened. He sniffed, trying to keep from crying. Not here. Not in front of Uthari and Malek and all these damn mages.

Uthari, with the ears of a bloodhound, looked back, as if he'd heard that sniff. Maybe he had.

Jak blinked a few times, not letting the tears fall. Uthari's face was as frosty as an iceberg. He hadn't yet spoken to Jak, neither out loud nor telepathically, but Jak could tell he was a lot angrier about the kerzor and Tonovan's loss than Malek had been.

Jak had seen Malek's face when he'd taken Shikari's chain from the anchor so he could lead the dragonling into the sky city. He hadn't wanted to do it. Even though Jak had originally felt betrayed by him, he couldn't bring himself to blame Malek. Malek was in a tough situation, and it almost made Jak regret his choices, but he couldn't bring himself to wish he hadn't attacked Tonovan. If Jak died tonight, at least he would know he'd helped take one evil mage out of the world. He hoped Uthari wouldn't find someone equally odious to promote into his position. If the world were fair, *Rivlen* would take Tonovan's place.

When the group entered the large audience chamber outside of Uthari's suite, he strode to a throne at the end. During their previous visit, Uthari had taken them to a private sitting room, but perhaps he only treated his prisoners to such cozy surroundings when he wanted something from them. If Mother had crafted his longevity potion for him, Uthari had no need for either of them anymore.

"Put the boy there." Uthari pointed at a rug in front of the throne. "I will have his thoughts and learn exactly what transpired, from his point of view."

A part of Jak wanted to resist the mage guards as they stepped forward, and Mother glanced at him, silently offering support if he wished to do so, but Jak would rather Uthari focus on him than Shikari.

Directed by Uthari, Malek took Shikari off to the side of the chamber. If Uthari had the parasite with him and threw the dish across the room, would there be time to protect Shikari?

Jak brushed off the grips of the mages, using a touch of his magic to push them back from him, and strode forward of his own accord. If Uthari wanted his thoughts, so be it. Let him see what Tonovan had done to Temrok and how he'd stolen Tezi's axe and been a coward on Nargnoth and tried to kill Malek. Jak would show him everything that had happened and perhaps far more than the wizard wanted to see.

"Kneel, boy," Uthari said, his power pressing down on Jak's shoulders.

Jak thought about resisting again, and he sensed his mother gathering her power to protect him.

It's fine, he told her. *I'll give him what he wants, as long as he leaves Shikari alone.*

As Jak knelt, another voice spoke into his mind.

Jak? Where are you?

Vinjo? Jak carefully pinpointed his response toward the docks. Vinjo's contact came from that direction. *I'm in the castle and about to be questioned, so I'm a little busy.*

We're stealing the gateship, and we're going to rescue you.

We? You and... Tinder and Sasko? Jak grimaced, remembering that there were four mages on that ship. Vinjo was a great engineer, but he wasn't a powerful fighter, and neither Tinder nor Sasko had dragon-steel weapons. *You better not. Just stay out of it. Be glad Uthari didn't drag you in here too.*

He did something to the portal.

I know. I think it's your device. Jak eyed Uthari, hoping he wasn't catching any of this, but he was looking over Jak's head toward Mother. Her jaw was clenched as she glared back at him. Several mages had been assigned to guard her—to combine their power to keep her from using hers—and they appeared ready to spring. The zidarr Gorsith was also at her back, his weapons drawn.

Don't do anything, Mother, Jak repeated, worried for her. That zidarr wouldn't have any qualms about ending her life. Malek was eyeing Gorsith and his weapons, but Uthari had put him on the other side of the chamber—deliberately, no doubt—and he might not be close enough to act if Gorsith sprang.

My device? Vinjo demanded indignantly. *If it is, I can remove it easily.*

Maybe you should. Maybe instead of worrying about rescuing us, you could rescue the portal.

Uh. The gateship is somewhat camouflaged to people's and dragon's magical senses, but it's not invisible. We would be shot down if we tried to fly over the castle to get the portal.

Well, if something happens and if you get the opportunity, the portal wants to be taken back to Zewnath.

Yes, yes, the orbs, but I haven't had time to make the ship impervious to water.

Better start working on it.

Malek stirred. "There are dragons out there again. You may want to make this quick, Your Majesty."

"I sense them." Uthari lifted his chin.

Shikari moaned softly and plopped down on the marble tiles, his chin between his forelegs. *They come for me,* he told Jak. *They want to make me one of them.*

Everybody does, it seems.

I don't want to be a mean, tainted dragon.

Trust me, I don't want that either. You're my friend.

You haven't gotten to ride me yet.

I know.

Take this chain off, and we'll go fly. Far away where they can't get us. Shikari shared a now-familiar image of the orbs on the underwater pedestals. Maybe the portal had been talking to him too.

They're a long flight from here, Jak thought sadly.

"We're ready for them," Uthari said, returning his focus to Jak. "And if that engineer tries to steal my portal, he'll find out how quickly he can get himself and his ship incinerated. My courtyard has defenses."

Jak swallowed. Damn it, he'd been careful to keep his thoughts guarded and his communication directed solely at Vinjo. But he couldn't be surprised that a wizard might have ways to detect them. He'd been a fool to let himself be brought here. Escape wouldn't be possible.

Not when you've worked against me, boy. Uthari's cold gaze held his, and then pressure built under Jak's skull, power raking through his mind, stirring up his thoughts as it elicited pain.

Jak gasped, his first response to tighten up his defenses and hide everything, but he *wanted* the bastard to know how evil Tonovan had been. He vomited everything Uthari wanted and more into his mind, especially showing the times when Tonovan had acted against Malek, though Jak was even more indignant about the transgressions against his mother. And Rivlen and Tezi. Tonovan might not have tried to strike them down, but his torment had been just as bad.

Uthari absorbed his thoughts at lightning speed, merely gripping his chin as he sifted through everything. "You slept with Captain *Rivlen*?" he asked at one point, then looked darkly at Malek. "What is it about this family that's so alluring that they can suborn my loyal troops?"

Mother's eyebrows lifted, and Jak almost groaned. Of all the things Uthari could have latched onto...

"Nobody has been suborned, Your Majesty," Malek said quietly.

His voice was muted rather than firm. Did he feel guilty for his actions? Jak hoped not. If anyone should feel like a heel, it was Uthari.

A door opened, and a young mage hurried up to the throne.

Uthari scowled at him, then lifted his eyebrows and swore. Whatever they spoke about, it wasn't aloud.

Uthari looked at Malek as the mage scurried away. "We have a new problem."

"The dragons approaching Utharika?" Malek asked.

"The dragons building an entire floating fortress out of dragon steel in the Glacier Islands," Uthari snapped, though he frowned, perhaps reaching out with his senses for the first time. "Damn. There are eight approaching Utharika this time."

Malek nodded. "More than we've battled before."

It took a lot to make Malek appear daunted, but he did now. Face grave, he looked across to Mother. But she could only spread her arms. She didn't have a solution for those dragons. Uthari hadn't given her the time to find one.

Jak shook his head, wanting nothing more than to take the portal and seek out those orbs, but they were about to be trapped on Utharika with no hope of that. Trapped and about to die? Fewer dragons than this had destroyed Temika. Though it had been Tonovan who'd been responsible for dropping the city out of the sky.

Shikari rose to his feet and roared, startling the nearby guards. Malek tightened his grip on his chain but didn't otherwise react. Jak, mulling over the ramifications of Uthari's announcement, barely noticed. The dragons were building a *fortress*? Not just another portal?

They don't know how to make a portal that can access the network, Shikari told him, as if Jak had been sharing his thoughts with him.

Maybe he inadvertently had been. *They are the tainted. Even if they know how to make a portal, the old souls won't let them connect it to the others. If they want to travel again from this world or bring more of their kind, they must have* this *portal.*

"They're coming for the portal." Jak lurched to his feet.

Uthari squinted at him. "How do you know?"

"Shikari knows."

Uthari raised skeptical eyebrows. Shikari roared again.

"They're speaking to him. They like to threaten to make him one of them." Jak didn't point out that Uthari had also threatened that. Better not to remind him. Surely, Uthari realized it would take all of them to defend against so many dragons, and that Shikari could help. "Let me access the portal. If we can't use it in the battle..."

"Oh, you'd *love* that, wouldn't you?" Uthari asked. "The first thing you'd do would be to order it to strike me down again. Don't think I've forgotten what you did in my courtyard the first time you were there."

"I hope you haven't forgotten that the portal attacked you even when I wasn't around. You've made an enemy of it." Jak lifted his chin. "If you want to save your city, let me take that device off it and wake it up. It'll help us defend against the tainted dragons. It doesn't like them."

"It doesn't like *me.*"

"That's not *my* fault." Exasperated, Jak looked to Malek, hoping he could talk some sense into his ruler.

Uthari also looked to Malek, who nodded back at him.

"Eight is too many for us to handle without help," Malek said. "I'm ready to battle and defend the city, as always, but..." He extended a hand toward Jak and Mother. "We need them to coax it to help."

"Especially after you've chained Shikari," Jak said, speaking to Uthari rather than Malek, knowing full well who was responsible.

"The portals have the souls of dragons in them, and they won't be happy about their own kind being treated poorly."

Shikari clawed at the chain and his collar, clearly wanting it off for the battle.

Uthari narrowed his eyes, focusing again on Jak. Did he truly think Jak was going to worry about convincing the portal to attack him when eight dragons were on the way? Jak couldn't even give the portals orders. He had to request that they help and sometimes convince them that they wanted to help.

But he supposed it was possible the portal *would* lash out for what Uthari had presumed to do to Shikari. Whether Jak wanted that to happen or not.

"You will protect me," Uthari said coolly.

"Pardon?" Jak could sense all of the dragons now; they were flying rapidly toward the city. He didn't know what had happened in the Glacier Islands, but maybe the dragons knew their secret was out and felt compelled to act. Whatever had prompted them, they were coming fast.

"I will allow you to remove the device and activate the portal," Uthari said, "but I must then put my powers toward defending my city, not guarding myself against a vengeful artifact. So *you* will protect me."

"I won't order it to attack you," Jak said. "If it decides of its own accord to do so, I can't stop it. Maybe you should avoid standing by it."

"This is *my* castle in *my* city in *my* kingdom that I've built over centuries. I will *stand* where I wish."

Jak looked at Malek again. What was the key to getting the king to be reasonable?

"Do not look at my zidarr for guidance, boy. After what you've done, you don't *deserve* his counsel *or* his loyalty." Uthari stood abruptly.

Jak lifted his arms, in case Uthari attacked him physically as well as with magic. But Uthari startled him by striding past him altogether. He walked toward Shikari.

Fear made Jak whirl so quickly that he almost lost his balance. Did Uthari have the parasite with him right now? In a pocket?

"Uthari," Malek said quietly, "this isn't necessary. He'll help. His mother is here, and this is his kingdom as well. He won't want to see it fall."

"Oh, I believe that." Uthari continued toward Shikari as he dipped a hand into a pocket. "But you're naive if you don't think he wants to see *me* fall."

Jak ran after Uthari, but the wizard conjured an invisible wall behind him. Jak didn't have time to react and smashed face-first into it.

Uthari lifted a glass dish sealed with magic, glowing motes visible inside. Horror filled Jak, for he'd seen those motes before. Back at the ziggurat on Vran, they'd carried the parasite from the dead dragons toward Shikari, trying to infest him.

"No!" Jak cried, his voice ringing from the walls.

A whisper of power crossed in front of him—his mother's power. She tore down the magical barrier that Uthari had made, and Jak could continue forward. He ran, prepared to tackle Uthari. His mother stepped toward him, her hands raised. Gorsith sprang toward her.

"No," Malek barked, raising a barrier between the zidarr and Mother.

Trusting him to protect her, Jak ran toward Uthari.

"Don't drop it in this room full of people!" Mother cried, completely ignoring Gorsith and the threat to herself. She also sprinted toward Uthari.

But he'd reached Shikari, and Malek was too busy using his magic to stop Gorsith to focus on his master. As Uthari flung the dish to the marble floor in front of Shikari, using his power to destroy the protections Mother had placed around it, Jak raised a barrier around the dragonling.

Protect yourself, he cried into Shikari's mind, making his barrier as hard and impervious as diamond.

Shikari looked over at him with the most placid expression. And when he said, *Obviously,* Jak almost laughed. He sensed a protective barrier around Shikari in addition to the one he'd made. But would those defenses be enough against a microscopic enemy?

The dish shattered on the floor as Mother reached Uthari, using her magic to tear away his personal barrier. She lunged in and grabbed his shoulders.

Uthari whirled on her. "You *dare* touch me."

He jerked out a lesser-dragon-steel dagger and raised his arm.

Jak sprang for him, but Malek got there first. He gripped Uthari's wrist, halting the attack. Jak tried to bowl Uthari over, but his foot crunched on the glass from the dish, and he halted in horror.

Motes floated upward, and Jak scrambled back. No, something *pushed* him back. Shikari. His power blew Jak across the chamber. It was for his own protection—he understood that right away—but it didn't push back his mother or Uthari or Malek.

"Get back!" he yelled to them, able to see the motes rising up as Uthari snarled at Malek, trying to pull his wrist and dagger free.

But Malek's grip was of steel—*dragon* steel—and he only shook his head. "You will *not* kill her."

Jak tried to use his power to push everyone away from the shattered glass, but they all had barriers up as they struggled against each other. He could only watch in horror as the motes rose from the floor. At first, they probed Shikari's defenses, almost eager in the way they tried to get at him.

Shikari backed away, fear in his yellow eyes. Fortunately, they couldn't get through his barrier. Mother, Malek, and Uthari, all struggling against each other, ripped each other's barriers down. Gorsith tried to get close to Mother, but once more, Malek used his power to drive him back, even as he magically wrestled with Uthari.

The motes drifted away from Shikari and floated toward Malek's and Uthari's backs—and Mother's chest.

"Move!" Jak yelled, as the motes appeared to enter their bodies. "Get your barriers back up!"

Finally, his words got through to everyone, and they realized the threat they were in the middle of. All three of them skittered away from the broken dish.

Once Malek was sure Uthari couldn't reach Mother—at Jak's insistence, she'd once again raised a barrier like diamond around herself—he raised his hands, as if to throw a fireball at the motes. But they'd all disappeared.

Jak bent, gripping his knees, afraid it was too late. What he'd seen hadn't been his imagination. He was positive the motes had gone into Uthari and Mother. Maybe Malek too. He couldn't be sure, but Malek was right there in the middle of everything.

What would it mean? All along, they'd believed the parasites preferred dragons, but Mother had never ruled out the possibility that they could take other hosts.

"It only affects dragons, right?" Malek asked, alternately eyeing Uthari, Mother, Gorsith, and the shattered dish. He'd abandoned Shikari's chain, and it lay on the floor.

"We don't know." There was dread in Mother's eyes, as if she *did* know, and she was afraid to share the answer.

Will it be all right? Jak asked her silently.

She shook her head and ran her hands down her dress, as if to smooth out wrinkles—or brush off parasites.

"We still have a dragon problem." Gorsith glanced toward the ceiling. "Your Majesty?"

Uthari, who was glaring at Shikari and the broken glass,

wrenched his gaze away from him. "Everyone to their battle stations. Malek, Gorsith, report to the courtyard. You'll be our last line of defense. Keep our enemies from getting that portal. The whole world could be at stake. And *you*—" Uthari pointed at Jak's nose. "Get out there and make sure that portal doesn't want to be taken. You and your dragon will convince it to help."

Shikari had backed away from the broken glass and had his tail mashed against the wall. *I do not know if my barrier was enough to stop them. The other dragons... They all had barriers too.*

I didn't see the motes get through, Jak said, though his stomach turned, because he *had* seen them get through to Mother and Uthari. He eyed the chamber, searching for more motes and wondering if the parasites lingered in the air. Air that they were all breathing right now. *Will you help me with the portal, Shikari? We really don't want the tainted dragons to get it now.*

We don't, but they will try to infest me too. Shikari lowered his head. *Everyone wants to make me one of them, but I want to stay free. I don't want to be a monster.*

I don't want that either. We won't let them get to you. Jak ran over and knelt beside him, wanting to take off the damn collar. If Shikari needed to fly, the weight of the dragon steel would impede him.

Uthari was leading his people out of the chamber, Mother included, and glared in exasperation back at Jak but didn't yell at him for dawdling. Hopefully, he had too much to do to worry about his prisoners now.

Malek had a lot to do as well, but he was staring after Mother and Uthari with a haunted look in his eyes. Had he seen the motes enter them? Did he know that they might have also entered *him*?

How do I get this off? Jak patted around the collar but didn't feel a clasp or hinge or any hint of an opening. The blacksmith who had crafted it had been talented.

If I knew, I would have removed it, Shikari replied.

Jak growled in frustration. If it had been anything less than dragon steel, he could have ripped it off with his power, but that wouldn't work here. Shikari might have to wait until after the fight to be freed. Jak could sense the dragons drawing closer, less than two miles away from Utharika's walls now. They were splitting up to encircle the city.

A hand came to rest on Jak's shoulder, making him pause.

His eyes still haunted, Malek knelt beside him. Shikari turned his wary yellow eyes on him.

Malek slid his hand along the collar, finding a cleverly concealed button, and it snapped open. "I apologize for ensnaring you, Shikari."

Shikari rolled onto his back, almost knocking Jak and Malek over, and stretched his wings, swished his tail, and waved all four legs in the air, as if he'd been enrobed in a cocoon, not simply wearing a collar.

His gyrations didn't last long. *They are coming.*

He sprang to his feet and headed for the courtyard. Jak and Malek strode side by side after him.

"Do you know what will happen to Jadora and Uthari?" Malek asked quietly.

"No," Jak said. "Do you think... I couldn't tell if the motes went into you too."

"I don't know, but I'm more worried about them."

Jak was worried about Malek and his mother. He couldn't have cared less about whether parasites devoured Uthari from the inside out. If Uthari ended up dying, right after he'd swigged that longevity potion, Jak would find it a lovely twist of fate, but he couldn't bring himself to wish for that. If Uthari died—or was turned into a tainted monster from the parasites—Mother would suffer the same fate.

The thought threatened to bring tears to Jak's eyes again, but he firmed his chin and made himself think of the battle. If the dragons destroyed the city, and it crashed a thousand feet to the ground, it wouldn't matter who had been infested.

Tezi stared at the open hatchway to the communications cabin. Rivlen was in there, hunched over the orange light of the dome-jir, reporting to her superiors.

Meanwhile, the mageships were turning, the deck reverberating as they sped back to the north, fleeing from battle. Abandoning Colonel Sorath, Captain Ferroki, and the druids. But if what Rivlen had said was correct, they were already dead.

Legs numb, Tezi stumbled over to join the company. She felt compelled to report the news, but Lieutenant Sasko was gone, sent off with Jak and Vinjo and Sergeant Tinder. Who was the senior ranking officer present? Sergeant Words? Not sure, Tezi headed toward Dr. Fret. She would know.

But a cry of, "Dragons!" came from one of the mages on watch.

"Two of them to our rear," another said. "Coming in fast. Mercenaries and mages, be ready."

Tezi had a feeling there would soon be many more than two.

The deck's reverberations turned into shudders as the ship flew faster. Someone's rifle, leaning against a post instead of properly secured, went flying over the railing.

Tezi squinted into the night behind the ship. She didn't expect to spot the dragons yet, since mages always sensed them farther away than a person could see, but she picked out two winged shapes. They *were* coming fast.

Wanting to make sure no humans got away to tell the world about their fortress?

"Attacks incoming!" someone shouted. "Brace yourselves."

Though Tezi couldn't contribute to the barrier protecting the ship, she dropped into a crouch with her axe at the ready.

Grim-faced, the Thorn Company veterans ran to the railing with their rifles, ready to fire when they got the opportunity.

The new recruits—*Tezi's* new recruits, she reminded herself—might not have seen as many dragon battles, for they shared panicked wide-eyed looks with each other.

"Be ready to fire if the mages drop the barrier," Tezi told them, though they had to know that by now. She expected a sarcastic comment or snide mutter, but they joined the others near the railing.

A wave of power must have struck the ship, for it quaked, the mages responsible for maintaining the barrier groaning with effort. The deck tilted, and the framework creaked. The mercenaries knelt, bracing against the railing, their rifles ready.

The two dragons approached rapidly, one targeting their ship and one the vessel to their starboard side. They were still a mile back, but that was well within the range of magical attacks. Tezi wished her axe could fire projectiles or maybe branches of lightning, the way the portal did. But if it heard her plea for such attacks, it lacked the ability to cast them. The haft merely warmed in her hand, as if promising it was eager for close-quarters combat.

More waves of power struck the *Star Flyer*. Though the mages maintained the barrier, the magic rocked the ship, as if they were sailing on rough seas instead of soaring through the air.

No spies shall escape! a voice boomed in their heads. *You dared look upon our fortress, and for that, you shall die.*

"*I* didn't look upon a fortress," Corporal Basher drawled around her cigar. "Words, you look upon any fortresses?"

"We didn't even get far enough south to see an iceberg," Words replied.

"That a dream of yours, Sergeant?"

"Well, I've always wanted to see a penguin. I've read they live on the Glacier Islands."

"I don't think these dragons are willing to accommodate your interest in nature."

"That's a shame. Penguins are monogamous, and many mate for life."

"A real shame not to visit them then. Who doesn't want to see old married-couple penguins?" Basher pointed one of the new recruits to the deck beside her and thumped her on the shoulder.

Ought Tezi be thumping people on the shoulder? It wasn't her natural tendency, but perhaps in such a situation, it would be comforting. "Are mercenaries supposed to comfort each other?" she wondered.

"Only if you think you're all about to die." Rivlen had finished in the navigation cabin and stood nearby, her arms lifted. Channeling her own power into the barrier? "I wish I *had* seen that fortress. The report I sent to Uthari's servant was sparse. I have no idea what Uthari was doing, but he was too busy to come to the dome-jir." Her lips twisted, but only for a second before she gasped and stepped back, her arms wavering, as light flashed around them and another blast of power struck the ship.

The dragons were closer now. Tezi lifted her axe, longing to help, but their winged enemies were deliberately staying out of her range. They might have learned their lesson, learned to avoid the dragon steel. Or they'd gotten enough of it for their plans and didn't need to risk flying in close again to acquire more.

A new kind of magic struck the ship, something that caused people to drop to their knees and gasp in pain. Mercenaries and mages alike rolled on the deck, grabbing their heads. Protected by the axe, Tezi had no idea what it felt like—or how to stop it.

"Mental attacks," Rivlen snarled, her face contorted with concentration.

Tezi reached out and touched her to extend the influence of her axe. As a powerful mage, Rivlen probably didn't need her help, but there was little else she could do at the moment.

"Thanks, but they're not hurting me." Rivlen waved to a dagger sheathed on her belt. Was that the dragon-steel weapon Tonovan had stolen from the king he'd murdered? "Help the others if you can."

The rest of the crew and the mercenaries, their faces twisted with pain, were struggling to stand back up.

"Our barrier is down," Rivlen yelled to the handful of people still on their feet, leaning against the railing for support. "We'll try to get it up again, but fire now. We need a distraction!"

Corporal Basher, Sergeant Words, and two others who clung to the railing managed to shoot at the closest dragon, but Tezi couldn't tell if their charges did anything.

Hoping to help, she ran into the middle of her writhing comrades. "Everyone who can, touch my axe—or just touch me."

Only half the people could respond, staggering or crawling to Tezi. Hands pressed against her, and several people gripped the axe. She struggled not to pull away, though a surge of claustrophobia came over her. But people gasped in relief and thanked her as their pain ceased.

Yelotta, one of the new mercenaries, rocked on the deck, the heels of her hands pressed to her temples. She met Tezi's eyes but couldn't seem to rise.

Careful not to dislodge the others, Tezi knelt to grab her shoulder. The axe flared blue, as if drawing on its power to better help everyone who needed it.

"Thanks," Yelotta rasped, clasping Tezi's hand back.

Some of the mercenaries managed to fire their rifles onehanded as they maintained contact with Tezi. Several realized that if their legs or backs touched her, it was enough. Their magelock charges lit the night as they streaked toward the dragons. But their enemies flapped their wings lazily, unconcerned.

"Land ahead!" someone cried.

They were almost back to the southern edge of Zewnath, but it mattered little. Tezi had seen it as they'd flown over it and knew there were no cities or outposts. No help waiting for them.

The mental attacks lessened, but that brought little reprieve. The dragons might have worried that the mageships would find help if they reached land, for they renewed their other attacks.

"Help me get the barrier back up!" Rivlen shouted as a great crack came from the framework of the ship flying next to theirs.

A huge chunk of its hull tore off and catapulted through the air toward the *Star Flyer*. Tezi hefted her axe, as if she might knock it away, but it struck Rivlen's barrier and bounced off, tumbling into the sea below.

More cracks came from the other craft, as well as terrified shouts from its crew. Many of them were still twisting and writhing on the deck. There was no one over there with a dragon-steel weapon to help them, and they couldn't get their defenses up.

"I can't extend our barrier to your ship without more help," Rivlen shouted to an officer in their forecastle, her voice strained from the effort she was already expending. As useful as the dragon-steel weapons were, the dagger couldn't help her conjure more magic.

The mage's face was ashen as he saw his own death. One of the dragons flew in closer, latched its jaws on the bow of the ship, and tore off a huge piece. Meanwhile, its talons raked more wood free, and its tail smashed into the rear of the craft. With its great muscles flexing, the dragon tore the ship to pieces.

Rivlen wanted to help the other ship—Tezi could see it in her eyes—but she had to channel her efforts into defending the *Star Flyer*.

Even that was too difficult. Their dragon launched more and more attacks at the ship, and Rivlen screamed and collapsed onto the deck.

"The barrier's down!" someone cried weakly.

There were no mages left to do anything about it.

"Come and attack us face to face!" Tezi shouted at the dragon, hefting her axe.

Had it been closer, she might have been tempted to throw the weapon, but the dragon was too far above, and she couldn't lose her axe, not again.

Power like a battering ram struck the back of the *Star Flyer*, blasting into the hull and smashing into the magical power sources that kept the ship aloft. Screams came from the engineers who worked below.

"We're not going to make it," Basher said, looking toward land.

The shoreline was still miles away.

Tezi looked at Rivlen, fallen and unconscious on the deck. Without the captain or the mages to protect the *Star Flyer*, it was going to crash, and it didn't matter if it was over the water or land.

A great wrenching came from below, and the deck splintered with boards flying everywhere. Tezi lost her balance as there was abruptly nothing supporting her feet.

Her head cracked against something, and as she fell, all she could think was that she had to keep a grip on the axe. If she died, so be it, but she would die with the weapon in her hands.

30

Jadora reached the courtyard ahead of Jak, Malek, and Uthari and hurried to the portal, her pockets clanking with vials. As if anything she had in them could help with the dragons. Already, she could feel their enemies casting magical attacks at the city's defenses. Fire and white flashes of energy struck the convex barrier protecting Utharika, and mages on the walls groaned and cursed as they added their power to it.

The portal still lay dormant, and Jadora searched for the device Uthari had placed on it. There.

A memory from Zelonsera crept into her mind with instructions on how to break an energy link. Jadora slid tendrils of power under the device like a spatula, then twisted it free. She hurled it across the courtyard, though maybe she should have destroyed it so Uthari couldn't put it back on later.

The portal stirred, emitting the same kind of confusion and grogginess of a person waking from a deep sleep.

We have a problem, she told it, resting her hands on the surface and relaying the threat.

It wasn't until Jak ran into the courtyard that true wakefulness

—and was that even delight?—surged from the portal. For some reason, Jadora had the impression of a dog wagging its tail as Jak joined her, resting his hands next to hers.

Shikari bounded in as well, the chain and collar gone. He leaped onto the portal and then into the center, almost disappearing, except for his horns and eyes as he peered toward the sky.

Two dragons were visible above the castle, pouring fire down at the city. For now, the barrier was holding, but Jadora's skin crawled at the sheer power being directed at them. Not only at the city in general but at the courtyard. This time, the dragons knew what they wanted and were focused on it.

The portal shared an image with Jadora and Jak, the now familiar orbs on underwater pedestals.

We know, we know, Jak replied. *But we have to get out of our current predicament first.*

Release the portal into our care, humans, a female voice boomed into everyone's minds.

It was so powerful that it made Jadora and Jak wince.

It was not your place to take it, and we will punish you for your impudence. Those of you who don't die when your city falls will serve our kind... until we grow hungry and eat you.

Jadora might once have called the cackle that sounded in her mind pure evil, but now she realized it was madness. Maniacal madness.

Would the same thing happen to her? She'd felt those motes pierce her defenses and then her body, passing easily through her skin and into her bloodstream. How long until she too went mad?

The portal doesn't want to go with you, Jak responded. *Leave us be.*

"We need the barrier down to attack," Jadora said.

Uthari stood nearby, his arms spread as he gazed up at the sky. "We'll open a portion over the castle so that you can attack without endangering the entire city. I'm calling the fleet to help."

Even as he spoke, mageships came into view, and lightning attacks streaked toward the dragons.

Professor Freedar? Vinjo asked from the docks.

Get out of here, Vinjo, she replied. *It's not safe.*

Oh, we know that, but we were talking to Jak, and... do you want us to try to sneak in and rescue you?

If she hadn't just been infested by that parasite, she might have yelled an emphatic *yes*, but she couldn't leave on a tiny ship without a real lab. If they survived this, she was going to have to renew her study of the parasites and figure out how to destroy them soon. Very soon.

No.

No?

The city has to survive, and then... We have some things to figure out. Jadora looked at Uthari again. She'd seen the motes enter him, as well, and she feared they'd caught Malek in the back too. Their fates might all be intertwined now.

"Now!" Uthari yelled as he peeled open a hole in the barrier. "Before the dragons see the opening and take advantage."

Jak was the one to compel the portal to attack, though it seemed eager to do so. Four bolts of red lightning streaked through the hole and sailed off in four directions, crackling toward different dragon targets. Three struck enemies, flashing red as they impacted their barriers. The fourth dragon whirled in the air and dove quickly enough to evade the attack.

It arrowed toward the hole in the barrier. Uthari flexed his hands, as if to close it, but the lightning was still flowing from the portal. Unlike the mercenaries and mages who practiced starting and stopping attacks in sync with the barriers rising and falling on their ships, the portal didn't know to pull back. It kept pouring its attacks through the opening at its enemies.

Several dragons screeched and flew away, their defenses faltering. But the diving dragon slipped through the hole.

Two bolts of lightning struck it in the chest, one from the portal and one from Uthari. But it kept coming, accepting pain and risking its life to reach its target.

Talons spread, it angled for the portal.

Shikari squealed and ducked low, but he also threw a magical attack upward, a ball of energy that struck the dragon in the chest with enough power to deter its flight. Instead of snatching up the portal, it crashed into the ground and tumbled sideways, hitting the courtyard wall hard enough that bricks clattered down.

Gorsith and Malek ran toward the dragon with their weapons drawn. It rolled to its feet and crouched to spring away from them, but Jadora used all the power within her to smash a wall of condensed air down on its back. She tried to grind the dragon into the flagstones to keep it from escaping.

The dragon's legs wobbled but held, and it roared at her, a blast of energy accompanying the cry. She shifted from attack to defense quickly enough to get a barrier up, but the dragon's crushing power still knocked her to the ground.

Malek saw her go tumbling across the courtyard, and he roared himself as he sprang onto the creature's back. Jadora scrambled to her feet and got her defenses back up in case of a second attack, but Malek had the dragon's attention now. He drove his sword and main-gauche between its scales, his face set with fury and determination. Gorsith dove and rolled under the dragon's belly, trying to find a weakness from below.

"We need more power." Jak glanced at Jadora.

Back aching from the fall, she rushed back to join him. What she could add, she didn't know, but she sensed Jak and Shikari funneling their power into the portal. It gathered and amplified that power, and its lightning bolts grew thicker and stronger. One hammered into the side of a dragon flying overhead and ripped through its barrier, scorching a hole in its side.

The creature screeched and dove toward the courtyard, but a

mageship coming in from the side intercepted it. The crew threw fire and wind attacks, knocking it away from its target. The dragon landed on the barrier above the castle, missing the opening to the courtyard.

Jadora's knees grew weak, and she siphoned more and more of her power—of herself—into the portal, willing it to best use the energy. It seemed omniscient, able to see all of the dragons at once and pick out which ones were the largest threats.

Soon, more mageships filled the sky, all drawn to the castle, defending it and their master from the attack.

Your defiance is pointless, a dragon cried, a male voice this time. *We shall have the portal if we have to destroy every human on this world. We are the deserving heirs to eternity.*

Imagery came on the heels of the words, fires scorching all the lands of Torvil as all the floating mage cities tumbled from the sky, burning as they crashed down in ruin. Millions of people died under the horrible assaults.

If not for the portal to lean on, Jadora's knees might have given out. The cruelty of the visions was almost worse than the painful power that came with them, ricocheting around in her skull.

"We've almost got them," Jak panted. "They're making threats because they're desperate."

They're making threats because they're vile, a young voice added. Was that Shikari?

Later, Jadora would ask Jak when he'd started being able to communicate with words. But for now, she wiped sweat from her brow and flexed her fingers on the cool dragon steel of the portal. If Jak was right, they were close to victory—or at least driving off their attackers for now.

A thump came from behind them, startling her. The dragon had flung Malek off its back and was rolling close to the portal. Blood ran from its eye—Malek's main-gauche protruded from it.

With his sword in hand, he ran toward the dragon's exposed belly as it rolled, but his enemy only rolled faster to escape him.

Jadora and Jak scooted away as the dragon struck the portal. It crashed to a stop, but it quickly flipped to its feet, its long neck snapping toward the center. Toward Shikari.

"No!" Jak leaped onto the portal and cast fire at the dragon as its maw opened, its fangs gleaming.

Jadora summoned her power to place a barrier between it and Shikari, but she feared the dragon would be able to pierce it—just as Shikari had pierced Tonovan's barrier several times in the past.

That huge maw snapped right through her magic, and she gasped as the barrier broke. But Shikari rolled to the side within the portal opening, having just enough room to dodge the bite meant to kill him—or maybe infect him.

Before the dragon could draw its head back out, Shikari leaped up and bit it on the side of the snout. Bit it and hung on. He was so much smaller than his foe that it would have been comical if Jadora hadn't been so afraid.

The dragon snarled and shook his head, but Shikari, his short but sharp fangs dug in, didn't let go. Jak jumped from the side of the portal to the top of the dragon's snout right beside where Shikari's teeth were embedded. On all fours, he scrambled to the top of the dragon's head, but he didn't have a weapon capable of piercing scale.

"Jak!" Malek yelled to draw his attention, then threw his sword.

Fear lurched through Jadora as she worried her son wouldn't be able to catch the sharp weapon, but Jak used his power to guide the hilt into his hand as the dragon reared back, shaking its head even harder. Jak wrapped an arm around its horn and leaned out, trying to find the angle to drive the blade into its other eye.

Jadora searched for a way to help him, but he couldn't reach the eye without releasing the horn. The dragon kept thrashing, trying to loosen Shikari's grip, so Jak dared not let go. Instead, he leaned back and turned the sword so that he could drive it downward, between the scales on the top of the dragon's head.

Seeing the opportunity to help, Jadora channeled her power into him and his arm, hoping to give him the strength to sink the sword in deep. Jak yelled as he did so, plunging it through scale and bone and into the dragon's brain.

Its entire body thrashed so hard that he couldn't hang on. He and Shikari both flew free.

Malek rushed in and pulled his sword from the dragon's skull, then crouched, ready to attack again. But those thrashes were death throes, and after a few more flaps of its wings and tail, the dragon lay still.

"Yes!" Uthari cried, not for their battle but his own.

High above, a dragon he and the portal had been attacking with lightning plummeted. It landed on the barrier near the hole, its body bouncing twice before sprawling akimbo, wings and legs outstretched. Thanks to the translucence of the barrier, it was a bizarre sight, the fallen dragon appearing to hang in midair.

Jadora ran to Jak's side, looking him over to make sure he hadn't been badly hurt. Malek and Shikari joined them, everyone bracing themselves for more battles.

But the remaining dragons seemed to realize they were outmatched, at least at the moment, and they flew off into the night.

Jak glanced at Jadora. *Vinjo wants to know if he should try to come rescue us. He thinks it'll be too late to sneak away with the portal, but maybe he can get us.*

Tell him we appreciate his offer, but... Jadora looked toward Uthari, not surprised to find him studying their group with narrowed eyes. *We need to stay here where there's a good lab, and I... I need to determine if Uthari, Malek, and I have a new problem.*

Jak grimaced. He must have seen the motes slide into them.

Technically, she added, *I had better check the blood of everyone who was in that room.*

Yeah. Jak looked at himself and then at Shikari. *I'll tell Vinjo that there's no point in coming. There's... no place for us to go.*

The portal apparently disagreed for it flashed the vision of the orbs into their minds again.

Even if those orbs could help, Jadora doubted there would be time to get there. If the parasites were inside her and affected humans the same way they did dragons, she likely had a limited amount of time in which her knowledge and power could be of use.

She rubbed her eyes, not surprised to find moisture in them, and slumped against the portal, great weariness filling her. When would this battle ever end?

Wet, in pain, and with a headache throbbing behind her eyes even before she woke fully and opened them, Rivlen grew aware of sand in her mouth and encrusting her eyelashes. She drew a shuddering breath and almost inhaled water as the tide surged up all around her, lifting her for a few seconds before receding and leaving her higher on a beach. Something hard poked her in the back. A shard of wood. All that remained of the *Star Flyer*?

Sobs came from elsewhere on the beach. One of her crew? One of the mercenaries?

Rivlen hoped everyone had found their way to shore, but she doubted it. After that crash, she was surprised she had.

As she pushed herself to her hands and knees, she tried to spit out the sand, but her mouth was dry. Another wave came in. She crawled away from it, vaguely aware of trees above the beach, a dense forest with no signs of civilization. It was still night, but something flashed orange in the undergrowth, highlighting the trees before plunging them into darkness, then highlighting them again. Maybe there *was* civilization nearby. A druid encampment?

She hoped whoever was out there had a dome-jir. She needed to contact Uthari and give him a more thorough report. When she'd reached out before the attack, he'd been busy, and she'd only had time to relay a terse message to one of his staff. But the *Star Flyer's* dome-jir was likely at the bottom of the sea with the rest of her ship.

Tears threatened her gritty eyes. The odds had been over-whelmingly against her, but it frustrated her that she hadn't found a way to win—or at least escape with her crew alive and her ship intact. She'd needed to win a great battle; instead, she'd lost every-thing. After all that had happened, she couldn't expect to be given another ship or even retain her rank. She'd failed.

She wished Jak were with her, lending her magical strength or simple moral support. Cracking inappropriate jokes. Smiling. Offering to map this beach. Anything.

Maybe it was selfish to wish he were stranded on a beach with her, but Rivlen doubted he would mind. As crazy as it seemed, it might have been better for him if he were there. Better out in the wilds fending for himself than in Uthari's castle.

As Rivlen crawled up the beach, half-blinded by the darkness and the sand in her eyes, she didn't see the body until she bumped into it. A broken piece of metal from a railing thrust upward from the officer's chest. It had pierced his heart. Lifeless eyes stared blankly upward, the dead man's face coated in sand. Even so, she recognized him. Captain Hevlor, the officer who'd been put in charge of the fleet.

Rivlen swallowed. Despite her failure, she was the senior-ranking officer here now. She was in command.

Whoever was sobbing farther up the beach might be the only person left alive for her to command, but the knowledge that she was in charge filled Rivlen with determination. When all this was over, she might be demoted or kicked entirely out of the fleet, but for now, she had to gather everyone, treat the injured, and find a way to survive until help arrived. If they had to, they would build new mageships so they could fly back to civilization.

The distressed sobs almost pulled her in that direction, but she needed to contact Uthari before tending to any one person. The entire world was in danger and would remain oblivious to the new dragon threat if she couldn't deliver a thorough report. She kept crawling up the beach, hoping the flashing orange meant someone lived here, someone with magic who could help.

But as she maneuvered over logs and ferns toward the source, passing wreckage that had somehow been hurled miles from the battle, she realized there was nobody here in this remote forest. That was her own dome-jir, or perhaps one from another mageship. And it was damaged. It shouldn't have been flashing.

Maybe she could get her report out before it died completely.

As she crawled closer, however, she could make out a fracture along its surface and a piece of crystal gouged out of one side. It hissed and clicked as it flashed. If Vinjo had been there, he could have waved a wrench and fixed it, but she'd sent him away, the same as she had Jak.

"Just work for me for ten minutes," she whispered, grimacing as she clunked her knee on a mossy log.

She climbed over it and rested a hand on the dome-jir, but as she envisioned Uthari's face and commanded the device to make a connection, it clicked one last time and went dark.

"*No.*" She slapped it on the side. "I need ten minutes. *Five.* The world has to know about the dragons."

The dome-jir remained dark and cold.

Rivlen slumped down in the dewy foliage beside it and rolled onto her back, staring up at the canopy. The terse report she'd managed earlier would have to be enough. She *hoped* it would be enough. She doubted the druids had survived or managed to send a report to anyone.

A distant roar floated over the rumble of the sea. The triumphant roar of a dragon?

Maybe they knew they'd won, that Torvil would soon belong to them.

EPILOGUE

MALEK RESISTED THE URGE TO PACE, INSTEAD WAITING WITH HIS hands clasped behind his back as Jadora bent over her microscope, running blood tests on everyone who'd been in the room when Uthari unleashed the parasite. Jak, Gorsith, and Uthari were also in the lab waiting. Shikari, too large to enter this part of the castle, remained in the courtyard.

Uthari had been quiet since the battle, not making any demands of anyone, not issuing any orders, other than to have his people get rid of the dead dragons and make sure the defenses were ready in case the rest returned. Malek wondered if he was thinking of his own mortality, the possibility that, after all these years of avoiding death, something his body couldn't fight off might have afflicted him.

But the parasites wouldn't kill him, would they? If they worked e same way in humans as dragons, they would make him more ressive, maybe cruel and a little mad.

fter his experience with the death-darter bacteria, Malek 't wish that on anyone. Remembering how he'd lost control of his emotions—of *himself*—still made him shudder when he thought about it.

Jadora rubbed the small of her back and grimaced. Had they been alone, Malek would have offered to massage her weary muscles. He was tempted to do so anyway. It wasn't as if Uthari hadn't figured out that they were romantically involved. Maybe Malek should have cared more about hiding that, but he was tired of doing so and irritated with Uthari for endangering himself and Jadora.

If the parasites *had* infested them—and possibly everyone in the room—was it possible the Jitaruvak extract would halt their advance? Malek doubted it. If that worked, the guardians on Nargnoth would have used it on the dragons long ago.

Sighing, Jadora leaned back and slowly turned to face them. She barely glanced at Uthari and instead held Malek's gaze.

"You're fine," she told him.

"Clearly," he said, attempting a smile, but the graveness in her eyes kept it from manifesting, and he waited for the inevitable bad news.

"So are you, Jak." Jadora smiled wearily at him.

"And Shikari?" Jak waved toward the courtyard.

Jadora had also taken a sample of the dragonling's blood. Perhaps fortunately, Shikari had been scraped up when the larger dragon attacked him, so she hadn't had to worry about finding a needle capable of piercing scales.

"He's fine too. No sign of the parasite."

"Has enough time passed that we can know for certain that negative findings are truly negative?" Malek remembered how quickly the parasite had grown in her dishes, but he assumed would take time for them to multiply and grow into a measurable amount within a host.

"Given that others *did* show signs of infection, I believe" Jadora pointed at Uthari. "They are in your bloodstream."

He scowled. "You're sure?"

"I'm sure." She lifted what was presumably his slide. "I've also been infected."

Malek closed his eyes and dropped his chin to his chest. He'd been afraid of that and shivered at the idea of his academic and even-keeled professor turning into a monster.

"How did Malek avoid it?" Uthari asked. "He was standing right next to us."

Standing wasn't quite the appropriate word. Malek barely managed to point out that he'd been grappling with Uthari to keep him from killing Jadora.

It frustrated him that he hadn't been fast enough to get to Uthari before he shattered the dish, but Malek wouldn't have forgiven himself if he'd failed to save Jadora. The woman he loved. The woman who was now, thanks to Uthari, in danger of turning into a crazy monster, a monster who had recently been gifted with great power. She and Uthari *both* had great power. What would Malek do if they lost control of themselves and became the same cruel murderers as those dragons? Kill them to save the world? He couldn't imagine it.

Maybe he would have Jak create a couple more of those kerzor. Never would he have thought that would appeal to him, but then, at least, Uthari and Jadora wouldn't have access to their power. They could be locked away in a room where they wouldn't be a danger to others.

Locked away to go mad together? Dear Shylezar. Malek shook his head.

"Just luck, probably," Jadora said, though she regarded Malek oughtfully, as if she wondered if there might be more to it.

Malek didn't know what it would be. Once, he might have eved that his strong zidarr immune system could have fought n invasive parasite, but he knew better after the trip to

Nargnoth. When it came to microscopic enemies, he was as vulnerable as the next man.

"So we have to find a solution." Jak wiped his eyes as he looked at his mother. "Now more than ever."

"What solution?" Uthari snapped.

"A way to kill the parasite." Jak spread his arms. "We were *always* supposed to do that. We just... can't delay now. We have to fix Mother and all the dragons."

Uthari scowled when Jak didn't mention *him*. Malek snorted. After all the grief Uthari had given the boy, he couldn't expect Jak to care about him now.

"We have to do it before the parasite spreads and turns you into... something," Jak said, "and we have to stop the dragons before they do... whatever it is they're planning in the Glacier Islands."

Malek didn't know the details of that yet and wondered if Uthari had received an update from Rivlen or one of the other commanders.

"Taking over our world, it sounded like," Mother said grimly.

Jak nodded. "We have to take the portal back to Zewnath and visit the Orbs of Wisdom and hope the answers are there."

A hint of hope entered Uthari's eyes. Before, he might not have cared if the dragons were ever rid of their parasites, but he now had a reason to care. Intimately.

Uthari turned toward Malek. "Take the portal on the gateship if it'll fit—it's the only thing we've got with magical camouflage. I would send the whole fleet with you, since you're going to be more of a target than we are, I suspect, but if you go alone in that ship, it's possible the dragons won't be able to sense you out there."

Malek nodded, though his mind hurt at the thought of trying to carry the portal on a ship that had been designed to go *through* it. He would hope Vinjo could perform some magic to make work.

"Take *them*—" Uthari waved at Jak and Jadora, "—and all the equipment she needs. Figure out this parasite, Malek. Before it's too late for those of us who were infected." *Before it's too late for me,* his eyes said.

"Yes, Your Majesty."

Malek didn't mention that Jadora and Jak had wanted this all along. Uthari knew what he'd done, the choices he'd made. There was no point in rubbing it in.

"I guess Vinjo didn't have to sneak in to get us after all," Jak said.

"Go to the gateship, and tell Vinjo and the others to prepare for another journey," Malek told him.

"Right." Jak hugged his mother, then jogged out of the lab.

"I'll get the best chemists and biologists and *exterminators* in Uth working on this problem too," Uthari said, "and I'll let you know if they discover anything."

"Yes, Your Majesty," Malek said.

Uthari nodded, his back straighter as he walked out, a plan of action firmly in his mind.

Thank you for your support in this, Malek, Uthari added telepathically, after he'd left the lab. *I know you've been... divided.*

Malek blew out a slow breath, remembering the look of pure fury that Uthari had given him when Malek had stopped him from driving his dagger into Jadora's chest. *You know I care for her and Jak, but it doesn't mean I want anything to happen to you. I regret that you are now in danger.*

I did it to myself. It was an act of desperation.

Did you truly fear that Jak would be able to get close to you with a razor?

That is not what I feared, no. Though I maintain that he's a threat. Uthari paused. *I feared I would lose you, Malek.*

You will not. Malek hoped that was the truth, that Uthari wouldn't transition into someone Malek would be forced to kill, for the safety of the kingdom and those he cared about. He hoped the same for Jadora, for having to kill both of them would destroy him.

I understand that now, Uthari said. *Carry out this last mission for me, and I'll release you from the zidarr vows if you wish.*

Malek blinked. *Your Majesty?*

So you can marry her, have a family, do whatever things young men wish to do.

Malek almost pointed out that he was in his mid-forties and hardly *young* but reminded himself that Uthari had lived three centuries. To him, most trees were young. Besides, Malek was too busy being stunned by the words to quibble about age. Zidarr weren't *released* from duty. It was unheard of. They swore their oaths for life, to serve their king and follow the Code until an enemy's blade or old age took them. And very few zidarr had ever survived a lifetime of dangerous assignments to die of old age. Malek had never even imagined it.

But... was the idea of a family unappealing? Of Jak and Jadora, and would she be interested in having another child one day? With *him*? Would he want that? Would she? Maybe one? She was a little younger than he but at the older end for having children, but then, between her new power and that longevity potion, she might be capable of childbirth for years longer. Jak, Malek decided, would be a good older brother.

But as Jadora slumped against the counter, he reeled his thoughts back in. It was far too premature to think of such things. Between the parasite and things escalating with the dragons, the odds of either of them surviving the next month were poor. He walked toward her, offering an arm.

Though I may insist that you help me train up some replacement first, Uthari added from his suite. *Gorsith is fine but not as one* zidarr.

I understand, Your Majesty.

Good. Just do this last mission for me. Thank you, Malek.

I will.

Jadora closed her eyes and leaned against him as he pulled her into an embrace.

"I'm so tired," she whispered, "but I need to pack, and we need to go right away."

"I know. I'll transport the portal over to the gateship shortly."

Despite their words, neither of them moved. Malek rested his face against the top of her head, her thick hair cool against his cheek.

"I'm sorry this happened," he said.

"At least it's compelling Uthari to send us on our way, as we wished. Maybe there's hope that we can find an answer in time."

"How much time do you think we have?"

Malek remembered how quickly he'd descended into madness back on Nargnoth. This was a different parasite, so maybe it wouldn't take root as fast, but he doubted that. It would take days to fly back to Zewnath and possibly more days to figure out how they could equip the gateship to survive traveling underwater—if that was even possible. If it wasn't, how would they get to the orbs? And even if they got to them, would whatever information the orbs could offer be enough?

He feared they would be, at best, a starting point and not the final destination. He couldn't imagine that the parasite would take hold so slowly that Jadora wouldn't be affected long before that. And if she went mad, who had the knowledge to defeat this microscopic enemy?

Malek drew a shuddering breath, afraid he was going to lose Uthari was offering him something unprecedented, freedom future in which he could be with her, but that could only n if they could save her and save the world.

on't know," Jadora said. "Once we're underway, I'll try to ways to slow down the spread of the parasite."

"Good." Malek thought about mentioning what Uthari had offered, as it might be an incentive, but he doubted she needed any incentives. She just needed support. "I'll be there for you." He swallowed. "I love you."

She squeezed him tight. "I love you too."

THE END

Made in the USA
Monee, IL
25 June 2024

60618698R00329